STIFLE

By Bee Nicole

Dedicated to those who've read, and loved along the way...

CHAPTER 1: CONNOR

She was texting my phone again. It vibrated violently on the table, and I watched the light blink with indifference. I took another drag on my cigarette and blew it into my laptop screen in front of me, a retaliation to the glow that was burning my eyes as I struggled to stay awake, nowhere near making my deadline for this book. My cursor was blinking too, goading me, trying to incite some sort of revelation onto the page. My phone went quiet. *Twelve new messages,* the screen shone at me for a moment before turning black again. The bar had closed hours ago, and I'd had to move my operation to the nearest Denny's to utilize their smoking section and unlimited coffee to its full potential.

Sure, we'd gone out a few times, mostly to the movies. Social conduct prohibited talking in the movie theater, so it was a win win for me. She hated my smoking. She hated my wardrobe. She hated my hours and availability, but she'd giggle with her friends and wave to me valiantly across the bar, making all the guys around them clench their jaws in jealousy, scoff and turn to shun me... which, if I'm being honest, was another win. And she left me twelve new messages when I had dumped her two days ago. She was my roommate's good friend who'd had a class with me back as an undergrad and thought I was something special, maybe a shy recluse she could change with a trip to the mall and an insightful conversation over a Starbucks cappuccino. Luckily, my roommate was moving out tomorrow, and I didn't have to pretend anymore. So bye bye Claire, it was nice knowing you. I'd used the word "nice" generously. It was actually completely uneventful knowing you.

I had no particular interest in what was being said to me, or going on around me. As far as I could remember, I'd never had any interest in anyone. My apartment situation was strictly business.

Jeff, like myself, needed a place near campus to make life convenient. He was a bartender at a pub a few blocks away from the school, reaping the benefits of the party lifestyle college students were infatuated with. Ironically, it was the same party lifestyle that made him drop out when we were both still Sophomore undergraduates, and now it was financing his half of the rent. That was the bar I'd just left a couple hours ago when they closed for the night. I couldn't go straight home to the apartment. Roommate-Jeff would always bring women back to our place, filling our small living room and empty hallways with idle chatter and obnoxious high pitched, drunk laughing. I was eagerly awaiting next week when I'd only know him as Bartender Jeff.

I looked to the bottom right of my screen and cursed under my breath, putting out my fifth cigarette in the ashtray next to my mug. It was 4:00 am. I had a mind-numbing summer session creative writing class to teach in 6 hours. Maybe teach wasn't the right word; "pretend to be interested in." Stories and poetry were piled on my desk at home, riddled with aimless ambiguity and no plot structure. Rhyme schemes with strict iambic pentameter with exoteric descriptions of cats and how much the writer hates their phone charger because it denies them "bootie calls and leaves blue-balls." Students taking an easy A to fill their schedules with convenience. Shocker for them, most of them were failing, except for a few scraping by with C's. A "Ch" escaped my lips in utter disgust, remembering their shitty work. I placed my head in my hands, frustrated, tired, dreading the stack I hadn't graded yet, the finals. It wasn't my fault they chose writing as an easy grade, mocking literature.

"Do you need another cup, Sweetie? You look like you're workin' hard." Waitress Emilia came by my table with a warm pitcher of coffee. The best woman I'd met since leaving for college. I looked up out of my hands, staring through her, my mind still drowning in the sorrow of grading papers when I got home. She wasn't perturbed by the black bags under my eyes, or the stench of alcohol and cigarettes permeating through my jacket, or my disarray of black hair. Emilia refilled my mug without an answer, and slunk into my booth. She looked excited to talk to me, a bright woman my age, probably another grad student in a different department, working her way through college. "Connor, do you sleep? Like, ever? What are you always writing?" I continued to stare, lacking the energy or patience to speak. I cared just about as much for Emilia as I did Claire, and I guess I'd made the mistake of exchanging names and opinions on the weather the other day ordering breakfast. Once the coffee had transitioned from her possession to mine, the indifference kicked back in. She seemed to get the message and scooted back out and away, back to the kitchens to gossip and carry on, but unoffended. I liked Emilia enough.

The absolute worst papers to grade were the love poetry. It made me suicidal. The diction radiated a perfume of sickeningly sweet flowers and sunshine that should only be alluded to in toddler cartoons. The rhymes were worse, forced. Love makes the sun shine out of asses in undergrad creative writing workshops. I lit another cigarette, continuing to watch the blinking of the cursor on my screen. My energy was drained in the first 6 chapters I'd written the night before. My phone decided to remind me of my 12 messages again. Even the ones that came out descent, in a literary fashion, with depth and less shallow insight, were wrong. They described love as lasting, infinite, infused with the concept of destiny and fate. My stomach made a gurgling sound, protesting my choice to chase hours of alcohol with coffee. A balanced food diet wasn't a part of me, coffee, and alcohol's exclusive club. It wasn't their fault really. Even the best authors, the staples of English Literature, often wrote of love in a sickening fashion.

Shakespeare's sonnets; "But thy eternal summer shall not fade, nor lose possession of that fair thou ow'st....When in eternal lines to Time thou grow'st". What a fuckin' joke. Love wasn't lasting, or infinite, or fate bound. *Love was*...I sat back in my booth arching my back slightly for a mild stretch, putting my arms nonchalantly behind my head leaning back, blowing out some smoke. *Love was...*

Like a bell in the distance I pictured a smile in my head. The sideways smile he would give me when I rumpled his hair, and he'd push my hand away laughing. My eyes widened and my cigarette dropped from my lip slightly. I hadn't thought of him in years. I shook it off carelessly and put out my cigarette. I was still buzzed, sleep deprived...getting nowhere on my book. My editor was going to give me an earful the next day, a repetitive chastising from hell. I 'ctrl' saved my document, and shut my laptop. I needed to get home and grade those papers so I could get a nap and a shower in at least before the 10 am class. I purposely didn't think about Liam, or his sideways smile, or whatever happened to him. I didn't have time for that shit, I made sure of it. *Fiction. Love was fiction.*

The next day the class was brutal, as always. Everyone turned in their final portfolios as I passed back their grades. My momentary relief of getting them all finished in time was traded for a new stack of bullshit. At least in the portfolios there would be no surprise 'blue balls' rhymes wanting me to stick my head in the oven. I walked the three story flight of stairs to my apartment, shifting my bag of student portfolios on my shoulder slightly. I had my own final at 5 pm and a phone meeting with my editor in about an hour. I'd written five good books since I'd graduated high school, and one really shitty one. The last two were just starting to sell decently and my editor was constantly up my ass, thinking this might be the break the publishing company was looking for. I had gotten a few decent checks previously, but I'd sent them to my little sister overseas. I wasn't too concerned. This wasn't about that.

"Connor! Ayo!" Jeff was naked in the kitchen with a bath towel wrapped around his waist, looking through the cupboards. He must have just showered. "Where's that one mug?" I dropped my bags on the floor and fell into the couch facing the kitchen. I didn't answer. So far it was a stupid question. He followed up "The blue one with the brown handle?" My voice was still raspy from lack of sleep, I was about to tell him I didn't know. "Oh, never mind, here it is!" He set it into a box on the counter. There were packed boxes all over the place. Jeff was the kind of guy who had a lot of stuff. I wasn't sure if it was because he was sentimental, or a pack rat, or just too lazy to throw anything out. A couple seconds later he pulled it back out to put coffee in. I caught a whiff of it as he sat down in the recliner next to me, it smelled delicious. "Dude. You look like shit." I laughed. Jeff wasn't too bad. At least he spoke his mind, and he wasn't sore on the eyes.

"Yeah, hangovers do that to you. I feel like my bartender should probably have cut me off. What a dick." My head was pounding too. I wished my shoes and coat were off, but now that I was already down, it was way too much energy to bother with. Jeff took another drink of his coffee. The smell of a tangerine-mango girly shampoo someone must have left by accident. He must have used it because it was within arms reach. I'd used it last night when I got home too. I needed to go shopping. There just wasn't enough time and I hated grocery stores. 24 hours a day was not enough.

"It's gonna be really fuckin quiet around here without me. You gonna be ok? I mean... if you die, would anybody pop in enough to find the body before it started to rot?"

"Yeah" I said, mustering enough motion to kick off my shoes, "The new roommate should be here sometime tomorrow, so make sure you get all your shit out by then."

"I should be done moving in the next couple hours, these are the last boxes. I feel like your kicking me out. Cheers to the end of a beautiful friendship!" He pouted with a laugh and made a motion with his cup. "But then I remember how sweet it's going to be living above the bar, and I don't give a shit." This was the most we'd spoken outside his place of work in over two weeks.

"If you take my coffee pot, I'll kill you." It was all I could muster.

"Where'd you meet the new roomie again?"

"I put a flier up at the bar, and a few in the English building. Emailed a couple times."

"I don't understand why you wouldn't demand a hot chick with a deep belly button to do recreational shots out of as part of the rent."

"Yeah, me neither." It was a half-assed reply but the heaviness of my eyelids finally won out and they shut. I heard Jeff put the mug down on the coffee table and felt him toss a throw blanket on me. Maybe a small part of me would miss him, we had been acquaintances a long time. No, maybe friends. Being roommates sort of made us friends. I heard him blast techno music from his bedroom as he finished packing, and he yelled on the phone with Claire over the music; "No, his phone was working earlier. He's probably avoiding you. I don't know. Did you not put out or something? I don't know Claire, he's just sleeping in the living room, ask him yourself!" A few minutes passed. My phone rang and buzzed violently again, and I decided I wouldn't miss him after all. It was the last thing I heard before I passed out.

I must have been dead asleep. I didn't hear him move the boxes out, or holler goodbyes when he left. When I finally woke up, I realized I'd missed the conference call with my editor. She'd left me a text threatening my life if I didn't make the next deadline and I was a little grateful I'd missed hearing that in real time. I'd slept all day. Oh well. What time was it? 4:30. I jumped up, slipped my shoes on, grabbed my school bag from my room and ran out the door. I barely made it in time for the final, but I was pretty sure I aced it, even half asleep. Since Jeff was gone now, I had no qualms heading back to the apartment right after class. Three flights of stairs and a few minutes brewing fresh coffee, motivated me to get to grading those portfolios. It only took a few hours, some Chinese delivery, and two cups of caffeine to get them graded (in a ridiculously nit picky fashion resulting in many low C's again) and online. A refreshing shower and some sweat pants later and I was back at my laptop trying to make up the hours I'd lost.

Thank god it was Saturday. I was back to the zombie like version of myself I'd grown much more comfortable with over the past few years by the morning. I'd finished quite a few chapters, then realized I'd fucked up a major plot issue and had to go back and essentially rewrite a variety of pages throughout the novel. I leaned back in my desk chair and angrily lit a cigarette. The smoke filtered out through the window next to me and I looked out to see the sun coming up behind the campus buildings across the street. I had a great view here. The sky was mutating from a bright orange, urging forward the potential intense brightness that would singe my irises after staring at my laptop all night. My cursor blinked at me in a brand new position, in the exact same fashion it did the old one. I pondered that for a moment feeling tired. I let my cigarette hang slightly in my mouth as I surged ahead, gathering new words from the crevices of my imagination, pasting them together with sentence structures ingrained in my mind throughout my education, desperate to convey my thoughts with 100% efficiency, painting pictures in a way that inspires no misled interpretation, that can lead the reader to only one concluding image; my image. Transferred directly from my mind's eye to theirs. My cigarette died out all on it's own and I placed the butt in the overflowing ashtray on my windowsill. I was just going to rest my eyes for a second on my desk. Just a moment of reprieve before my next burst of explanation and vivid imagery...

I heard the door buzzing through a groggy tunnel. Someone needing access to the stairwell to come up. I tried to shake off the sleepy sloth-like morning confusion that lingered. When had I fallen asleep? I sat up and stretched. My shoulders and back were killing me, in cahoots with my diet and smoking. I lit another one and meandered to the door, remembering how much I hate people. I pressed the button to talk to the person downstairs.

"Hello?" There was no response. I was annoyed I'd stood up for this. I pressed it again to speak. "Anybody there?" My voice sounded a little dead. I blew smoke, slightly pissed off. Maybe they'd pressed the wrong room. I started another pot of coffee and went and sat on the couch with my phone, finishing my smoke. I looked in my email to see when the new room mate was supposed to show up. I figured I should be able to show him the apartment and small talk for a moment or two before hitting up the grocery store and then the bar for a beer. "Re; I'm here, buzz me up?". There was a gentle knock on the door, as though someone were hesitant for anyone to hear it. Good! I didn't have to wait around to start my day. I pushed myself up from the couch and wondered for the briefest of seconds if I should care that I'd be meeting my new room mate half dead from an all nighter, shirtless, in sweats. Nope, I didn't give a shit. I blew smoke and answered the door.

"Hey, I just got your e-" my cigarette dropped out of my mouth. He made direct eye contact, and his voice was soft with a familiar British accent, deeper, more firm, I thought. I couldn't remember right then. I couldn't break eye contact.

"Hey." There was a fake chipper ring to his anticlimactic 'Hey' I instinctively hated. He stepped on my cigarette, squishing it into the hardwood floor. *Liam?* I stared at him, confused, annoyed. This couldn't be him, for starters, Liam was shorter. And more lanky. And frankly a bit of a putz. The guy standing in my doorway was, fuller, more confident. Another few inches and he'd have been as tall as I was. He was glowing almost, with an annoying bright aura that made me want to slam the door and go take a nap. But that smile he was shining at me was the same, and those blue eyes. I hadn't realized I was cocking my head with irritation radiating off of me. His smile faded into a polite concern.

"Is this a bad time?" he asked, looking back and forth slightly for an indication that I was busy, or had company. *Is this a bad time!?* My mind repeated. *Um. Yeah. Yes. This is a bad time.. Ya know, I didn't have a whole lot going on from 2012 to 13, so maybe some time in there.* I still stared at him. *Is this a bad time.*

"Go fuck yourself." It came out of my mouth as more of an exasperated comment. Where was my coffee? I noticed the silence exuding from my apartment behind me, the lack of dripping sound, an indication that I had a fresh pot, was comforting. I turned around and left him standing in the doorway. Maybe I should have shut the door, locked it, waited for him to disappear. But I didn't. I just turned, went into the kitchen. I needed coffee. *What time was it anyway? Who 'stops by' unannounced early in the morning? Or nine years later without a word.* I needed coffee. *Where the fuck had he been for nine years anyway? Here? In the U.S.?* I poured a cup, I needed coffee. I heard the door shut quietly behind me and I didn't want to turn around.

If he had left... with nothing else said, nothing explained, would I regret it? I wasn't ready to know. I poured my coffee. Directly above my pot was Jeff's cupboard. I opened it. That beautiful bastard had left me a full bottle of whiskey and half a bottle of Smirnoff. I grabbed the whiskey and filled the rest of my coffee cup to the brim. I didn't care that it was disgusting, even the least compatible friends will put up with one another in times of need. I needed a new cigarette too. I wanted to drink it all in one fail swoop, let the alcohol blur my mind and the caffeine activate my autopilot like it did around stressful deadlines, but it was still hot as shit.

"It's a little early to be drinking isn't it?" His voice was a life vest. He'd slid into the apartment before shutting the door. A relief I hated to acknowledged melted inside me.

"It's a little late to be showing up, isn't it?" *Cool down already, cool down*. I thought I was referring to the coffee. There was a pause.

"I thought it might be..." *Yeah, no shit Sherlock*. "For you maybe." Liam's voice grew softer and more hesitant, more familiar; " But it's not for me." I turned around; he was leaning his back against the door with his hands pushed down into the pockets of his jeans, staring at his shoes. I couldn't see his eyes behind his hair, they were pointed directly toward the floor; but the tips of his ears were slightly red. *Son of a bitch.*

My reactions were involuntary and impulsive, I couldn't stop myself. He didn't see me walk back toward him. "Con-" he started to say, about to look up. I lifted his face to mine and put my mouth on his. The second our lips touched a warmth came flooding through me. It resurrected the memory of his taste that I hadn't known I was desperately clinging to all these years.

———

13

"I just don't get why you can't go to school here, like a normal person. What does the UK have that we don't?" I was angsty, I didn't like this at all. Not when it was my baby-sister. Jen smiled and went to wave away my overprotective worries.

"It has-" I cut her off, annoyed, glaring cynically.

"Sex crazed lunatics, that's what it has Jenny, looking for an American piece of ass. What if the family you stay with are a bunch of murderers. Like Jack the Ripper." Anyone else would have thought I was dick, but she knew better. I thought I was talking quiet enough for this to be a personal conversation between me and my little sister. I was holding her hand like I used to when she was little, squeezing it a little more anxiously, and she knew better. Jen was 2 years younger than me, just starting her sophomore year of high school, but she was my solace. From the front seat of the car my mother laughed.

"Con! Watch your mouth!" It pissed off my dad that she never scolded me seriously. He made this "Ch" sound that radiated through the car making the girls feel uncomfortable, and shook his head in disapproval. I, on the other hand, always felt uncomfortable. Jen didn't say anything, but she squeezed my hand back, and tried to comfort me with a smile. I wanted to pull out a cigarette, but neither of my parents knew I smoked. "This is going to be great for her, she'll be fine. She'll make all sorts of connections over there for when she graduates. It's only for the school year. Show some support, Con." She glared at me slightly and flashed Jen a comforting grin, a warm one only mothers can toss around in such a nonchalant manner. I'd always thought this, but every once in a while I thought it more intensely than usual. She was way too good for Dad. Jenny and I often joked that Dad had ordered a Japanese mail order bride.

I had a habit of emulating my father's "Ch" sound. It seeped out my mouth like vomit, surprising me with it's echoing familiar sound that made me slightly hate myself, and him. I looked out the window, watching the cars pass on the opposite side of the freeway. I couldn't look at her, I was pissed, even at her. I felt like she was betraying me. She was my baby-sister, my best friend. Leaving to go halfway around the world as a foreign exchange student. But I wouldn't let go of her hand. When we got to the airport, my Dad wanted to drop her off at the curb, wave at her from the car as she disappeared through the glass doors. Fuck that.

"We still have to pick up our new kid for the year, Hank." Mom reminded him. We parked and Jenny and I took her bag out of the back for her. It felt light.

"Are you sure you have everything? Is this your way of saying you don't want to go?" I half jokingly tried to put her bag back in the trunk.

"Connor! I'm going! Oh my god." Her teenage 'oh my gods' sounded strait off the childish movies she still watched. But she was still smiling. She was like a tiny little Mom, and Mom looked so young herself they could almost pass as sisters.

My parents hugged her and coddled her in front of the security check, Dad included. He really loved Jen. Me I wasn't totally sure of, but definitely Jen. "Be good. Study lots," were his deep parting words of advice. Mom squeezed her till I thought her head would pop off. That image would forever be burned into my eyes; Mom squeezing her, Jen looking up at her for reassurance to calm her own nerves. She shook her slightly in a dancing motion. "Don't grow too much!" she warned, "You'll be fine. You're strong, you're brave, you're capable! You're *my* kid." She winked at her, "You'll be fine, no matter what." Jenny smiled, clearly feeling empowered. I knew she was almost 15, I knew that. But every time

I looked at her I saw an adorable little three year old who fell and scraped her knee and couldn't stop bawling from the shock. She came to me for her goodbyes.

"Connor, I swear to god, I'll kill you if you make me cry." *Make her cry!?* I was a grown 17 year old man on the verge of tears without a cigarette, God Damnit. I pulled her into a hug and kissed the top of her head.

"You're strong, you're brave, you're capable." I repeated, then I pushed her away. "Now get out of here." I winked at her too. The three of us watched her anxiously totting her carry-on through security, looking much too small to be capable of anything. I was ready to go; I turned to walk back to the car. This was too much. Dad turned too.

"Hey! We're not done!" Mom said, grabbing my elbow. I wanted to be done though.

Dad muttered an "I'll be in the car" and walked away in his fancy business suit. He was eager to get back to work. I didn't even know why he came. It made me angry, he should have been comforting Mom. She looked fine, she looked tough, but she couldn't have been. She had just sent her youngest child on an airplane to the UK by herself.

"We have to pick up our exchange student. Liam? I think that's his name? Or is that short for William?" she said. *Screw Liam*, I thought. But I didn't leave with Dad. I stayed as she looked through her purse to find the paper with the gate number our foreign exchange student would be arriving in. I wished I had a cigarette, my heart was seeping into my stomach picturing Jenny stepping nervously onto a plane without me. I wondered who would be picking her up, then remembered the family she was being sent to was super rich. She'd probably be picked up by a butler or something.

We walked to the baggage claim we were supposed to be at, but it was empty. There was just a kid with finely combed light brown hair standing by the chairs against the wall, unsure of what to do with himself, dressed like he was heading to church. The, clearly ironed, shirt with perfect creases and starched slacks were a big sign that he couldn't have been comfortable. From a distance he looked incredibly sad, bewildered. He'd lift his head, daring to look around for a moment, and then it would fall again and he'd be staring at his shoes. Mom pulled out her piece of paper again, to make sure we were at the right place. She tugged at my arm; "Con!"

"What?"

"I read the fucking paper wrong!" My mother's where I'd inherited my mouth. She only ever swore around me, it was our little secret. "His flight got here three hours ago!" She yelled it in a whisper fashion, another mom technique; loudly being quiet. She pulled me into a jog toward the lost looking kid.

"Liam? Are you Liam!?" she asked worriedly. He sort of nodded, with courteous smile, not daring to look either of us directly in the eyes, like he'd caused great misfortune upon us. "I'm so sorry, Liam." Mom said, immediately pulling him into a hug. One that I sort of imagined she'd hoped would be mirrored on Jenny's receiving end. "Welcome to America!" This direct contact seemed to shock him a little and threw him off balance, making him literally laugh out loud and I saw a red tint creep up his ears. He finally looked up at her with a sideways grin. "Were you waiting long?" she asked. Liam acknowledged me with a glance as well, his accent was thickly English.

"Not at all." He blatantly lied. "Hello", he said to me. He didn't look away as I looked down on him, our eyes locked for a moment, making *me* feel vulnerable, like the outsider in my own country. I felt like he was looking at me for an assurance I wouldn't give. He didn't wait for me to reply "But I've I misplaced all my luggage." His face was almost glowing red with embarrassment and an anxious disposition, preparing himself for a lecture. I watched his fists ball up at his sides in nervousness, probably a substitution for fidgeting. I said nothing. In a strange way I guess I forgot I was there, like a fly on the wall observing.

"Don't even worry about it." My mom assured him, keeping her arm around his shoulder, trying her best to make him feel welcome in a strange new place. She started leading him toward the exit to make our way back to the car, and I followed behind, watching them, unsure of how to feel. "Con's got plenty of old clothes that will fit you till we can go shopping tomorrow! It'll be fun, you, me and Connor will go pick you out some new stuff until they find your luggage." It was unlikely that she'd be able to successfully rope me into that.

He looked out of his element with her hanging on him like that, like he wasn't used to being touched. But he didn't push her away, and his ears stayed a tomato red. He tilted his head looking behind him, trying to glance at me again, with that contemplative look burning behind his blue eyes, a little pleading. Why would I need to reassure this guy? It wasn't my job. I looked away, with a discriminate smirk, shoving my hands in my pocket and following them out to the car. My father didn't say a word to him all the way home, earning scathing looks from Mom.

I didn't say anything either, feeling awkward, replacing the feeling with utter dismissal, and resting my chin on my hand as I nonchalantly stared out the window, waiting to ignore them all again. I could feel him stealing glances at me all the way home in the back seat. It made me much more uncomfortable than usual, and I decided I disliked him immensely. My hand moved of its own volition toward him, and I patted his head in a patronizing way, rumpling his hair. Was he really fifteen? He seemed too fragile and guarded, not like anyone I'd ever met before. *Is he really only two years younger than me?* Reaching out to him startled even me in a strange way, and I turned to look at his reaction. My eyes widened in surprise at the relieved smile he threw at me.

My mom laughed at the "Ch" that echoed out of me as I looked away again.

Back at the house I went straight from the car to my room. I shot him a glance beforehand, and there was that look again; the "please don't leave me with these people" look that I ignored. I pulled out a spiral and flopped down on my bed, chewing on the end of my pen, thinking. I wanted to write about how pissed off I was that Dad switched kids with a business partner. His company had been working with Clarke Co. for years, so when big CEO Clarke mentioned the idea to the lowly, small-time, recently-bloomed CEO Hank, Hank was all too thrilled to suggest the foreign exchange idea. This stabilized their relationship on a more personal level, strengthening their business Partnership. Jenny hadn't mentioned it even once, but he just assumed. I guess he assumed right. She was all for it. Who was I to be pissed? I jotted some notes in my spiral. Good for her. And good for him. I guess you had to sacrifice a kid or two to be successful, right? I dropped the spiral. I wasn't getting anywhere on this story, and it wasn't a priority by any means. I wasn't a part of any clubs, it wasn't an assignment. It wasn't giving me credit or furthering my education, I guess it wasn't important. I laid on my back and stared at the ceiling, watching the ceiling-fan spin around and around.

I pulled a cigarette out from under my mattress, took it to the window, and blew some smoke out the screen. I wondered if Liam was settling into Jenny's room, or if he was going to bunk in our guest room. Probably the guest room, huh? I opened my door, intending to peak my head out and check. He was standing there, I'd almost hit him with my door.

"I was about to knock..." He said, trying not to seem awkward or creepy. But he wasn't, at all, to begin with. Those blue eyes were so innocent and sweet, darkening my own spirit in comparison. His awkwardness gave me a confused smile, that didn't quite feel fitting on my face. "I was going to." He assured me.

"What do you want?" I thought I was being nice, kinda. My first thought was to say 'ok' and shut the door, so this was a step up for me.

"Erm. Nothing."

"K." I shut the door, and sat at my desk. What a weird guy. He was going to be here for a year? Knock, Knock. I answered.

"What?" I asked again. I should have been annoyed but I wasn't. It made me laugh lightly. He looked more embarrassed than ever.

"I needed pajamas." He was looking at me this time, which was nice. But it sort of made me feel embarrassed instead, which annoyed me. "I'm sorry I didn't say it the first time. I get the feeling you're not fond of me being here, I'm sorry about that too. But I promise, once my luggage comes in, I won't need to bother you." He wasn't exactly a bother. I stared at him, noticing his red ears again, in his church-going clothes. There was an odd relief in not being alone with my parents.

"Yeah? That's good then." I went and grabbed him some of my older clothes that I thought might fit, and a couple pairs of clean boxers. When I handed them to him, his face turned a new deeper red that I hadn't seen yet. Maybe it was just the accent that was throwing me off. *Have I ever known anyone with a British accent before?* It sounded kind of neat, especially in full sentences, the words ringing off one another, the vowels very distinct. He took the clothes and went on his way.

We didn't speak much the next week. I thought it was a good thing, the way he'd avoid me around the house, sticking to himself, spending all his time in his room. Mom didn't cook often, and wasn't home often. She'd gone to the mall with Liam, but apparently he just couldn't bring himself to let her buy him stuff. Other than that she was at work, and Dad, of course was always "working" through the night. Most (almost all) nights he never bothered to come home. His job was two hours away. We had a lot of money since he had been moved up to CEO, so I guess he could afford hotels. For god knows what. God and me.

School started the next week and I was grateful. I don't know when it was that I started feeling like the guest in the house. I'd leave often, in the afternoon, twice at night, and take walks around town to think. I'd usually walk up to the school, sit in the football stadium a while, look out over the empty field and contemplate on how serene it was, without the bushels of jeering crowds and hyped up jocks. This usually cleared my head and let new ideas sink into my writing, not that it was important. It was just something to pass the time, to fill it in. The days felt like time slots and sometimes I'd just keep a record of stupid shit I did, or I'd make up some shit to fill a piece of paper. I never knew what to do with myself in my free time. Jenny used to come with me sometimes and get advice about her insecurities. I wondered how she was doing.

His luggage came in three days later just when I'd gotten used to seeing a stranger in my clothes. He started dressing in what I guess was his normal attire but it looked exhausting. They weren't all church looking clothes by any means, but clearly high dollar clothing, clean cut, model clothes that all seamed tailor made. They were just jeans, nice shirts, clean cut jackets. I already knew the younger girls at school would go nuts over him. I felt a little sympathy; it was evident he wasn't super sophisticated in his socialization. Even his lounging clothes were *nice*. No basketball shorts, or loose T's. I half expected him to sleep in formal wear. Liam woke up early, went to bed early, and really only needed to ignore me for the brief few hours that my lackluster, lazy summer schedule intertwined with his.

The house only felt like mine again late at night. I'd greet mom when she got home. It wasn't anything special, but I'd always pretend to be looking for food in the kitchen when she'd walk in. I'd ask if she wanted something to eat since I was apparently already preparing something for myself. But I was never hungry. I'm not sure why I did shit like that, why I couldn't just say 'hey, how was your day? I waited up for you'. But she seemed to know. She'd let me make her a sandwich, and she'd reach up to brush the hair out of my eyes, laugh, tell me again that I should get a 'fucking haircut', kiss my cheek. Then she'd take her sandwich and a bottled Dr. Pepper out of the fridge to her room to finish something up on the new laptop Dad had bought her. It had been a long long time since we felt like any sort of family, normal, dysfunctional, what have you. We were all just roommates, drifting in and out of each others lives occasionally, solely out of proximity. I'd lounge around the dining room, listening to the background noise of the news drift in a mumbling fashion through the house.

A few years ago I heard her one night, after Jen had gone to sleep. This was long after Dad stopped coming home, back when mom hadn't been working and we lived in a much smaller house. I wondered if she'd found out finally. But mostly I wondered how she hadn't already known. I don't remember the exact moment I'd found out, legitimately, but I'd known Hank was fucking his secretary for years. I was young though, I mostly thought; *Good riddance. More time without you.* I'd never thought about how Mom might feel, not knowing for sure, not till that night I heard her crying. I'd probably never forgive him. But this house was much bigger, more spacious. I heard the news still, but I doubted that I'd hear her crying anymore, if she ever did. I'd become paranoid over the idea.

I found it strange that he owned a guitar, let alone brought it with him. He barely spoke and I couldn't even imagine him singing. A small part of me wanted to hear it though, his voice, ringing with melody, the distinct words meandering in the air. He probably just strummed and a small part of me wanted to hear that too. But he never talked to me, after that first night, never said a word. He was congenial with my parents, and he smiled at me politely if we passed in the hallway, heading back to our individual cells. I wouldn't smile back on principal. One day I found my clothes folded in front of my door, and I took them back into my room and set them on my dresser. However, I couldn't stop myself from thinking that he should keep them, to relax in. No, I didn't care. I was antsy, eager for school to start.

"Connor?" he asked, while we were sitting in the living room, putting our shoes on, our book bags alongside us. Mom had meticulously gotten his school supplies for him, triple checking his book lists, grabbing my hand-me-down literature from various book shelves throughout the house. He seemed uncomfortable in his clothing, nervous, but looked normal to me. Maybe he'd previously gone to a private school? It made me jump. That's how little he'd spoken to me, it was like I'd forgotten he was capable. I looked at him, he had my attention finally. "I won't speak to you at school if you don't want me to."

"Of course you won't." I picked up my bag and walked out the door. He hurriedly followed me out, locked the door behind us

23

with a key Mom had given him, and followed at least three steps behind. He pissed me off.

———

I felt my numbness, my indifference, fading away. Liam pulled his hands out of his pockets and wrapped his fingers in mine, taking my hand away from his face, but holding me there, frozen in a drizzling warmth where our lips pressed together. A throbbing radiated through me, my heart pounding on my eardrums, demanding the evacuation of all other thoughts, anything not Liam was no longer welcome. I felt like I was showing a weakness I didn't care if he saw, that I needed him to see. I needed my warmth to reach him, I needed it to tell him all the things my words couldn't. I pressed my body against his, pushing him slightly into the door, and he let me. He pushed back, just a little, slipping his tongue inside my mouth, breathing me in, and I felt his own desperation. I wondered briefly of all the things he needed to tell me, all the things he couldn't say. My blood raced from my head downward making me dizzy, euphoric, high. My free hand wrapped around his waist pulling him closer. I broke us apart, and pulled him to the couch. He let me. Without a word. I kissed him again, more quickly this time, melting into the cushions. I trapped him under me, putting my knee between his legs, feeling his heat against my thigh, drinking in his scent, melting in the pounding of his heartbeat that drummed against me. I was in a frenzy, I couldn't think. He wrapped his arms around me and pulled me into him. Next to him. He turned sideways on the couch with me, I thought he might fall, but we were too entangled, too entwined. He put his leg around me and I felt the heat from his groin against mine. I kissed his neck, ran my fingers through his hair. Everything was floating, swirling, fading in and out of reality, but I needed this, of all things, to be real. I needed him to be real. His voice echoed through me.

"Connor?" he pulled just a little away from me, became level with my eyes, gently brushed my hair out of my face. When did I become so weak and pathetic? His cheeks were rosy, flushed, with a tint devoid of embarrassment, a glossy intensity in his eyes that excited me, made me forget it all; the years, the anger, the resentment, the pain... the numbness that had followed. My hands were at his zipper, unbuttoning his jeans, needing him. I slid my hand into his pants, and felt his intake of breath that I cut off with another deep kiss. I felt a shiver go through him, his back go slightly rigid, his chin tilt up. "Connor, hold on...wait..." I even felt his nervousness creep back into him, like the very first time. "Con..." he couldn't finish his thought. I kissed him again, I couldn't stop, I couldn't risk letting him find himself in the chaos of my affection. I slightly bit his ear, and whispered to him with a rasp still caught in my throat,

"I think I've waited long enough."

The door flew open.

Bartender Jeff walked in with an unassuming nature.

"You really need to start lock- What the fuck?" He stood there, dumbfounded. Liam jumped up faster than I thought humanly possible, almost taking my hand with him. He zipped up his pants in a hurry, with a naively admirable amount of hope that, at this point, this could possibly be construed as anything other than what it was. *Jeff, you're an asshole.* A loathing grimace enveloped my face as the numbness crept back up inside me, the anger re-situating itself. The reality settling back in. He should have knocked. Definitely should have knocked. Liam stuttered

"I erm... It wasn't.. shit." He put his face in his hands, hiding his overwhelming embarrassment even if for just a second, which made me chuckle slightly, earning a very interested, shocked look from Bartender Jeff. Something clicked in Liam's head and he looked back at me, then Jeff, then back at me. "Why...oh shit...what the hell Connor?!"

"Yeah Connor, what the hell?" Playful, obnoxious, Bartender Jeff made himself at home, in his former home, with a smile playing on his lips. He sat in the recliner next to the couch and put his feet up on the coffee table, enthralled in the situation. Nonchalant as always. I sat up, glaring at him viciously. He didn't live here anymore. "And who might you be?" he asked Liam, who seemed more nervous than ever.

"I erm... I'm nobody. I didn't know, I'm so so sorry. I mean, I should have known, but I didn't."

"He's nobody. Get out Jeff." I felt like Liam was misunderstanding. I couldn't read his expressions well, but he looked more apologetic than embarrassed now, and it irritated me. Not that I should care, but my heart was barely tapering off from being aroused.

"Piss off, Con." There was a quiver in Liam's voice, a forced calm, but his eyes betrayed him. They were welling. He was definitely misinterpreting unnecessarily. *God damnit.* "You could have just fucking told me. You didn't have to fuck with me first." Jeff was such a dick, he played along like this was a game. He didn't know my heart was tightening, writhing in anticipation; because, unlike Liam my expressions were much more practiced in the art of not giving a shit. They'd had years and years to develop, before ever meeting him.

"Yeah *Con,*" He'd never called me that before, nobody here did, but the fleeting micro-expression of Liam's jealousy appeared to be too intense a temptation for him. "You could have just told me too." Jeff laughed.

"Jeff. Get. The Fuck. Out of my apartment." I was ok, I was calm. Jeff was always like this, having his fun.

"Relax, I just left a few boxes in my closet. It's not like I knew you had... 'company'." he pushed himself out of the chair and went back into his room. Liam made a motion to leave, ignoring us, shaking slightly, a quivering. Fury? Excess energy? Nervousness? Was he about to leave again? Would he come back? Probably not, right? But it was his own fault, arriving at unnecessary conclusions, assuming the worst. This wasn't my problem. Jeff hollered from the back,

"Ya know, Claire said something about you being gay. I just thought she was being a bitter bitch though. I mean I've lived with you for years. Absolutely no indication man." I rolled my eyes. He really was a nuisance at best. Liam had gotten to the door, and looked back at me as Jeff spoke, confused. "It's really actually a little fucked up Connor, I'm pretty sure you've seen my dick."

"I've never seen your dick, Jeff." I sat back on the couch and lit a cigarette. Judging from the conversation, Liam would stay now, right? He wasn't a complete moron. I leaned back, and put my feet up. *What a fucking morning.* But he didn't stay. He shook his head and turned the knob. Before I knew what was happening my body moved on autopilot again, jumping up and slamming the door. I turned to look at him, but he wouldn't reciprocate. He was still shaking, hands now balled in fists at his side. I reached down toward his chin again, just to tilt his face toward mine, so he could see I had no intention of letting him walk out, but he shoved it away.

"Stop fucking with me Connor. I get it, alright? This was a grossly undermined mistake." He looked at me, the quiver in his voice shining through his eyes. "It was different for me then it was for you back then. And I'm sorry that it went... the way it did. And I'm sorry for everything that happened, but I just thought, that maybe after all this time you'd realize that it wasn't my fault." Liam caught his breath, "But you clearly haven't." He forced a smile at me, an ironic one. I really fucking wished I knew what he was talking about. Even a little. What wasn't his fault?

Jeff came out holding an average sized box under his arm. With no shame whatsoever he walked up to us, ignoring the conversation, and stole the cigarette out of my mouth, putting it in his.

"'Excuse me guys," he motioned us away from the door and opened it, "Hey, Mr. Accent, is that your guitar outside? You should play at the bar sometime, everyone loves British musicians, you'd kill it. Look at the Beatles." He repositioned the box. "See ya, *Con.* " He flashed me a charming grin, enjoying my reaction at my own cigarette drifting out the door and away with such an asshole. Usually my cigarettes were such loyal friends.

I stuck my head out the door to see what Jeff was talking about. Liam's familiar guitar was propped up by the door, and a prim looking luggage bag lay at its feet. It took a second for everything to click.

"Holy Fuck. Liam, are you the new roommate?" He didn't say anything. I pushed my own hair back out of my face, only for it to fall in a tuft.

"No."He shrugged and bitterly laughed, looking calmer. Looking done. A composure that scared the ever living shit out of me. "Definitely not". he pushed passed me, grabbed his stuff, and was leaving.

"LIAM!" I yelled down the hall, hurting my throat. Everything inside me wanted to follow suite, but watching him go felt so familiar, the shackles of a painful memory locked me in place, a prisoner in my own head. As I had always been, though, at least before this moment, a willful ignorance was there to comfort me. And I was pissed. So angry that he'd showed up here, just to make sure that I knew, and acknowledged, that I'd always be alone.

But in the guise of my future roommate? That wouldn't make sense. I pushed my hair back out of my face. But he had to have been. Because no one else ever showed up.

CHAPTER 2: HELLO AGAIN

He's an asshat, really. I slowed down to a jog, panting. I
don't even know what I was expecting now that all was said and
done. Maybe a 'Oh my gosh Liam, it's so good to see you!', or a
'It's about bloody time Liam, here, let me help you with your bags.'
I shifted the bag around my shoulder and repositioned my guitar
case. They were getting quite heavy, starting to weigh me down.
Truthfully, I expected myself not to be a blubbering idiot. It all
went so smoothly in my head, an excellent plan. I knock, he
answers. I step in, I kiss him; a hey-remember-me kind of kiss. I
bring in my bags like I own the place, tell him I'm moving in.
Done. He re-falls in love with me all over again through sheer
proximity. Winners all around. Show him I wasn't the shy little prat
I used to be, show him I wasn't giving up that easily this time
around. It was an inner-bargaining chip really, my confidence. I
kept telling myself; *Liam, it's ok to be a fearful pansy and not tell
him it's you in the emails, just so long as you grow some fuckin
balls in person.* I saw how that played out.

And then I'd gotten all upset, and angry. *Jeff.* What a stupid
fucking name. *Hi, I'm Jeff, I work at a burger joint and wear
sleeveless T's and skateboard to work with my jeans falling off.*
Though, frankly, he actually held himself with rather impressive
sophistication. I kicked a can that someone had littered on the
sidewalk laughing bitterly at my shitty American accent inside my
brain. As I walked passed, a younger girl with bright pink hair was
smoking in front of a coffee shop. She paused to watch me walk
by. Girls were always doing that; it made me uncomfortable. Like
perhaps my shirt was on inside out, or I had a 'kick-me' sign taped
to my back. *And I surf.* Yeah, I bet he surfed. And I bet he was
good at it. Like really good at it... and I bet if he did cook
hamburgers for a living they were delicious, and everyone loved

them. And he wasn't bad to look at, a little bit of an ass, a little charming. I bet he cooked at home for Connor and they laughed and drank whiskey together, and he taught him to skateboard, and surf, and other stupid American things in their stupid American apartment, at their stupid American college that took me three applications to get into. And now I didn't even have somewhere to live at! I bet Jeff wasn't so bad.

I came here technically to check on him. Make sure that he was doing better than I was... I came to apologize and make sure he knew the truth. That he didn't hold onto any false ideals, haunting him or goading his isolation. I knew Con when we were younger. I really knew him... back then. That's right. The plan had been to come, check on him, and then leave, go home... maybe pick up somewhere new, again. Move on with my life. And then I'd seen the fliers, on a whim. The very first coffee house I'd stopped in, it was lying right on the table that I happened to choose... "Apartment for Rent- Contact Connor Shay: Shay.Connor@unt.edu". Then I'd felt awfully brave all of a sudden.

The universe was clearly on my side. Maybe this meant something? And on a joyous whim I started to think, starting as a tiny little seed, blooming into a giant oak of stupendous idiocy... maybe he could love me again. The next thing I know I'm actually believing that maybe 9 years was enough, maybe he didn't hate me. Maybe I'd show up with my bags and he'd be happy as a clam. I felt queasy thinking about it... a huge wave of nausea, self hatred, and embarrassment. Like there's any bloody way the fucking universe has ever been on my side. I thought maybe I'd made amends on that bridge; maybe it was throwing me a bone. No. Connor still absolutely hated me... and I lost the opportunity to even do what I came here to do. I never told him the truth. I never apologized. And then there's Jeff. Who was Jeff to him anyway?

And Claire, who was Claire? I stopped walking, feeling more dejected.

I was in front of a patio seating area in front of a restaurant, and I pulled up a seat, set down all my stuff. Technically, it was all the stuff that I'd owned in this world. I sort of wanted a cigarette. Not because I smoked, but because I still had Connor's smokey scent on my clothes, and the taste of him slowly fading away in my mouth, and I hated it. My body was aching everywhere that he'd touched me. My nerves fought urgently not to forget the feeling of his skin on mine, almost in a panic. In case that really was it, that was the end.

Why had he kissed me if he didn't still have feelings for me? Because he knew I couldn't let him go? Because he somehow figured out that even just the sound of his name pressurized the blood coursing through me and amplified the bursting of my heart in my eardrums? He wanted my hope to engulf everything, to seep its way into all my doubts, to expunge them... only to crush my soul all of his own accord. To play me like a fiddle. To embarrass me? To taunt me? To showcase a side of me that the rest of the world already perceived as disgusting, to showcase my shame? Did he really hate me that much? My throat constricted, remembering an unpleasant first week of high school in the US. I thought about the old Connor. How intensely I loved him. *It really wasn't my fault, Con.*

I put my head in my arms on the table and felt a clutch in my chest. It hurt to even breathe. I thought of how easily I folded, how quick I was to melt at his touch, his taste, his warmth. I'd wanted him so badly, I didn't even stop to think.... the way I'd felt when I said his name, when I'd wrapped myself around him, when I'd moved his hair to see him better, to see him again. And was he laughing on the inside? Was he delicately hiding his contempt and loathing? I crouched even further inside myself.

I heard music playing across the street and looked up. It was early afternoon, so it somehow felt out of place, in an exciting way. In the same way that I did. It's not like I could just get up and go home, back to my father's house. I couldn't beg for his forgiveness the same way I could Connor's. I didn't actually want it. Being gay really wasn't a choice, it wasn't something I'd gone out of my way to do, something I could control. It was the same as being in love with Connor. I wanted to despise him, curse his name, piss on his future grave. Or worse yet, to be indifferent towards him, to briefly acknowledge him as a stranger. But I just couldn't. I needed to stop this; I couldn't go down this negative rabbit hole. I couldn't be that person. I couldn't afford to. I knew, even as a dumb little teenager, fresh from home-school tutoring all those years ago, that I'd always be his. Whether he'd have me or not. And that was the inescapable truth of the matter.

I grabbed my guitar case and headed to the bar, having to double back for my luggage that I'd almost forgotten. Bars were a comfort zone for me lately; I'd recently frequented quite a few of them with my bandmates back home. Somehow I'd make this all right. But at the moment I just needed to vent, to brighten my spirits. The bar was fairly empty save for a straggler sitting up at the bar itself, face folded into his arms. The music I'd heard was booming out of some speakers from the back.

"When I said to come play at the bar, I didn't mean immediately, Kiddo." Jeff had walked in through a back employee door on hearing someone enter. "You seemed pretty busy after all." He gave me a knowing wink as he walked behind the bar and started moving things around, rearranging glasses and cleaning smudges when he noticed them with a hand towel. I didn't say anything. I wanted to be mad at him, like he'd wronged me somehow, but I couldn't, could I? Connor wasn't mine. In fact, he may very well be his. Which would mean, in a way, that I'm the home wrecking cheater. When you put it like that...

I moved toward the bar and set down my things, grabbing a seat. I was 23, but I didn't drink. Anymore. I managed to make a fool of myself perfectly well without altering my intoxication levels. There was never any need to hand over my dignity on a silver platter these days. Jeff had this arrogant smile playing on his lips that made me uneasy. Was he angry? Well duh. That's a dumb question I guess.

"Jeff? It's Jeff, right?" I asked. How terrible would it have been if I got his name wrong too, on top of making out with his boyfriend on his couch in his apartment. *An apartment he was moving out of. Had he and Connor broken up maybe?*

"Aye Lad, 'tis Jeff." He was mocking my accent. Except... he sounded Irish.

"I'm not Irish."

"Oh, you all sound the same." He was kind of an ass too. Maybe he and Connor were made for one another. Though, in his shoes, I wouldn't even have spoken to me. I looked down at my hands, rather ashamed, wondering how much he'd actually seen, in that split second walking in. Enough, probably. Was the sarcasm and the condescension a defense mechanism? Was Jeff actually hurting?

"Listen, I'm really really sorry about what happened. I honestly didn't know that Connor was seeing anybody. And that, what you walked in on, was never my intention." *Maybe a fantasy,* I added silently, shrugging in my head. "I don't know if you've already broken up, or there's a good chance that I've ruined it for you guys, but... I... I don't know, mate. *Literally,* I know nothing." He continued to let me talk, and I couldn't let there be a silence. It was too awkward now. I had to keep going, didn't I? Even if my face was burning and I could feel steam rising off the top of my head. Did I have an obligation to this stranger, to not just leave right then, find somewhere else to kill time? I guess if Connor loved him, I couldn't exactly hate him. *If Connor loved him.* The thought was so heavy it nearly nailed me to the ground.

I looked back up at Jeff. "If you love Connor, you can't let stupid impulsive episodes chase you off. He's a dick, but he's got a good heart, even if you can't always see it. And if he's close to you, I don't know... I think it means something." *Yeah, it means there's not a chance in hell he loves me anymore.* "The Connor I remember never got close to anyone." *Except me.* For obvious reasons I left that part out. I tried to shake off the intense jealousy. The self loathing. The overwhelming disappointment. The feeling of death crawling into my bones. "It didn't mean anything. I'm sure he was just dicking around. I wouldn't let this... ruin everything if I were you... I guess is what I'm trying to say..." The thought of sharing my special place in Connor's heart with this annoyingly amiable jerk in front of me made my blood boil, but... what rights did I have here? If Connor was happy now, if he loved him...

"Oh God, okay, stop talking." He put down the glass. He wasn't entertained anymore, I could tell. "You are disgustingly honest and straightforward. And so so gay. Like super gay." *What?* "Nothing has, or will ever, go on between me and Connor. Like...ever. You see, I've got an insatiable taste for women. Tall, short, sweet, slutty, chunky, skinny, you name it, all different kinds, but definitely with all their lady parts." I was a little confused, and it must have shown. "Mr. Accent. I'm not gay. I'm like the opposite of gay. I'm like a Lesbian, if anything." He thought for a second. "Well, wait, that would mean I *was* gay. Ok, not like that then. I LIKE WOMEN. End of story." My heart beat loudly again.

"You're not gay??"

"I'm not gay."

"Then you're not with Connor?"

"Aye lad, I'm not with Connor." I laughed then, loudly, and not at Jeff's pretend accent.

"You're totally straight!" I couldn't help repeating a little, convincing myself. He did a 'there-you-have-it' motion with his hands and smiled. "And you do understand I'm not Irish, right?" He laughed.

"Yes, I'm fucking with you." He went back to moving things around, laughing to himself. I just watched. I knew I was grinning like an idiot, but again, I was used to it by now. "I didn't even know Connor was gay till like 40 minutes ago. Didn't see that coming." Jeff handsomely shrugged. "But honestly, in this area I don't totally blame him for keeping it to himself." I was ignoring him now. Maybe Connor wasn't into guys anymore? But... I'm not sure he was ever into guys. I mean, he was into me at one point, but no one else. *Who cares? Jeff isn't the enemy.*

"Jeff, do you work here?" I was smiling at him. My friend Jeff. Yes, being not Connor's boyfriend made him my friend. Even if Connor still hated me, I was just a little step closer.

"Work here, eat here, drink here, sleep here." He smiled. "I live in the loft above the stairs, that's why I moved out. I'm working on buying it out. If I can raise enough revenue, come up with new marketing platforms to get new business, I think think I can pull it off." I didn't know him well but it still felt strange to hear him talk about something seriously.

"Do you think a nice Brit with a descent voice might be just the ticket?"

"It couldn't hurt. Lets see what you've got." He came around the bar to sit on one of the stools as I pulled out my guitar. "Do you want to know what the weirdest part of all of this is to me?" He asked me as I made sure my strings were still in tune.

"What's that?"

"In all the years I've known him, I don't think I've ever seen him smile. And I don't mean like the 'I'm about to walk over and murder you in the face' smile he makes when he hasn't had coffee. I mean *really* smile." I tried with much difficulty to focus on my guitar tuning. I still didn't know who Claire was. I still didn't know if I'd ever get Connor to forgive me. I didn't know where I was going to live, or where I'd be staying that night. But I knew Connor wasn't dating Jeff, and that was enough to keep me going for now, I guess I'd just have to figure out the rest, right? That's what I'd come here to do in the first place. And now I knew I'd made him smile.

———

The first week or so in the Shay household wasn't so bad. I felt an odd sensation on the back of my head a great deal, and girls in my class giggled a ton nearby. I couldn't shake the feeling they were giggling about me, though I don't exactly know what they had found funny. Probably how I dressed? Or spoke? Or was it something I *wasn't* doing? It was a little suffocating to be honest. I wasn't used to being around so many people all the time. But I found that if I focused on my shoes, and recited a poem in my head, everything else would go decently quiet and I could calm down enough to make it through. Even if they made me uncomfortable, it was nice being around people. Not alone in that big mansion back home. It was nice living with people that were home too. Right down the hall. Hank and Maggie were more than hospitable.

I didn't have anything to say. Expressing was griping, griping was irritating, and irritating people wound up alone.

When I was very young, there was an afternoon I'd spent out in the courtyard. I used to have nightmares back then. waking up in a cold sweat, feeling panicked… always feeling like I'd lost someone I'd never had. I'd shake it off… try to entertain myself, play outside, watch a movie. That day I'd exhausted all of my indoor solitary activities and gone outside to cheer up in the sunshine. I'd balanced on the small brick walls of the garden planters, jumping off and rolling around. Killing all my excess energy. The cook was in a nearby kitchen, she could keep an eye on me from the window. She was elderly and rarely spoke. I'd been alone for weeks... My parents had traveled to Spain to watch the Running of the Bulls festival; whatever that meant. And I'd missed them. I always missed them. I exhausted myself, finally... my heart pounding in my chest as I collapsed dramatically in the grass. I stared up at the sky feeling small... delicate...and alone. I spoke words, gibberish, and it faded off into the wind. I yelled. It faded off. I sat up and looked around, seeing and feeling noone. The last surviving human on the face of the planet. I started to shiver in the warmth, pulling my knees up to my chest. I closed my eyes because the world started swirling and I was becoming lost again.

And then I heard the gates opening at the front of the house, saw the driver pulling up with my parents; unmistakably them, curving around the side courtyard to the front driveway. I shook off all the bad feelings, pulling myself up, running into the house, wanting to jump into their arms...ask them never to leave me behind again. I stopped dead in my tracks noticing my clothes were stained with grass. I ran upstairs to my bedroom, ripping them off, throwing new ones on. By the time I'd gotten back down the stairs, my parents where in the kitchen with Ezzy. My mom's voice rang through the doors, giggling, laughing, as she always was. The consistent echo of Dad's follow up laughter ensued. I paused before running in there, happily listening. I started to make out words.

"Oh it was just absolutely Lovely, so exhilarating, Esme."
Esme was my Ezzy. She didn't reply. Dad followed up,

"Lovely? It was gruesome. And it was loud. But I love that
you love it, Dear." There was a pause. I was immediately
comforted by the sound of their voices. I'd missed them so much. I
went and sat by the door. Just to hear a little more.

"And how was William?" Mom asked. I heard Ezzy answer
with her thick Irish accent.

"He was sad, Miss. He's a lonely, lonely boy." I heard Mom
scoff and Dad grunt slightly. My heart started beating a little faster
and I was straining my ears more, leaning into the door.

"What a terrible thing to say, Esme. How awful it is to
come home after such a lovely trip and be bombarded with your
negativity." I heard her heals on the granite tiled floor, moving
around in the kitchen. "And It's not our fault, really. If he just...
weren't so whiny... so needy...so codependent. We might have a
mind to take him with us." My Dad stood up for me;

"He'll become a man soon enough."

"Yes. But till then what a terrible thing, to have to come
home and spend all of our energies coddling. It makes me want to
plan our next trip to Barcelona, every time I walk in the door...
someone has got to teach that child that griping is irritating and no
one wants to tote around an irritating boy." My heart was beating
out of my chest now; I was frozen.

The door swung open on it's iron hinges as Ezzy came
fuming through with the most flustered look on her face. She saw
me sitting by the door and a wave of sympathy cleared her
expression. She didn't blow my cover, she didn't say a word to
me...as usual. She kept walking. I didn't go in to say hello to my
parents. I'd slowly made my way back up the stairs, to my
bedroom, and quietly shut the door. I compulsively picked up my
toys around the room. I placed them delicately on shelves, in

drawers. I folded all my clothes that I'd thrown about. I didn't know what 'codependent' meant... but if it was bad, I didn't want to be it. If it meant dirty... I could be clean. They never came in to tell me they were home.

I didn't see Esme again. My mother let me know the next morning that she had quit...and she asked me to go easy on the next cook and housekeeper. To be less 'codependent'. And even though I changed everything about myself and never bothered anybody... they still never took me to Barcelona.

And Connor. It's difficult to describe how it felt living next to another person. I used to lay awake at night in the mansion, and sometimes I'd sing just to hear another voice in the house, an echo across my gigantic room. Sometimes I'd sing too loudly, and the echo would take just a millisecond longer to boomerang back to me, making me jump, startled. The weekends were the worst, where the maids usually didn't come in, so I lacked even the sound of tinkering through the house. The first night I was here I awkwardly crawled into the small (in comparison to the one I had at home) bed. I wanted to sing, to hear something, but I was too embarrassed. The silence was suffocating too. I lay there, staring at the ceiling in their guest room. Unfamiliar walls, with a strikingly familiar emptiness that I naively didn't think America would have. And then there was a light squeak, a tiny one that I'd never be able to hear in the hustle and bustle of the daytime, the opening of the door next to mine, easy footsteps down the hallway and the opening of cupboards in the kitchen. It's a strange feeling you get, knowing you're not alone; it's calming.

It didn't take me too long to notice that he'd leave his room at the same time every night, to make sure he was out in the kitchen when Maggie got home. And he'd wait to open the cupboards. It made me laugh every time. I wonder if he really thought she didn't know he did it on purpose. I gave her much more credit than that. That was really quite nice of him, going out of his way to make sure she never felt alone, making sure she knew she had a family to come home to. Or at least a son to come home to; I found it odd that Hank was never home with his wife, but maybe that was just a cultural thing I wasn't familiar with. My parents were always together, at least, usually away on business, or astoundingly long vacations.

"Clarke?" It was really really sweet actually. I smiled just then thinking about it. I wondered what he did in his room all day. Why he didn't come out. "Clarke?!" I wanted to talk to him, but I barely knew how to speak when addressed. Starting conversations was terrifying, being the first to speak, interrupting their thoughts. I'd already interrupted his life. I was staring at him again, across the gym. The seniors were playing half court basketball on the other side. If I did see him back at the house he was reading, or scribbling away in a current novel or notebook, or taking a nap on the couch in the living room, and I'd slink back into my own room as to not disturb him. It was odd really, watching him run, jump, fake out his classmates, dribble a basketball, make a shot, sweaty and focused in his school PE uniform. Clearly I was no expert, but he looked to be good at this, and his height was a huge advantage. I wished I had that ability, I was terrible at all sports ever invented. It was my father's greatest disappointment in me, besides the other thing. Connor paused for a moment and looked my way, we locked eyes for a split second. Should I wave? I started to. "CLARKE! CLIMB THE DAMN ROPE!"

I turned around. The seniors continued on with their basketball, all except Connor, and the other boys in my physical education class were staring at me, whispering to one another, laughing. The coach was beat red. "What the hell are you looking at?" he asked me.

"Nothing sir." I looked down at my tennis shoes feeling the inescapable blush crawling up me.

"You a gay-boy, Clarke? Would you rather have pom poms and a skirt and be cheering for our seniors?" *Absolutely not, that would be mortifying.* Everyone laughed again. I wanted to crawl inside myself, disappear into the floor. I was getting light headed, about to have a panic attack and couldn't think properly.

"Yes sir." *No Sir! I meant no sir!* I shook my head, shaking off my response, "No sir. I meant no sir." But everyone was already talking, whispering, pointing.

"Then climb the damn rope."

"Yes sir." And somehow, by the grace of the gods, and with a great deal of struggling, I did. Halfway up the rope, Coach blew the whistle and class was over, and a small part of me thought he might have done that on purpose.

I was late getting to my next class which was really a shame because it had become one of my favorites. I knew that Connor had already read all of the books we were reading. Maybe twice, judging from the different colors and combatant ideas in the side notations. Alot of them had turned out to be books he'd already read for other classes and even had his notations and analysis in them for questions being asked in class. It was comforting to not look like such an idiot for once when called upon. His handwriting was a little difficult to make out sometimes, but I managed. It was comforting in other ways too. I felt like we had had tons of conversations throughout the book, and he often made me laugh throughout the stories. I hadn't cared too much for reading back home. Whether it was because I lacked imagination, or because I lacked the proper books to be interested in, I wasn't sure, but it was a different experience when Connor was essentially leading a commentary on everything. Maybe it was creepy, but sometimes I'd even forget that, in reality, we never spoke. He had also probably completely forgotten that he'd even written these notes by now. He was a freshman three years ago right? So technically it was past Connor I was getting to know so well on adventures with Tom Sawyer and Huckleberry Finn.

"Liam, why are you late?" The teacher interrupted her own lesson to ask me this question as I quietly shut the door behind.

"I'm really sorry." I heard a boy at the back of the class mock my accent rather terribly, somehow maintaining his thick southern drawl I imagined coming straight out of an old western movie, "I'm *reeeeaaaly sorree"*, and a few other people laughed with him. I looked at my shoes again, they were the most familiar image I'd etch into my brain here in America, I was beginning to think. "I got caught in a bit of trouble with the PE rope." I thought she was going to laugh at me, or ridicule me too, but she didn't. She turned to the boy that had made fun of me.

"David, go to the office."

"What? Are you serious?" The boy looked dumbstruck.

"I'm done with your attitude, I told you last time." This boy had been teasing me all week, and glaring at me across the classroom. He was also one of my classmates laughing at me back in gym. It appeared to me that a girl he might have taken a fancy in was going out of her way to sit next to me, so I at least understood where he was coming from, and I felt bad for it. I needed to do something since it was kind of my fault.

"It's ok Ms. Gilly, really. He was only having a bit of fun." There was only one empty seat left in the class and it was next to said girl, so I made my way toward it, anticipating the warm acceptance of blending into my classmates. But David stood up, grabbing his school bag.

"I don't need some faggot standing up for me."

"DAVID JENNINGS. Get out of my classroom." Ms. Gilly's wide eyed expression and stern posture got him out of his seat.

"Well he is one of 'em. He told the whole gym last period. And he's a creep in the locker rooms." *Was I creep in the locker rooms?* I remembered being embarrassed about how my muscle tone was seriously lacking compared to the other boys. I never did anything strenuous back home. I never even had to clean really, let alone manual labor. So I'd changed in the bathroom the last couple days. *Was that creepy?*

"I didn't... that wasn't..." I started to say, looking around for a second for some confirmation, but inevitably dropping my eyes to the floor. David had already picked up his bag and made his way to the door. He gave me one last glare as he slammed it and left. I sat down in my seat and slouched gratuitously, wishing everyone would stop staring at me. Ms. Gilly tried to go on with her lesson, her aura still fuming. The girl next to me comforted me.

"Don't sweat it. Everyone knows he's a jerk." I opened my book to a random page and read one of Connor's scribbles in the margins; "A broken clock is right twice a day." It was clever, and the situational irony made me laugh. I smiled at her, gratefully and kept flipping through my book. "We're on page 56."

"Right. Thanks." I caught up with Ms. Gilly and the rest of the discussion. It was very sweet of her to show concern for me. Maggie at the house, too, with bursts of parietal concern I was clearly not accustomed to, and this girl next to me who's name I could never remember. *Ashley? Amanda? Something with an 'A'...* People weren't so bad. I couldn't let one jerk in a single classroom get me down, I just had to try a little harder to fit in, blend in with the crowd. In fact, I bet I could just speak to David, apologize. We could even possibly be friends, right? Perhaps he wasn't such a wanker after all? If I could just speak to him.

Listen, David, I'm really very sorry about the misunderstanding you and I appear to be having, is how I would start. Yes, that sounded sincere. I don't know why it wouldn't since I meant it. I stood at my locker, grabbing my book-bag to head home. *And the locker room too. I should apologize for that as well.* The sophomore lockers were on the second floor and mine was closest to the windowsill facing the front of the school. I looked down below at all the students filing out, chatting, joking, playfully pushing each other around, couples holding hands, or waists, or necking. Waiting for each other at designated locations. They made it look so easy, like in the movies...and here I was planning out word for word an imaginary conversation that I wasn't sure I could even start. I couldn't afford to blunder this up further. Why was it so easy for everyone else? I sighed, took a deep breath and re-situated my bag. *If they can do it, I can do it.* I caught a glimpse of Connor down below, not speaking to anyone, leaning lazily against a tree. A group of girls stood near by, throwing him glances, sharing giggles between each-other in such an obvious fashion I couldn't be mistaken in assuming Connor ignored them on purpose. He evidently hung out by that tree a great deal.

I made my way down the empty hallway. Everyone else ran out of this place rather quickly once that last bell rang, to meet up with friends outside. But I still hadn't mastered my lock... or had any friends to meet up with. Turn it twice, no, one left and twice right, then go around once to the seven.... something like that. Everyday it felt like sheer luck that I managed to open it at all. At least Connor's consistency made him easier to find at the end of the day, to follow him home. I felt extremely vulnerable walking by myself, and frankly I knew how spacey I was and how likely I was to get lost. I had no idea where to look for David. Maybe I'd have time to attempt to talk to him in gym tomorrow?

45

I walked out the side exit at the bottom of the stairwell intending to circle around to the front outside, so as not to get lost in the hallways. A Texas wave of heat took me by it's usual surprise because of the phenomenal air conditioning in the school building. I put my hand up to shield my eyes from the sun as well, for just a second, and tripped over apparently nothing. My bags went slamming to the concrete with the rest of me and I barely managed to shield my face from the floor with my arms. *Crap.* I really was clumsy. I heard some laughing above me and looked up. *David.* And a few of his friends stood over me. They must have been just beside the door as I walked out or I'd have seen them. Did they trip me on purpose?

"Pardon." I said, trying to gather my books off the sidewalk. "I'm sorry, I didn't see you there." I was on my hands and knees, my heart racing, trying to fit all my books back in my bag. I didn't want them to see the rosacea rising in my face or to notice how embarrassed I already was.

"That's because I fucking tripped you, Idiot." David's friends laughed with him again. I looked up at him in surprise. I'd never been tripped on purpose before. He looked like a mean guy. A big mean guy. Was he really only a sophomore too? I tried to shake it off. No one liked an over-reactor.

"I was... I was actually just looking for you..." I started. Now was a good time to apologize right? For however I'd offended him? The pressurized thudding was rising in my ears, and I tried to calm it as I started to stand up, to dust myself off. I was getting light headed. I couldn't breathe right. Luckily I'd already prepared my words. "Listen, David, I'm real real sorry about the misunderstand-" He pushed me back to the ground before I could fully get up. His friends crowded around me a little and they all looked huge, at least... from this perspective. I tried backing away from them on the ground, to get out of their small circle. But there were four of them and they just moved with me. *Everything's fine.* I told myself, rebelling against my panic. "I just wanted to apologize." My mouth was working, somehow detached from the rest of me.

"Oh, you were? Well never mind. Hey guys, he was going to apologize. I reckon stealing my girlfriend and making me look like a fuckin' moron is okay then!" He kicked me in the ribs, knocking the breath out of me. A darkness threatened to envelop my sight for a split second and I fought it off. The blunt force knocked me completely down and I clutched my side. I'd never been kicked before. I'd never been hit. Fight or flight was kicking in, and I was under no delusions of grandeur. I looked around frantically from the floor for some kind of weak spot, an opening to escape. "Get him up." He spat the order at his friends, who were happy to oblige. Why wasn't anyone else on this side of the building? What had I done? They held me on each side, holding my arms back and a panic ran through me. I tried to squeeze my way out of it, to pull, maybe even wiggle away in a pathetic manner, but they were too strong. I stopped struggling and everything froze. I stared at him in sheer awe. *What had I done? Why was this happening? Wait. Wait a minute.* My brain was hollering, trying to escape my lips. I didn't think I'd ever been this afraid before. It succeeded in an almost whisper.

"Wait. Wait a minute." I managed. "David, I didn't do anything. I swear, I didn't." I was trying to piece together clues, some indication as to why he'd hate me *this* much. I didn't even know him. He upper-cut me in the stomach and my body clenched up as I felt his friends grip tighten on my arms. The darkness threatened my sights again, and my hearing became distant. All I could hear was the pain. *Shit...* I never should have come here.

"You see, it's just like my daddy told me. Y'all are an abomination." *Y'all? What was I a part of? Who was I grouped*

with? He's mistaken, he's confused. It's just me. I'm just me.
"Freaks of nature. And we're not needing you're kind in our school, around our girls..." I squeezed my eyes shut in anticipation and he hit me again, this time on the side of my face, his knuckle landing on my right cheekbone, throbs of aching force rippling through my eye socket to my brain, through my jaw too. The side of my mouth nicked a tooth and I could taste blood. It was enough to make the pain go silent. "And especially not in our locker rooms." Then it dawned on me why he was so upset. Which group it was that I was apart of. My eyes shot open, and I looked at him; his brow furrowed, his eyes blazing with fury, anger, disgust. The bludgeoning strike of the realization hit harder than any blow he could have physically inflicted. *An abomination. Freaks of nature.*

"Because I'm gay?" I thought about my admiration for Connor, and how, if I was being honest with myself, I knew it was more than that. How I'd happily listen to his sounds around the house, and pinpoint him out in the crowd. I wanted to retract my feelings, bury them deep inside until they suffocated and died. I'd never felt so dirty, so *unclean*. I closed my eyes again. I wanted to go home, back to England.

"Ut oh." The guy on my right said quickly.

"What the fuck?" there was surprise in David's voice, and I opened my eyes. Connor was there, and he'd pushed David back, away from me, against the side of the building. He turned to the two boys holding me.

"Let him go. Now." They listened. He was an older intimidating senior. I didn't say anything. I couldn't.

"This is none of your business Shay, back off." David tried to push passed him and Connor slammed him into the wall this time. He was skinnier than David, but much taller, with a foreboding calm intensity.

"I'm making it my fucking business."

David's friends had let go of me and run off but I hadn't noticed. All I could do was stand and watch dumbly.

"Why do you care what happens to this fag?" Connor bent over him, staring down at him sinisterly.

"Are you deaf, you fucking hillbilly piece of shit?" He grabbed him by the collar of his shirt. "I said I'm making it my fucking business." David pushed Connor away from him non aggressively, and Connor backed off and pulled out a cigarette. "If you and your loyal pig-fucking friends ever touches Liam again..." he took a drag, "and I mean lays a fucking finger on him, I'll beat the ever living shit out of you."

"Oh yeah Shay? You think so?" The buff sophomore tried to look intimidating. Connor laughed.

"No. No not really. I'm not getting a record because of this dumb shit. But you're dad works for my dad doesn't he?" David deflated a little, starting to understand the gravity of the situation. "I'd hate for him to lose his salary paying job in my Dad's company. I hear it's really difficult for felon's to find decent jobs in today's economy." he spoke slowly, with confidence and an air of condescension, taking another drag, smiling.

"Jesus Shay, we were just messing around." David's whole demeanor changed almost instantaneously.

"Oh yeah Jennings? Doesn't look like it." Connor turned to me, reminding me that I existed. David glared at me with a seething hate. "Were you guys just palling around?" David's eyes burned toward me and my shame rose back in my throat.

"Yes." It came out almost inaudibly and Connor's brow furrowed angrily.

"Yes what?" he asked.

"Yes, we were just palling around." Connor put out his cigarette under his foot, crushing it into the ground with a temper.

"Oh ok Liam. My bad. Carry on then...excuse the fuck out of me." He shoved one of his hands in his pockets and waved at me with the other, brushing me away in the air as he tried to walk away passed me. My arm instinctively reached out and grabbed the nook of his elbow as he passed, stopping him. He couldn't just leave me here with David. I hadn't realized I was shaking till now, and I don't think he had either. Connor paused and his gaze zoomed in on me, tracing my features; a small amount of blood I could feel on my right eye, the bruising I could feel forming under my skin, the tense cramping of my shoulders in an effort to move as little as possible as the rippling ache of my ribs woke up in my body.

"See Shay, me and the Fag are just good buddies. No problem right?" Connor whipped around, jerking himself away from me, and closed the gap between himself and David in less than a second. He decked him in the mouth, and kneed him in the stomach. David slunk down into a crouch holding his sides with a "fuck!". Connor knelt down next to him and tilted his face up. I could barely make out his urgent whisper from where I was standing, bewildered.

"What's that Jennings? Oh don't worry about it, we were *just messing around.* You and I are just a couple of good buddies." He walked back to me and put his hand on my head lightly, without saying a word, and I knew he meant it was time for us to go home. I walked next to him to the front of the school to get his bag that he'd left by that tree. The one he stood at every day. The one I realized he'd designated as our meeting spot. I no longer staggered three steps behind.

I couldn't believe she'd done that. But there she was, fussing over me, looking at me so closely that I could smell her lavender shampoo permeating off of her long black hair streaming

50

it's way out of the bun she'd tried to wrestle it into. She looked so young. Much too young to be a mother. I'd never been fussed over before.

"That son of a bitch. Who the fuck even does that?" She cupped my face in her hands and kissed my cheek lovingly. "Liam, don't you let those assholes get to you. They're just a bunch of woodland hicks." Connor chuckled from behind me, sitting on the counter eating an apple. He'd called Maggie to ask her where the first aid kit was when we'd gotten home and she'd driven home from work in a rush. Not only that, but she'd stopped at the Jenning's household and given them a scolding. "Seriously, you're perfect just the way you are; goofy fuckin' accent and all." She ruffled the top of my hair.

I laughed and the smile made my face hurt.

"And then you know what that bitch Jennings had the nerve to say to me Con?" she whipped around and glared at him accusingly and my heart skipped a beat. Had I inadvertently gotten him in trouble? Was I causing problems? "She had the nerve to tell me you'd started it."

"Did she now?" Connor took another bite of his apple and I was worried for him.

"And then that little shit-for-brains pudgy fuck came lopping around the corner looking all bruised and 'victimized'." Maggie used dramatic air quotations on the word 'victimized'.

"Oh man... I wonder what happened to him. Crime in these parts run rampant..."

"And she starts hollering at me, telling me to keep my 'faggoty-ass' kids in check, that white trash piece of shit calls *my* kids faggots." Connor tilted his head at me in an amused fashion. *Had he heard everything David had said? Did he know?* As she talked she was whipping open the fridge and pantry, taking out

51

groceries to cook for dinner since she was already home anyway. I didn't know what to say. I was frozen. *Did they know?*

Maggie scoffed. "If I'd only be so lucky for you to turn out gay, Con. Then I wouldn't have to deal with those obnoxious shit-for-brain bimbos you used to bring home." My inside went numb with the double edged sword that dove through my chest. She didn't know I was gay then, but Connor was definitely strait, and bringing home girls. *Which is fine.* I told myself over and over, trying my best to calm any unnoticed recesses of hope from inside me. I'd really known all along right? Maggie kept going. "As if my apathetic, delinquent, son would waste energy even noticing that little shit without provocation. And really Con, you should have hit him harder. And a lot more." She motioned to me; "Look what he did to *my* kid!?"

The way she kept referring to me as hers lit a strange flame inside me. It made me blush, the rosacea climbing in my cheeks, scaling up my ears. My parents had only ever referred to me as "your kid." They'd argue at the dinner table politely, back and forth, on the very few nights they made it back to the house. My own mother would say "Listen, what are you going to do with *your* son? He's wasting his potential in this house. How is he supposed to be a decent, well rounded, *normal* citizen worthy of passing on the family name?" and my father would then reply; "Darling, *your* son will be just fine. There are programs we can enroll him in, in the church, to *fix* him...". And here was this beautiful Japanese lady, fussing over me, claiming me with no obligation as *hers.* In a very immature, childish way I wanted her to kiss my cheek again. My mother had never done that before.

But she didn't stop her ranting there. "I told her if her kid ever touched mine again I'd crawl through her fucking window and break her damn jaw."

52

"That's not.. um. Thank you Mrs. Shay, but I'm really ok. Honestly." She looked at me half sympathetically.

"Oh Liam, I'm half joking. I'd ring the doorbell." She winked at Connor and they passed some sort of silent message between them. Was she serious? "What started all this anyway Liam?" Connor spoke up for me.

"T'was an apple." He he said, tossing his apple core into the garbage can at the other side of the kitchen.

"Swish." His mom said absentmindedly. "It's always a girl huh?" She muttered under her breath and I had a hard time hearing her. It sounded like "That's surprising". More directly to us she added;"You teenage boys need to find something better to fight for. Like truth, justice and the American way." She side-glanced at Liam. "Or the Britain way? English way? You know what I mean. Did you at least hit him back too, Liam?" Her gaze was penetrating and made me feel ashamed of myself; ashamed of how easily I'd just given up, like I'd disappointed her.

"No ma'am." She stopped cooking and came back over to me and put her hands on my shoulders.

"Liam, as long as you're in this house, you stick up for yourself, and you stick up for your family. Do you understand? You don't let anybody put you down. Not always physically," She threw a dagger glance at Connor, "but you fight for who you are, what you want, and you never give up." Connor hopped down from the counter as she kissed my cheek again and went back to her cooking.

"Welcome to our little cult, Liam. You're strong, you're brave, and you're capable." He used a mock-dictator voice and ruffled my hair again, let his hand linger for just a second longer than I thought he would, before he walked passed and went back into his room.

My one-track teenage mind couldn't help but whisper to me sadly; *But what I want is him.*

———

I'd helped Jeff close the bar hours ago, wiped off tables, stacked chairs. He had to yell at some girls in the back to leave so we could close, and they'd laughed and asked for our numbers before they'd finally left. Jeff poured us some shots of whiskey, and ended up taking them both because I didn't drink. It made me think of Con pouring his whiskey into his coffee this morning, which I'd hated. I wondered if he drank a lot, if that was an everyday thing.

"Liam. Liam, right?" Jeff must have been annoyed earlier, when I hadn't remembered his name, or he was pretty scatterbrained. "You sir, have the voice of a fucking angel. And you're guitar is the shit. If you weren't batting for the other team you do realize you could literally get any chick you wanted, right?" He didn't wait for an answer. "But either way, you're gonna make me fucking rich. I'll have this bar in no time. Did you even notice the broads hanging all over you tonight? Just from a set? Fuck man. Seriously. They were eating up that hot, well dressed, british guy shit like fat-camp kids around cake. Where'd you learn to do that?" We were shutting off the lights and heading up the stairs.

"I just sort of picked it up I guess, the singing and the guitar. I had a lot of free time back home, and not a lot of distractions. It's the only thing that really keeps me grounded."

"Well, whatever it's doing, it's doing really fucking well. You've gotta keep playing here. Maybe learn some happier shit though?" I did tend to stick with the slow songs, the soft ones. I'd tried playing in a band once that played rock back home last year, and I loved it, but without a group the soft songs were easier. And I

54

felt them more. Especially now. Jeff had asked me up to his apartment a while earlier, when I'd mentioned I wasn't sure where to spend the night. He started terribly humming the chorus to a song I'd played earlier, and it echoed in the empty apartment, making me laugh. Over all, I'd had a half decent day, we were both relativity tired, in just a few minutes were were ready to pack it in, call it a night.

"You're absolutely fine with me staying here?" I asked as I unrolled some blankets on the floor of Jeff's studio apartment.

"Sure, why not? Any friend of Connor's is a friend of mine." He pulled off his shirt and threw it on a bar-stool he must have stolen to have a bit more furniture. "But not the same kind of friend, so you keep your happy ass down there and we'll both make it out of this without any trouble, right?" I laughed. He fluffed his pillow once before nestling into his bed. I turned off the light and, true to my word, crawled my happy ass under the blankets on the floor. It wasn't so bad. He threw an extra pillow at me in the dark that landed on my face, and I happily accepted it. When I breathed in I couldn't help but smile, and close my eyes feeling more comfortable than I had in years. I hated that time was dissolving the memory of Connor from earlier, first the taste, then the scent... or maybe I could still smell it faintly. I inhaled. I could definitely remember his scent. It was on the pillow.

"Did you steal this?" It came out as a chuckle.

"What are you, a fuckin' bloodhound? Go to bed." I was exhausted, but I couldn't sleep. There was no way. Jeff's apartment was never completely dark since the bar's neon sign shone through the window with a luminous fluorescent light that swept in comfortably, protecting all the potential stubbed toes from the threat of late night trips to the bathroom. "Liam, are you scheduled for classes yet? You're enrolled, right?"

"I've enrolled, but I haven't signed up for fall yet." That was the plan, though I still had no idea what I wanted to do.

"You know what might be fun?"

"What's that?"

"Summer classes. You can still sign up for the second summer section till Monday."

"Honestly I don't know what to sign up for."

"Well how about something to help with your music? Earlier those were your own songs right?"

"Yeah."

"I'm just saying there's a really cool creative writing class open. I'm pretty sure it's not full." Jeff laughed out loud to himself, "The guy who teaches it is a hard-ass so it's usually pretty open." I rolled over on my side and propped up my head in my hand. I couldn't see up on the bed from this angle so I absentmindedly glanced around at the shadowed objects along the ground; mounds of clothes mostly, and unpacked boxes.

"Jeff?"

"Damnit, do you already know?"

"Know what?"

"Nothing. What were you gonna ask?" I shook off his suspicious behavior lightly.

"Why are you doing this? Being nice, letting me play downstairs and stay here?"

"Honest answer?" I heard him rustle and I imagined him rolling over and propping up his head as well. "Because I know Connor well enough to think it'll piss him off. And I just can't pass up the opportunity."

"Why?"

"I don't know, that's just how our relationship works. I think deep down we both get a kick out of it."I heard him lie back down. I wanted to ask a million more questions about Connor;

how'd they become friends? What was he like now? Who was Claire? Did he ever mention me?

"Hey, how-" he cut me off.

"Liam?"

"Yeah?"

"Shut up and go to bed."

"Alright. Well thanks Jeff, I really do appreciate it, regardless." He made a grunt sound and I could tell he was already falling asleep. It was a really cool, really strange feeling that I was about a block away from Connor. I wondered what he was thinking about, lying in bed, if he was in bed. I'd left in such a crappy way, and I needed time to muster the confidence to apologize. And I needed to gather my thoughts, think things through this time. Maybe being swept away wasn't the best response for either of us. Maybe we needed to slow things down. We couldn't just skip all of the hard parts, the talking and figuring each other out to go straight back to physical stuff; the kissing, the touching, his body pressed against mine, the sound of his voice in my ear; *I think I've waited long enough.* I shivered and felt myself melting again, just remembering.

I seriously needed to get my shit together.

CHAPTER 3: THE LUXURY OF A FEELING

I seriously need to get my shit together. The bathroom was still spinning and I could smell the faint aroma of too much drinking all over me; the cold sweat, the barf near the toilet seat. *That's gross. I'm a fuckin keeper.* I tried to stand up and everything churning in my stomach burned up my esophagus as I leaned into the toilet. I made it that time, *Swish,* and fell back against the wall in front of the toilet. I slid down and buried my head in my knees. Everything was cold and I wished I had a shirt on at least. I hugged my sweats close to me and chuckled.

There wasn't a splitting headache throbbing through me, or a piercing in my brain, and I wasn't as disgusted with my bathroom floor as I should have been. That could only mean one thing; *I'm still drunk.* An alarm started going off in the pocket of my sweats and it startled me. I fumbled around to grab it, flipped it over and my heart *dropped* into my groin at the flashing lights. A note popped up with the annoying alarm vibration and beeping; CLASS. *God damnit.* I tossed the phone across the bathroom and looked around again, thinking I could stop the room from spinning by sheer stubborn will. It couldn't be Monday, there was no way; it was Saturday yesterday. I'd just seen Liam yesterday, and he left yesterday. Unless I'd drank for 48 hours...

I had to get going, I had to go to class. My class? *I'm teaching...* I had no lesson plans. I was supposed to do that Sunday but apparently time skipped a day screwing me over. I laughed again and sort of swung my body over toward the bathtub, crawled inside and lay there for a second. Had I at least turned in my finished manuscript to Folly? I sat up and reached out to turn on the water, leaving it on cold. I squeezed my eyes shut in anticipation of the freezing droplets falling on me, but my body still went rigid and tensed up when they did. My sweat pants were soaked and it still took me a while to remember I hadn't taken them off. *Why'd I drink so much??*

I hated my inner dialogue, I loathed it. The shower pounding down on me was clearing my thoughts, slightly washing away the dizzy room and giving my asshole conscious an opportunity to breathe. I was being a little bitch and feeling sorry for myself. *Boo-hoo, Liam left.* He came back, and he left again. He was probably back in England by now... since it was Monday. Not that I cared. But I felt my throat constrict and burn in a way that had nothing to do with my stomach acids. *Fuck him.* God I was pissed. I was pissed that he'd felt so familiar, I was pissed that he'd changed so much, was bigger, more fit, more confident. I was pissed that I'd had no self control, that I hadn't been the one to tell him to get the fuck out, I hadn't been the one to push him away. My anger joined forces with the water and somehow got me on my feet. I peeled off my sweats and boxers and threw them in a heap on the tile floor in front of my sink for future Connor to give a shit about later, then looked up at the water and let it freeze out the rest of my thoughts.

I was feeling a little better as I worked my way to the kitchen. *Pants, check, shirt, check, jacket, check, bag, check.* I made my way to coffee, my rebound fling to replace the emptiness in my heart from the abandonment of alcohol. Alcohol couldn't handle my life, couldn't handle my schedule, my responsibilities, and it left me as soon as the money ran out. Alcohol was a gold digging whore. Kind of like Liam right? Extract the financial issue, insert emotional stamina and the likeliness is striking. When he needed me I was there. When I needed him, when I was broken, he was gone. He just left and crumpled the shattered remains of what was left of me under his sneakers as he ran out. The first time. But this time was different; he came back specifically just to break me. *Fuck him.*

I poured the coffee and my stomach made a weird sound as it hit the bottom of the mug. I wondered briefly when I'd last eaten. Coffee fixes everything...except dehydration. I was too god-damn pathetic to make it through my day without it either way. I threw on some aviators Claire had bought me at the mall last week, and headed out the door.

I concentrated really hard on that saying 'you gotta put one foot in front of the other' and followed it with a literal translation. The sun was killing me, I could feel a headache setting in. Thank god my class was in the same building as last sections, there's no way I'd be able to walk around searching for it. My head was so light it felt like I was floating, and yet the amount of energy it took to keep my legs moving and maintain a vertical position was just astounding...and the headache was kicking in. Thank god I had nothing in my stomach left or it would have been all over the pavement by now. Shower or no shower I must have looked alarmingly like the incarnation of death. Like the grim reaper. Which, to some of these underclassmen I probably was. I was fine though. I was fine.

I was fine after high school, I was fine all through college, and I'd be fine now. *Without him.* I wasn't a 12 year old girl who had the luxury of pinning over a little crush. I was a grown man, with a job, and a career, and an education. I felt the nothingness creep inside me, the uncomfortable comfort that settled there and made camp when I remembered that anything ever changing was highly improbable.

He was gone, and that was it. I needed to focus on more important things; staying vertical, not puking, making it through class. I was done with him, I never wanted to see him again. I meandered through the hall, watching the tiles as I shuffled, looking up made me dizzy. I heard the mumbling sound of sleepy, energetic underclassmen permeating through the big wooden door and I took a last breather before opening it. My headache boomed with the full on chatter, which may only have been whispers. I didn't bother looking up, I didn't bother taking off my sunglasses just to give the florescent lights the satisfaction of twisting my stomach to knots. The chatter died down.

"Sorry I'm late," I said to my desk, flopping down in the wooden chair in front of the class, facing everyone. "Welcome to Creative Writing, 2110." Nope, that wasn't right. "2260". Nope that wasn't right either. "Some number on the syllabus, look it up if you need it." One of the students responded, but I still didn't make eye contact. I vaguely wondered if I looked as debilitated as I felt, but it was inconsequential regardless.

"It's 2113, section 3."

"Is it on your syllabus?" I snapped.

"Yes sir."

"Then I don't care." I leaned back in my chair and tilted my head back, staring at the ceiling. I missed my apartment, my bed, or my couch. I wish I hadn't fallen asleep on the floor. My bed sounded like a whimsical dream-land of delicately soft marshmallow-pillows. My throat hurt. "We're going to be moving the desks into a circle, so it's more of a workshop setting. This isn't going to be a lecture class, most of you will read what you've written and, as a class, we'll critique. If your uncomfortable sharing your work or I deem it inappropriate you can meet with me after class during my office hours. I assume if you've signed up for a writing class you can already read..." The words flowed out in a robotic fashion, "And if not, so help me god, get out of my classroom. Read the school safety regulation information on your syllabus by yourselves, and let me know after class if you have special needs or require special accommodations." I paused. What was I forgetting?

"And don't copy garbage from the internet." I added. The screeching of chairs made me jump; I'd forgotten how loud they were. I whipped off my sunglasses and buried my ears in the palm of my hands looking at my desk. *Son of a bitch.*

I knew anger was fuming from my expression at the poor undergrads for doing what I told them to do. But I felt no mercy. About 20 people stared at me with apt attention, big eyes desperate not to miss any instructions. I glared around the circle for a minute; it would take me a while to learn all these names, become accustomed to their styles of writing. It always felt a little intimate reading the projects of the other students. You get to know things about them that even their best friends, their families don't necessarily know.

"You've gotta be fucking kidding me." My mouth cut off my train of thought, and everyone stared at the seat in the circle I was seething toward.

"I swear to God, Con," He put up his hands in a 'stop' motion, "I didn't know you taught this class." My mouth kept moving forward and broke my eyes away from him. *Fuck him.* I wasn't going to let him bother me anymore, I wasn't going to let him in. And I felt impaired, I didn't have the energy to analyze this situation, put the puzzle pieces together. But already, I felt a heaviness inside me lessen. The lack of finality, the idea that he hadn't already jumped a plane back to England nestled it's way into my chest.

"We're going to start this class by going around the room, explaining why you chose it. What writing is supposed to do, or what it means to you." I was already flinching just remembering last sections shity responses. I knew to keep my expectations low. Why was he here? "And after that you're going to follow a prompt that I put in the syllabus in the calendar section for today. We're starting with poetry this week..." Why was he enrolled? "Next week we move on to essay format, the week after that is short story, then you'll need to put together your portfolios which I'll cover more extensively when the due date gets closer because frankly, I don't care enough today to waste our time, and it's in the syllabus."

They filed through the hoops, one after the other, humoring themselves with responses they perceived as witty, listening to one another to scavenge answers and maybe sound better on their own turns. It was a little adorable and simultaneously annoying that they thought any of this mattered. I purposely started on the girl to the left of Liam. It annoyed me that the girls had flocked next to him. I had a sneaking suspicion that they wouldn't get higher than a C in my class. The ever dependable head throbbing commenced. When the circle came all the way around, I barely let the girl on Liam's right finish her last sentence.

"Alright, so here's our first prompt," I had fished a piece of chalk out of my bag while I was pretending to listen, and I stood to turn to the blackboard. The sudden movement was too much for my dizzy, light headed, barely mobile body to handle and I fell back into my chair, my hand slipping out from under the support of my desk. Liam shot up, concerned, and made a motion to come near me and I felt like I'd puke.

"Sit down." He did. Everyone was staring aptly at our interactions and I knew I needed to tone it down; try not to draw any more attention to it. One of the girls next to him, an overbearing hipster girl with bright pink hair, stood up for him.

"You can't talk to him like that. And you didn't even let him have a turn to tell us who he is or why he's here, or wants to write." I caught Liam's miserable expression toward her, clearly wishing she hadn't said anything. Mostly he looked concerned though, worried... an aura of nervousness and foreboding anticipation floating over me in winds and gusts. Did I really look that terrible right now? I laughed out loud. He broke eye contact and looked at his shoes.

"Is there something you want to say Liam?" He shook his head no. "Who are you, why are you here, why do you want to write better?" I shot the questions at him in a bored robot voice I'd hoped he'd reject and ignore. But, of course, he didn't.

"Liam Clarke, I'm a first year student here, starting a little late. I chose a writing class because *my friend* suggested it would help with my music. *My friend* also picked the time, and decided this *specific* class would fit best in my schedule."

"Nice of you to join us." I said sarcastically, a feigned bored. So it was Jeff. One of the guys sitting on the other side of the circle snickered. He probably already didn't like Liam because of his magnetism for the female attention. "Hey, are you done with your prompt yet?" I snapped at Snickers McShutTheFuckUp. I had to keep myself in check, remind myself I was at work. "Everyone please just write your responses to the prompt, in any of the four formats, and either turn it in by the end of class, or tomorrow morning. Set it on my desk as you walk out, or turn it in our class assignment board online that I opened for you last night." I was exhausted, I didn't want to be here anymore, I needed sleep. Real sleep. I was barely holding it together and I knew I was getting worse. The AC was full blast in the building and I was sweating profusely. The pink haired girl spoke up again, annoyed.

"You didn't open it last night, I already checked." She was probably right. I didn't even remember last night existed, let alone remembered my class responsibilities.

"Then turn them in as hard copies in the morning. When you're done, you can leave." I knew every single one of them would pick poem, because it was shortest and the least amount of work. I was glad because I really didn't feel capable of extensively analyzing and grading twenty short stories at the moment. Snickers wrote for ten seconds, then stood up, set a piece of paper on my desk and walked out. Must have been a haiku. Most of the other students followed suit, a few stragglers took the assignment seriously, as they always did, and ran out the class time. Liam didn't. He didn't even touch the spiral he'd brought with him, or the pen. He just watched me, scrutinized, with a genuine concern that pissed me off. I was fine. I was fine the past nine years and I was fine now.

"So, Liam," The pink haired girl had finished writing like ten minutes ago and was clearly waiting for him to leave so they could walk out together. "There's a really great coffee place down the road if you want to grab some?" His gaze broke away from me and I didn't realize that I was watching so intently. *Do it Liam. Go with her. Do it.* He smiled really charming at her, really fake. The amount of strain it took him to be dishonest with people made my spirits light up with nostalgia... but I still hated him.

"Thanks. But I'll pass. I don't particularly like coffee." He spoke so softly and shyly looked down toward the ground with another smile. It made me want to deck him in the mouth with how humble and alluring he looked.

"Do you like food, we could grab something to eat?"

"Maybe another time? I have to talk to Mr. Shay after class about the assignment." She laughed.

"Screw him." *Oh, he already has,* I thought. "Just turn in anything. It's pretty obvious he's just a useless drunk." *She's not too far off today.* It made me chuckle on the inside, but Liam's smile was murdered with unmasked irritation.

"Honestly, you seem nice, but I'm not interested in getting food with you."

"What's your problem?" The look he gave me made me smile. I couldn't read it, had no idea what he was alluding to, trying

65

to communicate to me, but still, it made me grin, lean back in my chair, and fold my arms.

"Want me to start from the beginning?" He was still really soft spoken, but with more confidence, the confidence that I didn't remember very well.

"Well whatever, maybe tomorrow then." She grabbed her bag haughtily and left in a fashion that she must have thought maintained her dignity. It didn't, poor girl. It was probably one of the more awkward moments in my life, watching Liam get hit on in front of me..and just a day or so ago my former roommate walked in on me with my hand down some guys pants. The universe hated me and its enthusiasm for tossing me updates on this decision was keeping up with the rat races. Rats made me think of dirt, dirt made me think of dirty things, like my apartments bathroom floor and the smell of vomit. I put my hand on my mouth and swallowed hard to keep the bile down my throat. I guess there was some left. I closed my eyes to calm the room down again for a second.

When I opened them Liam had grabbed the trashcan in the corner of the room and was next to me.

"I don't need that-" and then my body doubled over and I heaved into the can. It wasn't my brightest shining moment. He stood and held the can close to my face as it happened, and tried to rub my back, but I swatted him away in the most pathetic motion imaginable with my freehand that wasn't holding my side of the puke can. I paused before looking back up to regain my composure. "Maybe I do. Maybe I do need the fucking garbage can. But you know what I don't need? You showing up to my classes." He smiled, that fake smile again, but more anxious.

"Technically, It's one of my classes now too. I'm on the attendance sheet."

"Fuck the attendance sheet."

66

"Are you sick Con? Is it the flu or something? You really look terrible." There was the look, *that* one, the one staring down at me in my chair, the worry, the confusion, the analytical, overtly considerate, painfully honest look in his eyes just exhausted me. And I was already sick feeling, already pissed off and drained and the weakness I was showing was just pissing me off more. I couldn't deal with it.

"Take the class, don't take the class, I don't care." I stood up way too quickly again and leaned my weight against the desk to not fall over. His arm went around me to catch me, and I pushed him back. "Stay away from me."

"Piss off Connor! There's something seriously wrong. You can't even stand! You look like a ghost." he pushed back my hair and felt my forehead, and my arms no longer had the energy to obey my brains screaming orders to push him away again. And my legs ignored my orders to keep me standing, and my body ignored my orders to stay away from Liam as I fell into him. My control center was insubordinate.

"Con!? Hey, look at me!" He put his face near mine. His four faces that I could make out as my vision blurred, colliding into each other, becoming three, becoming four, becoming three again, then two, then one. There he was. "Con..." I felt his hand slap my face a few times. Somehow he kept me on my feet and grabbed my bag.

I didn't remember getting back to my apartment, and I can imagine it being very difficult to get me there. I looked up at him from my bed where he'd dropped me and he was sweating and panting harshly, from half carrying me all the way back.

"Go away." I mumbled, and rolled over into my fantasized soft, marshmallow-pillow. And he did. But a few seconds later he came back in with a wet washcloth and wiped the sweat off of my face. I was feeling worse...and worse and worse and worse like a spiraling pit of matter crushing itself into a black hole.

"Con, when did you last eat?" I didn't want to waste my energy thinking about it, but I did. Sunday morning? Friday? Two or three days ago? "There's nothing in your fridge." I didn't want to look at him, I couldn't. Just the sound of his voice stung when I compared it to the silence of him leaving. I couldn't stand him being there, couldn't stand feeling close to him next to the idea of being alone again.

"Go away." And there was silence. I opened my eyes but still couldn't sit up. I hadn't felt like this big a piece of shit in years and years. I heard the apartment door open and slam quietly shut. *Good, finally. That's it, leave again. At least you're consistent.* I didn't need him. But he could have said goodbye this time at least, he could have said something. I'd be fine. My face was moist again, without the sweat, my lips tasted like salt, and my throat hurt. I fell asleep.

"Wake up. Hey, Connor, wake up for a second." Liam was sitting on the edge of the bed. It didn't feel like more than an hour had passed. He didn't leave? "Con, I need you to eat something. And drink something. I sat up a little and immediately felt nauseous. *No.* Toast and a cup of ice chips were sitting on an area of my bedside table he'd cleared off. "Hey, I need you to eat."

I took the cup of ice chips and let them melt in my mouth. I hadn't realized how dehydrated I was. I cleared my throat.

"Did you hear the part... where I told you to go away?" I was startled by my voice. It sounded like the crackling of a dying mans last words.

"Did you hear the part where I told you to eat something?" I grabbed the toast and took a few bites. It didn't want to go down, but I was a pissed off dictator. How many more times would I have to go through the motions of watching him leave until he just...stayed gone. Nine years. I'd gotten over it in the nine years he was gone, I'd buried it all deep, forgot about it, forgotten about everything, forgotten what it felt like for people to disappear and now every time I turned around he was here, and then gone, and here again. Hopes and the wishful thinking of good fortunes were complete utter bullshit but they seeped into me when he was nearby, making me hate my own naivety.

"Liam. Go. The fuck. Away." He frustratedly rubbed his eyes with his elbows on his knees but made no motion to go. "Leave!" He turned to look at me with a boiling anger I'd never seen in him before.

"Connor! You're *fucking* sick! You literally look like *fucking* death. I get that you're pissed at me. I get it. But I... literally... *cannot* leave you like this. I *can't*." Liam stood up. "Even if I wanted to I *couldn't*." His hands balled into fist. I felt the rebellion uprising of my stomach again, and he grabbed a big pot off the floor he must have brought to my room from the kitchen. I barfed again, disgustingly, half dry heaving. When it was done I felt his hand on the back of my head, his fingers in my hair, and I closed my eyes, locking the feeling in my memory. I slouched back down under my comforter and he took the pot, and headed to the door. *Where are you going?* I tried to ask, but the acids in my throat made it difficult to speak. A small panic inside me made me try again.

"Where are you going?" I knew my face wasn't blank. I knew this fucking hangover from hell was making me it's bitch, stealing all my power, my resilience. My competence. I didn't know what expression I'd made per-say, but when Liam saw it he set the pot down in the hallway outside the door and crawled into my bed with me. He pulled me close to him, and I let him... not that I had the energy to pull away regardless. My head fell into the

crook of his arm, and I could smell the laundry detergent and faint
sweat on his t-shirt. I was pathetic, and I knew it. I tasted my own
uselessness in my mouth, I felt it against the dry sweat on my skin.
But I was buried in Liam's shoulder, with the ringing of his voice
in my ears; *even if I wanted to I couldn't* and somehow, in seconds,
I was dead asleep.

I woke up feeling slightly less miserable. Liam was still
beside me, having fallen asleep himself. I looked at the clock on
my bedside table. There went my Monday too. He looked peaceful
sleeping; much more like his old self. I remembered him sneaking
over to my room in high school, after Mom would get home from
work and already lock herself in her bedroom. He'd crawl in my
bed and I'd pretend to be asleep at first, then I'd move impulsively
and pull him into me. I'd wrap around him and fall asleep calmly to
the smell of his hair. I remembered having never slept so well. I
couldn't remember when that started. I crawled out of bed, careful
not to wake him, and clumsily moved to my dresser, grabbing a
fresh pair of boxers and basketball shorts, and carefully walked to
the bathroom for another shower. The pot that I'd watched him set
down in the hallway was gone.

My bathroom was spotless. Even the disgusting puke
around my toilet had been cleaned, and my shower was scrubbed.
My toothbrush was pushed back against the mirror next to the
mouth-wash and hand soap... next to another toothbrush. I opened
the mirror cupboard and the neosporin, the bandaids, the razors and
shaving cream, were all in order. There was a second razor, a
second can of way more expensive looking shaving cream. I shut it
and leaned against my sink looking into the mirror. Dark circles
sagged under my eyes and I was surprisingly pale and grungy.

My took another quick shower, brushed my teeth, and stared
at the second toothbrush. Wondering vaguely what it meant.

Clearly Liam had cleaned while I was sleeping. That meant that I'd fallen asleep with him and he'd woken up, gotten out of bed and away from me, fiddled around the house, and then made the executive decision with no prodding or suggestion to crawl back under my comforter and fall back asleep. I grinned like an idiot and I thought I heard my heart laugh.I chastised myself for it. I made my way to the kitchen, and the hallway, the living-room, the tiny dining area was clean too. *Jesus, he was busy.* I needed coffee. I knew I was still dehydrated, I could feel it in the cracking of my lips and the tiny miniature nausea that still clung to the crevices of my head keeping me dizzy. I'd just have a little coffee, like a fourth of a cup, then I'd make the short walk to Denny's, or the store and get food. But I needed coffee, just a little. I grabbed a coffee liner from the cabinet and went to put it in my dependable coffee maker, my savior, my life giver. But it was gone. *Real funny.*

I scoured through the lower cabinets, it was nowhere to be found. I slammed the last cabinet I looked in an leaned on the counter. *Fine.* I guess I didn't need coffee right then. I'd grab some at Denny's in a minute, when Liam woke up, after I threatened his life to retrieve my coffee machine from wherever he was hiding it. Till then I just needed a little pick me up, a small one. I'd have to be a complete moron to get drunk again. *You were a complete moron to get that shit-faced the first time.* I opened the liquor cabinet, which is what Jeff's old cabinet had been named the second he left. There was just a bushel of yellow bananas in it. All the liquor was gone. *What?* I'd have to actually kill him when he woke up. I felt queasy, wobbly, I needed something. At least my cigarettes were still on the counter. Liam sleepily walked out of the hallway, scratching his head. He'd found a pair of my basketball shorts, making himself right at home.

"I know you think you're being cute, but where the fuck is my stuff?" I glared at him.

"You lost your privileges." He walked to the fridge I hadn't seriously used in a very long time. I doubted anything was in there. When he opened it the light inside shone on a gallon of milk, a carton of eggs, a bag of salad, a damn pineapple, orange juice, and other food you'd see a shitty-actor kid smiling at with perfect teeth on a dumb commercial. He'd gone grocery shopping?

"Liam. Where's my coffee?" He shut the fridge.

"You lost privileges." He repeated. "Want me to make you something?" he thumbed toward the fridge. *Yes. A pot of coffee.* "You have to eat something, and drink real fluids or you're not going to feel better...that's kind of how dehydration works."

"What are you doing?"

"I'm about to make you eggs."

"What are you doing?" I repeated. He leaned against the counter as well, the same way he'd leaned against the door the first day he'd come in. He looked down toward his bare feet and put his elbows on the counter behind him.

"Con, I'm sorry."

"Yeah? For what?" I snapped.

"For just showing up." *So he regrets it too.* My heart sank into my stomach.

"Then leave." I went to brush my way passed him and he grabbed my elbow.

"How long are you going to stay pissed at me?" he asked. I turned around and looked down at him,

"Are we doing this right now? Having *this* conversation?" He didn't say anything and I grabbed his for-arm, pulled him into the living room, and pushed him into the recliner where Jeff usually chose to piss me off. I sat on the couch a few feet from him, so we wouldn't fall into the same inevitable trap as last time. Proximity wasn't necessarily our ally when it came to communication. "What are you sorry for, Liam. Tell me, exactly."

Liam's blue eyes looked startled and he fidgeted nervously. The feigned confidence I saw earlier in the classroom had clearly dissipated.

"For showing up without calling. I didn't know how to tell you." But that wasn't it.

"And?"

"And... leaving in a fit." He genuinely looked embarrassed. "Con..." No, I wasn't falling for it this time. I wasn't going to. Not yet.

"Why were you mad?"

"Because I thought you and Jeff were a thing, I thought you were just screwing with me to... hurt me." A bland aching hit me. It felt strange to think that that's what he thought of me now. I couldn't think of anything that would make him think I was so spiteful, so malicious. *Why would I do that?*

"Jeff asked if I'd seen his dick. If we were fucking...don't you think he'd have known whether or not I'd seen his dick? You didn't pick up on that?"

"Well I wasn't coherently listening, was I? And then he said something about a Claire and I didn't know what to think." I laughed and it eased his nerves. I laid longways on the couch with my head propped up on the other side, my hands behind my head. We looked like therapist and patient. And maybe we were. Liam smiled at me, remembering something probably, and I wanted to ask what it was, but I didn't. I was so sick and tired of being sick and tired.

"Why'd you crawl in bed with me?" His face went beat red this time.

"I uh.." He paused, and I waited. "I thought that you wanted me to." I smirked at him in feigned condescension.

"Oh, did I?" I remembered wanting him to. I didn't remember telling him that. He didn't skip a bit.

73

"Well I certainly did." He chuckled, embarrassed. "Con?"

"Yeah?"

"I'm staying here. I'm not leaving." I didn't answer, forcing him to fill the silence. "I could lie and say it's because I'm already on the lease, and my half of the rent has already been paid for, which is the case, but..." *Wow, what an presumptuous asshole.* "But the truth is, after today, I can't leave you alone." *You can't leave me alone? HAH.*

"What do you mean you can't leave me alone?"

"You looked terrible. You still look terrible." *Thanks.*

"Liam, I'm a grown man. I can take care of myself."

"No offense, but not from what I've seen." He made direct eye contact, searing me with a blue intensity, daring me to argue. It's impossibly difficult to argue with someone who just held a bucket while you were puking your guts out. I shrugged. *Well, that's not **not** true.*

"Oh. For the two whole minutes you've been around? I don't know how good you are at math but fractionally, two minutes over nine years is a pretty vast... *marginal error.*" He uttered a fake hollow laugh and tried to shrug it off.

"If you don't eat, you're just going to get gross again. And I'm pretty finished with cleaning up your puke."

"Well, to be fair, no one asked you to." Liam stood up, and walked toward the kitchen, frustrated and antsy.

"Connor, just fucking stop already. I'm exhausted too. Other people in the world *fucking* exist and have feelings, and get fed up with your bantering bullshit." This combatant Liam wasn't the one I remembered.

"Touche."

"Listen, I didn't mean that. I'm just tired." He leaned over the counter and rubbed his eyes. "Con, I can't not be beside you. I know you don't want me here but I'm not leaving."

"Yet."

"What do you mean yet?" *What the fuck does he think I mean? Yet. As In 'going to'. YET.*

"You're not leaving yet. You will eventually." He looked confused and it pissed me off. *I know he's leaving, he knows he's leaving, why the smoke and mirrors, why the games?* I was too sick for this. "Why'd you come back? And not since the other day, I mean at all. There's a great big world out there. There were no other colleges you felt like going to? No other skeletons in your closet you could flush out and play with a while?" I guess it was his turn to be blank, to cut off his emotions, pretend that I hadn't hurt him. He didn't answer. I sat up to further my point, drive it home. "Liam just *fucking* GO HOME."

He couldn't hold his blank expression as long as I could, he was no professional. For the first time in years I felt remorse for the tears that welled up in his eyes and his pained expression. For the first time in years I'd wished I kept my mouth shut to spare someone else. Something broken started ticking in me somewhere and the sound resonated through me. It was disgusting me that I blatantly, cared.

"I did. That's why I'm *here*." It turned out I wasn't a professional either. The pathetic look on my face, the awe, the surprise, the shock, the happiness, the inability to hear anything else over the new-found ticking... it was all there, scribbled on my face. Come to think of it, maybe I'd always been easy to read and only he knew the language. He came and knelt down by the couch and put his lips on mine. The ticking grew louder, more profound inside me. It wasn't passion, it wasn't lust, it was tender and unselfish. It didn't convey a physical yearning. He didn't want anything from me, he wanted to give me something. It was pure comfort, familiarity, reconciliation, apologetic for anything wrong that had ever happened. For *all* the wrong that had happened. For leaving me when I'd needed him most.

I kissed him back, snuck my tongue in his mouth, grateful that Past-Connor had brushed his teeth. I nudged him on top of me and he held himself directly above. I pushed the hair out of his face, just like the other day. Liam rested himself on top of me and his skin touched mine, warming me from the core outward, replacing any of the cold left from my hangover with a burning that made my heart blunder. The second the blood started rushing toward my waist, the dizziness multiplied and I felt like I was going to hurl everywhere.

"Liam..." He touched the inside of my thigh.

"I thought you were fine?" He teased me, smiling.

"I thought you were finished cleaning up my puke." I laughed back at him. His hands froze. He quickly stopped arousing me at the thought, and just lay sideways in front of me, letting me hold him like I used to.

"I'm not going anywhere, Con." I couldn't hold back the sigh of relief that escaped me.

"Prove it."

"Stop trying to get rid of me. I'm stronger now... but it still hurts." It's funny how much easier it was to have a conversation when we weren't looking at one another. The tenderness of his voice floating up to me, instilled it's own swirling image in my head. I was smiling. It took me a while to notice it, myself, but I was, and I couldn't stop. I laughed.

"I'll try. But you really piss me off." He laughed too. We lay there a while and were both starting to fall asleep. He'd given up on force-feeding me, so technically I'd won. I shook him a little.

"Liam..." he let out a sleepy

"Mhmm?" and held me a little tighter.

"You know you still have homework, right?" He chuckled.

76

"I hate you Connor, I really do." When he happily pushed himself off of me I saw his muscles flex and wondered seriously when he'd gotten into shape. I closed my eyes and listened to his sounds. The refrigerator open, the rustling of pans, the clicking of the stove, the cracking of eggs. I hadn't won at all.

Son of a bitch.

CHAPTER 4: OH, SURPRISE SURPRISE

It took everything inside me to keep up the confidence I was mustering through sheer performance skills alone. I wanted to just run away, give up, just to be sure I wasn't bothering him, or making things more difficult for him, but I couldn't. Honestly, before I'd left England this time, I'd given up trying. Yet here I was, living with Con again.

Seeing him sick messed me up inside. I couldn't help but feel responsible for the damage I'd done on multiple layers. It was the literal least I could do to take care of him... and it was the absolute most I could do to not tell him everything, beg his forgiveness, and beg him to love me again. But he should be healthy, right? And then the way things had played themselves out... I just couldn't. I was too disgustingly happy, and hopeful. Maybe I'd never have to tell him. It all happened years ago, right? He seemed so happy... I couldn't destroy that for him? No. It was an excuse, I was just scared. I couldn't lose him.

That explained why my conscience couldn't let anything more happen between us. I'd slept in my own room, in a sleeping bag on the floor since I hadn't been able to buy a bed yet. It had been a week, since I moved in. I'd avoided him for the most part, at an expert level. Excuses came rhythmically; I was running late for work, I had to pick up shifts at the bar (Jeff had hired me on as a second bar tender in between sets), I had to do laundry downstairs, I had to meet up with Britain to peer edit our short stories for next week since I'd already missed Con's first assignment and he was a hell of a grader. He hadn't liked that excuse. Britain was a little abrasive, loud, and confrontational, even in class. Con hated her essentially, from her voice to her obnoxious pink hair.

A gentle brush against him in the kitchen. He'd pinned me against the wall yesterday, and I'd almost lost myself again. But I somehow slipped away, guilt ridden, aroused. I couldn't break. I wanted to be swept away, to feel him again. In fact, I'm not sure there's anything I've ever wanted more in my entire life. But I couldn't...How would he feel if I told him the truth and he couldn't forgive me? He'd have to carry that with him his whole life; that he'd slept with the person who'd taken away the most precious thing he'd ever clung to. Whether that were true or not wouldn't matter in the long-run, only how he felt about it. I'd summon the courage to tell him somehow. I would... Later.

He must have thought I was just shy, trying to take things slow. It wasn't an absurd notion, for normal people without buried pasts. He didn't seem to understand how profound my affection was for him. Connor Shay was the dumbest smart-person I'd ever met, honestly. Or I was just the biggest prat, and had no idea how to show him.

I stared at the marked up piece of paper on the coffee table with my guitar situated on my lap, mindlessly strumming different melodies, riffs. I'd read the words on the paper and try to feel if they sparked with the sound reverberating off the acoustics of my old guitar. I really had done Con's first assignment, I just didn't have the confidence to turn it in. Not to him. But maybe it would make a decent ambiguous song for the bar. I needed a chorus of some sort. And maybe to change the 'Him's to 'hers' to fit the general consensus. But I didn't want to. I set the guitar down and read through it for the millionth time, wondering what to change, what to skew;

If I've learned anything
I've been schooled in unforgiving
An animal behind the bars of anxiety
The suppression that feeds the intolerance
The haze of solidarity in the judgment of their eyes

Oh surprise surprise
He sees me, he knows what I am; alone
Or was till now.
I can't ever be again.
I can't ever lose him, or I lose myself.
I can't tell him or I might.
If I stay silent, I stay his.
Oh surprise surprise
I'm yours but you're not mine.

I needed a chorus. And more rhythm. And it probably wouldn't work as well from a hetero perspective. I crumpled it up and tossed it across the room, it wasn't going to work for a song. I needed to get to the bar and meet up with Con. He was there writing, as usual, constantly struggling to keep up with himself. I knew he was drinking, which I guess was fine. I wasn't the boss of him. I just wondered if he'd ever let himself be well enough to work out what he was running from. I knew him well enough, I knew he was broken inside. I was just terrified of breaking him further. I picked my apartment keys off the counter and headed out the door, locking up behind me.

"Liam!" Jeff called from behind the counter. "Liam come quick, some cougar's stealing your cupcake!" Thank god no-one was paying attention to him. I waved at him and smiled at his daring nonchalance. The very last thing I needed was everyone knowing Connor and I were... living together? Dating? A couple? Come to think of it, what the hell were we? *Wait, cougar?* I panicked for just second.

Across the bar in a booth near the back corner I saw Con smoking a cigarette with his laptop closed with an older woman across from him, probably in her late thirties. She was motioning around enthusiastically with a smile on her face, her mane of curly blond hair bouncing, and an empty lipstick-smeared beer mug in front of her. For an older lady, she wasn't bad looking. The pant suite she was wearing gave her a look of sophistication, a look of business that was in total paradox with her excited, childish, disposition.

"I'm telling you Shay, this one's going to be big. Really really big. Everyone at work is talking about it and it's been cycled through five different editors just to be sure."

"What's going to be big?" I scooted in the booth next to Con and he pushed his laptop toward the wall to make more room for me.

"Nothing important." His cigarette had burnt out and he put it out in the ashtray by his laptop. The lady ignored my question.

"Who might this be?" she asked with a smirk that could have been an attempt at being seductive. I wasn't totally sure... I was never very good at taking flirtatious subtle hints.

"Nobody." Conner said, leaning in on the table and resting his chin on the palm of his hand. *Oh, so that's what I am. Nobody. Mystery solved.* I felt his other hand on my knee, quickly but delicately journeying to my hips and when I felt his fingers slipping into my pants the surprise made me jump, hitting my knee on the table. She gave me an awkward suspicious incision with her glance.

"Hi, erm, I.. I'm Liam. I'm Connor's new... roommate." There was a smirk on the edges of Con's lips, making me blush slightly.

"I thought the annoying one was your roommate." She said, looking to the left at Jeff behind the counter, who was rubbing a spoon and trying to get it to stick to his nose, inciting laughter from a couple girls at the bar. The girls and a group of guys at a table a few feet away were the only afternoon drinkers today.

"This is my new annoying one." His answer probably deserved a glare, but I was used to him.

"It's nice to meet you Liam." She'd finally directed a comment at me, and it made me like her a little more. Discomfort creeping under my skin always linked itself to people talking about me as if I weren't there. "I'm Miranda Folly, Shay's editor. Everyone just calls me Folly, so I guess you can too."

"It's a pleasure meeting you Ms. Folly." Folly's smile grew huge.

"You are just absolutely the cutest thing I have ever seen." She reached across the table and grabbed my hand and held it. "You're so polite and sweet! Where'd you two meet Sweetie. Did Shay kidnap you or something? You seem like unlikely friends." Folly was batting her eyelashes and making an uncomfortable type of eye contact. Then I felt her slender foot, under the table, rubbing up my calf.
Connor knocked her hand away from mine on the table.

"Knock it off. He's too young for you." Ms. Folly stopped playing with me under the table.

"But Shay, that accent. Mmm." she bit her lip slightly as Jeff chose a ridiculously awkward moment to approach us. But he came bearing presents, a new mug of beer for Folly and a water for me, knowing me well enough by now to not waste his alcohol. Con was still working on a whiskey on the rocks.

"Staying out of trouble Folls?" he asked, grinning toward the enigma across the table.

"Trying not to." she pouted, taking the mug of beer.

"Oh Folls, don't waste your time on this one." *Oh no...* "When you could have a real man like me." He winked at her playfully. *Whew.* Ms. Folly dismissed him and looked back at Connor, realizing something.

"Nothing important? You just said it's 'nothing important!'"
She took a drink of her new beer. She appeared a little bit tipsy. I
looked up at the clock on the other side of the bar and chuckled; it
was only a little past noon. "Shay, do you not understand that this
is about to make your career? This is one of those pivotal moments
in a writer's life! You should be celebrating! Your last two books
have had THREE reprints, they're tearing off the shelves! Nothing
important?"

"Congratulations *Con!"* Jeff shot him a grin looking
genuinely happy for him. Maybe just excited to have something
new to celebrate. I liked Jeff, but I didn't like the sound of Con's
shortened name on his tongue.

"And his next book is even better, I swear, it's going to be
huge." She was ignoring us now and talking just to Jeff, her
companion in arms, her energetic affiliate. "They're estimating the
total of what four reprints would take, to start." The familiar 'ch'
escaped Connor on the side of me.

"Folly, you're fired." He sipped on his whiskey, "Your
confidentiality sucks."

"Con! You can't..." I started to seriously defend the woman
I didn't know. What was he thinking? He couldn't just run around
firing people, causing them trouble on a whim.

"Oh, suck a dick, Shay." She laughed at him and took
another drink. "No one else will put up with your bullshit." Jeff
spoke up again.

"She has a point, Love." I wondered vaguely if he meant
she had a point about him sucking dick, or people being unwilling
to put up with his bullshit, and then laughed to myself. If I didn't
like him saying 'Con', I really hated him saying 'Love'. It must have
shone on my face because Jeff winked at me charmingly, assuring
me I had nothing to worry about.

"Jeff! Birthday girl needs another round!" The girls from the bar called to him, and giggled to themselves. "We *need* you!" He sauntered gallantly to the rescue, throwing Con and I another grin. I guessed that play firing Ms. Folly must have been a common occurrence, and I blushed at my own useless valiant behavior.

I'd never tell him, but I'd read all of Connor's books, even though we weren't a part of each others lives. It didn't surprise me that people would be tearing them off shelves. Though, I'd personally had to order mine on Amazon. They were actually what gave me the courage to come back, they planted the seed of doubt that maybe I hadn't been forgotten, that maybe I wasn't the only one missing something. I'd perused through all of his annotations through that year I'd lived with him, in the margins of his old school books, in his spirals of work when he'd left them around the house. They were often dark, but not hollow, like his newer books. The ones he'd published right after high school were full, brimming, at least, with sadness. As he went they had less and less,.Just echos between the hollow covers; a dark pulsating nothingness. He'd always been his writing.

"Well, the point you should be interested in, is the big fat check you're going to be getting soon." She reached into her purse bag sitting next to her, hidden under the table and pulled out a crisp envelope. "This is a letter from our editor in chief, thanking you for choosing our publishing company. I'm sure the bulk is a pre-written default 'thank you' template, but he signed the bottom...and all the money you're bringing us in is a good indicator that he means it."

"Keep it." He took another sip of his whiskey, and I reached out for the letter. It just seemed like a big deal to me, a great accomplishment. I hadn't made any of those yet, and I was really bloody proud of him.

"I'll take it." I said, grabbing it quickly and shoving it into my pocket before he could grab it and discard it. Con looked at me surprised.

"Are you starting a fuckin scrapbook or something?"

"No, it's just... it's neat, that's all." I don't know why I grabbed it and wanted it so badly. It reminded me of when Con would come home with a paper he wrote and Maggie would save them all in a filing cabinet in her room, the proud mother. I felt a pang in my heart remembering. Connor sighed and shook his head, smiling, earning a confused look from Ms. Folly. She then eyed me suspiciously.

"You're the new roommate? Is that it? Are you related?" she asked.

"No ma'am. My last name's Clarke."

"Clarke? Why does that sound familiar?" Con answered for me.

"Our company works with Clarke.Co shipping as one of it's venders. They cover a lot of publishers distributions. That's his dad's company."

"Holy shit. You're dad is the CEO of Clarke.Co? Like the founder?" *Crap.*

"So you must be loaded...What the hell are you doing here, kid?" He spoke for me again, playing off my puzzled expression.

"Just wallowing in the problems of the common folk probably. Life experience. It's his 'walkabout'. Our dads work together. I'm practically babysitting." *Babysitting?* I could kill him. I wanted to. All I could do was glare. He put his hand on my head and ruffled my hair without making eye-contact. The condescension was palpable. I kicked him harshly under the table. "Son of a bitch!" he muttered, scooting away from me.

"I'm not loaded, my father has a bit of money, yes. I'm here to I guess, to broaden my music... I'm a musician." I offered.

Ms. Folly looked at us suspiciously again, and began forming another needless question behind her eyes. Luckily her phone rang.

"Shit. I'm late." She answered with her name, "Folly.... Yes, of course. I would never forget you Ms. Gallegos, I'm on my way, traffic is terrible..." she took one last swig of her beer and scooted out of the stall. She mouthed to Con, "Keep it up! Hear from you soon! Pay for this." giving him the thumbs up, pointing toward her beer, and leaving the bar on her way to the duped Ms. Gallegos. Without Ms. Folly we were sitting on the same side of the booth by ourselves.

I was still for a moment and Con put his arm behind me, resting on the backrest, and his fingers found their way into my hair. He always had to be fiddling with something, smoking something, drinking something, typing something. He always had to be moving. Being one of his 'something's gave me a fulfilling purpose that filled a confusing void I'd been carrying around all these years. But I could feel the imaginary eyes pressed against us, hear imaginary voices whispering behind our backs. I scooted away from him, out of the booth and he pulled up his laptop as I sat on the other side.

I laid my chin on my arms on the table and watched him type. He must have been in the middle of something before Ms. Folly showed up because he needed no prep time. His fingers were enigmatic, clicking away quickly, the light on his screen illuminating his facial structure. His interested expression, the furrowing of his brow in concentration. He'd stop for a second and raise his hand to his mouth in a small fist, resting his chin on his thumb, rereading a sentence. He used to do that when he'd write in his spirals too. I didn't want to interrupt him, to ruin his creativity...but I wanted to ask about his new book. When did he finish it? What was it about? Was he excited about his books selling well?

"What are you staring at?" He didn't break eye contact from the screen.

"Nothing." I hastily sat up, I'd forgotten I existed again... he did tend to have that effect on me. I should have gone over to Jeff and hung out with him so I didn't bother Con.

"Stay." He said, clearly sensing my thought process, still not breaking from the screen. I did. Then was annoyed with myself.

"I'm not a dog. I don't take commands."

"Stay please."

"Why?"

He looked at me in a way that had my face burning red and I halted. It was a lonely type of need, an expression of missing me. Con kept typing. "This'll just be a second."

I looked around the bar again as he worked, and watched Jeff fraternizing with his female patrons. It felt nice being with Con in a public place, where I didn't have to have an escape route if things started going too far. I didn't have to have excuses prepared. Seeing the empty stage, I wished I'd had my guitar. He finished his work with a last clicking and shut his laptop again, grabbing his cigarettes and lighting a new one.

"Are you playing on Saturday night?" he asked me, starting conversation. Jeff had signed me up for the main attraction this Friday. Just in the week I'd been there, people were bugging him about when I'd be playing next, asking him to request me. I guessed I was doing pretty well.

"No. Jeff wants me to learn more covers. He says drunk people need songs they already know the words to, but I think he's going to let me play some of my own stuff... once everyone's too drunk to hear the music anyway." Just the opportunity was amazing though. I had no idea getting to perform would be this easy. Everything just seemed to fall into place with minimal effort. I was grateful.

"Well, he's not wrong. He's a smart guy when you let him be." I wondered jealousy if he thought I was a smart guy. "Personally I've always enjoyed your work better than your covers. It's more honest when you're singing. Maybe I'm biased." He leaned back in the booth and blew smoke up toward the ceiling. That was probably the most straightforward, nicest, thing Con had ever said to me. I looked closer to see if he had a fever, or was sweating. If he was sick again.

"Are you feeling ok, Con?"

"Jesus Christ." He shook his head annoyed. I guess I'd asked that question a few too many times. Seeing him ill really had scared me.

"Sorry."

"Liam, I know you're taking things slow, but..." I didn't want to talk about it now, I needed more time to think.

"I'm just busy and stuff, getting accustomed to the neighborhood and work..."

"No, I mean..."

"Listen, let's talk about it later, I should go call Britain, see if she's free to work on our projects..." I went to scoot out of the booth and he reached across the table and grabbed my arm, losing his temper.

"Could you hold still and shut the fuck up for two seconds?" I did. "I'm talking about your music, Moron. I mentioned you to Folly the other day and she said she has a friend downtown that intermediately looks for new people." He was speaking as though being forced, like he really didn't want to be telling me this. I felt embarrassed for assuming it was about us. I didn't know where downtown was, or how I'd get there, but the idea of playing more, in front of more people and getting slots at multiple venues excited me. That would be amazing.

"Did you get a number? Should I call?" Con shifted uncomfortably and let go of my arm.

"She emailed me a number. I'll forward it to you later." One of the girls from the bar laughed obnoxiously loud and grabbed my attention. She looked like she was about to fall out of her seat. I couldn't help but think it might be a waste of a birthday for her if she was already piss-drunk by one o'clock. The little bell on the door rang and another guy and girl walked into the bar. Jeff practically jumped out from behind the bar and scooped the girl into a huge hug, twirling her around, and kissing her on the cheek.

"I haven't seen you in ages ClaireBear! Where've you been all week?" In an irritated way she pushed Jeff off and straightened herself out. The guy she was with was extremely good looking. His hair was slicked back with a moderate amount of facial hair giving him an edgy, rugged look, and he had tattoos on his arms showing with his short sleeves. He wasn't particularly built but he looked like he could handle himself. I got nervous even thinking about talking to him. She was very pretty too. Alarmingly pretty. Her strawberry blonde hair shone even in the crappy lighting of the bar and she pulled off a mini skirt and nice blouse, still managing to look high class and not slutty, which I think is an appealing attribute for a girl. Or so Britain had told me the other day after class.

Con's eyes traced my line of sight for just a second and then meandered back to me, uncaring.

"Folly said he wasn't looking for anyone until next month."

"What?" I'd gotten distracted by the couple.

"The guy downtown. He doesn't have any openings until next month." I pulled my gaze back toward Con and smiled. Connor Shay never had to try to look attractive...at least, to me. He

89

didn't need tattoos, or slicked back hair, or to dress like a model. Years after knowing him, a year after living with him, loving him, even being his, I'd get embarrassed with myself and be at a loss of words just from a glance. It was disgusting, really, the sick puppy-drunk affection I had for him. And he didn't have to try for it, for anybody. It came by accident and he regarded his attraction as a hindrance more than an asset, never using it for anything and dressing it down in basketball shorts and T-shirts. And for some illusive reason that I'll never fully understand, he was choosing to sit there with me. I felt like I was in high school again for just a moment...except he'd gotten even more attractive since then. *Is he really mine?* The poem I'd crumpled up earlier shot into my mind, dimming my random happiness. *Oh surprise, surprise. I'm yours but you're not mine.* He couldn't really be mine until he knew the truth, even if he wanted to be.

"Liam, knock it off." He took a drag on his cigarette, irritated, taking another look at the guy with 'ClaireBear' and looking back at me. *Oops.*

The girl finally brought her attention to us and she signaled to her hot boyfriend to go sit with his friends, with an 'I'll be there in a second' wave. She completely ignored me sitting there and Connor didn't take his eyes off me, ignoring her in return. Yet there she stood, glaring at him.

"I left you 20 text messages." He sighed and drew his attention toward her in a bored, rude manner.

"Yes. I know."

"Did you read any of them?" ClaireBear was fuming, her hands on her hips, and her face getting red in anger.

"Nope." He took another sip of his whiskey and I sat there quiet as a mouse, trying not to cause problems. I was feeling bad for the girl. *ClaireBear? Claire?* I remembered then, Jeff's name drop that first day in the apartment. Who was she to Con? I looked

90

at her again. She really was pretty, even on the verge of furious tears. She took a breath and calmed herself.

"You're a piece of shit Connor. A drunk, useless, piece of shit." Claire became less and less pretty to me by the second. A calm maleficence smoothed out her words and made them sound louder the softer they became, slow and calculating. Just soft enough to where no-one else would hear her being ugly. "And one day, surrounded by your shitty books that no-one even remembers as a passing fad, everyone around you is going to see what a completely worthless person you are... And you're going to die *empty* and *unloved*... with no friends, no family...*all alone*." My heart stopped and my body jumped up involuntarily. But words wouldn't come out of my mouth, I was too furious. All I could do was hate her. Hate her for picking at the one thing in the world I knew Con feared most.

I hadn't noticed everyone in the bar stopping to stare at us. If she weren't a girl I'd have have hit her... I'd have really hit her. Then I heard a familiar sound.

"Ch." Conner shook his head, annoyed, and stood up too. He leaned unhesitatingly across the table, lifted my face toward his quickly by my chin and kissed me on the mouth in front of everyone; Claire, Jeff, the drunk birthday party, the hot guy and his friends... My rage at Claire swirled together with the billions of other emotions cascading out of Con's mouth and into mine, twirling my insides like a tornado. He pulled away gently, leaving me standing dumbly in a taste of whiskey and cigarettes, and turned back to Claire with a bored but scathing expression.

Claire didn't say anything. He practically whispered his rebuttal.

"I *highly* doubt it."

He sat back down and was bored again as though nothing had happened, and Claire had finally had it. Her eyes welled and spilled over as she whipped around and ran back toward the bar. Her boyfriend stood up to come comfort her, to look mean and intimidating toward Con, but Claire ran right passed him to Jeff and cascaded into his arms, bawling. Jeff gave Connor an annoyed smirk and friendly-flipped him off behind Claire's back. Everyone was still looking over at us, and I thought my head was about to explode. I sat down.

"Con... maybe we should go..."

"Why?" He was either genuinely unmoved or completely oblivious. Hot-guy's group of friends were pissed, seething our direction and talking loudly amongst themselves, not bothering to lower their voices to a whisper, spouting all sorts of hateful garbage.

"I think we should go." Lazily, he put out his cigarette, slid his laptop into his bag, and finished his whiskey in a last swig. Con stood up out of the booth, paying no attention to anything. I followed behind, stealing a glance over my shoulder at the looming table of new-found enemies before leaving.

———

The next few days following my incident with David were rather uneventful. His friends that were there that day would occasionally knock books out of my hands while passing in the halls, or purposely target me in gym, but David himself stayed clear and left his hazing to an occasional glare here and there. Overall I didn't mind terribly. I was glad that nothing terrible had happened to Connor to be honest, no repercussions following an assault on school property, no punishments at home for causing trouble. The relief was striking. And no-one bothered asking about my bruised face, which I found to be very polite of them.

In Ms. Gilly's class I was careful not to sit next to the 'apple' that had angered David to begin with. But I smiled at her politely if our eyes met, hoping she would understand it wasn't about her; I was grateful for her attempted friendship. She eventually chose to sit next to David again, despite having previously called him a jerk. I was happy everything had worked out for them, and I'd even tried to smile at David when our eyes met by accident one day, thinking that perhaps we could put everything behind us. But we couldn't. He flipped me off while Ms. Gilly's back was turned. It was disappointing but Ms. Shay had told me that under no "fucking circumstance" was I to attempt to apologize for anything. So I didn't. I mostly focused on my studies at school and looked forward to going home.

I knew Connor was straight, I knew that, really. But that didn't stop me from enjoying being around him. It was almost a relief to get the fact out in the open, to crush any feelings from getting stronger or more pronounced right off the bat... before anyone got hurt. That's what I'd consistently told myself, if I ever let myself think about it long enough. The topic made me feel sick, or dumb, or anxious? I couldn't place it.

"Why didn't Bassanio just offer his own pound of flesh, while they were negotiating the terms of the loan to begin with?" I asked, watching the sidewalk in front of me, keeping in step with Connor on our way home.

"Because Shylock didn't hate Bassanio, he hated Antonio for spitting on him. And the story would have lacked half it's plot." I couldn't figure out why anyone would smoke in this weather. The sizzling end of his cigarette just made me sweat more thinking about it. Connor had lent me his "Merchant of Venice" book... along with a 'No Fear Shakespeare' accompaniment so I'd be able to understand it.

"I just don't understand why Bassanio wouldn't be responsible for his own actions. And if he loved Antonio, I don't think he should have left him behind for some woman." The book had really pissed me off. Even with Connor's notations to keep me company. "How does he love Antonio anyway? Brotherly? As a friend? Family?" He considered the question I'd asked him.

"What do you think?"

"I don't know." I thought I knew but I didn't want to be the one to say it. "But I hope he goes back for Antonio. I feel bad for him. I hope he doesn't marry the Portia lady." Connor laughed.

"I think I need my books back. Something important's come up." He took a last drag of his cigarette and crushed it under his foot. He looked down at me. "Liam, you're melting." I really felt like I was melting. This state got entirely too hot. It had apparently been a late summer and would barely start to wind down a month or so into the school year. Surely my body would acclimate soon. But not yet. Connor was sweating too, but not nearly as gross. He even pulled that off smoothly. My backpack was soaking the back of my shirt as I counted the seconds I thought it would take to get home. My companion only carried a single book with him, one he was reading for pleasure. He clearly didn't have homework to take home, leaving his backpack in his locker for tomorrow. I eyed a lawn sprinkler longingly.

"Hold on." Connor bent down to retie his shoe that had come undone, right next to the sprinkler, surely just to torture me with it's dancing droplets. He was taking forever. Every second felt like an eternity in this heat, and the sprinkler just kept ch, ch, ching away, watering the grass, cooling down the ground while I was dying in the sun-rays. I couldn't take it anymore. I set down my backpack and looked both ways to make sure no-one was watching. I'd just rinse the sweat off my face a little. That would suffice for the rest of the way home and make me feel less gross.

Connor was standing now with his arms folded, watching me from the sidewalk. Rotating, the sprinkler hit me off guard and soaked the entirety of my front, making Connor laugh. If it weren't so hot and I wasn't so desperate, I'd have been embarrassed but the cool water on my skin felt too refreshing. I let the sprinkler hit me one more time, feeling loads better, wiping the water off my eyes. He picked my backpack up off the sidewalk and handed it to me, smirking.

"Feel better?"

"Yes, very much." he laughed again, and we kept heading home. Maggie was outside watering the foliage at the front of the house. It was strange seeing her doing yard work, even if was just watering. My mother wouldn't be caught dead doing yard work, and my father paid a decent amount of money to make sure it never came to that.

"Liam! Is that sweat? Should I have picked y'all up?" Connor spoke for me.

"He got in a fight with a sprinkler today."

"Damnit, another fight? Are you trying to hit a quota?" She laughed at her own joke and sprayed a different bush.

"Hey, why are you home so early?" Con asked her.

"Your dad's coming home for dinner tonight, it must have been an easy day at work." I really hadn't seen much of Hank since I'd gotten there, so I was interested. I looked up at Connor to read his expression and any remnant smile from watching me get hit with the sprinkler had vanished. He'd become his normal, blank, self.

"I know something at his work that's easy." He mumbled quietly and Maggie didn't hear him. I didn't know what he meant, so I took it as gibberish.

"Hey Liam?" Maggie called to me as we were about to walk away. "You missed a spot." She sprayed Connor in the face

95

with the hose she was holding, soaking his clothes ten times worse than mine and I couldn't stop myself from laughing at him. She watched him with big eyes, a 'Whatcha gonna do?' expression and he was fighting a smile. He looked at the book in his hand, completely ruined, and didn't seem too perturbed. I couldn't stop myself. I was feeling awfully cocky.

"You feel better?" I asked, looking up at him. He shook his sopping hair at me, whipping me with a strip of water and I laughed, shielding myself.

"Hey Con, when you go inside can you turn off the oven? The lasagna should be done, I think the timer should have gone off by now." He didn't say anything and we went in the house. It was quiet and dark compared to the sunshine and shenanigans outside. I watched him look at the oven apathetically from across the room and then purposely keep walking toward his bedroom where he shut the door. The timer had indeed gone off. I ran over to turn the oven off...deliberating over all of the buttons since I'd never used an oven before. I found it, wondering if being sprayed with the hose really had bothered him that much.

I went into my own room and set down my backpack. I took out a folded piece of paper that had a song I'd been working on in class. It wasn't going anywhere great, but I at least had a rhythm I seemed to like. I hadn't played my guitar in ages, not since I'd gotten here, and it was the longest I'd ever gone without practicing. But I couldn't bring myself to play it where people could hear me, and I didn't have the house to myself nearly as often as I had the mansion to myself back home. So there my guitar sat, withering away with neglect. I heard the shower go on across the hall and I did my best not to blush. He looked so happy laughing, and smiling, when he'd let himself. I wondered why he didn't let himself be happy more often. So far, his life looked happy enough. It stumped me why he was such a recluse.

'The Merchant of Venice' was still sitting on my bed from earlier this morning when I'd been reading it before school. There were so many notes scribbled in the margin, in different colors. Connor must have read that book a great deal. Did he really need it back right away? Or had he been kidding because he didn't want me to figure out what happened with Bassanio and Portia? I heard Maggie come in from outside and fiddle in the kitchen a little more. Then she went back in her room and I heard the shower go on in her master bathroom, and I thought how different it was for everyone to be taking showers in the afternoon here.

The sweat had dried in the air conditioning on my skin and it made me feel sticky. I guessed I needed a shower too. Maybe Mr. Shay coming home for dinner was a big deal for the family. He must have been really busy. I knew I would get excited when my parents would stay home for a meal, or any time period because I rarely got to see them. The excitement would dissipate as soon as I was actually near them though, since they ignored me regardless. They were just as distant in the same room as me as they were in Barcelona.

I grabbed a towel off of the chair by my desk and bumped into Connor in the hall, coming out of the bathroom. His towel was wrapped around his waist and because I was startled, I stared for just a second at his disheveled wet features. He eyed me suspiciously as my face burned red and my heart stopped for just a second. I pushed passed him with a polite "Excuse me," and locked the door behind me as I went in, leaning against it until my heart died down. Did he suspect me? Could he hear my heart thud? It was strange how I felt like I was legitimately hiding something, being dishonest. I wasn't plotting to murder Connor, or rob him... I was just stifling feelings that would never in a million years be reciprocated, and that wasn't dishonest or shady. I used logic, calming myself down.

I rinsed off in the shower and got changed into some clean clothes, completely forgetting how hot and uncomfortable I'd previously been. There was a sweet, floral, scent permeating faintly through the house; a perfume. When I went back into the living-room, Maggie looked absolutely stunning in the kitchen, styling a beautiful, baby-blue, summer dress. Her makeup and confidence in her appearance had her glowing and her blue eyes were popping against her dress, her necklace sparkling, her hair down for once, slightly curled for a wavy appearance. And she was swaying back and forth as she grabbed plates and silverware, singing to herself lightly and smiling.

"You're beautiful." It cascaded out of my mouth independently, with no effort or forethought. She looked at me and smiled.

"You think? I bought it a couple weeks ago." She did a childish little twirl showing off her dress and I smiled at her. Clearly, Maggie was spectacularly excited for Hank to come home. It struck me as sweet, and serene. So different from what I was used to. A different kind of elegance infused with motion and rhythm, and an astounding amount of feeling and care. The lasagna keeping warm in the oven, the plates laid out on the table with the silverware, a little vase of sunflowers in the middle of the table that she'd probably picked earlier while watering. Her happiness was contagious and it filled me with a comforting warmth. I knew Hank, Connor, and Jenifer were a lucky family. She flipped on a small radio on the counter and switched musical numbers. The Beatles rang through the house and she turned it up.

"Ooh, Liam, you know this one?" 'It Won't Be Long' rang through the house, bouncing off of her smile toward me.

"Of course. The Beatles. It's all us British people listen to back home..." I joked, laughing shyly, slipping my hands into my pockets. Connor must have still been in his room, as usual. The

98

living room was spacious, but there was a coffee table in the middle. Maggie came over and made a motion to move it, and I quickly jumped to her aid. She gave me her hand, exaggerating on the performance of the matter. Normally I'd have declined instantaneously. My mother had pushed me into all sorts of ballroom dancing classes when I was younger, hoping I'd turn out a regular, wealthy, prince charming. But I was much too clumsy. However, I had a gut feeling that Maggie wouldn't mind. I took her hand, and we danced obnoxiously together, with no class, no grace, and only a slight resemblance to rhythm. But my body moving, the heat coming into my cheeks and the spinning room made me a pleasant kind of dizzy. I was grinning like an idiot as I let myself fall onto the couch. Maggie plopped down next to me.

"Oh Liam, it's great having you here. It really is." She hit my arm lovingly. "Con used to dance with me like that when he was little. It's been ages." A voice popped up behind us.

"I think my moves were a little better..." I turned around to see Connor leaning against the doorway. *How long has he been watching?* My cheeks went red for a different reason. It was probably the most I'd ever been embarrassed in the history of time. He smiled at his mom.

"Oh, you think so?" Bouncing up, she walked around the couch and took his hand, pulling him onto the stage. But the upbeat song had ended and it was replaced with a slow one. It didn't deter either one of them. Connor's height gave him an advantage and he twirled her out and back into him, flashing her a grin. She laughed and hugged her son and they slow danced, very smoothly, very suave. Their matching dark hair made them look like movie stars to me, their similar features made the moment all the more surreal, like a moving painting, and I very rarely ever saw Connor more happy. I became a fly on the wall again, watching them.

He moved the same way he moved while playing basketball at the gym the other day, nimbly, gently with an air of control. And he was smiling so warmly. I wondered why I never saw this side of him before, and I wondered how I might ingrain this moment in my memory, to remember it forever. His hand on the small of her back, the way she melted into his chest and their fingers folded into each others on the other hand, leading her in tiny slow circles around the living room. For just a split second I imagined myself in her place, and Connor smiling warmly at me. But obviously not as his mother, as his... something else. I shook off the thought harshly. The song ended and Connor did a fake half bow to the lady, and Maggie ruffled his hair lovingly. She turned to me, reminding me I existed.

"You see Liam? I'd have never gotten Con to dance with me if you weren't here... all those living-room dancing lessons as a kid would have completely gone to waste."

"Oh, they've come in handy a time or two at school dances. You've made me the ultimate lady-killer." He winked at her and my heart fell into my stomach again. Maggie looked up at the clock on the wall and my gaze followed hers. It was five o'clock.

"He said he was getting off early. Maybe he got stuck in traffic." She went to the oven to double check the lasagna and Connor sat on the couch next to me, his smile relatively erased again. When she'd opened the oven, the smell of lasagna reached my nose and reminded me I was hungry.

"He should be here any minute, boys. Then we can eat. I'm going to go freshen up again." she'd gotten a little sweaty dancing like a crazy person with me. It was adorable how meticulous she was about her looks for her husband. It made me smile. I looked over at Connor and his expression was the opposite, a furrow of annoyance. *What's his problem?* I thought we'd all been having such a nice time. We sat there a moment by ourselves, his mind in a different place.

"The lasagna smells very good." I offered.

"It is. It's her best dish." He paused. "You know it's something special when she pulls the lasagna card." He looked up at the clock and made a 'ch' sound, pushing himself off the couch and retreating back toward his room. When Maggie came back out, refreshed, she gave me a puzzled 'where's Con?' expression. I shrugged and looked toward his bedroom.

"Hank should be here any minute." She went back into the kitchen, to perfect something or other, and found nothing to do, so she came back to me in the living room. "Liam, can you move the coffee table back please?" I did. We sat together a while. "Are you liking it here so far?"

"Yes ma'am. Very much." It wasn't a lie. School aside, and David aside, everything else was going well. I had an odd sense of happiness in their home, being a part of something bigger than myself.

"Is Con being nice? He's got a bit of an attitude sometimes." *No he didn't, he was perfect.*

"He's been great." In fact, my only selfish complaint was that I didn't see enough of him.

"Well I'm happy to see you two getting along. I was a little worried that with Jen gone he'd completely shut himself off and become even more of a hermit. He doesn't get along with many people." I thought about all the girls that were constantly giggling around him, and the mentioning of so many females around me. At dances, girls he used to bring home. I doubted he'd be a hermit. She must have seen the doubtful expression on my face. "It's true. He has absolutely no guy friends, and all the girls he brings home wind up hating him. I think my son might be a male prostitute, Liam. I've really been considering." Her whole dialect became

101

somewhat different when it was just the two of us. Her language cleared up and became much more civil, less sailor prone. It was like she only swore around Connor, a twisted way of showing him her affection; only being herself with him. But the twinkle of potential vulgar word-vomit was very real, sparkling in her eyes. And now I was considering whether or not Connor was a prostitute.

"Yeah maybe..." I looked down at my shoes.

"I'm kidding." she assured me. "What about you? Do you have a pretty girl or two waiting for you back home? Do you miss your friends?" I may have answered too quickly.

"No."

"Any boys?" she winked jokingly. I laughed nervously and answered much too quickly again.

"No." I felt guilty, but again, I wasn't lying. There really was nobody waiting for me back home. "Do you mind if I go work on some homework before dinner?" I asked. Her questioning was sweet but making me nervous.

"Of course not, go, go. I'll get y'all when Hank gets home." She propped her feet up on the coffee table and smiled at me. I felt a little bad about leaving her to entertain herself, but she looked fine enough; still excited. I went back in my room and tried to find something to do to kill time. I couldn't hear any movement from Connor's room. I plopped on my bed and picked up 'The Merchant of Venice' again, and kept reading, getting lost in the pages...getting literally lost in the dialogue, having to reference the 'No Fear Shakespeare's almost every other monologue. I wanted to go next door, and read in Connor's room...so I could just ask him what they were talking about, and hear his take, but of course, I couldn't. His annotations made me feel like I was seriously missing something and I felt stupid. It only made me try harder, delve deeper. Try to put myself in the character's shoes, wonder what I'd do in the characters situation. I bloody well wouldn't have left Antonio. When I looked at the clock again it was 8 o'clock. Maggie had never come to get us for dinner.

I meandered out of my room and to the kitchen. The lasagna was out on the oven, and the smell wasn't permeating anymore. It must have been cold. The plates on the table were unused, and the dining room light was off. Connor was still in his room and the house felt empty. Had Hank not gotten home yet? I went back to Maggie's room and knocked lightly.

"Mrs. Shay?" I heard a rustle and then a small stuffed-up voice.

"Sorry Liam, I'm not feeling very good. Help yourselves." *Is she crying?* I heard the mumbling of newscasters push through the door suddenly and I knew she'd turned on her TV. I turned to Connors door and knocked.

"Erm... Connor?" He came to the door, looking just as expressionless as ever. I whispered to him. "I think your mom's upset..."

"Who saw that coming?" He shut the door in my face and I was left there puzzled. *Where's Hank?* I went back into the kitchen, but it was all dark now. A gloom had rested over everything and I suddenly lost my appetite. I knew at home, the house keepers would put leftovers in little dishes for me for later, in case I got hungry when they weren't there. I looked through the cabinets and found some Tupperware. I didn't totally understand what everyone was so upset about, but I felt the compulsion to help where I could. The compulsion to clean, to fix the environment. To be there. I thought about how excited Maggie had been, fun, free-spirited, her grin from ear to ear. If Hank hadn't come home, I could see where she would be disappointed. It really was strange that he was never here. Maybe it wasn't a cultural difference. Maybe it was just *off* in general. I covered the lasagna with some tin foil from their pantry and put a salad she had made and left out in the Tupperware. I put away the unused plates on the table where I'd seen her take them out, and I put the silverware back in its place. And then I sauntered awkwardly back into my room, to hide from the gloom.

I took my guitar out, needing to fill the silence. The mumbles of the news weren't enough to sustain me, keep the tension at bay. I strummed quietly as I could, careful not to bother anyone. I hoped Connor wouldn't be too perturbed. I sang in almost a whisper, songs that I'd memorized, written, attempted to make up on the spot. Every so often I'd pause and listen to the house. The gloom was somehow seeping under my door like a gas. We'd all been laughing just a couple hours ago, dancing, spraying hoses at each other. My heart hurt for Maggie, crying alone in her room, but I didn't know what to do, or how to comfort her. Why hadn't Hank come home? I killed more time, trying to shake my thoughts enough to grow sleepy, but they were relentless. *Had Connor seen this coming?* Is that why he was so annoyed when he saw how happy his mom was? How often did this happen? Hours passed and I heard nothing in the house.

There was a creaking at the front door echoing through the house. I'd almost missed it behind lull of my guitar. I heard the door close. The light clunking of unsteady footsteps and the opening of the fridge. I heard Connor's room door open, and his lighter steps down the hall to the kitchen. Curiosity dragged me out of my room and instilled a relentless, anxiety driven impulse to move. I silently went after him and stood out of sight in the hallway.

"Hey Con. How long has the lasagna been in here?" a slurred voice I recognized as Hanks quietly penetrated the silence.

"Hours."

"Good." I heard the refrigerator close.

"Are you seriously drunk?" Connors voice was a steady calm, but accusatory.

"None of your business. Go to your room." I heard Mr. Shay rustling in cabinets.

"She came home from work early... She cooked dinner... She bought a dress."

"Go to your room."

"She was so fucking happy. You should have seen her...You're a piece of shit."

"Watch your mouth. Go to your room."

"It's the ultimate *least* you could have done, just fucking shown up... Or not come home. It's the *fucking least.*" They were keeping their voices down, so Maggie wouldn't hear them, I assumed. Hank didn't reply. "Does your secretary fuck *that* crazy? Good enough make you forget you have a fucking family? A fucking wife?" My heart sank. I started to understand. I heard a strange thud and couldn't resist looking around the corner. Connor was standing next to his dad, looking sideways at the floor like he'd been hit. His hand went up to his face, touching it gingerly, unperturbed. He laughed ironically. Hank looked disheveled, kind of blank. For the first time I saw a similarity of expression in the two.

"Go to your room." Hank whispered threateningly. I almost didn't hear him.

"Go *FUCK* yourself." He threw the word 'fuck' at him like an object, hitting him with it. And then he spit on him. Hank moved instantaneously. *Connor!* Mr. Shay was slightly taller than his son, much heavier built. He threw Connor up against the front door by the collar of his shirt and my legs moved toward them, fighting the desire to run in my room and hide. Hank's back was toward me but Connor could see me. He shot me a look that stopped me dead in my tracks. Connor looked at his dad, still calm, still apathetic. His ability to remain unmoved on the outside while experiencing the assumed emotional trauma on the inside impressed and hurt me in a way. I'd never trust Connor's words again. I'd never believe him when he said he was okay.

"I told you to watch your *fucking* mouth and go to your *fucking* room." Hank's voice was a low intoxicated growl. Connor's eyes narrowed.

"In front of a *Clarke,* Dad?" He seemed confused for a second, then turned around and saw me standing there. "What will CEO Clarke say when his son tells him what a shitty, disheveled ship you run? Great qualities in a business partner." Connor could apparently be very manipulative, very concise in his words. Hank let go of his son. And turned to speak to me.

"There's discipline in every household Liam, your dad is sure to understand that." As an afterthought he added, "But I wouldn't bother bringing it up." I didn't especially like my father... but I had a new gratitude toward him, knowing that he definitely would *not* understand. He'd never hit me. He'd never mistreat my mother.

"I don't think that he would." I said truthfully. I was scared, for Connor. Of the situation in general. Things were happening above my teenage capacity to fully understand. Mr. Shay grabbed his suit-coat that he must have set down when he came in and headed toward the front door. Connor sidestepped out of his way, letting him go without further confrontation. He stared at the door for a moment, after his dad had left. Probably thinking. I was afraid to say anything, I just stood there.

I didn't think it was right for me to expect Connor to say something first. After what he'd just gone through, I knew I'd have to man-up, break the silence myself. I didn't want him to feel like he had to sugarcoat anything that had happened just for me. Because he really didn't have to. One of my old tutors used to constantly tell me, "Don't piss on my back and call it rain,"and I liked the expression because honesty was the only form of communication I was truly comfortable with.

"Your dad's an asshat." I said the first words that made their way from my head to my mouth. He turned around and looked at me. I saw something broken in his eyes that pissed me off. It angered me more than anything in the world ever had. I hated Hank. I was finally understanding how this house functioned, how Connor's brain worked. He smiled at me in a way I thought might be genuine.

"Yes. He is." Connor wiped his face with his hands and felt his cheek again where he'd been hit. "Liam...what were you playing earlier?" The quick subject change gave me whiplash. And I didn't know he could hear me very well through the wall between our rooms. Of course, I could always hear his movements too. I wondered why I'd never considered it working both ways.

"It was nothing." I lied. "Connor, are you okay?" I asked for the first time. Certainly not the last.

"You want to show me that song?" I didn't. But I could tell he was deflecting. I could tell he wasn't okay, and that I needed to be there for him. And I knew now not to believe him.

"You want to tell me what happens between Bassanio and Portia?" I forced a soft laugh toward him that he appeared to appreciate and we went back to my room.

He plopped down on my bed and I sat at the foot of it with my guitar, strumming more melodies I'd memorized. He asked me how far I'd gotten in the book. I told him. He asked what I liked about Antonio, and I told him, honestly. He asked what I hated about Portia... and I told him. I genuinely felt, maybe with a biased opinion, that Antonio and Bassanio were lovers. I felt like Bassanio never should have left Antonio, that he should have stayed in Venice with him, and forgotten all about Portia and riches. I told him that I thought love was more important. That I felt like they should have treated Shylock better. That they should have apologized. My suggestion of apology made Connor laugh for some reason. I just kept picking at my guitar. Having something to do with my hands made it much easier to contain my nervousness around him. His head was at the foot of the bed the way he was laying; on his stomach, his arms folded in front of him, resting his chin on his elbow. He was situated close to me so we could talk quietly and not wake Maggie, if she had fallen asleep. The story bothered me immensely, getting under my skin.

"He never should have left Venice." I repeated. "You don't just leave the people you love."

"Someone should have told Shakespeare that." Connor considered for a moment. "He probably would have just killed him off instead."

"Bassanio's an asshat." I said, unable to shake off my annoyance. "I just don't get it I guess. I feel like... if you have someone that loves you, enough to risk a pound of flesh for your happiness, why would you let that go? Why would you treat them like garbage by trying to go off and seduce some other woman? I can't fathom that. Listen, why-" I turned my head to look at him while I asked the question and he'd scooted his body forward toward me on the bed, so when I turned, his face was next to mine. He took my chin in his hand and kissed me quickly on the mouth. I'd never been kissed before. Everything erased from my mind.

Startled, I tried to push away from him. Was he making fun of me? Was this a joke? He must have known I had feelings for him. But he crawled off the bed without a word, and took the guitar out of my hands. I watched him move, I let the guitar be taken and set down away from us. He kissed me again on the mouth, and I knew my face was flushed. I couldn't fight it. I didn't want to. *Am I asleep?* But it wouldn't feel this real if I were dreaming. I wouldn't feel the warmth in his touch, or the energy of boiling emotion beneath his kisses. There was a faint taste of cigarette in his mouth, and it only made me want more of him. We slid sideways onto the floor. His body lay lightly on top of mine, his knees on the ground around my waist. I felt the pressure of his body against mine. I didn't know what was happening, everything was igniting in my head, driving me to a frenzy, and somehow, deep in the crevices of my mind lay an overwhelming embarrassment that I physically, mentally, emotionally couldn't rebel against. I was already getting hard and I couldn't bring myself to worry if he noticed. I could only slightly acknowledge how self-conscious I felt. I kissed him back, having even lost the ability to be suspicious. He pulled away gently and looked at me, running his fingers through my hair, and I wished he wouldn't. I knew my face was beat red, I knew I couldn't hide my expressions as well as he could and the bashfulness, the lust, the inability to push him away, was all written there; a gallery for my vulnerability. It made me suffocatingly more self-conscious, and my ineptitude of self control made him smile in a way I'd never seen before. A look of revelation, bewilderment in his expression that lit a comfort inside me I'd never dreamed would crawl into me midst the chaos of intimacy.

Connor pushed himself off of me, and I felt like maybe I'd done something wrong. I sat up and sat next to him. I didn't know if I should say anything. If I *could* say anything. I felt guilty again… like somehow I'd taken advantage of a situation, as though I'd used what happened with his Dad somehow to get what I wanted. But *he'd* kissed *me*, hadn't he? I hadn't come on to him. I'd sat on the floor, he'd asked me to play, and I did. I'd done everything *he'd* wanted. I was scared to look toward him, scared of what I might see. Would he be ashamed? Angry even? Regretful? Embarrassed? I couldn't stand not knowing. I looked.

He was smiling. He'd pulled his knees up close to him and was resting his elbows on them, staring at his hands in front of him. His cheeks were kind of feverish, even around where Hank had hit him earlier, but his expression looked confident, not embarrassed. And he was smiling.

"Con...?" I asked, hesitantly. Connor didn't look at me.

"Liam?" he replied with a chuckle. He finally turned and was startled at the look I was giving him. Maybe he could sense that I wasn't sure how he felt. He leaned toward me and kissed me softly again, lingering just a second. He looked at me again, smiling. "Liam..." he said again, looking down toward my waist. I was still incredibly hard, and you could see it protruding in my jeans. My face somehow pulled a new, darker, shade of magenta out of the deep recesses of it's capabilities and I quickly pulled my knees up, leaving me sitting the same way he was. Con laughed again, still unable to control his smile. Suddenly I realized I was still staring at him and I quickly turned my head down, looking at the carpet. He put his hand on my head, ruffling my hair like he'd grown accustomed to doing.

"I'm headed to bed. See you in the morning." He stood up and started to walk out of the room. I felt strange. Like if he left, none of this would have ever happened. I stood up quickly and grabbed his hand, slightly panicked. He turned back around and kissed me again, just to be sure. I had to extend upward because of our different heights, even with him looking down toward me, but he put his hand on my lower back and breathed me in all the same, and I was completely and utterly dumbfounded. Con pulled away away from me again.

"Goodnight." He walked out the door. *What just happened?*

CHAPTER 6: ALL OF THE FUCKS

Liam had grabbed my hand when we got to the sidewalk and was almost pulling me, hurriedly down the street. He was all wound up again, something or other bothering him in his head. He had a concentrated look, trudging along and his steps like stomps, tugging us forward. It was a little amusing. I'd grown tired of him ignoring me, in general, and his sheepish attitude in public. Clearly he cared what other people thought, but that was never something I'd been concerned with so I felt he should get over it. His hand was gripping mine roughly, and I smiled because he didn't notice we were holding hands. I pulled him backward throwing him off balance and he fell back into me. I held him, wrapping my arms around him from behind. He ignited something vulnerable in me just with his mere existence, the least I could do was irritate him.

"Con... you're going to get us in loads of trouble. You know that, right?" Pleadingly he caught his balance and pulled away, looking at me. Trying to read me.

"Am I?" It wasn't my fault anyway. He was the one avoiding me in the apartment all the time. Besides, Claire had provoked me. Liam had too, so really it was his fault. I saw him looking at Claire's new boyfriend with that stupid expression, ignoring everything I was saying. How could I not kiss him? People were always trying to but in to affairs that were none of their concern, so it was simply an expression of 'back the fuck off, he's mine'. I wasn't an idiot, I knew the consequences. I understood that Liam was now one of my students and I'd probably lose my job at the school if people knew we were 'fraternizing'. Win-Win as far as I was concerned. I didn't particularly hate my job, but it was becoming a distraction from writing, along with all of the other distractions... so I didn't particularly like it either. I did, however, enjoy kissing Liam.

"You're going to lose your job. " He said, turning away from me and walking angrily again, this time without my hand. It was less amusing when we weren't touching, and more annoying.

"Oh no." I said sarcastically, purposely slowing down behind him. *What's he hiding? Why's he avoiding me?* The one thing I was certain of was that he was pissing me off immensely. It was excruciating to have him next to me, in the same apartment, walls apart, waking up to him every day, after being pent up for so many Goddamn years. He was the one who decided to stay. I didn't understand why he was so hesitant to throw all his fucking cards on the table. I'd thrown mine.

Maybe I had to cheat like he did, and poison him so he'd be sick too, and I could extract all the information cycling through his brain, causing his anxieties. Poisoning was frowned upon. I stared at his back, slowly keeping up behind him, wondering when the hell it was that he'd stopped following me and I'd started following him. If relationships were a game of 'cat and mouse' I was definitely *not* the fucking mouse. But the mouses didn't chase the cats... so I was the mouse? The whiskey was resonating. I jogged up to him and grabbed his hand again. But he pulled away again.

"Class is going to be so weird once this gets around." He complained. *For you maybe.* Because Britain wouldn't be up his ass all the time? Because herds of adoring fucking Liam fans wouldn't follow him around and write their numbers on his prompts, or turn in shitty love-at-first-sight poetry alluding to his stupid fucking accent and charming humility? I didn't reply to him, or try to hold his hand again. Those students weren't doing well in my class.

I was beyond trying to convince myself that I didn't need him. It was pathetic, and grossly sentimental in a way that inspired pure self loathing and rage in my writing, but I also wasn't ignorant and I knew when to give up when I'd lost. We were passing a coffee house and I turned into it, escaping the heat and letting Liam continue on without me, probably talking to an imaginary presence he thought was still following behind. The air conditioning and aroma of the ever loving cocoa bean was comforting. I got in line. The heat made the whiskey inside me much less enjoyable.

I hadn't just mentioned him to Folly. I'd specifically asked her to feel around, put her business networking tentacles out into the ocean-Esq music scene to suction-cup some sort of opportunity for Liam to be successful here. Literature was a land-sport and I'd never learned to swim. Being a one-trick pony had made me terrestrial...but Folls was amphibious. I wanted Liam to be successful, to be heard. Mostly so he wouldn't leave. I'd even bribed her with a two point higher percentage of my book sales. I hardly knew what to do with the money regardless. I'd cashed the first check I'd gotten from the second book that needed re-prints, and the other checks I'd received I just sent to Jen, thinking she'd find a better use for them than I would. I wondered vaguely how long it would take Liam to realize I wasn't behind him, and turned to look at the door. He was already there, looking at me angrily as the barista asked for my order.

"Just a regular coffee. Black." I ignored him. There was a soft chatter throughout the coffee shop, being so close to campus. Students were around, talking pretentiously about authors they knew very little about, reciting almost word for word what they'd read that morning on Wikipedia. There were the few legitimate patrons with their laptops out, typing away and I vaguely sympathized with their troubles, having to consciously detach themselves from the freshman buzz. I looked over to Liam, as the barista handed me my coffee.

"Did you want me to get you something?" I asked him, amused again at the heat in his cheeks. Coffee in hand I walked back toward the exit, ignoring him once more as I left the shop. He followed behind me and I felt like my world was at peace again. I felt his hand slide into mine when I wasn't paying attention, and when I looked over in surprise he was purposely avoiding my eye-contact, staring off somewhere. I attempted to sip my coffee to hide the smirk on my face and, as I did so, he reached over, grabbed it out of my hand and dropped it into a trash can that we were passing like clockwork.

"Now we're even." B*alsy.* They new found confidence in Liam was... frustrating and exciting. He'd have never done that nine years ago, or even thought about it. In fact, he'd have most likely apologized if he even accidentally *bumped* my coffee.

It was my day off, and I'd just finished my goal for the day at the bar. Liam didn't work today either. The last place I wanted to go was back to the apartment. It was like watching your least favorite sitcom episode on repeat all week; driving myself to irritation in my spiraling, corkscrew thoughts that circled around to themselves, attempting to interact with Liam, hearing a bullshit excuse, and ending up alone in the apartment, replaying the scenario in my head, wondering what was getting in the way. I'd get pissed off again, pull out my laptop and just keep working, with small thoughts pricking my conscious like burs stuck inside a cotton shirt.

"If we go home, are you going to miraculously remember something completely unimportant that you forgot to do and leave?" Cogs wrestled tirelessly behind his eyes trying to think up some sort of evasive maneuver that wasn't too transparent and I sighed. Everything with Liam was transparent. "Is there anything you want to go do today?"

"What's around here?" Claire had dragged me around various shopping malls in the few weeks we dated, probably hoping I would buy her things to attach sentimental value to and embellish our barely tangible relationship. Jeff had dragged me to an eloquent piano bar once, trying to impress one of his fuck-buddies. I'd gone to a school basketball game or two in the time I'd been at this school, and a few concerts in the school of music on the other side of campus when I needed to clear my head and create space between myself and a project. Thinking about what I did for entertainment made me consider for a moment whether or not I was a boring person. It didn't bother me either way. I did a lot of people watching, I often got in my car and took impulsive road trips if I had time off school and work...by myself, mostly as research exercises for novels. There were poetry readings at a few of the bars downtown that fellow literature students had invited me to. I had attended a few with little to no enjoyment. "Con?"

"I don't know."

"We could see a movie." *We could see a movie.* Why hadn't I thought of that. "Britain was telling me about a really funny one that premiered last week, it could be fun." I tried to entertain the idea of a circumstance where I would be enthused by a movie that Britain perceived as funny, and it was difficult, even in theory.

"Liam, what are your hobbies now?" He looked at me like I might be sick again.

"Music..."

"Besides that."

"Erm..." He appeared to be at a loss for words too, which was heartening. He avoided eye contact again for reasons I didn't understand. "I picked up playing soccer back home... and basketball." Judging from his body language it wasn't difficult to guess why. I'd sometimes still shoot hoops in the apartment courtyard, very occasionally, if I needed to think and wasn't thrilled at the prospect of going far. My basketball was sitting under a pile of clothes in my closet. This was feasible, and I started to like the idea. We used to play in that year we were together, and I tried my damnedest to get him to not suck, but it was in vain. I wondered if he'd gotten any better...surely he had. I wasn't under any delusions, I knew that I'd physically declined somewhat. I remembered how muscular he'd gotten. Surely he'd gotten better.

"Basketball? Do you suck any less?" I asked. He grinned at me, probably relieved I didn't ask him why he chose that sport. Was it because of me? What was going through his head when he left the first time?

"Slightly."

"You wanna play?"

"Basketball?"

"No, dumb-ass, hopscotch." He grinned again and then took a serious look at me, scrutinizing. "Jesus Christ Liam, I'm fine. I was sick a week ago. I'm really fine." Physically, that wasn't a lie. Emotionally, mentally, I'd briefly considered the possibility that it may have been. Having him near me drudged up memories of my past that I'd thought I'd successfully intimidated to an irreversible submission. I didn't keep pictures in the house. I didn't even see Jen often. I didn't go home. I didn't want to be without him because showing up had opened Pandora's box of emotional bullshit and even I had to admit that I was literally fucking terrified of facing alone. Again. Especially since Saturday was the pitfall. Claire's voice had been echoing in my head like sonar, ricocheting off of everything else since we'd left the bar. *No friends, no family, all alone.* She was needy, obnoxious, a social chameleon devoid of all the small puzzle pieces that make a person complex and realistic. She was actually the equivalent of one of the characters one of my freshman creative writers, taking the class frivolously, would ideally create. Yes, I'd read her before, I'm sure, and she'd drained my red pen. She was all that and less. But the one thing she wasn't... was wrong.

116

I started to think that maybe a better idea would be to skip basketball, buy a new liquor bottle, and head back to the apartment. *Maybe two new bottles… and a bull tranquilizer.* The fact that Liam had shown up out of virtually nowhere, couldn't have been a coincidence. I wondered if he knew. If he remembered. I didn't know why he would; birthdays were just an obscure date muddled in the humdrum of all the others.

He was much better than I remembered. Though, to be fair, the bar wasn't set very high. Clumsiness still clung to his every motion. I wondered how someone so... ungraceful could enjoy performing. His shot was better, I'd admit. I watched as he jumped and arched backward, the ball slipping past the tip of his right hand, soaring through the air, and hitting the backboard and spinning on the rim before falling in. I caught the ball and looped around him, pivoting, jumping, visually latching on the net and pushing the ball forward. It arched into the air and fell strait through, seductively teasing the net as it passed. My hair was getting way too long, and the sweat dripping down finally convinced me to take the time to get a haircut later.

Liam's energy was endless and I tried my best to keep up, but my lungs were hurting. I guess I'd never pushed myself longer than half an hour by myself. I remembered really loving basketball in high school, as much as I loved anything anyway. It was a strange feeling not being able to keep up with someone on the court. I'd never experienced that before. I put my hands on my knees and leaned forward a second to catch my breath.

"I'm telling you Con, it's because you don't eat properly." He was dribbling the ball in front of me and he positioned himself to make a shot. I jumped and stole it in the air, rocketing around him to the other side of the court. *Swish.* I tossed it back to him across the court where he was standing and stepped off of the

pavement to the grass on the side of the courtyard. I purposely fell
into the grass on my back, putting my arms behind my head, eyes
closed, oranges and reds swirling into already forgotten images and
shapes on my eyelids. I hadn't soaked up sun in ages. It was almost
strange on my skin. I paid close attention to the air inflating my
lungs, expanding my ribcage, and was dismayed at the small,
heavy burn that tickled through them. Was I smoking too much?

"You're also smoking too much." Everything was changing,
causing a tangle of uneasiness to infiltrate my defense. It was as
though Liam hadn't just set up camp in my apartment, but in my
head, my thoughts, certainly my libido, and the throbbing in my
chest when he was around was a good indication that he'd also set
up camp in my...

"When did you become such a nag?"

"When you started needing me to be one." He pulled his
shirt back on and plopped down beside me. I liked the pricking
feeling of the grass on my skin too much follow suit.

An air of whimsy and adventure seared into me, the
tranquility that nestled in and calmed my nerves, relaxing my
muscles, and creating a chaos in my head, a panic of impending
doom. An ardent array of vehement calculation of the
consequences. I'd often felt something similar upon waking up in
the morning, jolting out of naps or finishing a good movie or book,
remembering with a suffocating remorse that I still exist.

I'm not sure when it was that I'd realized happiness was an
exchange, like anything else. For whatever happiness resides in the
world there is an equal and opposite amount of insipid
despondency. I was constantly trying to warn the masses
esoterically in my books, displaying the correlation with every
character, every plot. I was just another character. He was just
another plot. But regardless, for reasons I'd never be able to
contextualize, I freed one of my arms from behind my head and

claimed his hand. I felt his gaze on me without opening my eyes. I couldn't stop my fingers from intertwining in his, from squeezing slightly. I was lying to myself. I knew the exact moment I'd realized the true duality of happiness. Her face flashed in my memory, blank, staring...empty.

His touch briefly calmed the riptide of anxiety, inch by inch through my hand, my arm, my chest, my brain.

"Con?"

"Mhmm?"

"I don't know who Claire is to you...but she's a cunt." My eyes shot open surprised at his vulgarity, I turned my head toward him and the seriousness in his eyes took me off guard. "You're not going to die alone. Ever. I would never let that happen." He paused, and then reaffirmed, "I won't."

I stared at him. It's all I could do. Liam was gross and sweaty, glistening in the sun, searing me with his blue intensity, looking right into the thoughts and emotions I never found the motivation to voice, while calculating every micro-expression pulsing through my face. His muscles had a rigidity now, he spoke more self-assured, his actions were more confident, more assertive, and his shot was minimally better. He was different. Maybe that's why we couldn't just pick up where we'd left off, and act like nothing terrible had ever happened, because we were both different people now. But I was falling for this new Liam just as recklessly as the old one and though I knew I shouldn't, I also knew I was going to anyway. Just like before. The ridiculousness made me laugh.

"It's over, Liam." His expression burst with his own anxiety, lighting me up inside. "It's not you, it's me." I used my robot voice, "I'm not a place in my life where blah blah. We want different things. You deserve someone better. You're too good for me." I tried to think of more cliches to throw at him so he'd understand my joke, but I saw that it had resonated. He tore away from my hand and hit me, a smidgen harder than a playful swat.

"You're not funny, Connor." He used my whole name. I must have been in trouble. It made me smile. I sat up and pivoted toward him, crawling on top of him, holding his wrists down above his head. He was sticky with sweat and smelled like summer. Our hearts were still wound up from playing basketball and I felt his beating through my chest. I bent down to kiss him, the mutual heat of our bodies against each other driving me forward, but I stopped myself. Every time I'd wanted him he'd slip through my grasp like sand in the palm of my hand, evading me since he'd come back. I didn't want him to leave. He noticed my hesitation and was trying to read me as I digressed and let him go, falling back onto the grass, aroused and unfilled. Again. But at least, this time, of my own accord.

But to my surprise he maneuvered himself on top of me forcefully, pinning me to the ground.

"Damnit Connor." Liam's voice alone seeped into me, draining me of willpower, and I was still in trouble. His eyes were glassy. I could sense his acute control over his breathing. His shirt, his basketball shorts, they weren't enough to stifle the electricity that Liam was emitting, and I felt him against me, the pressure, the arousal, as he slid his tongue into my mouth. Liam wanted me as much as I wanted him. I'd felt it before, and I couldn't understand why he was fighting it so hard. I kissed him back, I let him take me. He kissed his way down my neck, pausing on my collarbone, working downward. Everything was slipping away from me, out of coherency. All that remained was the warm rippling effect of his kisses on my skin. A tickling evaporated into a shiver as he kissed my abdomen, and I resisted the impulse to writhe as he kissed my pelvis, intensifying the tremble.

"Oh shit." I heard the words escape him before hearing fellow apartment tenants chatting aimlessly as they walked toward the courts. Liam jumped off of me, startled, having clearly lost himself as well. *God damnit.* I was aroused to irritation. I stood up, ignoring my own boner and grabbed his wrist pulling him up with with me. I pulled him into a jog toward our apartment. I couldn't take this anymore, I needed him. No more fucking around, no more excuses.

We left the basketball, a casualty, a sacrifice for the greater good. I barely made it in front of our apartment. I pushed him up against the door in the hallway and kissed him again, tasting his tongue, and we were finally in an equal frenzy. I slid my hand into his shorts, feeling his erection and he exhaled into me. I pulled my hand back and reached for our door knob, twisting it frantically, expecting it to be locked, but trying anyway. It wasn't. I threw the door open and pushed us both inside, slamming the door behind us, breaking apart for only a second and coming back together like magnets against the wall. I couldn't get enough of him, I pushed in, closer, his erection between my legs, resting against mine, his arms around me, the tilt of my head toward his.

"Oh my god! Connor! Ew, stop. Oh my god, stop." A female voice penetrated our aura of exhilaration from the couch in the living room and I looked around confused. Jen was standing, having been startled with our entrance, covering her eyes with both hands and Liam broke away. This time I was the one taken aback, and red crawled into my face, up my ears, staring blankly at my little sister. I glanced at Liam and saw him in the same flustered state.

"Bloody hell." He uttered, "I erm.. 'ello Jen, I uh..."

"Liam..." she greeted awkwardly.

"I'm just gonna..." he pointed down the hall to his bedroom lamely, "I'll be right back." and he dashed, abandoning me to be scrutinized by my baby sister with a protruding boner and flushed cheeks. There really was a god, and he hated homosexuals. It was the only explanation.

Son of a bitch.

"I thought you said you were living with a bartender named Jeff?" She looked at me suspiciously. Trying to piece together if I had lied. "When did Liam get here?" The last time I spoke to her was months ago, and I'd been honest. Short, curt, and honest. I hadn't seen her in almost exactly a year. On the dot. Or would be this Saturday. "Why didn't you call me?" When was the last time I'd called her? Probably years. Probably 9 of them.

"It's good to see you too Jen." I said, smiling. It really truly was. Maybe it would have been *better* with a little notice and less of a boner, but apparently I had a big giant flashing neon sign over my apartment saying "No fucking calls necessary." I went to the counter to grab my cigarettes and joined her in the living room. God, she looked just like Mom. Especially now that she was older. The raven dark hair flowing down past her shoulders, her eyes, her soft skin, her laugh even, though I hadn't heard it in a while.

"So?" she prodded me.

"Liam's been here like a week. Jeff moved out."

"You know Liam's mom is flipping shit, right?" I watched in a trance as she delicately picked up a coffee mug by the handle that I hadn't noticed till now, leaving new rings on my stained-beyond-repair coffee table. Jen had made herself right at home, let herself in with a set of keys I'd forgotten I'd ever given to her.

"How would I know?"

"Good point." She folded her legs in a very grown up manner, leaning back on the couch. Sophisticated, an adult. She tried reaching for my cigarettes and I pulled them back away from her. *Not a chance in hell.* No baby-sister of mine was going to choke on smoke, slowly sucking away precious seconds off of her whimsical life like a trashy, middle-aged prostitute after a loveless fuck. *Absolutely fucking not.* I took another drag on my own cigarette. "You're early." I observed. Usually she'd show up a day before we left and we'd drive down together, back home.

My hypocrisy had her burning, flaming darts of dual sided love, hate, sibling relationship shooting from her green eyes. My baby sister had decided to finished her high school career in Britain, despite the expiration of the exchange student contract. Our beautiful, Japanese, southern bell had so impressed the filthy-rich Clarkes that they'd pulled some connections and let her finish in a boarding school, financing the whole thing. Though, despite the financial bondage to the family I didn't think she'd kept in close contact with them. Liam hadn't mentioned her. After she'd graduated she'd gotten a job in London through the Clarke networking market as well, in RTVF broadcasting for some overseas news-coverage channel I wasn't familiar with. It's the most I knew of her escapades. After what had happened, I didn't blame her for not wanting to come home permanently. There wasn't a whole hell of a lot to come home to.

"I'm early because Mrs. Clarke hasn't heard anything from Liam for months. She finally called me, bawling her eyes out wondering if I knew anyone he might have made friends with while he was abroad. And I thought that you might know something, so I came back early hoping you could help me track them down...but that seems a little unnecessary..."

To my knowledge, my nomadic, world traveling, TV, sister never got wind of Liam and I being close. But I wouldn't really know. Again....we hardly spoke. If she'd been in contact with the Clarke's all this time though, that must have meant that she'd known Liam over in Britain, that they'd spoken. But I doubted Liam would mention it. Jen reached into a very fashionable,

123

expensive looking purple purse and pull out a black, sleek, woman's wallet. A very clear image of the plastic hello kitty wallet she used to tote around with her in a Lisa Frank, glitter abused, handbag flashed through my brain like lightning, making me smirk. She handed me a gold credit card with silver lettering on it; "William A. Clarke". I knew the A stood for Alexander, but I hadn't needed to remember his middle name, and hearing it in my mind made me smirk again. *William Alexander Clarke III.* He sounded like a historical diplomat.

"She wanted me to give him this, when I found him. So she'd at least know he was taken care of. Con, you've got to get him to call her. She's a mess." From what I understood, Liam wasn't close to his parents and never had been. Plus, he was a grown adult for Christs sake. He had no obligations to keep in touch with them. And I certainly had no obligations to incite him to. The whole thing sounded alarmingly like none of my business.

"Did you say Liam hasn't been home for months?" He'd only been with me for a week.

"Months. She said about 6 of them."

"Half a year?" I repeated.

"No, dumbass, half a century. Yes, that's how fractions work." The familiarity of sarcasm woven into her tone made me swallow hard, feeling like home.

"What the fuck has Liam being doing for half a year?"

"No, Con, you don't get to be asking the questions." She cut me off, perturbed. "You just barged in with your tongue down another guys throat. I get to ask the questions. Since when are you and Liam a... thing? I mean, I knew Liam was, from what the cooks had told me living there, but I never knew you liked..."

"Rom coms?" I finished her sentence, amusement written all over me. An irritated 'Really?' radiated off of her face, egging me on. "Fashion designer clothing? Interior decorating?"

Stereotyping was frost-wedging to my patience, seeping in, freezing, expanding, tearing it apart little by little, and I saw glimpses of them in her expression as the cogs spun through her head rapidly. I took another drag, scanning for judgment. Jen was none too pleased with my passive-aggressive response.

"Dick, Con. I never knew you liked dick." Vulgarity spewing out of her mouth was the last age-faded puzzle piece of my mother's portrait, and it cut through me tersely.

"The most I can tell you is I like Liam." Simplicity at it's finest; the truth. Sexual exploits with other men were a very short list on my bedside notches. I'd fucked a lot of women. I'd done dirty, better-left-unmentioned things to fulfill a carnal need over the years with them, but Liam was the first and only in a variety of categories. It was only him, as far as I was concerned. I calmly took another drag. "And yes, by extension, Liam's dick."

"Is this why you and Dad don't talk? Does he know?" *God Damnit Jen.* Here was the reason I never called her, dredging up bullshit topics on a whim that I'd spent years digging graves for.

"Ch...This isn't family fucking story time, Jen."

"Fine, excuse the fuck out of me."

"Watch your mouth." I spat at her, and my soul burst into flames, killing me inside. I hated when Hank came out of my mouth. "I'm sorry." I put my cigarette out in the ashtray on the coffee table. She may have been the one who decided to live in Britain, but if I was being honest with myself, I knew that I was the one who'd left her; mentally, emotionally. I had no right to be irritable towards her. I had no right to be anything but apologetic. There was a pause.

"Do you love him?" She asked, seriously, looking at her nails in an attempt to avert my attention away from her burning curiosity. *God damnit.* My little sister grew up much too entitled toward the inner-workings of my subconscious, and her straightforward accusatory demands of information was a good indication of that.

"Hank? Absolutely not. He's a prick." I deflected.

"Liam." *Of course not.* He pissed me off, he made me uneasy. He destroyed the numbness I'd grown so lovingly accustomed to. He tore out my insides and gave me blue balls. Of course I didn't *love* him. What the fuck was 'love' anyway? A visceral transcendence to a fantasy land of hopeful beginnings and sun-shining, daisy-wreath, garbage.

"You don't have to love someone to fuck them, Jen." She was offended, whether by my indifference toward Liam, or by my shity attempt at lying to her, I'll never know.

"So that's it? That's all Liam is to you? A good lay?"

"Probably." I shrugged it off. If he wasn't...if he really wasn't going to leave... that wasn't any of her business. Jen smiled at me lovingly. She knew better, regardless. Jen always knew better.

"I call bullshit." she half muttered under her breath. Liam sauntered into the living room slowly, sitting on the couch with Jen, attempting that painfully fake smile I'd seen him muster in the classroom while I was hungover. His jaw was clenched and his brain was elsewhere as he avoided eye contact with me. He must have been eavesdropping. He must have heard me.

My throat fell into my stomach robbing me of speech. *What did he expect me to say?* I tried in vain to grab just a second of eye contact to transmit my affection toward him psychically, but he gave me no opportunities.

"It's good to see you Jenifer. Sorry for making everyone worry and getting you involved. I honestly didn't think much of it." He said politely, fiddling with his fingers on the couch. *Damnit Liam, look at me.* But he wouldn't. I lit another cigarette and stole Jen's coffee. They small-talked about how Liam's house had been since he left, which cooks were up to what nonsense, how many house cleaners his mother had fired. When Jen mentioned his parents, he changed the subject well, having been practiced in deflection and avoidance all week.

"Listen, Jenifer, are you staying here with us a while?" He asked her. I smoked and observed quietly while they chatted.

"Usually I'd just kick Con out of his bed and stay here, but I don't want to displace both of you for a couple nights..."

"Oh no. Connor and I don't sleep together. We're actually *just* roommates." He smiled and laughed softly. "Obviously I sometimes get confused on the matter... confused with a lot of things actually." Liam still wouldn't look at me, and for a brief second focused an alarming amount of attention on the wall as he spoke that sentence, not wanting to make eye contact with either of us. "Feel absolutely free to kick Connor to the couch and stay here. It's strange how we never were around each other back home."

"Are you coming with us this Saturday?" she asked innocently. I'd been planning on asking him to come, but I hadn't found the right moment with his ninja-Esq disappearing skills lately. It hadn't come up.

"What's this Saturday?"

"Mom's birthday." she looked at me confused, acknowledging how strange it was that I hadn't mentioned anything to him. Liam turned to me, with another hurt expression, locking eyes this time.

"No, actually, I didn't know it was this Saturday."

"But you were close with her when you lived with Mom and Dad?"

"Yes, Yes I was." I tried tuning this conversation out and forgetting about it, but It was too fresh and difficult. Too present. I interrupted them rudely.

"Why don't you call your parents before concerning yourself with mine, Liam." I handed him the credit card Jen had given me for him. "You have your own bullshit to work out before butting into new bullshit." Jen watched us back in forth, trying to gauge where the aura of discomfort was spewing from.

Situationally, this was the epitome of discomfort. A self-loathing somehow festered it's way inside me watching Jen and Liam sitting on my couch, discussing my parents. I avoided Jen on purpose. I love her, but I hated the sight of her, the sound of her, even her smell was familiar. And Liam. An innate need, an insufferable passion, made me cling to him despite the obliteration of my numbing-norm and my own disillusionment of happiness, but I abhorred this moment of drudgery, of an aching forgotten pain resurfacing to the present.

The rest of our conversations, or more accurately; their conversations, dissolved into pop-culture and pleasantries, as we ordered Chinese food and listened to my baby-sister chat endlessly about her RTVF job in London. Occasionally Liam would ask polite questions, some concerning her work, some concerning the whereabouts and gossip of the Clarke Household, or stories of Jen during her exchange into Liam's life all those years ago. I ate food with them and remained physically present... but mentally I felt myself sliding backward, consuming myself with thoughts of my writing. I was reciting details of my characters, my plots, my sub plots, utilized potential diction for specific circumstances, and I zoned out of their world back into my own.

I stared at Liam blankly as he chatted noiselessly with Jen, wondering what the fuck I was doing. I'd somehow managed to bully my anxiety into submission the past few days and it broke free with an unquenchable thirst for revenge. It shouldn't matter to me that Liam was here. He was nothing. It shouldn't matter to me that Jen was here. She was nothing. They were both just tangible memories. And the past was inconsequential.

When you constantly hold yourself apart from things, and focus on the bigger picture, everything appears small and unimportant. Numbness was just a rational progression of thought when the profound realization of how unimportant everything is logically descends upon you. As you shuffle experiences, memories, values, morals, ideals, dreams, and realism around to various different perspectives, you inevitably conclude that it only pertains to an infinitely specific spec of dust that is yourself, and nothing is important. Not my feelings. Not Liam's feelings. Not Jen's feelings, or any of us. And I could do without the excess garbage, distracting me from my work. That's where my irritation derived from. Everyone thinking their menial lives held importance. The seriousness with which everyone functioned. Really, did Liam think whether or not I loved him mattered? And what the fuck was I thinking? Caring if he left or not.

"I'm going out." I said, standing up in the middle of some joke Jen had been telling.

"Where are we going?" Liam asked, standing up as well.

"*We're* not going anywhere. *I'm* going out." I grabbed my keys and my laptop.

"Well where the fuck are *you* going then?" Jen asked incredulously. "I haven't seen you in a year, asshole. You're being rude."

"Stop coming then, Jen." I didn't bother looking at her expression. I knew how to hurt people, it was my specialty, I knew the ball would go in, I didn't need to see the *swish*.

"Connor!" Liam looked at me, pissed. Hurt. Confused. But it was his own fault, for letting me get to him. I didn't care. I had no obligations toward these people nestling into my apartment. I had no obligations toward anyone but Folly, and that was strictly for a decent manuscript in a couple months. *No friends, no family, all alone.* Claire's voice echoed in my head again through the megaphone of my annoyance and irritation. These stupid fucking people failed to realize that that wasn't my greatest fear anymore... that it was my *goal*. It had been years since I trembled at the thought of winding up alone, 9 of them to be exact. If Past-Connor could see me now, what I'd turned into, he'd probably hate me. He had so much to lose, so much to be afraid of, having never experienced pain. It was the fear of the unknown that drove him to terror. But I'd experienced it, lived through it, continue to live in it. I'd experienced pain, remorse, isolation, self loathing... suffocating guilt. Now I had nothing to fear. Now I had nothing.

When I took a last glance at Jen before leaving the apartment, all I saw was mom staring back at me in disapproval. Past-Connor was a simpleton. A love-struck, dumbass simpleton, and I didn't give a fuck what he would have thought.

———

I don't know why I'd kissed him. It was impulsive, I hadn't weighed the pro's or con's or made a concrete decision. He was just spouting random garbage that I must have subconsciously been dying to hear. It was all irrelevant, I knew, and about fictional characters, but just his resolution in everything he proclaimed had hit me during a time of retarded vulnerability. Under normal circumstances, I'd have probably never kissed a guy. And I'll admit, I watched him curiously since David had outed him and he hadn't denied it. I knew he had feelings for me. The poor guy had no idea how to mask his expressions or control that rosacea that crept up every conversation we'd had, every interaction. I probably should have found it creepy, but I didn't.

But I didn't regret kissing him at all. If anything, I was shocked at my own concern as to whether or not I now had to take responsibility for my actions. That was definitely a new array of concern I'd never encountered. I'd made out with countless girls with no regard to the consequences... their feelings didn't concern me in the slightest. If their feelings were hurt, it just sucked to be them. Hurt goes in circles through everyone, round and round like a carousel. But with Liam... I cared. I felt responsible. Responsible for his happiness I guess. As lame as that sounded. I watched him attempt to shoot a basketball and trip over himself.

"Jesus Liam." I walked over to show him how to stand for the millionth time. How to arch his back when he went to shoot, how to position his wrist. He tried again. He failed again. His motions lacked fluidity, they were jagged and uncertain with no conviction. I'd taken on an impossible task. But there was that resolution in his face again, egging me on.

"Pardon." He apologized, blushing, getting up to try again. "I've never been very good at athletics." He confessed. I dribbled the basketball a few times and passed it to him. It almost shook his body the way he caught it, slightly flinching.

"Stop being afraid of the ball." I laughed at him.

"Right." He failed multiple times, repeatedly, and got no better. But eventually he wasn't embarrassed, and we could both laugh at him.

He never spoke about what had happened a week ago in his room, and there was no indication that it was on his mind. Maybe he'd taken it for what it was; a moment of awkward dysfunctional family vulnerability. But every time he looked at me anxiously, every time he scanned for my expressions, or got too close, I found myself combating the urge to kiss him again, just to be sure. But it would have been irresponsible. I knew I wasn't gay. The weather

131

was nicer today, less scorching than it had been, but the exertion of mobility made us sweat like bandits anyway.

"I don't think I'm going to get it." He shook his head in dismay, giving up.

"Doesn't look like it." I admitted. But I threw him the ball again anyway, and hoped for the best. He went to shoot, tilting completely off balance and I was losing my patience. "Wait, Liam, like this." I went up behind him and gently nudged his feet into a position that granted him balance. I lightly touched the small of his back to get him to straighten up with better posture, and then moved up his arms in a way that would efficiently direct his trajectory at least somewhere close to the goddamn net. I mimicked a shooting motion around him. "And never stop looking at the net when you shoot." It came as a whisper because I was so close to his ear, I didn't want to yell at him unintentionally. I'd save that for on-purpose later when I really lost my temper.

I stood back to watch him shoot and saw that he was trembling slightly, because I'd repositioned him and he was about to fall? He didn't shoot.

"Liam?" He didn't answer and I circled around to see his facial expression. He was beat red embarrassed trying painfully to focus on the net. I realized that I'd practically been hugging him. I touched his arm, and his gaze fell on me, startling him into dropping the ball and losing the position that I'd so carefully put him in.

"Pardon!" he said clumsily, going to catch the ball that was rolling away.

"Liam." I grabbed his forearm and pulled him toward me again, letting the ball roll away. There was that motion again, an involuntary magnet drawing me toward him.

"Con, I'm sorry." He startled me with his abruptness. I stepped back, regaining my composure. That was close.

"For the other night... in my bedroom." *What?* "I feel like I somehow took advantage of you, after everything that happened with your dad, and how messed up everything was. I'm just really sorry." I'd kissed him. I remembered it vividly, there was no denying or misunderstanding the situation on my end. I'd wanted to kiss him, and I did... just like every other want I'd adhered to. Why was he apologizing? "I wasn't going to bring it up, or talk about it, because I thought that's what you wanted but I just can't stop thinking about it and I really owed you an apology." He had that earnest expression again, he drew his eyes away from mine and stared at a tree nearby to keep his composure. "I... I feel like you know I've had feelings for you, and it made it difficult the other night to not... erm... like the uh..." The poor guy was struggling so hard for words that have always come so naturally for me, just like he struggled so hard to shoot a damn basketball.

I understood that it was his compassion for others that drove him to such lengths; that overwhelming consideration for the feelings of everyone around him. It clearly killed him to come out of his shell and express himself, yet there he stood, apologizing to me for *my* actions. He cared for everybody, and I'd almost never cared for anybody. I reached out and held him close to me again, like I had the other night, giving in to my indulgences.

"Con, I-" I tilted his mouth to mine and kissed him again. No-one had ever considered me before, at least, enough to do something for me. Anything for me. Liam was startled, like the first time, but like the first time, he reciprocated. Since I was completely in tune with my senses, it was hard to argue with the unbiased, non manipulated yearning I had for him and it shocked even me. When I broke away from him he looked down at his shoes. "Connor, this...this isn't funny for me." His voice was constricted, and I could see his eyes welling. *What did I do?*

"Liam, I-" he cut me off.

133

"I know you're just messing with me, you're just playing, but... it's making me a nervous wreck around you." He looked up at me finally, and to be honest, I have no idea what he saw. But it made me realize something astonishing inside myself, and I blurted it out before I even had the chance to mull it over in my head.

"Liam, I like you." I wasn't ashamed of the fact. I'd never cared what anyone thought of me before, it would have been a hell of a time to start now. It made sense. I thought about him constantly, I wondered what he was thinking, what he was doing when he wasn't around me, when I'd see him next. I'd been fighting the urge to slink next door to his bedroom at night when I couldn't sleep. I'd lay awake listening to the sound of his voice and guitar through the walls of his room, and it was a solace I'd never experienced before. A sharpness in the dullness of my existence. I cared for him, I felt responsible for his happiness.

"You're an asshole." It wasn't the response I necessarily expected. But I wasn't shocked...And frankly, it was sort of charming the way he said it, his "a" coming out as more of an "o". I was kind of an "osshole". He started to walk away from me.

"Yeah, I am. But I'm not a liar." He stopped and turned around. "Liam, you're an idiot. And you're really fucking naïve, and hard to take seriously, but I like you. Alot." He eyed me suspiciously. "I've never given two fucks about anyone before, besides Jen or Mom. I give tons of fucks about you." I laughed at myself and my inability to talk in a sophisticated dialect when I deemed it important. "I give all of the fucks for you." I tried to use a mock serious tone but I ended up laughing again. No wonder he couldn't believe me, I sounded like an ignorant prick. I couldn't help it; *I was happy.*

"What does...what does that even mean?"

"I don't know, man. I'm sorry." I paused. "Don't apologize for me anymore though." I walked back over to him and ruffled his hair affectionately. Then I walked away and grabbed the basketball we'd let escape us while he just watched me completely confused. I started to leave the court and he jogged up to me, without saying a word. My cigarettes reminded me they were in my pocket with a slight rub against my leg and I pulled one out and lit it. Liam couldn't look at me, couldn't make eye contact...and I was okay with that because I felt a little stupid too. Like maybe I was the real idiot. What the fuck was I getting myself into?

So what were you supposed to do when you liked a guy? The same stuff that you'd do with a girl? Did you ask them out, and go on dates, and lamely hold hands in amusement parks and smile for fake-ass photos in photo booths? Did Liam even know? Had he had a boyfriend before? He was only 15, I doubt he'd have any idea...especially when it came to sexual exploits. I should have just let the whole idea die, just let him apologize for his magically materialized, exaggerated, inequities and kept going. But I didn't.

"Do you like people, Liam? You have shity social skills, but I can't tell."

"I don't necessarily dislike them." Honesty was his best policy.

"There's a party a couple streets over if you want to go." I guess it was my shitty attempt.

"What kind of party?"

"I don't know. I don't ever go to them."

"Then why do you want to go to this one?"

"I don't." He wasn't understanding my awkward failed attempt at asking him to a social gathering. I wasn't going to explain it. There was a long pause and I could tell he was trying to figure it out in his head. "Forget it, don't worry about it." I said that but I knew he would anyway. I knew he'd probably keep himself up all night worrying about it. And maybe that would elicit some songs to fall asleep to, so I didn't totally mind.

135

It wasn't brought up again. Everything went on as usual, with a little more amiability between the two of us, more jokes, more laughing. Liam was finally getting comfortable around me after his awkward as hell apology, but really, whatever helped him sleep at night. School was a little less boring. We didn't necessarily hang out at school, our classes were too far apart, and the senior, sophomore schedule discrepancies didn't really allow time for it. He'd waved at me like a total dork a few times across the hall, sort of shy, but unable to hide a smile and it made me smirk. I head nodded and continued on my way, sneaking out the back doors for a smoke break between classes. I turned my familiar corner outside and almost ran into a girl from one of my classes, Andrea.

She was leaning up against my wall, lighting her own cigarette. The sun had somewhat smudged her black eye-liner but it just made her look a little more wild, adventurous. Her hair was up in a messy bun, matching a punk-rock look she was pulling off pretty well. I'd sort of slept with her last semester and hadn't remembered till now. My intrigue in Liam was a little strange situated next to a girl I'd fucked in the theater room on an old matted green sofa during lunch break. I'm not even sure why I did it... probably because she'd asked me to and I had no tangible reason to decline. Why not?

"Big Shay." She greeted me while inhaling, cutting her breath short. The nickname she'd given me was odd, but it came from the fact that she knew Jen and spoke with her on a somewhat regular basis, to my dismay. Jen was 'Little Shay' and I was 'Big Shay'.

"Andy." She pulled the loose cigarette out of my lips and lit it on hers before I had a chance to ignite it myself, then handed it back to me, comrades in the disrespect of school discipline. The

136

only difference, I thought, was that she was a rebel to prove a point, to 'stick it to the man' and I was a rebel because following certain rules were just plain and simply inconvenient. I was a lazy asshole, not a punk.

"Missed you at that party the other night."

"You mean all of them, ever?"

"Yeah." I took another drag.

"You should work on that." I looked away from her at the empty campus. Everyone was already in class. Some picnic tables were in front of us, a display for some snack wrappers and spilled milk cartons. Andrea misunderstood my intention. She came onto me, holding her own cigarette in her mouth and handling my zipper. I pushed her away nonchalantly. "No thanks."

"Is the illusive Connor Shay finally tied down to some lucky harlot?" she laughed at me.

"Nope, just not you so much." She was taken aback. I guess she assumed we were more the comrade in arms, friends, two of a kind. I never really understood what she thought, but whatever it was I was fairly certain she was wrong.

"Well, when she breaks your heart, you know where to find me."

"Riding out the innocence of some up and coming youngster who doesn't know any better?" She put out her cigarette annoyed.

"Probably. Have you seen the new British sophomore kid? He's going to be a little hottie. Looks a little corruptible, doesn't he?" I laughed. "Oh shit, doesn't he live with you Big Shay?"

"Sure does. And I've grown accustomed to his not-so-corrupted presence, so lay off." I put out my cigarette too and we went back inside.

"Connor, for real though." She lightly pushed me into the wall and wrapped her arms around my neck. She got on tiptoes to kiss me, and honestly it required less energy to just let her, and leave without a confrontation than it would to make a scene, push her off, reject her. Andrea kissed me on the lips and felt right away that I wasn't reciprocating. "Wow. Have it your way, Limp-dick." and she turned and walked off.

"You just have that charming effect on me, Andy." I loosely saluted her a goodbye and walked to class. Typical day.

After the last bell I walked up to the sophomore hallway to meet Liam at his locker instead of outside, because I thought he might like to stop in at the library before we left. I had some books to return and a few new recommendations for him to read outside of class. But it turned out he'd beaten me outside. When I looked out the window by his locker I saw him standing by the tree we usually met at, with Andrea. He was looking around nervously, trying to ignore her to the best of his ability, but she was relentless, playing with his hair, draping over his shoulders. A simmering vat of green irritability bubbled to fruition inside of me, a feeling I'd never been befuddled with before. I immediately hated it. I darted down the hallway, down the stairs, pushing people out of my way rudely, through the schools front doors.

"Hey, Andy, fuck off." I said, slowing to a forced walk as I approached them. But she was still playing, enjoying the fact that she was getting my goat. "I'm serious."

"Oh, Big Shay's serious, Liam." Then she leaned in closer and whispered something in his ear that turned his face excruciatingly red.

"I'm...I'm... sorry Andrea, but I'm just not entirely interested." He reacted immediately to her pained shocked expression. Two rejections in one day must have killed her already fragile self esteem. The self esteem that she'd loosely thread together with a slutty persona and added, "You're very lovely, it's nothing to do with you, I just... you're not especially my *type*."

"Is this about Connor?" I knew, because of my previous interactions with Andy, that she was being sarcastic with him, trying to use their conversation to elicit a response. Liam eyed me surprised and a little hurt for some reason. "Shay screwed me, so now you can't?" The hurt expression was more poignant.

"No, sorry, I promise, I'm just not interested," He wiggled out from under her and walked away quickly. "Excuse me. Pardon." I quickly caught up to him and kept pace, and we left Andrea behind, to irritate someone else. He wouldn't look at me or talk to me.

"Something wrong?" I asked and he kept walking, watching his shoes.

"No." I didn't believe him, obviously, but I wasn't going to press it. It was his business.

"Making new friends?"

"She's a bit crass." I laughed, pulling out a cigarette. Our walking slowed to normal.

"She's a bit of a bitch."

"So I guess you're into that then?"

"Not currently, no." He stopped walking and looked up at me. I really wanted to... solidify whatever it was that was going on between us. So we were on the same page at least. I'd never done this with a girl though, attempted to establish a sort of... contract of understanding? But I didn't want Liam to think I was just dicking around. His psyche already teetered on the brink of negative self fulfilled prophecy and sheer Hit-and-miss-communication. Andrea wasn't helping much. And I was sure that if he started listening to any gossip around school my name was bound to pop up on different womanizing escapades. Such frivolities helped to alienate annoying people from befriending me, and any serious girls from attempting something insipid, so it was a win-win, usually.

We walked silently for a few minutes while I thought of solutions. Then it hit me. I edged my free hand toward his, slowly, an irritated nervousness crept up in me. I pulled back for a second. Maybe that wasn't the way to go. Contracts of understanding where really fucking awkward and out of my league. Fuck it. I took his hand. Unexpectedly he rejected me, pulling his hand back and staring at me in an angry disbelief. I wasn't understanding the sequential order of his thoughts.

"Are you bloody kidding me, Con?" Honestly, it was kind of what I was thinking too as I did it. I didn't blame him. Two guys hand-holding.... hand-holding in general was super lame. But I didn't think that he'd think so, so this caught me off guard.

"Maybe?" Liam could cut me some slack though. I was doing my best here.

"You think you can just run around doing whatever you bloody want whenever you feel like it?" It wasn't *not* true. I did essentially think that, but the accusation was harsher than I believed to be warranted. I took another drag of my cigarette and eyed him suspiciously. He turned on me and kept walking.

"Liam." He didn't answer. "Liam?" I trailed behind him. There was no possible way in all of existence that he was so intensely a prude that fucking *hand holding* would elicit this angry of a response. Fine then, fuck him. *This whole thing is stupid anyway.* I walked passed him and left him behind, not bothering to look back. When I got home, I went straight to my room, grabbed a paperback off my shelf completely randomly, uncaring what I chose, and plopped on my bed to settle in and read. I heard the front door open and close, he must have gotten home.

He knocked on my door.

"What?" He opened it and shut it behind him so he had something to lean against as he spoke, shoving his hands in his pockets.

140

"Listen, Con... I'm sorry. I saw you and Andrea kissing in the hall today, I should have said something." He wouldn't make eye contact. *So what?.* "It's none of my concern, really, none of my business. But I'm not...interested in being one of your impulses. I'm just fine as your friend. I'd like you to respect my boundaries from now on."

"Ok." Well that made things easier, didn't it? *Good call.* I went back to reading and he hesitated by my door.

"Was it true, what she said?" he asked timidly.

"Which part?"

"About you two... you know..."

"Absolutely." I didn't look up from my book. There was no point in lying, I wasn't ashamed of anything. I could tell he was about to leave and for some god-awful reason my heart was beating more quickly than usual. "Liam?"

"Yeah?"

"When I said I gave all the fucks about you, I meant all of them. As in, there weren't any left to give anyone else." He stared at me, still not understanding.

"Didn't seem like it."

"She kissed me, it didn't mean anything." Not that it was any of his business.

"Doesn't really ever *mean anything*, does it?" I couldn't read the smile he gave me, and somehow, I felt like I'd messed up. He left. *Good, now things can go back to normal.*

But my feet moved on their own, tearing me out of my room. And my hands turned the knob on his bedroom door, and none of my limbs seemed to give a shit what I thought. Nor did my organs, because my heart was about to boom out of my chest. Liam was sitting up against the foot of his bed with his guitar nearby and some notes in his lap, probably working on something. He looked miserable. Clearly I wasn't cut out for this 'being responsible for

141

other people's happiness thing'. I didn't say anything, I just grabbed his wrist and pulled him up to his feet, ignoring his protest, and I dragged him out the front door of the house, locking it behind me with my keys. He was confused and dumbfounded, a deer caught in headlights. I turned back to him, grabbed his hand and intertwined my fingers in his, and pulled him away from the house.

"Connor!?" He tried to pull his hand away from mine, but I wasn't letting him. "Con!?" I ignored him and kept going. "What are you doing?".

"I don't know." I wanted a cigarette but I'd left them in my room.

"Where are we going!?"

"To a movie."

"Con, we're um... we're holding hands... in public. People are going to get the wrong idea!" He tried pulling away again and I didn't let him, again.

"Good." I really needed a cigarette.

"CON!" He jerked away and pushed me back roughly. "You can't just do whatever you want! To whoever you want whenever you want to! I'm not a bloody play thing! For Christ's sake, I'm not a pet in the Shay household!" That pissed me off, I didn't think I'd ever treated him shitty. He was the one who moved into my house, disrupted my life, confused me with all his gay romance shit, subtle blushing, watching me when he didn't think I noticed...this was his fault.

"Then stop acting like a little...bitch!" I hadn't meant it that harshly. My writing brain thought of pet, which transitioned to dog, which transitioned to female dog, and spat out of my mother-grown-sailor-mouth as 'bitch'. Anger was overflowing out of him, his glare more penetrating than I'd ever imagined possible. Words couldn't escape him, and his hands were balled into fists at his sides. Instead of responding he turned around to walk away again and I impulsively grabbed his arm. He swung around and kneed me in the balls, causing me to double over in pain. My body tensed up and I crouched on the sidewalk. I didn't think the little shit had it in him. I held my breath as the shocking throb railed through me... then I laughed. "I... I probably deserved that." I admitted, half smiling up at him, half wanting to slam his face into the concrete.

"Con, I'm.. I'm so sorry..." he knelt down to help me up and I put my hand up in a stopping motion, keeping him away. I needed another second. "I didn't meant to... bloody hell." *I think...I probably deserved that.*

"Do you feel better? Are we even now?" I reached out for his hand to help me up and he politely obliged.

"A little actually." I saw him consider. "Yes, I feel much better." He smiled genuinely, and it was disgustingly adorable. I bent down slightly and kissed him, hesitantly this time, flinching away slightly in case he decided to hit me again. He chuckled onto my lips, and pulled away.

"Will you come out to the fucking movies with me then?" I asked, grinning. A car passed and Liam's eyes were distracted, following it a second.

"Yeah, but you have to stop with the public stuff... you're going to get me beat up again." I shoved my hands in my pockets and started walking. Liam walked next to me, watching his shoes.

"I don't know, I think you could handle yourself pretty well if you tried." My balls were still throbbing sensitive.

"Con... could you maybe not let other people kiss you?" I'd almost completely missed it, he whispered in such a translucent mumbling fashion, as though he didn't even want me to hear him.

"I guess. Could you maybe not let any other guys kiss you?" I shot back at him. "I guess if your tongue wants to explores the secrets of Andy's throat, that's your prerogative. Clearly she's interested." I joked. He laughed.

"Shut up. I'm not a tom like some people."

"A tom?"

"A slag..." I still didn't get it. "A whore." I reached into my pocket for a cigarette and found none, remembering I'd left mine at home.

"Thanks, for that." I laughed. "But I bet you are deep down... What's your kissing number at Liam?" I joked. His face reddened and he walked a little ahead of me.

"One." I stopped and he kept going. *What have I gotten myself into?*

CHAPTER 7: THE EBB AND FLOW

"LIAM!" Jeff came barging up to me as Jen and I walked unknowingly into his crisis. We'd waited at the apartment for at least two hours, trying to keep up light conversation, thinking that Connor would have a change of heart and come back, but he never did. I kept imagining him sick and decrepit somewhere, throwing up all over himself from too much to drink. He'd had that look in his eyes, the hallow one I'd seen between the covers of his books. I couldn't stand holding still and waiting around, and finally convinced Jen to go out with me to look for him. Of course, the first stop was the bar. "Liam, you have to help me."

Jeff wasn't any less cavalier as usual, but clearly he was in a bind. The bar was packed beyond belief, I barely recognized it. *Thank god I'm not working tonight.*

"What's wrong?"

"Andromeda canceled." I could barely hear him over the chatter of people. Andromeda was the name of an apparently well-liked local band I hadn't had the chance to see yet. But I'd heard a lot about them.

"What? They canceled? Why?"

"Fuck if I know," Jeff put his arm around me and started steering me away from Jen. "So there's a guitar in the back, you're going to have to fill their spot. I tried to tug myself away to stay with Jen in the bustling crowd.

"No, Jeff, I can't. Con's sisters in town, and he left and I can't find him..."

"Well we have the alcohol, I'm sure he'll end up here. It would be *irresponsible* for you to leave."

"What about Jenifer? I can't leave her alone..." I didn't think Con would appreciate it if I left her with a bunch of strangers in a crowded bar. He had trouble grasping the fact that she was a grown adult, and what he cared about, I cared about.

"Jenifer? Connor's sister?" Clearly he was only half listening to me. Jeff turned around and saw her for the first time. "Holy shit." His voice turned into a whisper. He pulled closer to my ear, "Liam... Connor's sister is totally banging." Jen pushed through the crowd after us, keeping up. I put my hand over Jeff's mouth.

"Listen Jeff. Do nooooot even think about it." He laughed and I felt like he understood.

"Jenifer Shay I presume?" Jeff greeted as he approached. He took her hand royally and kissed it. I wanted to kick him. Jen pulled it back.

"Jeff the bartender?" She was quick that Jen. He corrected her.

"Jeff... the one who got away. Or so you'll be saying years from now if you don't have a drink with me." Con was going to kill me. *Shit.* He remembered his current crisis as Jen looked at him with a pretense of disgust. "Liam! Please, for the love of God. Please, for real..." He apparently wasn't above begging. I looked to Jen to make sure she was okay, and I figured.... if she was Maggie's daughter she'd be fine.

"Go ahead, Liam, I'm fine! I wanted to hear you play anyway." She'd be fine. But my stomach hurt as I left her with Jeff. I politely excused myself through the crowd, careful not to bother anybody. It was inevitable that I'd bump a few people now and again earning a glare here and there, but I'd smile apologetically and they'd turn back around. There were so many people here...it was nuts. I kept looking around for Con, hoping I'd spy him in the crowd. Where would he go if not here?

I grabbed the guitar Jeff had told me about and snuck up to his apartment, sitting by his locked door so I could tune it real quick and make sure it was ready to go. Thank god I did, the tone's were way off. I wished I had my guitar. There were so many people... Andromeda must have really been a great band. All of these people were here excitedly anticipating a band that they weren't going to get to see... I was going to have to perform for people who were starting off disappointed and already hating me. Where was Con? I couldn't stifle the worry inside me. I hated that look he'd had. I wondered why he hadn't invited me to go with him on Saturday. Or at least mentioned it. *I guess I understand why.* I tuned the guitar, it was an electric. I was a little relieved, on second thought, because I was afraid my acoustic might not be heard over the potential booing and negative feedback I'd be receiving. I knew it said nothing of my own abilities; these people had been hopeful for a punk-rock girl band, and they were getting saddled with a timid British guy in jeans and a T-shirt. Surely Jeff would find some other replacement after a few songs when he saw terrible everything was working out. However, the guy had let me sleep on his floor, offered me a job, and was helping me get good publicity for no reason other than being a friend of Cons. I was actually lucky to be in a position to help him out.

I wished that Con would just talk to me. Tell me what he was thinking, why he was so hell bent on shutting everyone out. He'd been that way a little, when I'd first met him, but we'd already gotten past that once. Before I'd left the first time, he'd been completely honest with me, open about everything. His fears, his dreams, his gratitude, how he'd felt about me, his family, his sister, his mother... everything. I'd never been closer to anyone. I missed that Connor so much my insides felt like a crushed soda can. Leaving tore myself apart, abandoning my favorite part of myself. And I was never the same either.

The half I'd taken with me I'd tried to acclimate, to open up to other people. But it just... it didn't work. Nothing worked. One

147

day I would tell Connor everything I'd been through since I'd been gone, but I just needed him to feel like *him* again. And I needed to tell him that it was my fault, what happened. And I needed him to forgive me because I'd already tried to live without him and everything had felt lifeless, pointless, miserable, as hard as I tried. For nine years. So if he rejected me afterward, if he couldn't bear to look at me, I really had nothing left. My throat was constricting just thinking about it; I needed to get my shit together. I could hear the ominous hum of people downstairs.

I wanted to see the best in people, so I did. I saw the best in every opportunity, every situation, every person I'd passed on the streets of London, because I forced myself to. I refused to think the worst because it scared the crap out of me. I'd let myself once, and it'd almost killed me. I wasn't as strong as Connor, I never was. I heard Jeff on the mic downstairs.

"I'm so excited you all made it out here to see the one and only Andromeda!" Everyone hollered and glasses clinked together. "But! They're not going to make it." There were boos from the crowd. I tried to subdue my heart from racing out of my chest. "However! We have a very special guest, the young heart throb from the UK, our brilliantly talented Brit, Mr. Liam Clarke!" I knew that was my cue to go down there and man the stage but I could barely move. There was awkward dispersed chatter. "LIAM!" he called to me through the mic on the stage. I could do this, I could do this quickly to fill some time for Jeff, and then go find Con.

Jen was sitting at a table closest to the stage with a fruity drink in her hand. Leave it to Jeff to make sure a beautiful girl was accommodated. When I saw everyone staring at me, despite the contempt and judgment, I felt an oozing calm melt it's way through me. I loved the stage. My head cleared and I smiled, genuinely, happy to be there, happy to be alive. I pulled the covers I'd been

148

practicing from the back of my mind. Everyone was back to drinking in minutes, ignoring the fact that I was there, and it was a beautiful feeling, playing for them all without being intensely scrutinized, smiling to Jen in the front row, intermediately scanning for Con. Britain was there, in the crowd, chatting with friends. Jeff eventually got one of his employees to man the bar so he could sit and watch a while. Watching this big of a crowd, the ebb and flow of energy as one song seeped into the next, made me miss London, and my band, and my band-mate Brent, a little bit. I tried not to think about Brent. But mostly, I missed Connor. Every second he wasn't in my sight I missed him. I felt it, even on stage, that echoing void of needing him, even as my voice reverberated softly through the mic, smoothly, rhythmically with the strumming of my guitar.

Britain cheered at me from the crowd and I winked at her, smiling. More people were watching now, and I felt their apt attention. It was exhilarating. Jen was talking animatedly with Jeff, some of the patrons were leaving... it couldn't be helped, I was just one guy. It was hard to keep them intrigued. But I kept a lot of them too, and the fact that they were giving me a chance gave me the energy to keep going.

On a ten minute break Jen waved me over to the table with her and Jeff. They were getting along amiably, Jeff was respectful. A flirt, but respectful. He must have really cared for Con.

"You know what I love about your brother, oh fair Jenifer?" He asked her, taking a drink of his own glass. "He's real. He doesn't waste time on bullshit, he's honest, he doesn't worry about hurting feelings or judge anyone." *I love that too.* "And he's so completely fucking oblivious to the fact that he's absolutely, goddamn, miserably, broken. His oblivious nature is almost poetic." Jen and I locked eyes for just a second. "And I'm not saying I love his misery, by any means, but all the years I lived

149

with him I just couldn't help thinking, if this is how this guy writes at his worst, and functions at his worst... what the fuck is he capable of at his best?" I could tell Jeff was getting tipsy. "And I love him. He's like a brother to me. Love that guy." *Not as much as I do.*

"Con's fine." Jen assured him. "He's always been a strong guy. He's invincible." Of course she'd think that, he was her big, immovable, impenetrable brother. "He's sad sometimes, but he keeps his shit together. And plus, now he has Liam." She motioned to me with her glass. Was it my imagination, or was Jen getting a little tipsy too? Should I not have taken Connor's baby sister to a bar? She was my age though, she wasn't a baby. I smiled toward her.

"Yes, he does." I affirmed. It lit me up inside. She was right. He had me. And I wouldn't let anything happen to him. Weak, pathetic, loser Liam from back in the past didn't have the strength, or confidence to be there for him in the way he needed, but I'd changed since then. I'd changed. And I'd be able to save him from anything now, even himself. I'd unintentionally made sure of it.

I'd spent so many nights back home, on long walks, or sitting on benches under windy trees and knowing stars, staring up, begging them to tell me how he was doing. If he was fine. If he needed me. If he'd tolerate me coming home. Years went by. YEARS. And it felt like it never got easier, the not knowing. The wondering if he blamed me as much as I did. The guilt. I thought that maybe it was my house, the solitude, the emptiness of the mansion, the whispering of the cooks about Jen and her whereabouts that kept me locked to him. I'd felt a separation between me and other people way before I'd ever come to America. It was nothing extraordinarily new. My parents had convinced me something was wrong with me, made me almost too embarrassed to join society. And after feeling what it was like to be normal, a part of a family, however dysfunctional, I could never regain that complacent contentedness for anything less. Even after the years of therapy my mother had shoved me in on returning home, the attempt at church, the attempt at a military discipline.

So I'd left about six months ago. I moved in with Brent in a shitty apartment in the darker side of London, but that had led to a whole shit-ton of new problems and a bridge on a stormy night strung out on coke and alcohol. I didn't handle storms well. I shook off the thought, I wasn't going to do this, let it all back in. I'd given up that night, I was going to jump, but I didn't. Because I'd thought of Connor, and I knew, If I were really gone, he'd truly have nothing. I was his, whether he'd have me or not.

I didn't like drinking because it made me look stupid. And it made me act stupid.

"Liam, whats wrong?" Jen reached across the table and held my hand. "You look pale." She almost had to yell across the chatting around us. I grinned at her.

"I'm alright!" But I wasn't. I was worried about Connor. Jeff interjected.

"You better be, you have to get back on stage soon." He excused himself politely to Jen, throwing her a flashy-casual grin he'd perfected. The blushing in her cheeks told me she'd completely fallen for it. *Jesus Christ.* I liked Jeff, it was a bummer I'd have to help Con kill him later.

When I got back on stage, I felt like I was running out of cover performances. I only had a few more. I used them, and the crowd was suddenly glued to my music again after my break. I saw Claire in the crowd with that boyfriend of hers and they were both listening, laughing, smiling, talking, drinking. The boyfriends friends were there too, nearby, drinking. They all looked wasted already, having clearly pre-gamed before coming out. Claire was watching me intently, recognizing me from earlier. It made me nervous so I scanned a different area of the audience, back to Jen. Britain made her way over to the table she'd seen me sitting at and sat with Jen. It made me grin; I was glad Jen had company I knew I could trust not to attempt to get in her pants. I loved covers, as much as I loved music in general. I liked the familiarity of the words, the ability for anyone in the audience to sing along. But Con had been right earlier, I was less passionate about them than my own writing.

When you write a song yourself and you sing it, hearing the words come out of your mouth, feeling the honesty, the fear and anticipation of how listeners will react, whether or not they'll really hear you, really feel what you're trying to get across. It's like floating in a different dimension where you're not a person anymore, you're a medium. And your only goal in life is to transmit a intangible, untouchable, non-corruptible emotion from one heart, to another, without changing a thing. Singing other people's songs, that was great, but singing your own was ripping your heart out and holding it on stage for all the world to see. I finished the last cover I knew, and the audience was still rapt in attention. I looked to Jeff to see what I should do. He was looking at me, noticing the pause in my music. He made a rollover motion with his hands, the universal 'keep going' sign.

It irritated me ever so slightly. I needed to get going, I needed to find Connor, and make sure he was okay. I'd already spent hours here. Why was I the only person who was so concerned with where he'd gone off to? Con could be anywhere, and he was alone again. Maybe he'd done this often. Maybe, previously, there'd never been anyone around to notice he'd gone missing. *Can you really go missing if you don't belong anywhere to begin with?*

The last week had been blissful and I'd seen the happiness etched on his face, the relaxation in his glances, felt the familiarity of comfort in the way he'd held me. But when he left, that was all gone, and I knew he was wandering around empty and alone, left only with himself and the berating inner dialogue I knew was pounding him into a submission of numbness and solidarity. He'd been gone for hours.

"Liam! Liam! Liam!" Britain had started a slightly drunk rant, and everyone else started cheering. The sound of my own name coming out of the mouths of strangers felt odd. Back home, outside the mansion, everyone called me 'Lex'. William was left behind somewhere and I'd graciously welcomed Alexander into my mundane day-to-day.

I had spaced out for just a second. I looked out over the audience, stretching to the front doors, a little more spaced out now, and my heart leaped into my throat. I grinned from ear to ear. Connor was in the back, near the doorway, leaning against the door watching my set. How long had he been there? All of my anxieties slipped away and relief swept over me. I was out of covers. All I really wanted to do was drop the stupid guitar and go to him, tell him everything I'd been thinking, tell him the truth, hope to move forward, passed it all. But I couldn't, I had to finish the set. Though...there was a song I'd written in high school, one that I'd never gotten to show him. One that I sang solo, sang with my band, threw into all of my sets over years.

"I'm sorry you've been stuck with me instead of Andromeda." People laughed, and cheered for me all the same. "All of you have been very kind to me tonight." I said timidly into the mic. I wasn't as confident at public speaking. "And I have one song that's very dear to me I'd like to share with you all. I wrote it a long long time ago for someone very special to me." I tried my best not to look at Con, and stared elsewhere so as to not give us away. "It's called; *Convict.*" I started the intro, slow but powerful, sounding even better on an electric than an acoustic. The patrons of Jeff's bar quieted down, I'd successfully pulled them in. Connor hadn't moved from his spot, arms folded in the back, watching me play. There wasn't a drink in his hand or a cigarette hanging from his lips...feeling unfamiliar in a familiar place.

"I breathe you in, you give me life.
I taste you, you're my nourishment.
I hear your silent, anguished cries...
But baby, you are heaven-sent."

I wondered where he'd been all night till now, I wondered if he knew how worried I was. I wondered if somehow he knew how hurt I was having to leave him nine years ago.

"There's nothing more important.
There's nothing in this world.
There's nothing that could warrant
Me not being next to you."

The chorus clamored through me, battling with my guitar for headway. I closed my eyes and tried not to choke out the words, but I felt my throat hurting. I ignored everything around me, I was singing for myself, and for Con, and that was all that mattered. Not Jeff, or Jen in the front row, or Britain, or Claire, who I saw whispering to her guy friends, pointing back at Connor angrily. I pushed through to the last verse;

"There's no saving me without saving you;
You're a part of me, it's true.
In a darkened world, I'm seeing light.

154

And the flame inside me's you.
The flame inside me's you.
I breathe you in, you give me life,
I hear you silent anguished cries
And the flame inside me's you.

I really loved him.

And you burn, burn, burn,
through the dark
And you burn, burn, burn,
And leave your mark.
As I burn, burn, burn
The prisons down.
You're not a convict anymore..."

I paused, letting my guitar fade out, looking to Connor at the back of the bar. I couldn't make out his expression from where I was standing, and his body was motionless, head tilted toward the ground, no longer looking toward me.

"Cause you've got me."

The song ended. He turned abruptly and walked out of the bar as everyone else applauded loudly. Britain whistled between her fingers and I saw Jeff's wide claps, Jen's smile, and soft tears. *Where's he going now?* I stood dumbly on the stage as they quieted down. I saw Claire's friends all leave at once, quickly, together, in a group. My heart dropped into my stomach realizing where they were going. My gaze quickly landed on Jeff and we made eye contact as my face paled,

"Sorry." I said quickly into the mic, dropping it, whipping the guitar strap over my head, letting it fall down to the floor with a clanging, as I jogged off the stage. Everyone was trying to stop me, trying to drunkenly say hello, congratulate me on a great set. A quick glance showed me the worry in Jen's eyes at my abrupt behavior and I hoped she'd stay put. And I saw Claire again, with a smug smirk, solidifying my worry. People kept getting in my way between me and the door.

"Get the fuck out my way!" I pushed through them and slammed open the bar's front door, a soft cool breeze brushed against me, catching in my sweat from the set and cooling me. But my insides were already frozen. I looked back and forth, I didn't know which way Con would have gone. I headed the direction of our apartment in a jogging panic. Then I heard voices, movements between the coffee shop and gas station on the strip. *No. No, no, no...* I heard an unfamiliar voice;

"Say something smart now, Jackass!" I heard a rustle and a thud, more thuds, "Are you fucking listening?! You faggot piece of shit!" I whipped around the corner and saw the five of them, Claire's boyfriend was the one yelling, cursing at Con on the floor. He was on the ground, head tucked under his arms, and they all kept kicking. Claire's boyfriend already had blood on his face, Con must have gotten a few good hits in already.

"Con!?"

"Liam?!" Connor lifted his head slightly, just enough to see me. In the entanglement of swinging feet I watched one kick resound with a thud on the side of Con's head. I saw his arms go limp, I distinguished dark shadows of blood on the ground around him.

I instinctively ran at whoever was closest, elbowing them in the face, knocking them down. A terror rose inside me that made my senses haze out. I'd completely lost it, I wasn't in control, I barely knew what was happening. It was fight or flight and Connor was... I tackled Claire's boyfriend with all of my weight and it stopped the assault on Con immediately, grabbing everyone's attention. We went crashing to the ground and he managed to deck me in the mouth, but I didn't feel it. I wrestled my way on top of him and slammed my fist into his face. Again. And again. Ignoring the sharp pain in my knuckles and wrist. Again, one more time, and I felt arms reaching out around me, yanking me off, throwing me to the floor, a kicking on my ribcage, but I couldn't feel anything. Was Con...? I jumped back up, ignoring the pain. They'd surrounded me. I backed up, pushing the guy behind me harshly into the brick wall that was caging us in. I heard his head slam on the brick with the rest of his body, and I didn't bother turning around.

The last three were so much bigger than I was, but it didn't stop me. I went to hit one of them, but the other two were too quick, they grabbed my arms and held me immobile. I fought, kicked, tugged, to no avail. The third guy uppercut me in the jaw and I had a small flashback to my first fight, back in my sophomore year. I saw Con in the corner of my eye. The guy hit me again, laughing. He was the first one that I'd elbowed in the face; he was enjoying this. He laughed. I didn't care. I'd been in a lot more fights back home in London since high school. I thought back to everything Brent had taught me. With the two assholes holding my arms I was able to jump and kick the third guy with both feet, right in the groin. I headbutt the guy on my right and whipped around and slammed the other guys face into my knee in the brief seconds before the surprise wore out. The third guy was up on his feet again, and he'd pulled out a knife. Blood was dripping from his eyebrow where I'd elbowed him and he side-spit blood out of his mouth. But I didn't care, I didn't have the capacity.

157

I grabbed the knife first as he came at me, but the sheer force of his weight knocked me to the ground.

We landed next to Con. The guy was on top of me, pressing all of his weight on his wrist that I was desperately trying to fight the increasing force of, keeping the knife away from me. Blood was filling my mouth from where I'd been hit previously, and dust from the ground, mixing with the sweat on my brow was getting in my eyes. I turned my head, still staving off the knife, and I was looking right at Con. *Connor... Con!? Con...* He was just asleep, right? I needed to get to him, I needed to tell him the truth, I needed to tell him I loved him. *I'm sorry. I'm so sorry...* I couldn't....I couldn't fucking get to him! He was just out cold... He was going to be fine. He was fine... Unless he wasn't. I couldn't hold off the knife anymore, it was getting closer. The guy shoved his knee into my ribs and I heard a crack. This was it.

There was a sharp, resounding shot and my heart stopped. The guy on top of me fell off, quickly crawling away, dropping the knife, putting his hands up. I heard the sirens of police cars in the nearby distance.

"Liam?" Jeff's voice rang worriedly through the air. "Are you alright?" I couldn't answer him, I scampered quickly on the floor toward Connor and brushed his hair out of his face. "Jesus Christ, Connor..." Jeff pointed the gun at the guy who'd dropped his knife. He'd just let off a warning round into the air. "Don't you fucking move, friend."

"Con..." I couldn't breathe. I was fighting back tears welling in my eyes. They were burning uncontrollably from the dust, sweat, tears, blood. I put two fingers on his throat and exhaled sharply when I felt a pulse. "You're okay, Con. You're fine..." I was whispering it, more for myself than for him. "There's a pulse, he's ok. I felt a piercing in my chest, and I sat back, putting Con's head in my lap, waiting for the ambulance I was sure would come. Jen ran around the corner and she stopped dead in her tracks, seeing her invincible big brother covered in blood. She inhaled and the image hit her so hard she stepped back, paling immediately. Her wind-weathered hair blew across the panic in her eyes.

"Jen... He's okay." I managed to choke out. "He's okay, he's fine. Everything's fine." Jeff hadn't put down his gun, but it went limp at his side as he reached out toward Jen and pulled her into him. When the policeman got out of his car Jeff placed his gun on the ground. The officer immediately radioed for backup and an ambulance. I couldn't take my eyes off Con, I couldn't move my fingers from his from his pulse. I needed to feel his heartbeat, he looked so pale, so lifeless, and there was so much blood... The sharp pain in my side throbbed, and the rest of me ached, my head pounded, almost numbing the other pain away. I needed to feel his heartbeat... My vision was going blurry and I had trouble breathing, trouble staying awake. I felt the back of my head with my other hand and when I brought it back down it was covered in my own blood. It must have been my head I'd heard slam into the brick earlier. But I needed to feel Con's heartbeat... I saw Jeff coming toward me quickly,

"Liam? Liam!..." as I blacked out my body falling limp with Connor's.

———

Con and I had been dating. Actual, real-life, dating. We went to the movies that one day; he'd held my hand in the dark, stroking my index finger with his thumb without any indication of nervousness. It felt familiar, like we'd always been this way; a day in the middle instead of a day in the beginning. And the next week we'd gone to a football game... without hand holding. But the glances and the laughing made up for it. Neither of us cared much for football, but crowd watching and his narration on life was definitely worth it. He made up stories between cigarettes for everyone of slight interest that we saw...none of which could possibly be true without impending SWAT teams casing the area. It was the weirdest, most abstract, unbelievable, thing that I'd ever experienced. It came with that weird anxious feeling, like a roller-coaster...or how I'd imagined a roller-coaster must feel, exhilarating with the knowledge that it will end eventually and you'll have to sort out your stomach.

I'd been royally peeved before, with Andrea, with Connor's indifference and nonchalance toward everything, but the way everything was working out... maybe I owed Andrea an apology, or at at least some appreciation. If she hadn't riled me up that day, I probably never would have confronted Con about anything.

"Well I don't get it." I said, annoyed with myself for lacking the capacity.

"I'm not sure you're totally supposed to." He answered, flipping a page in his book, laying on my bed. "That's kinda the point. It's called 'Theater of the Absurd' for a reason... It's supposed to be absurd. I guess."

"Then why write it?"

"Something about the futile nature of existence, some shit like that. Nothing's important because everything's absurd. I wouldn't think too much into it." He flipped another page in his book, something else I probably wouldn't understand. He saw my annoyance. "It's depressing, Liam. You have plenty of time in the world be depressed. Don't go looking for it." I had to wonder if he was being hypocritical. I tried not to be too judgmental, but given what I'd read in some of his journals, and some short stories he'd concocted... he wasn't the happiest guy I'd ever met.

160

There was a pause as we read separately. I was sitting on the floor at the foot of my bed. I felt his hand on the top of my head, his fingers gently pull through my hair for a second, and then get back to his reading. I couldn't focus on the book, I was blushing. Again. I really needed to get the blushing down to a minimum, it was getting ridiculous. No one else seemed to have that problem.

"Liam?" He didn't bother looking up from his book but his eyes weren't shifting back and forth scouring the lines, just staring straight into the fold of Chaucer's The Canterbury Tales. "What do you want most? Like in the world? What do you want to *do*?"

"Like a profession out of high school?" I asked.

"Mhmm." I tried to think about it. The 'what do you want to be when you grow up' question. My father expected me to be a lawyer or a doctor, so naturally I held a secret cliché dream in my heart to be a musician, to play guitar professionally, to sing. In America. And recently I had a dream in my heart to have a real home to come back to at the end of the day... with Connor. I hoped that he was there, in my future. Probably more than I'd ever hoped for anything. I hoped that I'd eventually meet Jen; that she and Maggie would be standing by my thirtieth birthday cake smiling like idiots and clapping as I blew out candles with Connor holding my hand and teasing me all the while. But I couldn't tell him that.

"I'll probably be a fantastic lawyer, or a doctor." That sounded like a safe answer in my head.

"Bullshit." Con laughed behind his book, setting it down and looking directly at me.

"Then I'll be splendid accountant." I laughed back at him.

"Then I'll be a priest." He shot back. The irony sparkled in his eyes and sarcasm emitted from his smile. Con was sitting so close to me on the floor. I wanted to reach out and hold his hand, or rest my head on his shoulder, or just touch him in any way to

161

make sure he was real and this surreal happiness I'd stumbled upon wasn't a dream. Bloody hell. I needed to stop staring at him, tear my gaze away, but I couldn't. He turned away instead and picked his book back up. I felt a little left behind and silly, so I stared intently at my own, hating Rosencrantz and Guildenstern.

Connor re-situated himself, lying on his back, laying his head in my lap, tossing his book aside. I set mine aside more gracefully with calculated movements, trying to get my heart to stop nervously pounding. I looked down at him and couldn't stop my fingers from sliding into his hair, brushing it out of his face. He stared at me intently and I now avoided his gaze, looking away.

"You think you'll remember me?" He asked, his mood back to a pretend dispassion.

"Remember you when?" I hoped I was sounding as nonchalant as I intended.

"When you're up on stage. When your fangirls are flashing their tits at you and throwing their panties at the strait drummer you're harboring a crush on."

"What?" I hadn't told him I wanted to be a musician. He sighed and made his voice sound bored.

"When you're in your limo... at the end of the night... and your asshole manager is cussing you out because you clumsily dropped your guitar backstage... Do you think you'll remember me? Remember this? A fleeting high school romance." How did he do that? How did he always sound so poetic, so collected? So thought-out, like he'd planned to ask this a million times and rehearsed it in the mirror. When it was probably a whim. He either said nothing at all or everything I could I imagine in just two or three simple sentences.

So Connor thought this was fleeting. Connor thought this was temporary. A panic flowed through me instantaneously at his realism. I was almost angry that he'd even try to force the idea

162

upon me. It hurt to legitimately try. I knew I was young, naïve, half stupid really. But for just a second, I didn't care.

"Well, if I do..." I forced the words out, trying not to be too emotional, "Then you'd better remind me when I get home at the end of the night." I wasn't as poetic, or quick on my feet as he was, but I knew I'd gotten my point across by the delighted smirk that snuck through his facade. He lifted himself up slightly and pulled my face toward his by the collar of my shirt, kissing me more passionately, more appreciatively than ever before, and it gave me a confidence I'd never experienced. I pulled away slightly, just enough to whisper into him,

"You'd make a terrible priest."

CHAPTER 8: WAY TO BE FUCKING HUMAN

I stared at the water dripping through my IV bag and the monitor next to my bed, beeping appropriately. The room was dark, and the door perched half open with no windows. Just the stagnant smell of sanitation and white noise of echoing beeps and worn out nurses losing stamina near the end of their shifts. I'd been staring a while.

Jen and Jeff were both somehow asleep in uncomfortable chairs smushed against the wall. The kind with the plastic cushions and wooden arm rests. I had no idea what time it was. Her head was placed on Jeff's shoulder which unnecessarily churned my insides. I'd pieced together going for a walk… stopping in at the bar, hearing Liam play… Seeing Claire's cluster of fuckfaces coming at me from the doorway. Being cornered in the ally. They'd circled me like a bad 80's montage and I'd laughed. Literally laughed. They queer bashed and I smiled. They'd called me a fagot and I wasn't offended. I was reckless and numbly clever. I'd mentioned Claire had that kind of effect on people. And when her over-compensating, shit-for-brains, hipster, sex-toy had lunged at me, I'd nailed him in the face through sheer reflex and took pleasure in watching him hit the asphalt before tearing himself away from the ground and letting his friends beat the shit out of me.

And even lying on the ground feeling the soul-throbbing blows of boots and sneakers smash against my flesh and vibrate throughout my bones, it was an out-of-body experience. My human instincts immediately threw up my arms to cover my exposed cranium, but I honestly….could not have cared less. There was a part of me that may have even been hoping…. hopping a single punt would land horribly correct and snuff out the lifeless vigor of my surviving carcass that just kept fucking pulsating through the hours, days, months, years of my existence since *that* day. Until I looked up for a split second, and caught a glimpse of *him*. And panicked.

A panic that had slithered it's way on the vertebrae and ribs of my slowly recouping memory.

"Jen." My voice was cracked and a whisper. I felt the air through my throat and lungs; the softest sandpaper landing on my cotton-dried tongue. I cleared my throat. "JEN". She jumped slightly hearing her name, startled. Jeff woke up slightly disgruntled. She jumped from the chair.

"Connor, Jesus Fucking Christ". She ran closer and clung to my hand.

"Jen where's-"

"I swear to Fucking God Connor, if you'd have left me…"

"Where's-" I tried again; Jeff interjected.

"Holy shit am I glad you've made it. You've been asleep on and off for days. Wasn't sure you'd come through. You look like total fucking trash." *Days.* I didn't have time for this.

"Where's Liam?" I looked around the room, toward the door. No one answered me.

"Connor, Dad's here… he just left a minute ago to head to the cafeteria for coffee. He was really worried…" Jen offered, obviously ignoring me and her words didn't resonate.

"Where's Liam?"

Hank came through the door with a cup holder of 3 coffees. Clearly not expecting me to be awake. His expression did not alter; the stoic demeanor that defined my childhood, that dissolved into rage and intoxication in my later youth. But this wasn't the same Hank. This Hank was sullen, pale, shell shocked, almost ghostly and emaciated. His hair lay in thick wisps of gray and he appeared unshaven for the first time in my entire life. This was not the light

165

aftermath of a few days of parental concern. Hank looked as though he'd been haunted incessantly for years. As he should.

The words felt caught in my throat.

"I see you're awake…"

"Get the fuck out of here." it tore through me, dryly, soft and piercing. Jen took a step back. He was unphased and sat in Jeff's abandoned chair, unashamedly with the coffee. "Get THE FUCK out of here!" The boiling anger inside me meant it as an uncontrollable scream but it came out a pathetic, tired hollar. Hank locked eyes with me and without skipping a beat over the years,

"Watch your fucking mouth in front of your sister." The last time I saw Hank, I'd lost everything. Jeff had retreated to the empty side of the room and leaned against the sink, watching the interaction with a tired, worried, amusement. For once not saying a word. I broke eye contact with my dad. Panic was boiling in my chest, anxiety was closing in with Hank in proximity, the beeping machines getting louder and louder; the hallway hustle and chatter was like a megaphone bursting through the open door.

"Where's Liam?" I repeated, looking back at Jen. Straight forward and pleading. Why couldn't she answer me? She was thinking first, hesitation; why couldn't she just tell me? Hank lost his shit.

He jumped up from the chair.

"Clarke? Liam Clarke? You've got to be fucking kidding me, Connor." His booming voice in the small room made even Jeff flinch and my heart started pounding, reverting my entire demeanor back to being a 17 year old kid smashed against the kitchen door. He slammed the coffees to the floor and the brown steaming liquid splashed, covering his shoes and the foot of the bed; Jen's shoes and bottom of her pants. She jumped back in shock. She was the angel who'd still never seen Daddy angry. "After everything that happened Connor! After everything he put

166

our family though, you're still…. you're still…He's the REASON," He was fuming and losing his words. Jen's eyes grew too large for her body. There was a moment of fuming silence.

"The reason what, Dad?" She asked. Knowing. He looked at her as if realizing she were there for the first time. "He's the reason Mom…?" she faded off. Hank didn't even acknowledge that she'd spoken. I stared at him. With the dumbest expression, I stared…as though he had just sprouted a big nose and started juggling. He was sad…sad and pathetic, and deranged. After all these years. I turned to Jen and she looked terrified.

"No, Jen. Liam had nothing to do with Mom." I turned back to Hank, "You need to leave, Hank." I was calm about it. I didn't have the luxury to over react if Jen was going to suffer for it. He swallowed some sort hate; be it for me, or Liam, I'd never know. He looked at Jen and saw how scared he'd made his baby-girl.

"Fine Connor. I'm leaving. Your hospital bills are all paid for. Jenny, Honey, walk me out." He lifted his hand toward her, beconning her with his fingertips, and she took it, walking with him out of the room, ignoring the mess on the floor. He had her pulled into a soft hug and as they walked out. Hank stopped and looked back at me one more time.

"Con. I'm glad you're not dead." It was the nicest thing I could remember ever hearing him say to me. I heard the two of them talking as they left the room and I didn't care what was being said. I just stared at the empty doorway a minute, not even thinking. Just staring. It may have been the drugs, I couldn't tell, but I wasn't thinking, or feeling, or even really seeing. Anxiety had pushed me into overdrive and with the drugs my brain couldn't keep up. It just gave in and flatlined out.

"Well, since we're stating the fucking obvious man, I'm pretty glad you're not dead too," Pointedly Jeff added a "you fucking idiot" to the end of his kindness. I'd forgotten he was even there. "Your Dad seems nice…" Sarcasm rolled off his tongue nonchallanly as he gently kicked a cup on the floor walking toward my bed. He picked up the little button that calls in the nurse. Her voice came on the speaker,

"Yes, What can I help with?" she spat.

"Hello love, it seems we've spilled some coffee. Is there a mop around here somewhere?" She was extra snippy, "I'll send someone." and hung up.

Jeff leaned against the bed. "Liam's fine by the way. He did much more damage to the other guys, I think. He had a bit of a concussion but it didn't keep him out long." That's literally all I needed. I paused. Feeling oddly comfortable. I think the morphine was starting to kick in a next dose, just in time. I paused and we were just quiet a minute.

"Is he here? At the hospital?"

"He was yesterday. Jen told him your Dad was on his way, and he just left. He didn't say a thing, just high-tailed it out of here." I nodded my acknowledgement. That felt right. "That's how I knew I was really in for a treat meeting that hierarchy of Shays. The way Liam was looking at you, I thought he was going to ask the doctor to sew you guys together at the dick. Then suddenly, poof, he was gone. Like a magician." That felt right too.

"Has he answered his cell?" I asked, feeling like I knew the answer.

"No." Jeff looked away from me at the door, as the nurse walked in with a bucket and mop and started cleaning up the coffee angrily, not saying a word. We went quiet again as she worked. She slammed the mop angrily in the bucket and we pretended not to notice. She was gone again in minutes.

"Is he at the apartment?" I asked. Jeff looked at the door, probably secretly wishing the angry lady would walk in again.

"Nope, Buddy, he sure isn't." That felt right as well.

When Hank showed up... I lost everything.

"That sounds about right." I said out loud. He didn't have a sarcastic comment to throw out there. Now that I really looked at him, he looked tired. "Jeff, what the fuck are you still doing here? It's been days?" He laughed.

"How dare you, Con. I'm a sensitive guy. I care." I nodded sarcastically.

"Jeff. Are you trying to get with my sister?" He winked at me.

"What do you mean trying? You've been out for days..."

Jen popped in the door, unknowingly rescuing me from manslaughter charges.

"You pig." she said matter of factly, walking to my side of the bed. She leaned in and kissed my cheek. "Con, I just talked to the Doctor and he's fixing to come in here and check on you. But he thinks you can probably go home in the morning if everything looks good. And uh... about Liam," She looked nervous.

"It's fine. Jeff already told me. Is Hank gone?" She smiled and nodded.

"Great to see you guys getting along, just like the good old days." She chuckled at her own joke and started picking up a jacket and purse that she'd left on one of the chairs. "I'm going to head back to your place."

"Or my place." Jeff interjected and she laughed at him. I, however, didn't find it funny.

"Get some sleep Con. You get to go home tomorrow." I nodded. Thank God for the Drugs. It sounded like a pretty difficult place to go sober.

Jesus Christ it was. I'd always thought that my body hated me because I treated it like shit. Evidently all those shitty feelings

169

were it playing nice with me. Now I was really feeling it's wrath. Jen had cleaned up the chinese food from the other night; other than that it was the same. I immediately took a shower when I got home, robotically. Brushed my teeth. changed my clothes. Plugged in my cell phone. It was so far dead it would take a while to even pop up charging. I sat in the living room and pulled up my laptop. My email probably had a hate speech or two typed up from Folly. I'm sure she intricately described where she was going to shove my head after she decapitated me and fed my worthless brains to some starving wolves. She stuck to that threat a lot. There's a reason she didn't write her own damn books. But I didn't care about what she wanted from me right now.

Jen had left to see Jeff as soon as she dropped me off, to give me my space to rest and I couldn't even fight it. I didn't particularly care what she wanted from me right now either. If he was gone again, redundantly, everything was gone. I opened a new word document on my computer and I stared at the blinking pointer. It's consistency was rhythmic. Therapeutic. I didn't... really have words.

My emotional rigamortis was usually a comforting suffocation. But this time it wasn't. I randomly thought about that one time, after school, when that Jennings kid had cornered Liam with a bunch of his friends and beat him up. That look he gave me was always etched in my brain. It was scared, and hopeless, and guilty. I wondered if that's how I'd looked, when Liam jumped in to save me this time. I also wondered what the hell he's been doing all these years to be able to fight off all those guys at once. This rigamortis wasn't suffocating. This rigamortis was calm... and patient.

There was a knock on my door. My heart stopped. I knew he'd come back.

"Come in." I tried to put annoyance into my voice. The door started opening slowly, hesitantly.

Claire came in, practically shaking. She looked like she hadn't slept. I felt nothing. She had a hard time saying anything, tears welling in her eyes. She just left the door open behind her and came to the living-room.

"What?" I asked. She didn't answer right away, she just came right in, sat in my living room and stared at me with water edging out the corner of her eyes; already a very uncomfortable situation. Obviously, she expected me to hate her. But the thing is, you really have to care about something in order to hate it.

"Connor..." she started, and took a dramatic breath and stopped again because she was going to cry.

"Jesus fucking Christ, Claire. What?" It wasn't a weird thing to have her in my living room. She was here all the time when Jeff was living here. They were pretty inseparable. Apparently they'd been friends for a long time so she kind of came with the territory. I just never really thought about her. I set my laptop back down on the coffee table and tried to give her my attention for once. I... wasn't really doing anything else. I was spacey and lacked motivation.

"Connor, I'm so, so, so, so, sorry." She stared expecting a response. *For what? Why do you look so fucking sad?* I really didn't give a shit what she felt. I thought vaguely about Liam....how I'd hurt his feelings, and Jens, before I left the apartment the other night. How Liam cared about everyone. Guilt seeped into me.

"It's fine." There. I'd done my part.

"It's not fine." And there it was; the water works. "It's not fine and I should never have said those things to you and I should never have been so angry and got those guys riled up. I had no idea they were going to be so rough with you. And I just kept thinking,"

171

she took a deep breath and wiped some of her curly hair out of her face, "I just kept thinking if you didn't pull through, that it would be my fault!" *No shit.*

"That sounds accurate." She started legitimately crying. I could just picture Liam's face, shaking his head in disbelief at my insensitive nature. There was usually a strange pride in maintaining who I was, but, this morning, an obstinate guilt krept up inside.. *Fine.* "Claire." She sucked it up and looked at me. "How do I put this…..Clearly shitty things have happened to you in your life where you have the self esteem of a fucking ant. You're only attracted to empty pieces of shit because you, yourself, don't even think you're enough of a human being to treated like one." Her eyes were huge staring at me, she remained motionless. It was sort of out of character for her to really be listening to someone. "Fuck. Good job for being mad about it for once, kid. If someone treated me the way I treated you, and *did not care* at all…. which I still, abhorrently *do not*, I'd have beaten them up too. So yes. Yes, getting the shit kicked out of my was *your fault*. And Yes, it was fucking shitty. Congratulations on finally being a fucking human."

There was a long silent pause. I needed a cigarette. her eyes narrowed in confusion as she stared fixedly at the coffee table until she reached into her purse and pulled out a new pack of cigarettes. I eyed her lovingly. She opened them, pulled out two, and handed one, and the pack, to me. I accepted. She silently lit her cigarette, not bothering to wipe the tears off her face, then passed a lighter to me.

"Are these mine now?" I never liked this woman. I'd been around her, I'd dated her, I'd even fucked her. But I never, not even once, not even for the tiniest sliver of a second... liked her until now. She didn't answer the question, but motioned me a yes with her free hand and leaned back in the chair, oddly reminding me of Jeff. She took a few puffs and finally spoke.

"You really, really, really are…. a total asshole." By now I'd obviously lit my cigarette and leaned back and relaxed too.

"Yes. Yes I am. But I'm honest."

"I really had myself convinced that I loved you, Connor Shay." she was talking more to herself into the nothingness, dumbfounded. I took the most grateful puff of my cigarette that I'd ever taken before.

"Well, you never really struck me as clever, Claire." I could *not* even remember her last name.

"You actually are the most honest person I've ever met." She leaned forward again. "What are you thinking about right now?" *Fuck it. Why not?*

"Liam."

"The guy from the bar?"

"Yep."

"The Lex-guy on your emails from those fliers you posted?" I didn't remember ever telling her about that. Which she knew, adding, "I looked through your phone when we were dating." *Sounds about right.*

"Yep."

"Well…" This was the most I'd ever *really* spoken to her. She was clearly intrigued. And nosy. "Well what are you usually thinking about."

"Liam." I puffed. "William Alexander Clarke." She raised her eyebrows. "Yep… the third." I added the suffix because it always sounded so weird to me. The sophistication attached to such a goofy, clumsy, kid.

"Always?"

"Liam. Yes, always. That's it. That's all I think about." It…it really was all I thought about. "Liam. Liam. Jesus fucking Christ, Liam." I broke away from our conversation for a second and looked around the Liam-less apartment. She followed my gaze.

"Well… Where is he then?" *Where is he?* I didn't know.

"I don't know." It came out so matter of factly, so detached.

"Did he leave?"

"I. Dont. FUCKING. Know. Claire." She laughed at the anger in my voice. Not in a malicious way, in a really, really, funny way.

"Way to be a fucking human for once." she threw my words back at me. I didn't care. It was such a long weekend, and my brain was just so empty. She put out her cigarette in the ashtray. "For what it's worth, I am sorry for almost getting you killed. Whether you deserved it or not." I nodded. "And thank you for not hating me."

"I could never hate you." She smiled, genuinely, relieved. As if my deep affection for her had at last been revealed. And I just let her keep her self-fulfilled misunderstanding because I was done talking. Claire left like she'd never even come and the room felt just as empty.

My denial was slipping away and my 'when's turned into 'if's. I wondered if he was coming back. The last thing he heard me basically say was that I didn't love him. I told him to stay out of my parents business… as if they didn't mean just as much to him. As if she didn't… And then I nearly got him killed. Concussed, at least. If he didn't come back it would be because I was *not* the most honest person in the world. It would be because I was an Asshole. And a liar.

I went to my phone, half hoping, half not even daring to hope that he'd texted, or called. He hadn't. *1 new text message* blinked on my screen. It was from Folly. 'You better make it through this and feel better. Lots of of love. Please get back to writing'. I saw the email I knew she'd sent as a little envelope notification on my phone. That was it. Nothing else. I scrolled down to Liam's number.

I hesitated because I didn't know what I was going to say. It was going to be an apology… I just… didn't know how. I'd figure it out when I got there. I hit dial. And it rang.

Not in the phone, it rang, throughout the apartment. I followed the noise to my bedroom and didn't see his phone lying anywhere. I moved his pillow on the bed, and found it there, vibrating and ringing. Relieved and slightly panicked, I looked around the room more, searching for his wallet, for his house key. Those were gone. He'd just left his phone. Left his phone to go somewhere. So he'd be back. If not for me….for his celular device. After all I'd done for words, they owed me this. They would just have to get their shit together and help me figure out how to adequately say that I was sorry. How to formulate themselves into whatever fucking syntax or structure it would take to get him to stay.

I crawled into his side of the bed, laying my head on the pillow he frequently used. If he would just come home I could somehow get him to stay.

———

I woke up early to the sound of Mom getting ready for work. The familiar blow-dryer and Carol King emitted from her side of the hallway. Usually I'd roll over, put a pillow over my head and doze back off, but my arm was wrapped around Liam and he was dead asleep, no cares in the world; a human body pillow. My blanket had scrunched to the foot of the bed, and the AC had made it chilly in here overnight. I wriggled my arm free and reached for them, pulling them up to his shoulders and I buried myself in and put my arm back around him. The movement obviously woke him up, because he was smiling. He hadn't opened his eyes, or moved...but there was that little sideways grin that somehow contaminated my face too.

Jen's favorite book was always Peter Pan by JM Barrie. I read it to her 4 times when she was sick in bed with strep throat a few summers ago, over and over again. There was this 'kiss' that Barrie wrote about, right on the corner of Mrs. Darling's mouth that Wendy was obsessed with... and as fucking Gay as it sounded, half-asleep, I couldn't stop myself from thinking about it. I brought myself to his level and kissed him, pulling him against me at the same time. He breathed in, reciprocating, melting into me, still smiling and raised his fingers into my hair, breathing slowly, warmly evaporating into our kisses.

I pulled him under me and lay on him lightly in our little cave of blanket. I felt the warmth of my waist resting on his, I moved from his mouth, to his jaw, to his neck, and broke into a grin when I felt him squirm and emit the lightest laugh because it tickled.

Knock. Knock. "Con... hon?" Liam went rigid and slunk down lower in the covers silent as a
mouse. That made me laugh. She didn't open the door, just hollered through.

"Yeah?"

"Your gym clothes are washed and folded in the living room. I'm headed in a bit early."

"Ok, thanks."

"Love you, kid. You're my favorite biological son."

"You too, bye." Liam's body relaxed. I knew she wouldn't open the door because of a few extremely awkward moments when I was 13.

Then I heard her down the hall a ways...more knocking.

"Liam…" My gaze shot down at him. He whispered up at me, panicked,

"What do I do!?" I shook my head, still smiling.

"Hey, just pop out and tell her you're homosexual real quick and come back." I shrugged as I said it and kissed his neck again. I wasn't worried about it. I've always been who I've always been. I didn't think choosing to make out with a guy I stumbled upon an attraction to really changed that. It wasn't necessarily anyone else's business, but if they asked I'd tell them. How they took it was really none of my business either. Sounded like a personal problem. But Liam's face went pale as a sheet and he shook his head 'no' vigorously. I sighed as Mom hollered,

"Liam, are you awake? You're my new favorite non-biological son…" I heard her start to turn the knob and Liam slammed his eyes shut waiting for the world to cascade down around him.

"Hey Mom," I yelled out at her, which clearly caught her attention because she didn't open Liam's door. "Are you staying late tonight?" I pushed Liam out of the bed and pointed to the closet, he ran in there, and pulled the door shut, leaving a sliver open so the latch wouldn't make a sound.

"Are you naked or doing weird stuff?" she lightly knocked on my door again as she turned the handle. *I wish I was naked doing weird stuff.* I'd had to pull a pillow over my lap to hide some morning wood.

"Not anymore." Mom stood in the doorway with the door ajar. Her hair was tight in a ponytail, with some bangs hanging loose around her face. She was in slacks and a cardigan with a white blouse underneath, and every time she walked into a room her perfume would permeate through the air; her presence always enveloped everything. Made the air feel like home.

"I'm actually going to be home around the time that you're home. I gotta do some parenting shit, like grocery shopping. You wanna come? I miss grocery shopping with you. You're always busy now days." I... oddly really liked grocery shopping.

"Yeah. Sure."

"Do you think Liam will want to come." I looked toward the closet and remembered he had a project to do after school that I was already annoyed with because I knew I was going to be bored. And it was a writing project... one that would only take me like twenty minutes but would probably take him two hours. He already established that he wouldn't let me do it.

"No, I think he has a project." She smiled.

"I think it's pretty cute you know his schedule." She smiled knowingly. "Don't look now Con, but I think you have a friend. Of the male variety. That's new for you." I laughed.

"Yeah, you could be on to something there." I pushed some hair out of my face. I wished I could see Liam's expression in the closet. She was quiet and looked like she was really struggling with something. Contemplating whether or not she should share.

"What?" I asked. She came into the room and sat at the foot of my bed. She fidgeted with her watch a second, glanced toward my closet, and decidedly changed her mind.

"I just hope, ..." She started with such a serious expression I thought this was going to be a very awkward sensitive moment. But clearly she was just keeping me on my toes because she finished with "That you have such an *excellent*, informative, awe-inspiring day at your public education system." She jolted in a kiss on the cheek, and went to leave. "Hey, tell Liam to have a good day today, and that his teacher only had great things to say about him at the parent-teacher conference I went to last night." She started to leave, then turned back again, remembering. "And Connor, your teachers had other things to say about you.

Remember your peers are retarded and learn to just… feel sorry for them and be nice. It sure would save me the hassle of telling your teachers to fuck off."

"We're almost done with this whole school thing, it's my last year. Hang in there. You're doing great." She laughed and walked away. Liam wouldn't come out of the closet until he heard the front door shut and Maggie lock the deadbolt behind herself. And even then he hesitated. "The boogeyman's gone now; you can come out."

"I can't keep sleeping in your room. She's going to catch us soon if we keep this up."

"Liam, if you spent half the energy you use hiding your gay on your music, you'd have been a child prodigy." I could still see his heart beating out of his chest in an almost cartoon fashion. I fell back lazily into my covers. He said that every morning. Every morning I ignored it. I did threaten once that I'd just find my way into his room, and that I probably wouldn't exercise the same finesse that he did. I put my pillow over my head wanting to go back to sleep forever and never wake up. At least until school was over for the day. Then I'd happily get up, find food, smoke a cigarette and maybe write a little bit. Right as I reveled at the idea, the alarm clock on my nightstand blared the song of its people, ringing relentlessly into my eardrums and screeching it's insinuations of a long, daunting day of class-time boredom and time-killing. Liam almost tripped over himself walking over to turn it off. He paused over me and I could hear his smile in his words;

"Come on Con. You're strong, you're brave, and you're capable." I threw my pillow at him as he hurried out the room to dodge me.

"I'm skipping my study hall class today." I ashed my cigarette as we walked to school. Liam smiled.

179

"Your study hall class is during my lunch period."

"Oh. Is it?" a friendly sarcasm rolled off my tongue. I took a drag and didn't look at him. I had walked by the cafeteria yesterday during his lunch period, and saw him eating by himself. There were girls, of course, eyeing him from other tables and whispering, but no one seemed to have the guts to go be friendly. Which, I assumed, was incredibly fortunate and relaxing for him. I hated when people tried to small-talk their way into a conversation with me. I didn't like having to pretend, even a little bit, to be interested in other people. I was much happier when I was left alone to bask in the thoughts of Nathaniel Hawthorne, or more recently, Chaucer. Or better yet, just myself.

We started approaching the other kids walking in the front gate of the high school. I saw David Jennings push a smaller looking kid into the gate jokingly and walk off. I'd walked by the Jenning's household a few times and knew that it was a little run down and sore on the eyes. I also knew that his dad was an ex felon and his mom had a drug problem. Mom had let it slip a while back around the time Hank had hired him at his company. Both Mom and Hank had been friends with him back when they were my age, and he'd just taken a turn for the worst. I figured David didn't have the best home life and wondered if he knew what a fucking cliche he was. Liam slowed his walk. Obviously making room for a few more paces of space between himself and Jennings. Clearly he still thought about what happened after school that day. I kept walking the same pace. He'd have to go faster to keep up with me. I hated watching him care so much about the people around him.

"Hey, don't forget I have that writing project thing after school today."

"Yeah, I know." I put out my cigarette right before walking in the front doors. Liam would go left, and I'd turn right. I was still kind of tired; we'd been out of coffee the last two days. Part of the reason I didn't fight against going to the grocery store later.

We entered. Liam turned left. I turned left.

"You know, I could just write your project real quick during lunch." He pretended not to notice that I'd followed him down his hallway. "Merchant of Venice is a pretty quick thing for me."

"No, that's cheating. I'll write it. It's not a big deal. And I liked the book, it should be ok."

"Anything you want from the store? Tea? Crumpets?" I teased.

"Why aren't you going to class?" *I didn't want to.*

"I'm very busy." He laughed. I liked his laugh.

We got to his locker and he clumsily put in the code. When he opened it, a piece of paper that someone had tried to slip through the bottom came falling out. He picked it up and read it. His expression went blank and his face went red as he crumpled it up, slamming his locker.

"What was that?" I asked, going to reach for it. His aura pulled a 360 and emitted a disturbing kind of hurt as he jerked it away. "What is it?" I asked again. Why was he hiding it from me? Was it a love note or something that some girl had left him? I was irritated but didn't show it. Clearly something was upsetting him. His brow had furrowed; he clammed up, became jittery and looked around kind of paranoid. "What the fuck's wrong?"

"It's nothing. Go to class Con. I don't want you here." The 'I don't want you here' rang in my ears louder than my alarm clock this morning. That was the first time he'd ever said something remotely hateful toward me that wasn't warranted. I usually knew when I was being an asshole, and I'd been playing pretty nice with everyone lately in my happy state. He stared angrily at his shoes. Other kids were walking around us and we were impeding traffic now as the first period bell loomed closer. I laughed at him, and got a little closer.

"I *want you here…*" For a split second he almost laughed as his face grew red, but then looked around and morphed back into anxious.

"I have to go. I'm going to be late. Connor, please don't meet me for lunch. I'll be busy." I'd clearly just lied about being busy so I knew it was possible. He zoomed away from me into the sea of chattering students making the great migration to their classrooms, terrified of being late and receiving an arbitrary tardy slip that held no merit relatively in the real world. I stood in place, wondering what he was really thinking and trying not to smoke a cigarette.

I sat in my 3rd period AP math class with the giant math book propped up and Machiavelli's *The Prince* hidden in it's pages. It was the smallest edition I had of any of my favorite classics. I read and wondered simultaneously. I annotated and wondered, simultaneously. I was called out in class, answered a math question I was only half paying attention to...and wondered, simultaneously. I couldn't tell if I was irritable from the lack of caffeine or from whatever made-up understanding of the world around him that Liam was suffering through now. What the fuck made him feel like he couldn't tell me something? *He really pisses me off.* I thought about this morning in bed, and all the mornings in bed I'd woken up next to him lately. His scent lingered on my blankets now. Maybe it was all just an insipid performance of calm that was stretching over everything… it was a completely new perspective of the world, constantly trying to interpret it from Liam's perspective.

Next period was my study hall class. Andrea caught up with me as the bell rang, dismissing the begrudging cattle for a ten minute reprieve as they sauntered, mooed, bellowed and moaned their clanking bells and branded thighs to their next classes.

"Hey, Shay."

"Yeah."

"Is Liam rooting for the other team?" She didn't sound like her normal, facade of herself. Andrea was a Junior and had a kid brother whose name I could never remember that was in one of Liam's classes. She'd mentioned it a few weeks ago.

"I don't think Liam gives a shit about sports." I kept walking, not looking at her.

"There's alot going around."

"Of what, karma?"

"If Liam being gay is an act of Karma." I looked at her.

"Did you throw a social hissy fit because he wouldn't play with you?"

"Fuck you Shay. I'm only telling you because Liam carries himself like a sweet kid. Despite being a little shit. I thought you'd want to know. You said you didn't want him corrupted. So Man up and go look out for him you fuckin' prick." She pushed passed me and walked away. I considered Andrea for a moment. Maybe she wasn't just a girl with daddy-issues kidding herself into a tough, slutty act. I started walking toward the lunch room.

The hallway was pretty empty toward the lunch room, with kids either in their classrooms, or waiting in line for their food in the cafeteria. The tiles were checkered black and white with shoe skid marks here and there from the onslaught of hyper, hormonal teenagers. I vaguely remembered being a freshman and walking these halls for the first time... feeling kind of small with the high ceilings and the older seniors looking at me like I was some sort of obnoxious nuisance before I'd even done anything. I zipped my jacket slightly as the AC came blaring on with the intensity needed to cool down a thousand middle-humans at the same time. It was hard to believe that that was four years ago. Time sure flew when you were looking at it from the other side.

Even if I didn't particularly care for other people; it was comforting to see the other familiar freshman faces in the crowd that I'd gone to middle school with. They always looked scared shitless, which somehow heightened my ability to to maintain the idea that it's not that fuckin' bad. It occured to me that Liam didn't have that. Not a familiar face in sight. I remembered him waving awkwardly at me a few times when he first got here. Just me; that one familiar face in a sea of robust, loud, chatty strangers. And he was only a sophomore. And had been homeschooled... by expensive tutors. What kind of socializing did he experience before he got here? No wonder he was so fucking quiet. Did he have any friends back home? How had I never asked that before? I also hadn't thought about the fact that he was younger than me in a long time. He was 15. Where the fuck was I at 15? Reading somewhere... writing somewhere... avoiding people somewhere.

Our school cafeteria had half a hallway of transparent glass for a wall. You could see the entire lunch room through it; all the tables, all the lines to the shitty cafeteria food from this hallway, with big swinging doors that did a magnificent job at holding in the stampede of idle chatter. I could barely hear the rumble of crowds as I peered in; just the occasional burst of noise when people came in and out. I avoided that particular echoing, cacophony of bloated babble, box of hell. I'd spent many a lunch-hour out in the courtyard where the outdoor tables were; sprinkled between artistically seasonal trees in a small nook next a brick wall where I was able to smoke without being seen by the school staff. I'd sit, stand, lean, puff and fade just enough away from the present to feel good for a moment, a platform of amnesty. I paused, scanning the room for Liam. He sat alone,

He had his food in front of him and a journal he was occasionally writing in. His song journal. He looked content for the most part; his brown hair having grown a little bit shaggy since he moved here, hung over his eyes as he wrote. He'd tap his pen occasionally; probably to the beat to whatever song was seeping in bouts of comfort through headphones coming out of his ears. And just a hint of despondence. I could tell his emotions from just the slight slouch of his shoulders and the cocking of his cranium as he stared at the paper in front of him. A table away sat David and his circle-jerking devotees; a bunch of apes tossing leaves around and beating their chests. I watched as they mimmed eachother provokingly, telling David to do something. He finally got up and was walking toward Liam's table. He didn't see or hear him because of his headphones. I made a motion forward and then remembered how resolute he had looked telling me not to meet him for lunch. I paused, and kept watching. David reached out and grabbed Liam's journal out from under him, concurrently swiping his tray to the floor. Liam flinched distinctly and hesitantly got up from his table. He pulled the earbuds out of his ears and reached for his Journal to snatch it back from the gorilla. They were speaking back and forth but I obviously couldn't make out what they were saying on this side of the wall.

David pulled the journal back away from Liam, opened it to a random page, and started reading, taking moments to laugh between. He'd gotten the attention of the other students in the area, who were now eyeing Liam suspiciously. His gaze fell to his shoes. David kept reading, and started tearing pages out of the book, handing them to his friends that had gotten up and joined him. They took the pages and handed them out to the different tables. Liam silently looked up for just a second. Enmity and exhaustion boiled expressedly. The forlorn and hopeless burning that weighed in my gut.

I didn't know what I was waiting for... I just kept hearing Mom telling him over and over to "stand up for yourself and your family" and kept waiting for him to make a move. Andrea showed up out of nowhere and pushed me.

"You are such a Fucking Pussy Connor Shay." she whipped open the doors to the lunch room releasing the jeers and laughter that ensued, and I finally followed her. I did feel like kind of a pussy. And an asshole. In a totally different way than I ever had before. I heard streams of "What a faggot...", and low toned "Holy shit, he's really gay? I thought that was a rumor. Who do you think the poem was about?", back and forth chatter at every surrounding table diverting everyone's attention away from the humiliated, fleeing, british kid. Liam still hadn't seen me. He just turned, grabbed his backpack and walked quickly to the door behind him, leading to the courtyard. I saw Andrea in my peripherals approaching David. I heard her calling him a 'limp-dick piece of garbage' as she grabbed the journal back, but I wasn't worried about the journal in that moment... not as much as I cared about that broken, terrified expression Liam shot the crowd before he fled. *Jesus Christ.* Why hadn't I reacted sooner? I barely caught the door before it shut behind him, and he'd already made it halfway across the courtyard before I caught up. I reached for his shoulder and he jerked it away angrily before he'd realized it was me. We weren't in view of the cafeteria anymore; he'd reached the sanctuary of my smoking corner.

"*YOU* CAN'T BE HERE!" he yelled at me, slamming his backpack against the wall, refusing to make eye contact. I stopped harshly...he'd never yelled at me before. I'd never seen him so upset. I took another step toward him;

"Liam, it's fine." He paced back and forth a minute, fuming, looking anxious, hopeless... mad as fuck. I reached toward him, and he pushed me away.

"No, Connor, it's not fine. It's not fine at all!" He was irate. "You. Can't. Be. *Here*." The more he lashed out at me the less advantageous I felt capable of being, the disgrace of not reacting quickly enough welling inside me. I turned on my defence mechanism and went imperturbable as I reached out and grabbed him, trying to hold him still. He really slammed me away this time.

"Fuck. Liam, I'm *already* here! Clearly I CAN be here. Jesus Christ." I reached into my pocket and pulled out a cigarette and a lighter. He didn't relent.

"No, you can't. Because they're all going to see you! Everyone will associate you, with me, the fagot from overseas." He motioned to the cafeteria dramatically. "They're all going to see you, paired off with me, and they're all going to start whispering awful things about you in the bloody hall, and dropping crappy letters in your locker..." He reached into his front pocket and pulled out the wadded up piece of paper that he'd shoved in there this morning and threw it at me. It hit my chest and fell to the floor. I knelt down to pick it up and unfolded it. The word "FAG" was written in Red marker. Liam kept going. "They're all going to think you're a freak, and beat you up behind the school, and knock your books out of your hands, and lock you in the gym bathroom, and..." He was so angry he ran out of energy and leaned against the wall, sliding down to the floor and sitting on the concrete with his legs pulled up.

I lit my cigarette, with the letter still in my hand. "Who the fuck gave you this, Liam?" An unhealthy, seething anger blazed inside me as I held my composure. *David. Probably David.*

"I don't know. Look around and pick someone."

"I thought those assholes left you alone after I knocked the shit out of Jennings."

"They did... for a while. But there are alot of Jennings in the world, mate. It wasn't that bad so I didn't say anything."

"You should have said something." I looked down at him but he didn't look back up at me.

"Oh, and have Maggie crawl into someone's house and break their jaw? No, I can't do that. It would just cause more strife."

"What did David read from your journal just now?" He just shook his head angrily. I repeated myself, "What did he read?"

"Just a stupid song I wrote for you." *Oopf. Social suicide.* I was wracking my brain but I couldn't think of what to do for him. Clearly he excruciatingly cared what these fuckers thought of him. I couldn't even begin to imagine how exhausting it must be to be him. I was silent, thinking.

"You're fine, your name's not in it." he said, looking back down at his shoes, misinterpreting my silence. I didn't give a fuck about that. Let my name be in it. Let them all know, what did I care?

Andrea nonchalantly burst through the doors and joined us in our nook. Liam stood back up as she handed him the journal. There were pages sticking out; she'd clearly gone around trying to confiscate his work. The tragedy of his lost and ripped up writings descended on me as well and a whole new appreciation of sympathy washed over me. An overdrive of any emotion usually stabled me out. He'd never fully recover everything in that journal. That was his *writing*, that was part of him. And I'd just let it happen, right in front of me.

"Way to really be the hero, dipshit." She pegged me with that dart and it pierced right through. I knew she was right. I really fucked up in the moment. Liam, of course, stuck up for me.

"He's fine. He doesn't owe me anything. He's barely a friend, it's not his problem." *This fuckin' kid.* He was trying to protect me. He'd just gotten his heart ripped out in front of his entire graduating class and *he* was trying to protect *me*. I dropped my cigarette and stepped on it, self loathing enveloped my soul, sinking into my porous resolution.

"Boyfriend." It came out sounding sarcastic. My linguistics lacked the practice of sincerity. I didn't know how many more times, or in what fucking language I had to tell Liam that I did not give a shit. Andy grunted a laugh because she thought I was kidding.

"Too soon, Shay." She joked. Liam's eyes were huge, widening with the frantic 'no' head shake he was throwing at me every time Andrea looked away.

"No, I'm his fucking boyfriend and I should have done something. You're right." I looked at Liam. "I'm sorry." He still tried to cover for me;

"He's kidding, Andrea, honestly.." I stepped forward and I kissed him. Andy took a step back and was awestruck.

She let out a soft "holy shit", and then she laughed, "Holy shit, that makes so much more sense." Liam was shocked too. He just let it happen. I could see in his eyes that his mind-hamsters were on steroids, pushing their wheels to the absolute limit, trying to think of a way to back out of this. But he was still angry, and hurt, and confused, and I'd honestly have done *anything* to make him feel alright again. I went in to kiss him again and he looked up at me with pleading eyes.

"Con, I don't want them to treat you like they treat me. This is all my fault." *Jesus Christ.*

"Liam. Stop being a fucking idiot…. for Christs sake. I don't have friends because I don't *want* friends. *ALL* of my fucks, Liam. ALL OF THEM, they're just yours….. I don't know how to tell you this without sounding like a raving lunatic, but I could give a rats-ass what any of those small-minded pieces of shit think about me. Or what they think about you."

189

Andrea was staring at me like she'd never seen me before. I semi-consciously remembered I was inside her once.

"Plus," I added, "People here already think I'm an asshole, 'slag', anyway, right?" I smiled at him. Liam emitted a laugh that surprised even himself. He was definitely calming down. Andrea scoffed.

"Pff. Yeah, because being treated like an aloof, handsome, dude-whore is totally the same as being treated like a slut, or a fag."

"Thanks, peanut gallery...fuck off." Liam cut me off.

"But she's right though. I don't think you know what you're getting yourself into." *Didn't I fuckin' know it.*

"Oh no." I said sarcastically. And I winked at him and smiled.

"Con. For me. Can you just... not... out yourself? Please?" He was very serious, very adamant and firm. Fuck. Yes. I'd do anything for him. The transitional bell rang through the building, making Liam flinch again.

"Yeah, I can do that. Come on, I'll walk you to your next class. Today's like your worst fucking nightmare."

"What, no. No, you can't walk me to class, not after that." Andrea piped in again.

"Calm down squirt, I'll go with you guys. If anyone starts to talk I'll just grab one of your asses." Liam laughed again. The scars of worry peaked through his hopeful face like meerkats popping up in the Savannah, and it took an unequivocal amount of self control not to tell all the little shits muttering about him in the hall to fuck off.

"See you at home tonight."

"yeah." he said, not looking at either of us. "See ya." He took a deep breath before diving into the ice-cold fear of his peers.

Andrea was pretty quiet as we walked back to the senior hall. We didn't have the same class next so, at a certain point, the fact that she was stalking me started to become irritating.

"What do you want?"

"Connor, you love him." She said it matter of fact, like she was announcing the sky being blue or the theory of gravity. But I wouldn't use that word. I knew I might be able to, but I *wouldn't*. I didn't respond and an awkward amount of silence passed.

"Have you… have you acknowledged that yet? Like really thought about it." *No, not really. It doesn't fucking matter.*

"Wouldn't be your business either way, would it?" I kept walking and she kept walking with me. Ignoring everyone else.

"I don't know if you remember this, because you sure as hell don't act like it, but I've known you since the 2nd grade. I've never seen anyone get under your skin like that before. I've never seen you really 'with' anyone. Not… emotionally. You give "all of the fucks" for him? What a poet." I may have hated her.

"Shut up." There was a weird sensation tingling up my spine through my heels. One that made me kind of want to smoke, laugh, and trip her at the same time. It was the same discomfort I had on the way back from picking up Liam at the airport that Pissed me off. I wasn't used to this kind of energy and unfamiliar territory. It was like fighting a war on enemy territory; I had no vantage points, no foreshadowing of what was to come… no prior knowledge to formulate a strategy. And I knew somehow, through the devine intricacies of the universe, that that war had yet to come.

I stood outside the school by a small, billowing, tree that I'd usually wait for Liam at, knowing that he was ditching me for the sake of his education. He was cheating on me with my own literary mistress. I wasn't smoking, in case Mom pulled up. I honestly believed we both liked to pretend I had virgin lungs. I'd forgotten that I'd known Andy that long. I oddly remembered playing with her on the playground at recess. Freeze tag. I guess we'd been friends as kids. It was funny that I didn't remember that till now. Memory was a mysterious thing; it grabbed the parts you deemed important from your life, filed them away in the deep recesses of your brain, and classified them by relevance. How the fuck would a 6 year old know what was important enough to store away for a 40 year old in the future? It was a sick set-up.

The weather wasn't as hot anymore and the sun was starting to set much earlier. It was roughly 4 o'clock and I could already feel the anticlimax of day inching its way to the lull of evening. I stared up, watching the clouds mingle and disintegrate; the wind was picking up and the leaves were rustling around. Near the corner of a building they formed a small whirlwind. Fall was sneaking up at me... I'd filled out college applications pretty early. I wasn't worried about being accepted, my GPA was pretty high. All last year I'd been on the Basketball A team, I'd contributed to the school's only year of making it to State. There was a trophy somewhere buried in my closet. I'd written fairly compelling entrance papers as well. And luckily... I didn't have a preference on where to go. I could write anywhere, I could study English just about anywhere. A college with an emphasis on Arts couldn't hurt. There was one about three hours away, up in North Texas, on the shirttail of Oklahoma that I'd considered. Nothing fancy, just your run of the mill University... and I'd still be fairly close by if Mom or Jen ever needed me. But now... if Liam was going back to Britain at the end of the year, maybe there was more paperwork to be done. Either way, change was coming, and I wasn't dreading it. I... wasn't alone anymore and the universe sort of expanded before me, beckoning me into its folds. I could do anything. We could, anyway. I wasn't going to exist in a world without that measley, shy, naively distorted alien that crashed into my life.

I already had a passport from family trips as a kid. Unsure if I had to get it renewed. I'd never gotten hyped on Traveling before. I figured leaving the country would really excite Hank; I was sure he'd throw whatever money he needed to into that venture, probably tip the pilot to fly me out of here faster. "Really pump the gas" he'd say, slipping him a couple hundred inconspicuously... and the pilot would make a joke...and Dad would make a "Ch" and walk away without saying a word to me.

A honk ripped me back into the present. Mom's Fiat pulled up and she waved, beckoning, and smiling as I made my way to the car. I stopped suddenly and looked up at the school. *Fuck em, Liam. Hang in there.* I got in the car as Mom moved her purse from the passenger seat to the back seat.

I always felt somewhat younger in cars. Mom looked slightly more weathered than this morning, still energetic and happy to see me.

"How was school?" Oh the tribal dances and formulated rituals of suburban life. The 'How was school', was parent slang for 'Sup?'.

"Gross. They tried to teach me things." She laughed.

"Oh, I'm assuming those were the classes you went to."

"Yeah".

"You know, your wardens *call* me every time you break out of your cell". I hadn't really thought about it before. But none of my teachers gave me much grief when I wasn't in class. I'd just show up again, ace the tests, do the assignments, and not especially cause too much trouble. Unless they provoked me to speak. "They think you're a psychopath and that you have shitty teeth. Thank god you don't smile." When I didn't laugh she added, "I had to tell them you have periodically scheduled therapy with a counselor because your uncle touched you as a kid. And occasionally I mix it up with dentist appointments".

"I was meaning to tell you your imaginary brother was kind of handsy. You've really failed as a parent." She laughed again and I smiled at her.

"That's what they tell me at those parent-teacher conferences." She flipped on her blinker and leaned into the windshield to see better as she made a sharp left turn.

"Speaking of which. Is Liam being bullied at school?"

"Yep."

"God damnit. My poor little weirdo. What, he's too nice for the other kids? Too polite?"

"Yeah, I guess."

"Kids are assholes, Con. Glad you never were one." That joke struck me with a little more emphasis than it should have because I'd literally just remembered playing freeze tag on the playground. "Well… you *were* a cute as fuck little kid with your shaggy black hair and your little dinosaur shirts…" she looked over at me and grinned, probably seeing a toddler with big eyes, a blissful smile, smelling like smoke and wearing a dark blue jacket six sizes too big for him.

I knew beneath the thin veil of my shitstorm of arrogance that Andy and Liam were right. I didn't profoundly grasp the persecution that awaited me at the end of this flamboyantly homosexual rainbow. No human being can fully understand the plights of a degraded individual until they'd experienced it themselves. Especially no human whose parents always had a 401k, whose mother had always invested every second of her life making her kids feel dominant over the chaos of worldly tribulations… who seamlessly skirted below the radar of society by keeping to himself and living solely between the pages of 18th century lit. I *knew* but I didn't *understand* how my sexual

194

preferences were somehow indicative of who I was a homosapien. Like a nonsensical fact. I wasn't too worried about it, but the idea pissed me off. So long as the world didn't retaliate against my happiness by robbing me of all my pens, petulance, and preference for solitude… I wasn't concerned.

I reached out and turned up the radio slightly and my childish mother started singing, tapping her fingers on the wheel, turning to me at the good parts egging me on to sing too. Which I did not. But I watched, and I smiled, and I took it all in; the blaring 90's music on her pre-set station, the window down and the way she'd hang her arm out and motion a wave through the air, up and down and up and down…. the lavender car air-freshener hanging from her rearview mirror wiggling back and forth as if dancing to the robust energy of the car's favorite occupant. I harbored this rare, care free Friday-contentedness easing into the nostalgic familiarity of a grocery store stop-off with my Mom.

We struggled to park the car as the weekend-grocery-store fanatics plundered into every remaining spot, but victoriously swiped a recent vacancy near the front.

"How was work?" I asked; Phase two of the tribal dance as we walked toward the store.

"Eh, it was work." There was a very color-washed carousel horse next to the electric doors that my mother was just infatuated with, and I knew what was coming "Oh, Connor, look. You remember this? Oh you'd get soooo excited every time we took you here, right after Jen was born. I'd be struggling to get Jen out of her car seat and out of the car and you'd tug on your dad's sleeve pulling him to the store...begging him; 'Horsey, Daddy, Daddy'. And he'd laugh and leave us girls behind, lifting you up and setting you there till we caught up…"

"And I'd ask him for a quarter…" I finished for her. She grinned madly.

"Oh, no, you begged him for a quarter. You'd scream for it. He'd reach in his pocket soooo slowly on purpose, egging you on and you just waved your little hands around like a crazy person. He loved it." She stopped and started digging in her purse, "I've got one in here somewhere, come on for old time sake," She winked at me and I dragged her into the store as she laughed at me. A wave of cold AC and the smell of fresh vegetables hit us as we walked in.

"Where is Hank this weekend? Is he coming home?" She eyed me sideways, sweetly frustrated.

"Dad. He's your Dad, he's not a Hank."

"I don't think he's been my Dad since the last time I rode that fuckin horse." She scoffed.

"No, he hasn't been my husband since the last time you rode that fuckin horse, but he's always been your father. And he always will be."

"Ch." I grabbed a cart and strolled toward the vegetables.

"He's the only one you'll ever have, Connor. Whatever's been bothering you two for the past few years, you really need to work out before you leave for College." *Highly unlikely.* She didn't know he'd slammed me against the wall, she didn't know that he hit me sometimes when he got drunk, she didn't know that I knew about the secretary. He could have slammed me into a thousand walls, broken every bone in my body, spit on my grave, and I could have found some sort of paternal loophole to crawl through and find a way to forgive him if she asked. But I could never forgive him for hurting her. Never. She locked her arm in mine as we moved passed the lettuce, the onions, the turnips, the peaches, the pears, the strawberries… The smell of strawberries made her stop and throw a bushel into the cart. She grabbed more produce as we went.

Maggie laughed to herself. "There was this one time, that neither of us had your fuckin' quarter. I stayed with you outside, bouncing Jen in my arms as you cried and cried and cried on that damn horse. Other people kept walking by giving me nods of parental *solidarity* as you tantrummed your little heart out, and Hank literally ran to the back of the parking lot and tore the car apart trying to find one. And he didn't." She picked up a can, eyed it, and set it back on the shelf. " Next thing I know he's running past me again, with big giant panicked eyes, slaps me a kiss on the cheek and bolts through the doors only to get stuck in a 15 minute line trying to break a dollar. By the time he came back out, you were fine, and Jen was a maniac, wriggling and writhing, just screaming out her insides and you were down bellow, wet-eyed and scared." I had no recollection of this story. She kept going. "You had one hand grabbing my jeans and the other tugging at her little foot trying to comfort her, and you kept trying to get me to put her on the damn horse. Hank lifted you back up there, and I put Jen in your lap and stood behind you guys, as that tiny little deathtrap horse bucked and jolted. You just..." she paused and stopped as she grabbed a can of diced tomatoes. "You just stared at Jenny, wondering if she was happy. And Hank had his eyes glued on you, wondering if you were happy, and I was just a fly on the wall... wondering if we could be happy forever. Jenny broke out giggling and you laughed, and Hank laughed, and I laughed.... Jesus Christ, why didn't I have a fucking camera? I'd give anything for that picture." She kept walking and I couldn't bring myself to, not yet.

She turned around, noticing I wasn't beside her anymore. "He loves the shit out of you guys. He just stopped knowing how to show you by the time you started hoarding memories."

"I'm going to get coffee." I turned abruptly and walked away.

"Grab rice! And hot chocolate. Oh, and Apple Cider! Con?!" I gave her wave behind my head, acknowledging that I heard her.

I ignored the crowds and my tall stature parted ways like the red sea. I grabbed the usual French Roast at the coffee, grabbed the hot chocolate, grabbed the apple cider, and went looking for the rice. Purposely not thinking about Hank. I just kept gripping the fact that I hated him. I strangled it, keeping myself afloat.

I pushed myself to wonder how Liam was doing instead. His naivety usually had him bouncing back to his perpetual state of optimism pretty quickly... I didn't need to be worried. He was the exact opposite of me. Had he been Hank's son... I suspiciously thought he'd have forgiven him already. And probably would have granted him an apology for being a nuisance. Usually I'd tactfully ignore any thoughts of Hank that dredged their way up to the present, but remembering that stupid Fucking carousel was making it exceptionally difficult. Because I did *remember*. I remembered a time when everything made sense and the world wasn't a fucked up piece of shit.... just, unfortunately, that ended by age 5. Everything became hostile, the house filled with unspoken understandings that took me forever to understand, and the pain and resentment locked behind closed doors populated and infected every inhabitant of that fucking house. I grabbed the rice.

Except Liam. And his bright, infectious buoyancy. Caring about him wasn't easy... getting used to another person making camp in my head space was frustrating, at best. But having him made everything else around me less heavy...more natural and organic. He shows up and all of a sudden I'm laughing, or playing, or chatting seamlessly with my Mom nonchalantly, with little to no calculation. And she lit up; she glowed, and she danced in the living room, and she knocked on bedroom doors in the morning, like she hadn't done in years... she remembered carousels and took him shopping, and gullibly refound her faith in a home-cooked lasagna. We were all more ourselves with him in our house than we had been with each other for years. *God damnit.* That house was going to be so fucking soul-suckingly empty when he left at the end of the year. And if I left... Hank always had Jenny, but Mom... she always had me... *Fuck it, I'll figure that out when I get there.*

I found her in the frozen food section.

"How about one of these frozen casseroles? Will you guys eat this?" She eyed the box suspiciously, her blue eyes glimmering with the possibility of never cooking again.

"Yeah." We walked quietly a moment.

"Well, my heathen son, what's new with you? What's going on in your life?" *Obviously my insatiable thirst and affection for Liam.* I laughed at myself.

"Quite a bit." She peaked at me and smiled.

"This newness wouldn't have something to do with the fact that Liam was hiding in your closet this morning, would it?" I didn't answer. I'd really suspected that Mom wasn't stupid enough to not notice some sort of shift in our household paradigm.

"How'd you know Liam was in my closet?" She laughed.

"Because his teachers all tried to stress the importance of him *staying in the closet* at the parent teacher conference last night." I nodded. So, she knew. "But also, I'm not a fucking idiot Connor. The way that poor kid's been looking at you the past couple months kinda gave him away pretty quick." *Makes sense.* "I've gotta tell ya, Con, I'm conflicted."

"With what?" I was taken aback... and apprehensive.

"The whole Liam *thing.*" The way she said 'thing' struck me to my core. It wasn't a positive sounding 'thing'. I thought she loved Liam. I thought he was *her* kid now. Liam's feelings weren't a 'thing'.

"What *thing*?" We were headed to the checkout line.

"The Liam *thing*. He's obviously smitten with you, you let him sleep in your room, you're spending all this time with him and I'm happy your friends but, Con, you're also *you*."

"What the fuck does that mean? Stop speaking in Mom code." She started unloading the groceries on the conveyor belt.

"Listen. When I finally agreed to this kid swap out, I signed a contract to parent a stranger's child when they came into my house. And then it was Liam. With his overly polite aura and *readable expressions*,(what a fucking blessing that was) and need for affection. I fell in love with the kid. He's mine now. I love him as much as you and Jen." *Good.* " So I have to tell you, I'm conflicted with how you're not setting any boundaries. He's in Love with you. That's more than friendship. I know you're pretty aloof when it comes to other people's feelings and needs, so I gotta make it painfully clear to you that his little heart is going to be absolutely fucking shattered. You're impulsive, and you do whatever you want when you want, and maybe right now you just want to make him feel better because he's in a new place and you finally have a confidant besides your sister, but it's different when someone's in *love*. You have to take responsibility, set boundaries, and make sure he knows that you're *just friends*. If he gets hurt out of this, I'm going to be pretty pissed with you."

Maggie wasn't usually rude, but she was enthralled in our conversation and completely ignored the cashier, thrusting her debit card at him as she spoke with me. She thought… that I was indifferent. I vaguely wondered if she thought we were fucking and I was still indifferent, or if she thought I was just oblivious. We had not had sex yet. We'd come close a few times, but I could tell it wasn't something Liam was comfortable with, or ready for. It was funny that she'd spent so much time analysing Liam that she'd forgotten to analyze me. I didn't respond to her as we walked out

200

to the car. We loaded up in silence and I sat in the passenger seat. Feeling childishly indignant.

As soon as she sat down she turned to me and looked at me more sternly than I'd ever seen her look before. I started to realize that this grocery store endeavor was a plotted mom-attack. She was as concise with her words as I'd ever been; that's where I learned it from. But now that I realized she was running on half-formulated intel, it was amusing.

"Connor, do you know what you're doing?"

"Nope." I couldn't lie to her.

"Did you know that Liam was gay this whole time?"

"Most of it."

"Have you verbally, and concisely expressed that you like girls?"

"Yes." Technically I had, I'd expressed it pretty plainly after I'd kissed Andrea.

"Good. Then try not to send him mixed messages. You know, I've talked to that kid's parents; they're robots. They're apologetic for that kids existence." She knocked off the intensity and started the car. "I don't know why they even reproduced. All they do is complain about him…" And now she was purposely avoiding eye contact. "Con, since you're leaving at the end of the year… I was meaning to ask how you'd feel about me asking Liam's parents if he could finish out school here? Up through senior year. After I talk to him of course, if he even wants to. I'm sure Jen will love him when she gets back. I haven't told Hank yet, but fuck him, he's never home anyway. How do you feel about Liam?"

"I love him." It just pounced out of my mouth before I could stop it. Stupid Andrea planted the seeds of her girly vocabulary in my brain. But I also couldn't think of a good reason to stop it. She almost jerked the wheel.

201

"I never thought you'd take so well to a little brother."

"I wouldn't. I don't see Liam as a brother. *I love him.*"
Mom immediately put on her blinker and pulled the car over. I
heard the water melon she'd bought roll in the trunk.

"What?"

"His feelings aren't *unreciprocated.*" I didn't expect the
nervousness creeping up inside me. I honestly figured if I ever told
her, which I was not planning on doing, that it would be one of
those 'Hmm... that's interesting' conversations. Not a
'pull-over-the-car' conversation. She'd previously asked me about
my first kiss and I'd told her, and she wasn't surprised. She'd
asked me whether I'd lost my virginity, and I told her. Sometimes
she'd seen me with a girl outside of school and asked if I'd slept
with her, and I told her. And it had never mattered then. I didn't
think it should matter now. But now she was staring at me like she
hadn't, in fact, given birth to me and we were meeting for the first
time. Her expression was injured and her bright eyes dulled as she
looked away and stared out the windshield, thinking. *What had I
done to hurt her?*

"What's wrong? What did I do?"

"Why wouldn't you tell *me* something like that? Why
wouldn't you tell me you were Gay?" She wouldn't look at me, she
was clearly working something out in her own head.

"I..." I felt so unnerved at her reaction. I'd never lied to
her, I'd never been dishonest. I'd never been anything but myself
with her. Or anyone for that matter. "I didn't even know until
recently. If I even am."

"What do you mean 'if you even are'?"

"Fuck, Mom, I don't know. I don't just run around making
out with dudes all over the place, or am suddenly attracted to every
guy I see. I just met a fucking human and felt... comfortable. It's
just him."

"Don't mistake what I'm telling you. I've always loved you, and nothing can change that. It's just a bit shocking. I love you just as you are-"

"Listen, I don't need the gay-son speech. It's not a big deal to me. I know." She put the car back in drive and kept going.

"Good, I'll save it for my other stupid fucking son then." I laughed, and I saw her grin sneaking up on her face and immediately felt at ease again. Her phone rang and she answered it on her car speaker.

"Hello?"

"Hello, Margaret, this is Principal Collyher. I'm going to need you to come pick up Mr. Clarke."

CHAPTER 9: I HATED HIM

I sat on a chair outside the principal's office forever. A forever that, to anyone else, would probably only be 30 minutes. But I couldn't stop thinking about it. In the lunchroom, I was minding my own business, just jotting down some lines I'd thought of for a song. They really weren't any good, now that I was seeing them on paper. I was about to scratch them out and start again. I was just trying to calm my mind from the whirlwind of anxiety breaking out from hurting Connor's feelings at my locker. I wished I hadn't snapped a him. I wished I hadn't told him not to meet me for lunch. I just...didn't want to be a bother to him... once people saw him with me I'd have ruined his whole world. The exhaustion of fearing I'd run into David around every corner, or find myself alone out at the pavilion again was not something I wanted to share. David popped up beside me out of nowhere, snatching my journal and knocking my tray to the ground. My body tensed from the slamming of plastic on tile at my feet. I slowly stood up... I wasn't going to overreact... I wasn't going to be scared. The cafeteria was full of people; nothing bad would happen.

"Give it back, please." I reached out for the journal and he held it up and away from me. What was so awful about me that he'd hated me this much? That he couldn't just let me go... couldn't just ignore me. He wore a happy grin on his face as he looked over his shoulder looking for the appreciation he needed in the faces of his jeering friends. He started reading one of my poems out loud as the surrounding tables began to quiet down and listen. My face turned beet red, my ears burning. There was a teacher at the other end of the cafeteria not paying attention. My heart was racing and I couldn't stand the staring, the rosacea that crept up into me, the anger at everyone for not just leaving me alone. I felt like I'd followed their constructs; I didn't talk to any of the girls in my class, I didn't dare talk to any of the boys... I kept to myself, I started to not raise my hand in class, and be ever-so brief when called upon. I just... tried so hard to keep to myself and blend in. Why wouldn't they just let me? What was I doing that was so wrong? And then the note in my locker that planted the seed of unease and gutlessness in me. It reminded me what it had felt like to be staring up from the concrete, panicked and helpless. I really was the worst kind of coward.

One of the Principal's office aids walked by but didn't acknowledge me. I just stared at the tiles, acknowledged their speckles, thought about the incident in the cafeteria and wondered what was wrong with me. Why did I have to cause so much trouble for everyone?

All of my classes today were... difficult. Before lunch was fine; but after... people were whispering about me so incessantly, wondering if David was right, or what that meant. I'd heard my name so many times ascend the normal chatter and whispers of the classroom that I became paranoid that, even the kids out of earshot, were laughing at me as well. I couldn't bring myself to look up. And in science class I'd even seen that Ashley girl, the one David was friends with, that he clearly liked (that was initially so nice to me when I first started) passed around one of the pages that Andrea couldn't rescue from the rest of the class. One of the pages that I felt embarrassed even writing; a short excerpt about that first night that Connor had kissed me. The one where Hank had come home drunk.

I thought if I could just get it out in a few short sentences or phrases, that I'd be able to write a poem or a song about that feeling later. But...instead I saw it passed from Ashley's hand, back to one of David's friends, who shamelessly pointed my way and then laughed with his science partner. The teacher called them out on it and demanded their attention, but it remained elsewhere, on me... which somehow was made into my fault. Mr. Johnson sent me to the hall for the rest of the period. I didn't argue... I didn't want my voice to be heard today. I understood. There were twenty other kids in there he had to educate. I was distracting.

And... Connor had called himself my boyfriend. That was worth a million rumors, a thousand embarrassing moments, and hundreds of lost excerpts from my journal. Maggie had taught me that it doesn't matter what people are saying around you...it's *your* feelings that matter, how you feel about yourself. I...hated myself right now, but I felt pretty bloody good thinking about the term 'boyfriend' slipping out of Con's mouth. Conner would say "Fuck 'em". I had to, at least, live up to that...somehow muster the energy to show my appreciation for that one solitary uplifting moment. I really did my best not to care, like him.

After that class someone had tripped me walking out the door and my books went flying. I'd picked them up quickly, worried they'd get swept off again. I should have just gone home right after school, maybe borrowed Maggie's laptop and written my paper on there. But the After School Study Hall teacher was Ms. Gilly, who I'd also had my lit class with. She'd offered to help me write my thesis statement and come up with a good outline after school today. The paper was due Monday and I hadn't started.

And honestly, I just wasn't the writer. Connor was the writer. I could write a poem or two maximum and utilize all of my writing enthusiasm for the next few days. Having to write a full paper about The Merchant of Venice was quite a production for me. Though, I was honestly excited to get to share my thoughts on the book, on something I could keep forever, and hold onto. It was a dumb thing to be excited about, but I was. The Merchant of Venice technically brought me and Con together to begin with... it felt special. The study hall was hosted in one of the labs too, so I could print it as soon as I finished. My stomach growled because David had knocked my lunch on the floor. I was starving.

I walked into the lab and put my backpack on the chair. There were about 8 other kids in there with me. I recognized their faces from my other classes, but, again, I'd been trying to stick to myself. Ms. Gilly was sitting at a computer at the front of the class.

"Liam. I have your rough draft outline here." I smiled and came to her desk, feeling safe for the first time all day. I knew *she* wouldn't have any staring, whispers, or judgments about me. "The only thing that I'd change is moving this part..." she circled a few sentences I'd written half way down the page and moved them up in to the opening paragraph.

"Thankyou". She stood up and addressed the class.

"Everyone, Liam made a good point in his outline. You can't start the paper not knowing how Portia plays into the play as a whole at the end. You really have to incorporate the whole plot throughout the paper as you're defending your thesis statement." I realized then that we were all working on the same paper. There were unfamiliar faces from her other period classes.

I was walking back to my computer when this guy from my specific class period, off in the corner raised his hand.

"Ms. Gilly, where Basanio and Antonio gay?" She shuffled to the white board that was behind her slightly uncomfortable. My interest peaked. I thought they were and I was kind of hoping for some affirmation. I felt lucky that I didn't have to be the one to ask.

"It's been argued by plenty of scholars that they were. However, that's not something that's appropriate to talk about in our classroom. I'm sure you'll go over the play again in college." She laughed slightly, nervous, and my heart sank as I felt inappropriate for my grade. Another voice came out of a girl I didn't recognize.

"Why not. Liam's gay. And Isaac's gay." Her voice didn't hold malice; she just stated a fact. and I perked up again, just a little, feeling slightly stood up for…. until the room snickered and I slunk into my seat, wiggling my mouse so my screen would come on and I could melt into it. I didn't know who Isaac was. I didn't remember any Isaac's in my classes, and he clearly wasn't in this classroom to defend himself against the onslaught that was sure to follow.

"You know what, that's incredibly inappropriate for my class too. We need to veer back on topic here." She kept on talking about the book and I opened 'Word' on my computer, typing the header to my paper. Trying to ignore everyone like I had been all day. Two computers down were two kids, a guy and a girl, laughing and carrying on. They had Google up and were looking up funny memes.

"I heard Isaac had a thing for David as a freshman, and that's why he and Matt beat him up last year." There was gossip, but for once, it wasn't about me. It must have been easier to talk about someone who wasn't present. They kept going. "I heard he fucked that British kid in the bathroom last week." There we go, there I was. They lazily attempted to whisper that part more quietly, knowing I was nearby. It was not true. I'd have remembered that. I'd never had sex with anybody. I uncomfortably readjusted in my chair and tried to melt into my screen again, tried to stop listening.

"He probably couldn't get a girlfriend, because of his sister, so he just gave up and started blowing dudes." That was incredibly rude. I should have been happy that their attention wasn't on me. But I wasn't. Whoever this Isaac was, wasn't here. They shouldn't be saying things like that about him.

"I'm sorry, but if you could keep it down, I would very much appreciate it. I'm trying really hard to finish this whole paper in the next hour or so..." They just glared and turned away from me as the adrenaline of intervening made me weak. And they didn't stop.

"And that Liam kid has a crush on Connor Shay. Can you believe that?" He added.

"The hot one on the basketball team? Oh my god. How sad. Wasn't he dating that one fagot's sister?" The girl hushed her tone at the end of the sentence. The guy whispered softer.

"Liam didn't have a sister. Shay does...was that Jen girl slutty... someone could have told me?" He thought for a minute. "Gross, wait, that would be incest." He clearly wasn't bright.

"No, Isaac's sister, Andrea. Isn't Shay dating that slutty Andrea chick?' I'd stopped even pretending to be able to focus on my computer. Once Con's name was brought up, I wouldn't be able to tear my attention away. So Andrea's brother was gay...and probably being bullied too. It made sense now why she'd gone out of her way to defend me. She'd gone out of her way and now I would too. I couldn't tell if bashing Isaac behind his back, or the insertion of Con's reputation, or the gossip about Con's little sister somehow burrowed under my skin more. I stood up from my chair.

David, I couldn't stand up to. Our physical altercation had weaseled it's way into my anxiety and I couldn't quite get passed it... I was a coward. But these were complete strangers, judging this poor kid that wasn't even here, Andrea, who'd been perfectly nice earlier, and whispering about whether or not Conner's little sister was slutty. I was so tired, so exhausted from the social minefield and bullying that dragged me down all day.

"Just stop." I was loud, staring at them abruptly. "You don't know any of those people, they're all very nice. Stop talking about them." The lab was looking at me. Ms. Gilly was as well.

"Liam, you need to be quiet, people are trying to work in here." I sat down, slightly embarrassed but, for once, too tired to care. The two gossipers wouldn't stop. They laughed at me. It was fine. I was used to it.

"That was the Liam kid, right? The British one?"

"Jesus Christ, I can hear you." I turned and snapped at them, earning a harsher:

"Liam Clarke, settle down or I'll have to ask you to leave." I melted into my seat. I tried to focus harder on my computer and keep my head down. None of that was any of my business, I just needed to focus. They were just bored, with nothing else to talk about. They probably weren't necessarily bad people, just... bored teenagers. I shouldn't be so angry.

Somehow, by the grace of God, I'd angrily and terribly typed up complete rubbish and called it a paper... in just an hour. I submit online, and sent it to the lab printer, to hand to Ms. Gilly on the way out. There were 10 bonus points added for turning it in early... maybe that would save me. I picked up my stuff to leave, and the guy I'd successfully ignored got up at the same time.

"Hey Liam, can you help me on this one part of my essay right quick?" He pulled a slip of paper out of his pocket and unfolded it. "So far I have ' Oh with the burning eyes that scheme a lonely, drawn demise, first hide your hope and faith in me, hide your faith me...'" It was one of the songs that was taken out of my journal. Somehow it had landed in this kids hands after being passed around. "And I was thinking of adding this second part; let me know what you think; 'Oh, Connor Shay, whose slutty sister I couldn't get it up in, would you please oh please just get it up in me. Get it up in me. Get it up in me...'"

I shook my head angrily, balling my fists at my side."Piss off" I practically whispered it. I was seething.

"I'm sorry, what was that, I didn't hear you? Just one 'get it up in me'?"

"I said, PISS OFF." I grabbed my poem out of his hand and shoved him away from me.

"WILLIAM CLARKE" Ms. Gilly was up immediately. "GET TO THE PRINCIPAL'S OFFICE NOW!"

And here I've been...at the principal's office for the past 20 minutes. I heard the principal talking to Ms. Gilly about a zero tolerance bullying policy. Apparently I was the bully. She hadn't heard any of the stuff the other kid said to me, just my disruptions. She'd always looked out for me, done her best to help me with my school work. I wasn't upset with her at all. I should have just handed her my poem, that that kid had written on, added another disgusting verse. But I... didn't want her to see it. Miss Gilly had walked me down here, spoken to the principal, and left. Principal Collyher talked at me for a second... scolded me on disrupting the classroom and let me know he'd be calling my guardian.

I was a little confused as to whether they'd be calling my Mom and Dad at home, or Hank and Maggie... and I wasn't sure which was worse. My stomach was in knots...and still hungry. Mom and Dad already knew I was different...already thought of me mostly as a nuisance. This would just confirm their perception of me. And my perception of me. But if he called Maggie, and told her what happened, what would she think? And if he called Hank, himself...at the office.... I didn't know what would happen. I shouldn't have said anything. I should have just grabbed my poem and left.

I heard Maggie before I saw her, down the hallway. I couldn't make out what she was saying, but I could definitely hear the anger in her voice. Was it anger at me? She didn't check in with the administrative lady that was sitting at the desk ready to great her. She came and sat right next to me, to hear what I had to say.

211

My parents had never done that. Not once. I had this memory, of being very very small at a birthday party that they'd taken me to. I had to have been around 4. It was weird that I even remembered it. All the little kids were running around and I was happy and excited. I'd held this boy I didn't remembers hand and we ran around together. When we stopped I'd kissed his cheek. His parents asked me to come in the house and explained it wasn't appropriate and called my parents to come get me early. I was confused and they never spoke to me about it.

My tutors were always having problems with me. I didn't learn fast enough, I didn't study enough, I didn't play piano fast enough, I'd never learn how to dance... They'd file into my Dads study and he'd talk extensively with them. Never to me.

"Liam, what happened." Principal Colleyher heard Maggie outside his door, and came to great her.

"Ms. Shay, thank you for coming, we have some disciplinary issues to discuss."

"No, excuse me, I'm talking to my son right now." The words "My Son" rang through my ears, echoed off of the 15 years of emptiness that had been bestowed upon me by my own parents, all the way down to my toes, making my whole face blush a fuming red. I caught a glimpse of Connor as I tried to avoid eye contact with Maggie. The blush was clearly noticeable; Connor grinned and sighed, shoving his fists in his pocket and nonchalantly sitting in the seat on the other side of me.

"Mrs. Shay, Ms Gilly gave me a full account of what happened in the classroom, and it's William's actions that we need to discuss."

"With all due respect, Mr. Collyher, you can wait five minutes while I find out what actually happened."

212

"Margaret, when students get into trouble, it's highly unlikely that their version of events are unbiased." I felt very strongly that Principal Collyher would get along with my father.

"Excuse me? Liam's not capable of lying. Do you see his face? He's mortified just to be sitting here." She stood up, "And frankly I don't need your help talking to my kid, so if you don't mind waiting for me in your office, or sacrificing your office to *me* so I can talk to William, as his guardian, while you sit out in this hallway being ignored and feeling like crap about yourself after what can only be assumed was a shitty day, I'd appreciate it." Principal Collyher put his hands up to his face and rubbed his eyes; a confident exhaustion. It immediately granted my sympathies; he was just doing his job. But so was Maggie. I was the one who didn't turn over my poem to Ms. Gilly to tell her the truth. She was right, I didn't lie, I just... didn't know how to tell the truth without hurting anyone; including myself. The principal went into his office and shut the door.

The attention was back at me. Connor leaned back in his chair and stretched his arms behind his head lazily as Maggie's soul-x ray mother vision pierced through me. The Principal's office was clearly more comfortable for him than it was me.

"Liam. Tell me what happened." I could barely talk; shame and embarrassment cascaded through me, an infinite supply of of self-loathing.

"I pushed a kid in the after school study hall. Ms Gilly saw, and I'd interrupted previously so she sent me to the office."

"What did the kid do?"

"Erm... nothing really, picked up his backpack and went home I think..."

"No, before you pushed him. What did he do that upset you?"

213

"He uh..." I looked over at Connor who was giving me no support, just looking at the ceiling tiles. "He had taken one of my poems."

"He already had it?"

"Yes, he got it during my lunch period. David tore up my journal and passed it around." The poem was still folded up in my left hand; I'd been grasping it for dear life, terrified, all the way down to the admin office. Connor could clearly sense something about to happen; the same way that dogs can sense a storm more than an hour beforehand. He made a motion to get up and maybe wait outside.

"Sit." she commanded at him and he stayed put.

"Liam. Are you telling me that David Jennings stole your journal at lunch, ripped it up, and passed it around through the cafeteria?" *Should I say no??* I looked over at Con again, who shrugged at me, the least helpful being in the world. I couldn't lie.

"Yes."

"Were there teachers in the cafeteria?"

"Yes, but they didn't notice, they were helping students on the other side of the room and monitoring the lunch lines; it's not their fault." *Who else can I save?? Who's in danger?* Her gaze darted to Connor.

"And where the fuck were you, eldest son?" Connor didn't reply. I was quickly back in the spotlight.

"What's that in your hand?" I shoved my hand, paper and all, into my pocket, panicked. "Let me see it please." I looked at Connor again. Another useless shrug. I handed it to her.

She unfolded it and read it through; what I'd written, and what the other kid had written about her daughter, her son, and myself. The intensity in her blue eyes erupted, for just a fleeting micro expression, and then she became as naturally stoic as Connor. She handed me back the piece of paper.

214

"You keep this. I can paraphrase for Mr. Collyher." Maggie grabbed her purse and stood up. "I'm sure enough people have raped your fucking soul today with the contents of that Journal; he doesn't need to see it."

"Mrs. Shay!" I started to say; being scared and nervous made me intensely formal, "Maggie", I corrected myself. "Please, I don't want want to cause anyone any trouble." She just paused and sighed.

"Liam, honey... You're not in trouble, and you're not causing trouble. You, being exactly who you are, doesn't cause any trouble for anybody. It's these other people, being themselves, that need to get their shit together. Starting with Mr. Collyher." She opened the door and it shut behind her in a foreboding manner. I was so nervous, anxious, tired and scared I was sweating. Connor put his hand on my head like the first day they'd picked me up at the airport, to calm me down. The poem was still sitting open in my lap. He peeked in and read it real quick. Then he ever so seriously pointed to the last line gingerly,

"His pentameter was off". Connor was doing a literary critique of my hate mail.

"Are you... are you bloody kidding me right now?"

His laugh startled me. Nothing about this was funny! My heart was about to beat out of my chest, Maggie was about to find out form Principal Collyher that I was actually gay.

"I could, ya know. If you were ready for that sort of thing." He was clearly referring to the last line that the other kid had written... as if I weren't mortified enough! My brain didn't have any room left for any more!

"No! Stop, this isn't funny!" I hated his stupid shrugs.

"It's a little funny." He smiled at me and it...oddly started to quiet my anxiety. Maggie's voice came booming softly through the door,

215

"Don't you DARE tell ME to calm down!" I flinched. He pointed to the door with his thumb.

"Ooopf. Yeah, you really should never do that." Connor leaned forward and hunched slightly over, resting his elbows on his knees as he played with a lighter he'd pulled out of his pocket. He didn't light it, just twirled it between his fingers, not really focusing on anything. I heard more yelling in the office, but couldn't make out what they were saying. Moments later Maggie came to the door and called me in. Connor was prepared to stay in the hall but I grabbed his elbow on the way in and pulled him with me. I didn't want to go in there alone.

"Liam," Maggie was smiling at me. "Principal Collyher has something he'd like to tell you."

The principal sat on his side of the desk looking at least 10 years older than he had 10 minutes ago, before dealing with this crazy mother-bear. He folded his hands on his desk and made perfectly good eye contact which made me squirm.

"William, I wanted to apologize for the actions the school took toward you in calling you down to the office. Where any form of physical altercation is not tolerated on campus; the escalation of the situation should have been noticed and handled far before you were harassed in the cafeteria today. David's parents will be contacted, and so will Jonathan's." Jonathan must have been the kid who'd written on my poem. He'd never given me his name...just a very reclusive complex during any of my social interactions for the next few years. Everyone was looking at me for a reaction.

"Thank you sir. I'm sorry for the ruckus that I've caused today. It will not happen again." Maggie interrupted me.

"No, he's not sorry. And I'm not sorry. And Conner's not sorry. And Jenny wouldn't be sorry either if she was home right now. Thank you for calling me down here to address the situation, Mr. Collyher. Have a good weekend."

She motioned for us to get up and we left the office. I faintly heard an exasperated sigh of relief from our school's fearless leader. I was now anxious that I was in trouble for apologizing.

On the way home, Connor snagged the back seat of the car, forcing me to the front seat next to Maggie. It was a very silent drive home. When we parked, Maggie hesitated turning off the car.

"Connor, get out of here. I need to talk to Liam." And without any complaint, he just bolted. Got right out of the back seat, shut the door normally behind him, and I watched him walk into the house without me, no hesitation, no apprehension, no consideration for the fear shaking through my knees at all.

This was it. This was the moment I'd been dreading since I was first even offered the idea of coming to the United States; that my exchange parents would find out I was different, that they'd treat me different, or send me back, and my parents would finally digress into sending me off to that church school that would 'heal' me of my condition. And if that didn't work, military school. And Maggie. Why did it have to be her? I'd never felt so cared for in my entire life, and I already saw the looming distance growing between us, the detachment, the reconsideration of letting me join her family. She'd disown me...and send me home...and I'd never see Connor again.

"Listen Kid, we need to talk." *No thank you.*

"I'm actually very tired right now Ms. Shay, I really need to erm..." my hand was on the door handle and my words were getting caught in my throat. I had to escape, I had to avoid this so everything could keep going on as it was. So I could keep being happy. So I could stay here...stay at my real home as long as I possibly could.

"Not uh, Liam, sit." I took my hand off the handle and held my breath, avoiding eye contact. I already knew this would be the conversation ringing through my head...ringing throughout the whole empty mansion when she and Hank sent me back prematurely. This would be the conversation that I'd nestle deep inside as I agreed to go off to that bloody religious school, that I'd read on every line of the scripture they'd shove down my throat. That I'd carry in my heart until the day I died. I was shaking and I didn't say anything, I stared at my shoes on the floorboard of the passenger seat. "Look at me." My eyes were watering. I looked up at Maggie.

"Yes?" I asked. Even my voice trembled.

"I love you." my heart stopped. She'd always been kind. She'd called me hers. But she'd never said that out loud. My parents had never uttered that out loud...unless we were around company. "I love you, and I need you to understand that there's nothing in the entire world now... absolutely nothing that would stop me from loving you." I felt my eyes spill over slightly and couldn't stop them. He must not have told her. She must not have known. "And you're so so so so so smart and polite.... but you're stupid and frankly insulting if you really think I hadn't known you were gay this whole time." She smiled... she smiled Connor's smile. The one that melted me to my core. She reached over and wiped a tear away that had escaped out of my eye.

"The whole time?" I asked, incredulously.

"Darlin, I'm fiercely protective of Connor. I know when anyone has feelings for him within a 75 foot radius." My own laugh shocked me. "And you're not as sneaky or trained in hiding your emotions as you think." I laughed slightly. I *was* very bad at that.

218

"Are you... Are you going to send me home early?" I couldn't quite adjust to the thought of no negative consequences to being outed.

"No. Fuck no. I wanted to talk to you about staying here until you graduated from high school, even after Con goes off to college. Which, I don't know about now, since your school's been bullying you this whole time. I don't care that you're gay. I don't care that you have feelings for Connor (which we're absolutely going to have a separate conversation about later)", she made a dramatic hand motion to emphasize that fact. "But I do care that you don't feel comfortable telling me things; that you tried to just wait this all out all by yourself. I already have an emotionless monster teen in this house...there's not room for another one. I want you to be yourself; to be open, honest, and ridiculously clumsy at all times. And I want you to come to me when you need help. You got it?"

One part had especially resonated.

"You want me to stay? When Jen comes back, you want me to stay?"

"Do you even *want* to stay here after all the crap that school is putting you through?" I barely let her finish her sentence.

"Yes."

"You want to stay here, go to that school for another two years after this one until you turn 17?"

"Yes. Yes Please." She smiled, brimming, affectionate, and relieved.

"I was going to wait till I'd talked to your parents and Hank before I'd even brought it up to you...But Hank doesn't really call the shots around here. I think we can convince your parents that you'll have a better shot at university if you have the diversity of study-abroad graduation on your resume. We can talk to them." She was grinning, and I was grinning, and I didn't know what to do. It was a relief, a sadness slowly fading away from all the chaos of the day, a nervousness for school the following week (that I'd have to try 10x more effectively to fit into now that I might stay for two more years) and the unfamiliarity of being.... *known*. Let alone *loved*. She reached out and pulled me toward her, into the warmest, most genuine, most comforting hug that I'd ever been given.

———

When I'd seen Hank at the hospital it had suddenly occurred to me that it was Maggie's birthday the next day; and the whole family was here. She would be alone.

I'd heard the doctor say that Connor was in the clear, that he'd be ok. Jeff, Jen, and now Hank were all there for him; maybe Hank wouldn't have been the best support, but he had Jen. And I couldn't face Hank... not after everything that had happened. Connor would understand. Actually, knowing Connor he'd probably try to throw Hank out, have an aneurysm when Hank stubbornly declined and would just implode the next few days with his dad being anywhere near him. He wouldn't want to deal with that by himself, I don't think... But I knew that what he wouldn't want more is for Maggie to be alone on her birthday...and no one else seemed to remember. I didn't even know if it was something I should bring up.

I just immediately left the hospital, hearing that Hank was coming. Ran away. Just like before. I'd gone back to the apartment, grabbed my school bag, emptied it out and shoved in some clean clothes and a toothbrush, barely thinking about it; and a phone charger; I'd need that.

I didn't realize I'd forgotten my actual phone until I was already in a taxi headed south... headed to Maggie. It was going to be quite the bill on the credit card Jen had brought me, but I'd pay it back later. This was worth it; tenfold. The Taxi driver kept to himself, the radio was off and I was really alone with myself. I didn't know what I wanted to say to her. Or needed to say to her.

I hadn't gone to her funeral; I hadn't been invited. Hank had made it very clear that I was not to be there, or be anywhere near his son, ever again. Plus, I was 15... I didn't have say in anything. I was swiftly sent back home; I couldn't say anything to Connor before I was thrown in the back of a police car and driven to the airport. Hank eventually shipped me my belongings. With the burning secret inside me, I didn't even know what I'd say to Con even if I could speak to him. I'd have to speak to him somehow...face to face...or at least on the phone and I just didn't know where he was or what he was doing... and then I couldn't. Even if bravery *had* mustered its way inside me for the first time ever, I had no way to get ahold of him. I'd tried calling, just once, afterward, after weeks of building up the courage and Hank had answered the phone; screamed at me never to call again and told me Connor had moved out; not to bother.

Thunder crackled through the air and I rolled down the window of the cab to smell the storm that was headed this way, smell the rain that was coming in. This was fitting. It was raining the last time I saw Maggie too. I had the Cabbie drop be off at the only motel in town. I bought a room for the next night so I could stay here just a little longer. As soon as I dropped my backpack on the bed I instinctively plugged in my charger to charge my phone... and then felt incredibly stupid. I wondered if Connor or Jen had tried to call me. I wondered if I was needlessly worrying them... him. He had to know by now that I wasn't going to up and leave him again. Ever.

But still; I should do something. I went down to the office and asked if they had a public computer. They did. I found it in their small customer-office area by their Recreation room and I logged into my email. Sitting in my inbox were a few enrollment emails from UNT, from the financial offices, an email from Britain about one of our writing assignments...and a little further down were the emails I'd exchanged from Connor before he'd realized it was me. I read through them.... there was nothing insightful, nothing sweet...nothing incredibly sentimental, but still I read them;

LexWasHere463@gmail.com: Saw your ad about the room for rent. Available for immediate move in. I have first and last month's rent. When are you available to meet?
Shay.Connor@unt.edu: I'm not. Here's the number to the landlord. Give them your money and move in when you can. Current roommate will be out by Saturday.
LexWasHere463@gmail.com: What? You want me to move in without meeting me first? What if I'm a murderer or something?
Shay.Connor@unt.edu: Highly unlikely. I've never been so lucky. Move in or don't. Let me know asap.
LexWasHere463@gmail.com: I'll take it. See you then.
LexWasHere463@gmail.com: I'm here, buzz me up?

I clicked on Connor's email and started a new email thread:

Subject: *I Forgot My Phone*
Message: *I'll be back soon. Don't worry. Focus on feeling better. Don't murder Hank if you can help it. I'm going to see Maggie for her Birthday; didn't want her to be alone since you couldn't make it.*

I smiled to myself. Honestly just appreciating I was able to write Connor so easily. I'd lost count of the times I sat at my computer

222

back home, watching a blinking cursor in my email, not knowing what to say. Never sending anything. I'd found his email on the UNT directory his first year there; it wasn't hard to find. I'd found it again when I'd seen his advertisement. I may have been a little bit of a stalker. It was funny how happy I was to be writing an email when just a few days earlier we were lying on the grass next to the basketball court... I'd lost myself wildly with him, like we were teens again, forgetting everything but his smile, his taste, his warmth...

I miss you.

Maybe that was too straight forward. I deleted it. Maybe it wasn't straight forward enough. I rewrote it;

I miss you. I love you.
Love, Liam.

Two 'love's were definitely too much. I deleted it again and retyped it;

I miss you…
And I still love you.. you stupid, suicidal, trouble-seeking maniac.
-Liam.

I sent the email. I smiled again, hoping that I knew the expression he would make when he opened it. He was in pain, and needed to recover. For now he just needed assurance and support. Even if it might break him worse later. My smile vanished instantly. More thunder cracked outside and I looked out the window. The grounds would be muddy as hell. But there was no putting this off. I borrowed an umbrella from the hotel and left by

223

foot. I knew the graveyard was only a few blocks from here... Connor and I had walked by it multiple times when we'd lived here. On our way to and from school.

The water cascaded down harshly; my shoes and the bottom of my pants were immediately soaked. I could barely feel it. Cars drove by, indifferent, splashing gritty asphalt water in their wake. I avoided the splashes but cherished the sound of their presence zooming past. It interrupted my thoughts enough to remind me to breathe. I was terrified. I wasn't sure how my feet continue moving when everything else inside me was completely frozen.

The waist high gate to the cemetery loomed before me; and for just a second I stopped. Maybe I didn't have to do this? Not right now. Not today. The rain was pouring down, Connor and Jenifer weren't here... was this even a respectful thing to do? Would she have resented me all these years? For what I did? For what I didn't do? My feet kept going and my free hand undid the latch on the waist-high gate. I realized I didn't know what grave it was. I'd never been to see her. A gust of wind hurled water onto the rest of me, diverting the direct downward trajectory of the rain below the umbrella, rendering it useless. I wiped the water out of face and looked around. I started randomly reading the names on the stones, knowing I would find her eventually. For five minutes I wandered, aimlessly, reading the names as I went, vaguely wondering what kind of people they were...who missed them... who they left behind....

About 15 feet away I saw vibrant, soaked and now wilting sunflowers in front of a gravestone. I knew it was her. I kept making my way toward her.

Margaret Shay
Loving Wife and Mother of Two

That's all the stone said. That was it. All of her smiles; all of her perfumes, dresses, laughter, twinkling sarcasm that shone out of her eyes, her tenderness, her love, her ferocity... her hopes, her sadness, her dreams... her regret... her childhood, her motherhood, all of the affection, obsession, passion that she had for her little family in such a giant terrifying world... and all that was left of her was this gravestone and those carved out, cold words;

Margaret Shay
Loving Wife and Mother of Two

I had no right to be here. I had no right to face her, to come back for Connor, to pretend like I belonged to this family. I took a step back in shame, just staring… for a long time. But I couldn't leave. My feet were locked resolutely in the grass.

I remembered how she'd pulled me into her that first day at the airport, making sure I knew I was safe and welcome. Taking me shopping that first day, laughing openly at my clumsiness and social anxiety, just enough to make me feel normal. To make me know that I never made her uncomfortable. Dancing with her in the living room. The way my stupid, gay, little heart skipped a beat seeing her dressed up for the first time in that blue sun dress, for blushing at the way she smelled, at the way she smiled, at the way she loved me. Me. Of all people. I'd felt so safe... protected by such a small, fierce, woman. Thinking about her as an adult, I knew that she was just a human...just a person trying to do her best, suffering from depression and a neglectful husband, and just loving and caring so hard all the same. Just a small little woman. And I'd felt so safe. So safe that I didn't do anything.

There was a deep seeded sadness that prompted me to

mourn all over again... or maybe openly for the first time... but I couldn't. I didn't deserve to. I just stared onward, in the rain...remembering everything. I was the only one crazy enough to be out in this. The one who left the sunflowers must have gotten here earlier, before the storm. I wondered vaguely who did bring those flowers. I swallowed hard and it burned inside me. I opened my mouth to speak, and the words barely came out, completely inaudible with the crashing of raindrops ripping into the puddles of ground. I thought... that the gravestone needed to be able to hear me. As if it were a person, I tried louder;

"I'm sorry!" I knew she still couldn't hear me.

I just kept talking. To myself. Because Maggie wasn't here...she never was here, and she'd never be here. Because I'd been weak. Because I'd been helpless.

"Maggie."My inner dialogue spilled over to the real world. I still couldn't help myself though, as stupid and selfish as I knew I was being. Maybe I didn't even deserve to use her first name. "Ms. Shay..." I really was pathetic. "I know I have no right to ask you for anything... anything else... but..." I stopped myself. I was right... I couldn't ask her for anything more. *What the bloody hell was I thinking?* I felt the darkness that enveloped everything on the bridge back home that night that I'd almost taken my own life. I wish I would have. Seeing what Connor was going through since I'd been back. Watching him fight with himself, with his own anxiety, with the memories I'd inadvertently brought with me. But I loved him too much to leave. He made me too happy. None of this was fair of me. My grip tightened on the umbrella handle. *Jesus Christ.*

I wasn't like this just before I'd come back. I wasn't emotional, I wasn't pathetic, I wasn't weak. I'd focused on making myself stronger; eventually my parents had helped; sending me to a military school. Where Brent had accidently been dropped into my life, pulling me into the band, pulling me into The Factory (the MMA Gym I'd spent most of my days). For the longest time my mates and I had cheated time and killed it swiftly. But I never could run far or fast enough until Brent eventually introduced me to heroin...staved me off of heroin with cocaine, ecstasy, xanax... I hadn't really cared what he'd offered me; I'd have taken arsenic with the same satisfied smile to get Maggie's lifeless body out of my head. Maggie probably would have murdered Brent, hated him if she'd ever met him. But my own stupidity and meek ingratiating servility wasn't his doing; it was always my own... and he was running from his own Demons...gracious enough to take me along. I'd loved him too, in a way. Not like I loved Connor; I'd never loved anyone like I'd loved Connor. But he wasn't there, and Brent was, with open arms and an open bed to sleep in. I wondered why I was thinking of him now, of all times. I didn't want to be that person anymore. I never wanted to be a junkie, or hurt anyone, or beat up a bunch of homophobes in an alleyway. All I'd ever wanted was Connor and to be someone Maggie could be proud of.

I don't know if my hollaring into a ridiculous rainstorm, or my sudden traveling and over analyzing had just exhausted me, but suddenly, out of nowhere, I'd lost the energy to hate myself. I'd felt a calmness as I stared at her soaking stone, watching the water flow down her etched named. I felt...calm. I felt warm in the soaking breezes that slapped against my skin. I felt relief. I felt like I was sitting in her Fiat and she'd told me that she loved me for the first time. That she'd always love me. I was calm. I kept talking to her... I couldn't stop myself. I needed to talk to her. She'd told me to, she'd told me to rely on her, to not face things all on my own.

"Connor isn't doing well. At all. Everything is killing him inside.... I wish you could read his books. They're beautiful but they're full of you..." *and then the harsh realizations that you're not there.* "I guess...they're full of the emptiness you left behind.

227

He's... he's drinking a lot. He's smoking like a chimney." For a brief second I could just see her in my mind, smiling and rolling her eyes at the smoking bit. "OK, I know he's always smoked like a chimney... there's no saving that, is there?" I smiled back at her. "But he's...broken. And I don't think he'll ever be whole again." I thought for a while. Wondering what she'd say back. Still seeing her in my heart, knowing she couldn't speak. "A few nights ago he let himself get hurt." I told her. I told on him. "He let it happen, and I somehow knew he was looking for it." *He doesn't want to be here anymore. He wants to be with you. His anxiety doesn't let him sleep without whiskey, and his fear of always being alone doesn't let him stay awake without Gin. Or beer. Or diving into his laptop to hold on for dear life...* Though I'd maintained that calmness... that I couldn't help but feel she'd given me... I still felt guilt creep up inside me. "I know it's my fault." I confessed. "I just don't know how to fix anything." I was more asking her...pleading for the advice I knew wouldn't come.

I thought silently for a long time, listening to the rain, fighting the shivers of cold searing up my spine. I lost all hope, I fell from a calm, to a guilt, to a calm again, to a terrified, till I didn't have anymore emotions left to give her. To give anyone. Until the very last effort I had was just an awkward bravery. And maybe I hadn't ever had it before. Maybe she'd given it to me, there, in that graveyard. I stood up, and I tried to shake off some water as more just poured from the skies and absorbed into me. And very clearly, very distinctly I felt the presence of the phrase searing through my entire being;

"You're Strong. You're Brave. And you're Capable". I heard Connor's voice in the back of my head adding. "Welcome to our little cult...". I laughed. Out loud. To noone. I opened the umbrella and left it perched over her grave, stopping the rain from hitting her directly. I kissed my hand and and I placed my kiss gently on the word "Mother". The word she cherished the most. She didn't hate me. She hadn't hated me all this time. She'd never hate me. I was her kid. And as her kid, I made my way from the graveyard.

I wasn't running, I wasn't being pulled along anymore, I wasn't the obsequious piteous rubble dodging my demons by any means possible. I needed to face my past monsters head on. What I really needed, if I was going to be able to be there for Connor in any way...was to confront Hank.

I was knocking on the door loudly, competing with the white noise of pouring rain resonating on my old house. I knocked. And knocked, and rang the doorbell, determined. Until I remembered that Hank was at the hospital with Con...until I remembered that I hadn't even verified that he would still live here now that the kids had moved out and Maggie was gone. My fist was still pounding on the door as I thought, in a trance.

And it opened. And I was correct. A complete stranger stood before me, surprised, confused at the bruised up, soaking wet specticle before him. I'd forgotten I had bruises all over my face in that moment; residual swelling. The residential stranger was about my height; he was thin, seemingly in his 50's, with long brown hair pulled back in a light pony-tail, a mid length beard and reading glasses. He didn't look alarmed, just confused.

"I'm sorry, Sir, I was looking for someone else. Someone who used to live here." I backed up to start walking away. He smiled warmly at me.

"Are you looking for Henry?"

"No." *I'm looking for Hank*. Hank was a nickname for Henry… "Hank Shay?" I asked.

"Yes, he still lives here. Would you like to come in and dry off to wait for him?" I wasn't sure. I hadn't exactly planned any of this well. But the new found bravery was coursing through my veins and I gave into it's prodding.

"Please. If you don't mind." He led me into the house nicely… though I didn't need any leading. I'd entered that house hundreds of times before. I looked around and noticed that nothing had changed… not a single thing. Not a placemat, not a rug, or a couch, or a coffee table… not a single kitchen appliance. I hadn't walked through a doorway; I'd walked through a time warp.

He introduced himself. "I'm Gideon", he said, familiarly finding his way to the linen closet, handing me a towel to dry myself off. "Would you like a dry shirt to change into? Hank's son left a ton of clothes when he moved out, I believe they're about your size."

The AC in the house was making me cold.

"Yes, please, if you don't mind." I was a robot on repeat. I watched down the hallway as he walked into Connor's old bedroom. I imagined it being exactly the same. The whole house a museum of a happier time. I turned around toward the livingroom, eyeing the pictures that draped over the fireplace. Connor as a little kid, Jen as a little kid. A Picture of Hank and Maggie on their wedding day, smiling, holding one another. I noticed, there was an additional picture. Just one of them. And this stranger was in it; a selfie of Gideon and Hank at a Bar, smiling. I wasn't sure I'd ever seen Hank smile. The likeness to he and Con, especially now that Con was older, was off putting.

Gideon came back with one of Connor's old T-shirts. It didn't smell like him anymore, just like laundry soap and the musk of an old, wooden, drawer. I went to the bathroom and put it on; my pants were still soaked. There was a knock on the door and Gideon had found a pair of his old basketball shorts too, and smiled warmly as he handed them to me. I changed and felt very strange. Very not-myself. I came back out and didn't know what to say.

"Hank ran to the pharmacy just before you arrived to pick up some prescriptions for me. I've had a bit of a cold, you see." He pushed his glasses up the bridge of his nose. "Would you like some tea?" Usually when people asked me that, I knew it was a joke. A british reference. This time I knew it was sincere and with my skin refusing to shed it's dampness, I honestly would like some tea.

"Yes, please." He motioned for me to sit in the living room as he went to the kitchen and put a teapot on the stove. That, I did not remember being here when I was younger.

"He should be back any minute. Is he expecting you?"

"No, I don't believe he is." This Gideon was very kind, very soft, very warm. I liked him. I knew that Hank would be enraged that I was here when he got back... I felt the need to warn him before things got too incredibly uncomfortable.

"Oh. Pity. You may have caught him at a bad time. His son was in some sort of accident. He just got back from the Hospital late last night. Still hasn't shaken off that parental worry, I'm sure you understand." I did not. I couldn't imagine Hank really worrying about Connor's well being. Perhaps his career...his image, or persona, or livelihood. But not his well being. To give him credit, I could imagine him being glad that Connor wasn't dead.

"Gideon, I'm afraid that's why I'm here. I'm a friend of Connor's." He handed me my tea as he sat on the couch with me. He smiled warmly again.

"Then maybe he will be happy to see you."

"I'm uh... Liam. Liam Clarke. I'm not sure if he's ever mentioned me..." Gideon's eyes widened, but not in an anger, or anxiety... to be honest, with his hippie persona, I doubted he'd ever felt anxious in his entire life.

231

"Then perhaps he will not." He leaned back into the couch just a bit, sinking into a thought as he looked up at the fireplace. "He did mention you. A long time ago and then last night. I remember when you were staying with he and Margaret back when you were a teenager. Henry told me all about it." He wasn't making eye contact. Who exactly was Gideon? How long had he known the Shays? Connor's uncle perhaps? I was too amped up thinking about what I was going to say to Hank when he got home to dwell. There was a long silent pause. I noticed a book on the coffee table, laying open on it's spine; "You Can't Go Home Again," by David Wolfe. I'd never read it. Gideon must have been reading when I'd shown up. I thought that I should say something… but he beat me to it.

"Liam. I'm going to say something to you I've been wanting to for a very, very, very, very long time." He spoke *very* slowly, "I never thought I'd get the opportunity to, and I don't think I'll ever get to again, so I'm going to carpe diem, as they say." I had no idea who this fellow was, I didn't expect him to know me, let alone have any kind of message for me. "Margaret's passing wasn't your fault." *What?* "I respect Henry, but he handled that poorly, and I know, deep down, he regrets it. He was quite the alcoholic back then." I was dumbfounded. My own hand surprised me as it pulled my tea to my mouth. The heated, familiar, liquid cascaded through me, shaking the cold from my bones and bringing life back into my face. This stranger wasn't there the night Maggie was murdered. He didn't know.

"How do you know the Shays?" I maintained my calm disposition. Though, the blatant excavating of deeply personal memories shook me.

The front door unlocked and opened; Hank entered with a plastic bag in hand, folding his umbrella behind him.

"It's ungodly out there. And they were out of Bayer, I grabbed tylenol." He turned around and saw us on the couch. It took him just a second to recognize me.

"Thank you." Gideon stood up. "Henry, it appears you have company. This young man has come to talk to you about something." All of a sudden I was afraid! Where had my bravery gone! My soul looked wildly within itself, throwing everything around, trying to find it. Hank stared straight into me, shaking his head in disbelief.

"What the fuck made you think you could come back here?" He hadn't dropped the bag, or relinquished the umbrella. A small part of me worried he was going to beat me with it. Gideon walked up to him, taking the bag from him, rescuing me from an umbrella bludgeoning. He set the items in the kitchen. He also answered for me.

"Henry." Gideon was stern. "It looks like he has come an awful long way in a storm to tell you something. It's been long enough that you can sit down and *listen*." I was worried for him then. The Hank I knew would have hit him. But he didn't. He tore his seething gaze from me into Gideon, where it lightened and I felt an entire world of conversation take place in front of me as they locked eyes. Hank didn't say anything. He came into the living room, dragging a chair from the kitchen table behind him as he approached. He set it in front of me, opposite the coffee table and sat down. Leaning in on his knees. Not saying a word. I thought, with a fleeting terrified impending doom, that Gideon might leave us to our own devices. But he did not. He came and sat just where he did before, picked up his tea, and kept drinking.

"What?" Was all Hank said to me.

"I, um." *I don't know. Why did I come here? What was I going to say to him?* He looked so much like Connor.

"Well, that's enlightening Liam, thank you for coming by. Thank you for landing my *son* in the Hospital. Thank you for killing my *wife*." He sat up. "Now get the *fuck* out of my house." He didn't break eye contact. Gideon sighed, unaffected.

"Henry." he scolded him again. And I wondered yet again who Gideon was to Hank.

"I didn't land Connor in the Hospital, Mr. Shay. And I think you know that. I think Jen would have told you." I remembered the feeling I'd had at Maggie's grave. "And I needed you to know that I'm sorry for what happened with Maggie. More sorry than anyone could ever have the right to be. But I'm not going to leave Connor alone again. And there's nothing you can do to make me. I just need you to know that." The rage burning in his eyes was palpable. I swallowed hard but maintained my position. I kept talking, while I could, before it was too late. "I couldn't control anything back then Mr. Shay. I was a child." He continued to let me speak. "I asked her not to involve anyone in my bullying, I never asked her to approach the Jennings. I never asked her to make you fire that man. I never asked for any of it."

"Your excuses are all well thought out, Clarke." He spat at me, but I didn't let it deter me.

"All I ever wanted was to be a part of a family, left alone, and be free to be myself. I should have done more. I should have. I know that now, but I can't change anything. All I can do is be there for your son, and try to make up for you not letting me be there for him before." I thought deeply for just a second. If I'd said this much, I could say more; "And for *you* not being there the way you should have."

Hank shot up from his chair. And so did I. Even if I were wrong about everything else, I knew I was right about one thing. I wasn't a child anymore. I'd defended me and Connor in that alley,

234

I'd defend us here too. I wasn't going anywhere. I almost hoped that he'd swing at me.

Gideon coughed, with limited energy as though he'd been sick a while, which grabbed Hank's attention. "For heaven's sake, Henry. Calm yourself. Everything that happened was years ago. Sit down." To my surprise, he did. And I awkwardly followed suite.

"Why are you here Liam?" was all he asked me.

"Because I'm going to tell Connor the truth. And I wanted to tell you the truth first." He left me room to speak. I made my words pronounced, clear, and as poignant as I could, to resound in his head for days to come. "It is NOT all my fault what happened with Maggie. She was strong, she was independent, and she fiercely protected me the way any mother would. And I never once asked her to. You fired David's dad. You blew up on Connor that night. And you don't deserve to push it all on me."

"Get out of my house, Liam." I could tell he was desperately trying not to lash out. Not for me. Not for himself. But maybe for Gideon. But I was angry now, thinking about all of it, thinking about how long everything had solely tortured me all these years. I kept going, more vehemently.

"If you weren't such a fucking up-tight homophobe who cared more about his career than his own fucking Son, none of this would have happened. We'd have all been home that night. Maggie would still be here." He was boiling, his temple throbbing, his face turning red, so intensely his eyes glazed over, his bodice shook; a volcano ready for the the boiling spewing lava to cascade out of him. He was about to lose it. Gideon set down his cup, swiftly, calmly, making his way over to Hank. He put his hand on his face, pulling it toward him and kissed him on the mouth. I saw him fight, just for a second, to hold onto his anger but it simmered calculatedly. I was taken aback.

Gideon was... Hanks...

"You've got to be kidding me…" I stared wide eyed. "You've got to be bloody kidding me." I repeated. "Who are you?" I asked Gideon, who looked at me with a sad, assertive nature.

"I used to be Henry's secretary. I've been his partner for a very very long time." I couldn't and didn't say anything. I didn't feel, I didn't think. I wasn't supposed to know this.

"Why? Why would you…" I shook it off. I was not supposed to know this. I walked around a heated, bewildered Hank, eyes slightly darting at being outed… I went to the sink where Gideon had set my wet clothes, I picked them up, I put on my wet shoes that I'd taken off, in pure silence.

Hank called to me: "William! Don't you dare tell Connor." The phrase sort of echoed for me.

I turned and looked at him in disbelief.

"No, Hank. You don't ever get to ask that of me again." I exited the front door. I shut it behind me. I stared out into the rain, out into the lawn where I remembered Maggie watering the garden. I thought about how calm she was about Hank's arrangements, never coming back to the house. I thought about how they touched, loving, but never passionate. She had to have known. The whole time...she had to have known.

I must have been standing there a few minutes. In a shocked granite position, being lulled into my memories, my subconscious already trying to figure out how to tell Con. My final understanding of everything around me. Gideon opened the front door, coming out alone. Hank did not follow him out. He stood next to me, silent, for just a moment. I felt strange, not knowing what to do with my hands, one engrossed with my wet clothing.

"Did Maggie know, Gideon? Did she know the whole time?" I didn't look at him. He was still calm, calculated, and warm.

"Yes." More silence. Then he added; "I'd met her. She was a beautiful woman. I met her and Connor, and Jen, when Jen was just two years old. Hank had asked her for a divorce, we all sat on that same couch, talking it over. He hadn't realized he wasn't in love with her...not until he met me. And when he did, he tried to do the right thing. They were highschool sweethearts, they'd known eachother their whole lives. Their parents knew each other, they'd grown up together... they were closer than any two beings could ever be on this planet. He just wasn't in love with her. And frankly... I don't quite remember if she was in love with him either at that point."

"She was." I wasn't there, there's no way I could have known...but thinking of Maggie crying in her room, somehow, I felt like I did.

"She asked him not to divorce her. To be there for the kids, because they needed a father. Liam... don't misunderstand. Henry loved his family; more than anything in the world..."

"Except for you." It was a fact, it wasn't accusatory.

"Except for me." he agreed. Looking slightly ashamed. He tried very hard for the longest time to be there for himself, for Maggie, for Connor, for Jenny...until he hit the bottle for a little solace and it was all downhill from there." He paused, looking out at the rain with me. I noticed a pack of cigarettes resting on the ground, just out of the rain. I felt so numb and empty... nothing but a million questions burning through my mind.

"Do you smoke?" I asked him.

"No. Henry does. He always has, far back as I can remember." Another silence. "Liam..." He looked at me, slightly pleading this time, "If any of this makes it back to Connor; make sure to tell him... tell him that his Dad was never cold to him because he hated him. He was cold because he hated himself." I didn't nod, I wouldn't affirm. I didn't owe any of them anything;

237

Con didn't owe either of them anything, and Hank didn't deserve an ounce of Connor's forgiveness. He didn't deserve to be humanized. After a while Gideon asked,

"Where are you staying?"

"At a hotel up the road." I wouldn't look at him.

"Do you need a ride?"

"No. I don't need anything from you." I hated him. I hated Hank. I hated this house. I hated their pictures on the wall and I welcomed the rain, wishing it would wash away everything they had just told me, as I walked into it; down the driveway, down the road, past the graveyard. I couldn't even look toward Maggie's grave; my gaze held strictly to my shoes... all the way back to the hotel.

CHAPTER 10: ONE OR TWO PEOPLE

I was definitely surprised that Hank was home when I walked in the house. He was sitting on the couch with his work laptop in his lap, completely sober. I hadn't seen that in quite some time.

"What are you doing home?" It was a fair question I asked him. And I wasn't ramped up, or angry. I was still mulling over the conversations Mom and I had had at the grocery store.

"I got a call at work that Liam was sent to the Principal's office. I came home to make sure everything was alright and see that the Clarke's were informed about about whatever happened with Liam at school.

"Some kids were a jerk to him and he pushed a kid. That's literally it." I went straight to the fridge and grabbed a beverage. This was the most normal angst I'd had toward him since Jenny left...which I still blamed him for. But... that was also the same reason I'd met Liam, so I wondered silently to myself if I was still allowed to be angry about that specifically. I had plenty of other shit to dwell on and be angry with him for.

"That's it?" He looked up from his laptop at me as I unscrewed a Dr. Pepper bottle.

"Yes."

"Yes sir." he corrected me. And I literally laughed. He had to have been kidding. He smiled at me as if he were; it was a smile of jest, not of condescension for once. It was a weird smile. One I didn't know what to do with. I couldn't read him at all. "Listen, come sit down. I want to talk to you." I sat across from him in the living room instinctively. I always reverted to being a little kid around him, without thinking. If I'd thought first, I'd have just thought my way strait to my room, slamming my door behind me.

"What?"

"Listen, about the other night. I wanted to tell you I was in the wrong." He'd meant the 'other night' as in hitting me in the face and slamming me into the door. I wondered if he'd known he was in the wrong all the other times he'd come home drunk and hit me. If he even remembered.

"No shit?" He clenched his jaw at my swearing but didn't chastise me. "I'm a 17 year old fuckin' kid and you're a grown ass man. And my Dad." He still didn't correct my language.

"Connor. I'm trying to apologize." *Fuck you.*

"Fuck you. No. You don't get to do that." I got up and was about to walk off.

"SIT DOWN." I did. He'd moved his laptop from his lap and set it on the coffee table leaning forward seriously. "What do you want from me, kid?" he asked earnestly. "You don't want an apology. What do you want?" I thought for a minute, studying his features. He was chiseled, well kept, his hair slicked back, wearing formal business attire having come straight from work. I thought briefly back to the carousel horse; his faded blue jeans and weekend T-shirt. I thought about Mom watching her happy family, and Dad lifting me up... making sure I didn't fall.

"You're right. I don't want your fucking apology. Why don't you apologize to Mom, for ruining all of our God Damn lives." He wasn't surprised. He just exhaled and leaned back in the couch, exhausted of me.

"You don't understand anything Con. You really don't. You're just a kid."

That infuriated me. I did understand. I understood better than anyone; better than him, for sure. He wasn't the one who'd sit by Moms door as a kid hearing her muffled crying under the mumbling of the TV backwash. He wasn't the one sticking his ear to the crack under the door, trying to hear why she was sad but not being brave enough to ask. He wasn't the one who'd try his damnedest to distract Jen on Mom's 'Down Weekends' when she didn't want to get out of bed. He wasn't the one who noticed antidepressants when Maggie had asked him to pick up her prescriptions that time she had a cold a few years ago. He wasn't the one. Because he was never here. As much as I loved words, they weren't there for me in this moment. There was nothing I could say to him to make him understand just exactly how much I'd have fucking exalted to be a fucking kid all these years. I was silent.

"You're graduating this year, and we can't keep at it like this. You're about to be leaving the house; we have to get serious about picking out your college and helping you decide what you want to do career wise."

"Is that what this conversation is? Don't worry about it; I'm fine."

"What do you mean?"

"I'm going to a College here, to be closer to Mom and Jenny, so they have someone to depend on when you fuck up. I'm going to be a novelist. And a Professor. Eventually." He exhaled again as though talking to a toddler he could not convince to tie their shoes correctly.

"You know that writers don't make much money... neither do teachers...You really need to start thinking about engineering, or business. If you want to travel, or support a family one day. You have to be making more."

"Like I said, don't worry about me. I'm fine." It's not like I expected him to support anything I believed in anyway. Like Honesty. And not hitting your fucking kids. And not cheating on your fucking wife. I didn't need his approval. I got up to walk away, and no amount of astute bravado in his voice could have made me sit down again, like a timid dog at his command. He knew this too.

241

"We'll talk about it again later, Con." I didn't like when he didn't use my full name anymore. Like the world was betraying my hatred and letting him pretend to be a Dad.

"Talk all you want." I went into my room, and slammed down at my desk, instinctively grabbing a pencil, but not really intending to write. I was almost tired of always being so angry. I heard Mom and Liam come in and I barely heard Liam exchange a soft formal greeting with my father. I'm sure he smiled politely, and was perfectly well kept. I heard the happiness in my mom's voice as she greeted him, and imagined her lovingly touch his face before making her way to the fridge for a Dr. Pepper. She always had to be doing something with her hands as well, drinking something, fiddling with something. I could see the living room like I was still in there, and leaving didn't help at all.

Liam came straight to my room and shut the door behind himself, grinning like an idiot.

"Hank's home". He stated the obvious, still radiating with happiness.

"What? No way." I said sarcastically, wondering why the fuck that would make him happy. He didn't skip a beat. He came straight over to my desk and was just slightly taller than me since I was sitting in my chair. He grabbed my attention by placing his hand on my face and turning it toward him, kissing me. I was shocked that he'd initiate any form of intimacy. I tasted his happiness then, and couldn't help but smile. Whatever surly mood that was emaciating my insides evaporated and replaced itself with warmth… and hope. I turned away of my desk, mid kiss, and pulled him onto my lap playfully. It didn't matter that Hank was home; we were happy. We were happy and it didn't matter. I kissed him back passionately, and he pulled away.

"Maggie said I don't have to leave at the end of the year. I can stay here. In the States. While you're at college." I grinned up

242

at him.

"Yeah, she mentioned something about that." I shrugged like it was no big deal, but my heartstrings had left ropeburns on my voicebox the second I'd seen him sitting outside Mr. Collyher's office. He kissed me again and I pulled away slightly, still grinning."You know, if Hank walks in and your tongue is down my throat, I feel like Mom will have a harder time convincing him." But that didn't stop him. I'd never seen him so energetic. He got off me and went to sit on my bed, still bouncing animatedly. "So...not such a shitty day after all?" I asked. He shook his head no, too excited to speak. It was odd, to me, how he could love the household that I hated so much. It made me wonder, exactly how hope deficient his home in Europe was. How devoid and isolated he must have been there to thrive in the animosity and thick tension that nestled its way into my world. Or maybe that bright enigma of light that he projected through the darkest parts of me... shone for him to when we were together. Maybe that was what love really meant.

I felt like I kinda wanted to tell him that I loved him. His stupid goofy smile, and dramatic facial expressions, the light he brought into my world. Love had to be it; but I oddly had a distaste for the word in my mouth. I felt like it described a crippling weakness rather than a strength. I couldn't say it.

"Boys!?" Mom hollered from the living room, "Get ready to leave, we're eating out!"

"Didn't she just buy groceries?"

"I guess that was enough Adulting for her for one day." I laughed between my words at him. We'd just gotten home, so there wasn't a lot of 'Getting Ready' to be doing. I stood up and went to Liam on the bed, deeply grateful for his infectious joy and energy. I kissed him this time, pushing him over on the bed and crawling on top of him. A playful kind of passion, that I'd honestly never

243

experienced with any girl I'd ever been with. I did ravish the idea of him not going back to Europe, of staying close to me.

He pulled away slightly, "Con, we're about to leave."

"I'm not." I joked, kissing his neck and running my hands up his shirt. "I'm about to do something else." He laughed, sheepishly and wiggled out from under me. There was an adoration in his shining blue eyes that I wasn't sure I could ever live up to, and for the first time in my life I knew I'd do everything humanly possible to try. I wasn't there for him at school, when he needed me to step in and stop his journal from be torn and tossed around, and I was never going to let that happen again. If I was really going to take responsibility for someone's happiness I decided in that moment to really own it.

The drive to the restaurant was silent in the back seat with Moms parent chatter enveloping the conversation stage.

"I don't know what you want me to do, Mags. You want me to fire him because his kid's a little shit?" Hank asked her. She'd been nagging him to commit to talk to David's father.

"No, I just want you to talk to him. To call him, or talk to him at work."

"That's probably not appropriate."

"Well, his son laying his hands on my kid wasn't appropriate either." He made a 'Ch' sound at Mom's 'my kid'. Clearly Liam was not *his* kid. It didn't seem as though anyone felt the need to tell Hank about Liam's sexual preferences. Or mine for that matter. I never did have that cliché Father/Son talk about the birds and the bees... how shitty it is to accidently have kids because they ruin your life and are ungrateful little shits who grow up... who want to become writers.

I turned to Liam to avoid them. "Hey, how was your paper?" I asked. He looked down, slightly put out.

"It didn't go well."

"I thought you loved that book?""

"I did, but I'm not great at writing. It's done though, I turned it in at least." I was bummed that he looked so disappointed in himself. I ruffled his hair.

"Just rewrite it and turn it in again a little later. I had Ms. Gilly as a Sophomore. She'll appreciate that way more than a shitty essay. I'll help you." He smiled at me. *See, I could be responsible for someone else's happiness.*

Mom loved these kind of restaurants; she dragged us out to Cajun food, delighted not to cook. She glowed with radiance under the streaming- repurposed - christmas lights that hung all over the ceiling, the decor of hojpog junk on windowsills and countertops, the bluesey music that meandered through the crowd of fellow families and hungry folk. And she beamed at us across the table as Hank looked through the menu. I searched her face for some kind of dismay, some kind of *difference* since finding out that Liam and I were more than friends. But there wasn't one. She was happy, I could feel it. I hoped that Liam felt it too; I hoped that he knew that Maggie didn't have an ounce of hate or prejudice in her to care about something so trivial.

"I um. I was hoping that maybe we could not tell my parents about me being sent to the Principal's office today?" Liam offered, with both Shay parentals at the table.

"That's fine." Maggie offered, with no hesitation.

"No, that's not fine." Hank interjected. "Liam, if Jenny where to get into trouble over there, I'd want your parents to let us know. They have every right to know what you've been up to. What happened anyway?"

"I told you. Some kid was being a jerk and Liam pushed him. It's not a big deal." I interrupted him before Liam could speak." His gaze burned into me. "And frankly if you or Mr. Clarke wanted to know what was going on with your kids, you wouldn't have sent them halfway around the world so I don't think it's any your businesses." I knew that Hank wouldn't start a confrontation in a public place.

"Damnit Connor, just one nice night out." Mom interjected. "Liam, we're not going to talk to your parents about what happened unless you find yourself in trouble again. Hank is right, they do have a right to know what's going on in your life, but there's no need to worry them over a misunderstanding." She winked at him, and Liam just kept looking at his plate. The waitress came over and everyone ordered their food. We were all grateful for the distraction. What an excellent fucking family night out. So glad that Hank could make this one. I ignored him. I did realize that I was being a little shit and making everyone uncomfortable but I couldn't help it. He really brought the worst out in me. I felt bad for Mom, who was really trying to enjoy herself. I tried to reel it in for her and Liam.

I looked around at the other families. There was one to our left; an older gentleman and his wife, and what I assumed where their three teenage daughters. They were all laughing; the dad had told a joke and the mom was covering her mouth with her napkin stifling a laugh. The girls were smiling too, having side conversations and rolling up ripped up napkins to flick at their parents. I wondered what that was like. I sucked up all my pride, all my anger, all my angst, and thought about how happy I was that Liam was staying, after graduation.

"Dad." The word felt gross in my mouth; I didn't let it show. "How's work?" everyone looked at me surprised. I just...wanted to give Mom some sort of *gift*. Give her *something* and being nice to that asshole was all that I had to give. His eyes widened at the 'Dad'. I hadn't used that word in a very long time. He seemed pleased.

"It was fine. It's been hectic lately, trying to find enough distributors for the new client we took on, but Clarke Co has really been a valuable asset..." Liam continued to look at his plate. The food came and Hank continued talking about work. Mom continued to look interested. Liam and I didn't say another word. I subtly slid my foot on top of his under the table, just to remind him I was there and the tiny gesture put a smile on his face as he snuck a glance at me. I didn't smile back; I made an absurdly serious face and asked him to pass the salt. But inside I was laughing. Mom watched, half listening to Hank ramble about work, half watching me be happy for the first time in years.

Liam excused himself from the table to use the restroom. I continued to eat the green beans on my plate, trying to exude my inner peace treaty with my father by remaining silent and to myself. He'd be gone again before I knew it, I'd cheer Mom up all over again, and the road would go on and on.

"Mags," Hank turned to Mom as soon as Liam left the table. "I didn't want to tell you in front of the kid in case it somehow got back to his father, but I already had to fire Jennings. Yesterday."

"What?" She stared at him in disbelief, "Why would you do that? ... Hank I had to beg you to hire him in the first place! Why would you do that? I just wanted you to *talk* to him!" She was angry. Hank shook his head.

"It had nothing to do with David and Liam." He pushed his plate away from him. "He was stealing from the company, he was allocating large profits to an offshore account. He stole thousands." Mom stared at him blankly. "I've pressed charges. He may be going back to prison." Mom was silent. I wasn't sure how to feel. I never cared about the wellbeing of Hank's office. I heard Jim Jennings was a worthless piece of shit anyway... his son was a worthless piece of shit... maybe now they'd move. I wasn't perturbed. Liam came back from the restroom. Sensing the increased tension that had settled on the table, he eyed me quizzically. I shrugged. I knew that somehow, in the deep recesses of his own stupidity he'd manage to care, even about David, should he hear. I decided not to tell him. Somehow he'd think that was his fault to; or he'd make it his fault and beat himself up about it for centuries to come.

If I could just give him a fucking ounce of my ability to accept people as they are; to not unrealistically imagine the good in every human being and accept the fact that people are just new generations of fucked up people… he'd be so much better off, and I'd be so much more alone.

As soon as we got back to the house, we announced homework and escaped the penetrating gazes of my mother and father. The first thing he said, shutting his bedroom door behind him, was

"Con, your mother is wonderful." I laughed.

"Have you gotten yourself a new crush? Are we done here?" He picked up his backpack and set it on his bed. I picked up his backpack and set it on the floor, stealing it's spot. He got the message that we weren't really doing homework. I lay on the bed staring up at the ceiling, thinking about the day. Thinking about how Mom had told me I am who I *am* and described me as self centered. Liam lay next to me, watching the same ceiling fan, ignoring my crush tease. I thought again to the park a while back, when I'd told him I liked him for the first time. "Do you really think I'm an asshole?" I asked. I wouldn't be offended either way.

"Sometimes." He knew I meant it honestly, that I didn't expect him to lie.

"Do you know why?" He reached down and held my hand and I turned to look at him, he was sappy as hell with a serious expression.

"I think so." I let him take that one. I wasn't going to pry, or test him. Plus… if he knew the reason, more power to him. I didn't quite know the reason myself. It certainly wasn't because I enjoyed hurting people. I just didn't think about anyone enough to waste any energy realizing. I thought that's what it was.

"I'm glad you're staying."

"I'd certainly hope so." But I wasn't thinking about me. I was thinking about Mom. she'd need him here if I was leaving. She was accustomed to having two kids; she had too much care and affection in her heart to keep all to herself. She needed someone to take care of her, to listen to her, to wait in the kitchen and pretend to make food every night when she came home. And it couldn't be Jenny, that's just not who she was.

"Liam."

"Yes?" I was grateful he didn't look at me.

"I'm worried. All the time." He kept quiet… had no comment. "And I'm tired of being angry. I'm exhausted."

"I understand." I could tell he wasn't cutting me off, or was disinterested; he was letting me talk without shoving in his own dialogue. He was listening.

"Every sentence, every word that Hank says, I'm dissecting, breaking down, verifying the annotation and denotation of that word. I'm spot checking it against every memory I have, to see if he's meaning something else, if it could be construed as something else to her, and hurt her. Every gesture… every phrase, every movement. Most of all…everything he's not saying. Which is infinite." I paused, letting out a sigh. I continued more frustratingly; "And even when I find those brief instances, those nuggets of blatant negativity; there's really nothing I can do to protect her from the sadness. I'm always too late." I was listening to the light 'wherring' of the ceiling fan, watching the shadows of the panels chase them around in circles. "And I just... I fucking *hate* every God damn fucking syllable." Of all the words in the English language I could not think of a more appropriate, or a more specific word to describe hate. I meant it almost biblically, the kind of hate that seeps into the hearts of mankind, altering their souls and sending them to hell.

He still didn't look at me. He just repeated himself. "I understand." I held his hand a little tighter and felt some knots in my chest start to unwind. I'd never spoken openly like this to anyone. Not to Jenny...certainly not to Mom... not even to myself. They were truths that I didn't know were real until they came out of my mouth and I was forced to paste emotion fragments into sentences. I kept going;

"And that just...complete disregard and loathing I see in Hank...the fucking... *cognitive dissonance*... I see in Mom, the stupidity that keeps her magnetized to him, watching her die inside little by little... I see it in everyone. And I hate them all." He was still quiet, but ran his thumb over mine, reminding me he was present. "And if it were just me, if I were her only kid, her only tether to that fucking asshole, I'd off myself in a second so she'd be forced to go be happy because...honestly... I'm sick of this shit." I watched him seriously consider what I was saying. He wasn't startled, wasn't surprised.

"Con. She loves him. Even if you weren't here; she'd still love him. And he'd still be exactly who he is. And she'd just be all the more alone. You know, if you told her the truth, that he hit you... I'm sure she'd leave him." I laughed.

"No, she'd murder him. That's very different. She'd get 20 to life and plead guilty all the way through the trial." I really really laughed thinking about it. I was definitely jaded. There was a comfortable silence.

"I don't know what to say. I've never really *known* anyone but you. I've met people, obviously, and I've guessed at who they are, and why... but I've never known. Never...communicated." He paused and it was my turn to let him talk. "My parents seem nice, when I've seen them. They talk pleasantly... they do alot for their community, and they worship each other. I've never seen two people so molded into one humanoid." That part put a jolt of delight in his voice. He added matter-of-factly, "They just never really cared for *me* much. I don't think either of them ever really intended to become parents." I looked over at him and watched his reflective genuinity hover over his face, in his eyes, through his lips. He was always honest, always embarrassed. But right now... there was no blush. He wasn't hiding anything, he wasn't worried what I'd think, or about how I'd judge him. "Maybe..." He was trying to put a thought together into words; something much more difficult for him than it was for me. I wished I could lend him my vocabulary, my thirst for syntax. "Maybe how we feel toward our parents is how we end up feeling toward the world. Maybe *you're* destined to love one or two people *with a painful intensity* your whole life and hate everyone, and everything, else." That struck me, settling heavily over my heart, and I believed it to be true. He continued, "And maybe I'm destined to never feel like I was supposed to be here." He didn't need my love for words. He was my love for words.

I wanted him then. More than my young heart had ever wanted anyone. I didn't dare kiss him. I didn't dare touch him, because I knew I wouldn't stop. I'd always succumbed to what ever I wanted but this time it felt better not to, to let the yearning for him remain a feeling instead of an action. It pulsated through me as an emotional stimulation, a flywheel collecting and storing rational energy. My heart was a mechanically powered flashlight, and without even knowing it he was winding me. I felt like I might erupt in a giant ball of flaming light. I tried my best to stay calm.

"Connor?" I turned and looked at him, he was staring at me. "I love you." I tried not to say it back. I tried so hard because I wasn't sure my voice would even work, not with what I was feeling.

"I love you too." I could barely hear myself over my pounding pulse, beating it's way out of my chest. And I gave in. I turned to him, and I kissed him; as our lips touched all of the built up energy, the compounding light he'd built up in me, poured between us, tethering us together. A frenzy couldn't describe the chaos, the warmth and tangled nervous systems between the two of us. I kissed and felt my tongue in his mouth, felt him breathing heavily, felt him getting hard, trying not to make a sound, trying to convince himself that we should stop because someone might hear us. I kissed his neck, ran my hands over him. I took off his shirt and he let me. I tore off mine, wanting, as though it were possible, to be closer, more connected. I kissed him again, passionately on the mouth, I tasted him, I welcomed him into my soul, just emotionally pulling him into me the only way I knew how; needing him. I kissed down his collarbone, down his chest, and he let me. He was already shaking. So was I. I kissed his upper hip as I unbuttoned his pants, taking them completely off and he kicked them to the floor. I felt the warmest part of him in my mouth, felt his body tense, a deep inhalation of breath. His breathing quickened and I felt that bursting light inside me wind tighter the more excited he became. He put his hand in my hair, motioning for me to come back up, I did. He was beat red, staring at me, surprised at himself, at us. I pushed his hair out of his face and really looked at him. I did, I loved him. I loved him with everything I'd ever had. He was still trembling, he was excited, he was deeply embarrassed and open at the same time. It took everything inside me but I began mustering the courage to tell him that we could stop if he wanted to, that we could just go to bed… it didn't have to be tonight.

"Connor…" It barely came out as words, "Can we…" He gave no indication of stopping. He gave no hesitation, no want to call it quits. I took off my remaining articles of clothing, I pulled us under the blankets of his bed, I pulled him against me, feeling the warmth of his skin all over me, each touch bursting with a rippling effect of intensity; heat. I heard him laugh, comfortably, in complete disbelief, trusting me with every atom in his entire being… a metaphysical disarray of losing ourselves in one another. I heard his laugh turn into heavy breathing, I felt his hands, under mine, gripping into the bed….

And afterward, sweaty and content, we remained a single entity, wrapped up in one another, catching our breathing, still exalting, calmly and comfortably with our kisses, until we closed our eyes and just listened to the sounds of house. Hours went by, and we couldn't bring ourselves to part. It had to have been 2am before either of us said a word.

———

I woke up and the medications had definitely worn off. Why the fuck hadn't I stopped by the pharmacy and picked up the painkillers the doctor prescribed me? I had multiple bruised ribs, I had stitches, my whole body ached, deep seeded bruises that must have grazed against my bones. The inside of my mouth was even swollen. How had I not noticed this before? I didn't want to move, I didn't want to open my eyes, I didn't want to exist. I wanted to hold so still my body wouldn't even notice that I'd accidentally woken up. But to no avail. I was awake, still me, and still in an empty apartment. I pulled my phone out and looked at the time. I'd only been asleep a few hours. Just enough hours for the pills to wear off. I threw my feet out of bed first, pushing the rest of myself up, out of my room and into my kitchen. I pulled the whiskey out of the top shelf, hearing my shoulder pop as I reached up for it. I deserved this; I knew that I did, but self repugnance wasn't an anesthetic.

I poured it into a mug. I opened my patio door, and sat on the balcony with a cigarette. It wasn't too absurdly hot today. Maybe 80 degrees. Somehow, in the shade of my balcony there were still small puddles from the storm that apparently took place last night. I hadn't heard it from my hospital room. The trees and grass from down below still smelled faintly of residual rain aroma. The earth was still moist. I got up and went to grab my laptop, it had been charging. I went back onto the balcony and powered it on. I had to keep my hands busy to keep my brain from thinking. And I had to keep my brain busy to keep my hands from doing something stupid. My right hand was a bulbous, deep shade of purple and swollen. They'd done X-Rays and determined it wasn't broken, thank God. They could have wrapped it, bandaged it, done something for it but I wouldn't let them. I wouldn't be able to type with my hand bandaged. Though, as I typed in my password to unlock my screen there was a searing pain through my palm and up my wrist. It felt as though the small bones were rubbing together, pulling at tangled up veins. When Windows popped up on my screen, I did all of my navigating with my left hand, and left the right to the peon, entry level, cigarette responsibilities.

I didn't quite know what to do with myself on here if I couldn't adequately write. I guess I could proofread... but I knew I'd be forced to edit should I pull up my recent manuscript. I couldn't simply *read* it when there was always a better way to phrase everything. Always another sentence to add, dialogue to alter.

I clicked into my email to read Folly's life threatening macro. But it wasn't from Folly. It was from Liam.

Subject: *I Forgot My Phone*
Message: *I'll be back soon. Don't worry. Focus on feeling better. Don't murder Hank if you can help it. I'm going to see Maggie for her Birthday; didn't want her to be alone since you couldn't make it.*
I miss you…
And I still love you.. you stupid, suicidal, trouble-seeking maniac.

-Liam.

I read the words four or five times. Even mumbled them out loud on the last read. I leaned back in my chair, putting my hands behind my head, knowing my body needed to stretch, despite the pain, my cigarette hanging delicately from my mouth. I stared up at the rafters above me.. at the spiderwebs between the wood. The way it shadowed next to the deep blue backdrop of a storm ridden sky. *And I still love you.. you stupid, suicidal, trouble-seeking maniac.* I could hear him saying it, in his own voice, ringing through my ears. *And I still love you.* It was the first time he'd said it since he came back. How should I reply? I wanted to write him a whole novel in that email. I wanted to delicately type phrase my apology. The email almost felt like a scapegoat from heaven, to be able to write how I felt instead of wait for him to come back. But this hand wouldn't let me make it as eloquent as it needed to be.

And I didn't sound like myself. To be fair… I didn't feel like myself.

255

Message: *Please. Come **home** soon.*

Out of the billions of sentences I thought up, the beautiful descriptions of my ostentatious waves of guilt and remorse...that's all I put. I made 'home' bold. I *felt* bold, even having the fucking balls to ask him for that. To come home. They were the words I'd wanted to scream at him over the Atlantic Ocean after Mom died.

I felt awful that I'd missed Mom's birthday. I felt worse that I hadn't even thought of it. I wanted to blame it on the drugs; it felt fair but it didn't ease my conscience. My "con-science". I thought about my love for words, how it was inherited through her. I thought about how she'd held me in her lap in second grade, reading me a book as I tried to follow along. I'd never felt so inept, but I couldn't remember which one it was, and by the time I'd realized I hadn't filed away its title in my memory she was already gone. Instinctively I tried to push thoughts of her out of my head... and then scolded myself. Not after forgetting her birthday. She had taught me the word "conscience", which was poetic. She was the one that gave me one too. She'd told me it meant 'Con', my name, and 'science'. She told me it was defined as "the Science of Con". My own special word. I pronounced it wrong all the way through the 3rd grade. I'd never forgiven her.

I was glad he went. I wasn't just glad that 'someone' was there. I was glad it was him. He probably needed her as much as she ever needed him. I didn't believe in the afterlife. I genuinely believed that once someone is gone....they're just simply gone. No waiting for their loved ones in the afterlife, no haunting specific houses, or visiting people in their dreams. They just left, and ceased to exist. A Christian had approached me after the funeral, tried to convince me of the afterlife. He said that she was waiting for me, up in heaven, with Christ. It was disgusting, in hindsight, how badly I'd wanted to believe him in that moment, how badly I'd wished that was true. Especially when I realized, if it were true, the same man also believed I'd never make it back to her because of the love I shared with Liam. He believed her to be in heaven, and that I, a premarital, homosexual, fornicator would be sizzling on the grill of purgatory to celebrate the grand festival of eternity.

Somewhere, deep in the hidden folders of my laptop where a multitude of letters that I'd written right after Mom's death. To just about everyone. I didn't speak for at least a year... I finished out my senior year of highschool in a daze somehow; the motivation inside me purely driven by Mom's repeated yearning for me to walk the stage. Somehow, there was a childish wonder, stagnate in disbelief, harboring the thought that if I walked the stage, somehow, against all common sense and the somatic fixture that was the imperishability of death...she'd come back. And after graduation is when I'd really...really... broken.

Hank was the one who told me she was gone. He'd had me go with him to the hospital, down into the morgue. To see her. For closure. I knew that if death were a color, it wouldn't be black. It would be a fleshy blue. I knew that I'd never get that empty, blank, stare... her penetrating yolky eyes that once belonged to the illustrious Maggie Shay out of my head. I tried to shake it off. I went to sip on my whiskey, but I gulped it down instinctively.

Jenifer came in the front door, totting some fast food. She had the same distaste for cooking that Mom had.

"Hey, you're up." I came into the living room, leaving the patio door open to let some of the AC out of the apartment that kept me shivering to my core. Maybe it wasn't the AC.

"I'm up." I repeated, landing on the couch.

"I brought you food." I wondered where her recent hip attachment, Jeff, was. She didn't make eye contact with me; set the food on the coffee table and started rummaging through the bags.

257

She'd brought home hamburgers. I couldn't quite think of eating. She had another bag, from the pharmacy. She'd picked up my pain meds. I did take those when offered and swallowed a few down with a Dr. Pepper she'd brought me. "I'm sorry, Con, I never know what kind of food to bring sick people. Especially when fast food soup isn't really a thing…" she was fishing for things to talk about. I could tell. She spoke more quickly when she was nervous.

"Jenny. I'm sorry for what I said." She looked at me.

"What? When?"

"When I told you to stop coming. Never stop coming, please." I really didn't feel like myself. She clearly didn't know how to respond to the stranger I'd become.

"Of course I won't, Dumbass." She handed me some french fries and looked at me angrily for getting soft on her. It made me smile. It was either her acceptance, Liam's email, or the drugs that allowed me to smile. "Connor. We missed Mom's birthday this year."

"Yeah. I know. It's my fault. I'm sorry."

"Jesus Christ, stop apologizing. It's creeping me out a little. Are you dying?" I laughed.

"No. Not right now. We're all dying, relatively, but I'm not going out any quicker than anyone else." And then she laughed; my comrade in dark-humor arms;

"Well, kinda. With the amount of cigarettes you smoke. I'm sure you're dying quicker than most." She started to unwrap her burger. "I'm just glad she wasn't alone yesterday."

"What? You knew where Liam was? Why wouldn't you tell me when I asked?"

"No, Dad left and went home the night before. Remember?" She looked at me, gauging that I was really feeling ok. Everyone seemed concerned about me lately. First Liam, when I'd gotten really sick after binge drinking. Now Jenny, after putting myself yet again in a precarious situation of self harm. There was a correlation I refused to acknowledge. I couldn't tell if the difference between now and the past 9 years was just that people were around, or if, I was hitting some sort of 'two roads diverging in the woods'.

"Oh. Right."

"So Liam went to see Mom?" I nodded. She always had questions burning through her, she was always holding back. As intense and satisfying it would be to solve the mysteries that have been brewing over the years, she never cared more about the truth than she did about me. I knew she deserved to know. This was her God-given right since being born into the same family. And I was going to tell her, eventually. It was a fact I'd already accepted, a long time ago. I just wasn't ready.

"Jeff sort of explained what happened that night, about Claire." I wondered if he *really* explained. "She's a bitch, obviously. Not just for what she did that night, but for how she's been treating Jeff for the past couple years. I kinda hate her. You have a really dramatic life for a loner." She leaned back in the chair, sat criss cross applesauce like she did when she was little and it lit a calmness in me; a sort of safe space. It felt like lighting a candle of your favorite aroma. It would never be the thing it was pretending to be, but at least it smelled the same. She took a drink of her pepsi.

"What do you mean, doing to Jeff?" She stared at me sort of blankly.

"You know, the fact that Jeff's been in love with her since they met?" I didn't know that. "She's just been dragging him along in the friend zone all these years. I can't even imagine. He's flawed, but I don't think he deserves that." That was interesting. I thought back to all their encounters, the way he came to her rescue

259

all the time, the way he always answered his phone when she called, regardless of the importance of his current environment. *Huh. That makes sense.* I really had been self centered. I hadn't ever noticed. I wondered how he could be my friend…

"What about you?" I asked her. "You've been pretty friendly with him the past few days. Are you considering test driving that?" I felt like we were teenagers again, taking a walk toward my old High School football field.

"Fuck no." she laughed. "I make it a point not to fall in love with people who are already in love with someone else. That's retarded. You're just hurting yourself, and making their lives more complicated. It's stupid." She paused, then added, "He's nice though, I like him as a person. Alot." She chewed some food and kept going. "I don't know. It's gotten kind of lonely in Europe. I have friends, don't get me wrong, it's just that…" I could tell she wasn't getting emotional or anything, just trying to find the right words. "I don't know.'

I smiled at her. "You missed me?" She laughed.

"Yes. Fine. I fucking missed you. Are you happy?" It made me feel guilty for leaving her by herself in the world. I'd apparently hesitated too long. "Hey, Fuckface, this is the part where you tell me you missed me too." I laughed.

"I did. I missed you." The pain through my body was starting to feel less pronounced.

"Thank you. Shit. It's like pulling teeth." She was so relaxed, so open. She wasn't jaded. She didn't hide anything. She laughed when she wanted, she was kind, and she didn't appear to have hate in her heart. And every year she showed up, when she knew I'd be at my lowest, making sure I never landed in a gutter somewhere. And she'd lost her mother too. the same way I had. Maybe it was easier because she was never pissed off at Hank, or maybe it was easier because she hadn't loved so intensely and had her soul ripped apart at the same time, or maybe it was easier because she didn't have the traumatizing image of Mom's dead body forever crawling through her subconscious... but then again, maybe it wasn't.

"I've never asked you. Are you ok?" She cocked her head slightly, not understanding.

"Um. Yeah. I'm fine..."

"How?"

"How what?"

"How are you fine?"

"Regarding..." We weren't on the same wavelength. I didn't communicate as efficiently on pain pills and whiskey.

"I mean, you're just effervescent. Every year. On Mom's birthday." She thought for a moment.

"Because Mom was effervescent. I don't think she would have cared."

"Cared that she was murdered?"

"Yep." She took another drink of her coke. "Mom never cared about herself. All she ever cared about was us, and if we were happy, and if we felt 'strong, and brave, and capable'." Jenny laughed, fondly remembering and grabbed a napkin off the coffee table to be able to wipe up some of the condensation that was dripping off of her cup. So relaxed, in her blue jeans and one of my Tshirts she'd swiped. "Con, I don't get sad when I think about Mom. I did, for a long time, obviously. I'm not heartless. But after meeting so many people...hearing their stories. I just get happy. Happy to have had her to begin with. It's sad what happened, with that guy Dad used to work with... and I've always worried about you both. But She's gone. I'm not worried about her anymore. You can't keep worrying either, ya know?" I... I didn't know. I'd never once thought of it that way. I didn't know how to digest what she was saying. "Oh!" she added, pulling out her phone.

"What?"

"You'll never guess who I got back in touch with right before I came home!" I started eating some french fries. I needed to be fucking *doing* something...grading or writing or studying... I was wondering oddly if this was ok. If just... relaxing with Jenny in my living room in the early afternoon, eating fast food and talking lightly was ok...

"Who?"

"Andrea!"

"Woah, that's a blast from the past." I hadn't heard that name in a long time. I eyed her suspiciously. "Did you uh... 'get in touch with her', or *'get in touch with her'*?" I teased. She almost choked on her fries. And gave me a confident, condescending smirk.

"I'm not even going to answer that. I'm going to wait till you come and visit me, out of the goodness of your heart, and then I'm going to tear through the doorway, sucking face with a lady-friend, with my hand down her pants." I openly laughed then. A sound that startled myself, and it didn't stop. It was infectious, making her laugh at her own joke. She eyed my cigarettes, and looked at me, as if asking my permission. *Fuck no.* I still didn't like it. But I handed them to her begrudgingly. She wasn't just my little sister anymore, she was a fully grown adult. She took the pack and headed to the patio since the door was open. I watched her light it and lean against the railing looking at the road below. "This is amazing, you can really see this whole side of the campus from here! What were you like, Con? As a dorky little freshman straight out of highschool?"

I got up to join her, slowly, trying not to arouse any pulsating pain. I wondered how Liam was feeling. From what I'd heard, he'd taken quite a beating as well. I didn't ever remember being a dorky freshman fresh out of high school. I remembered being a broken mute; miserable, angry, and alone. I remembered learning the true definition of 'to miss'. To recall any sort of second of happiness was quickly followed by my atoms breaking apart and slowly sinking into the matter of the ground beneath me till I couldn't breathe, move, or feel. It was the whole world moving around me while I stood still, in the middle, watching the months on the calendar change slow and consistent. It was beating my conscience to death on a whim for not being able to remember the sound of Mom's voice, or how I felt the first time Liam and I kissed. It was this view… and my obsession with writing and literature that kept me waking up every morning and made the world endurable. I looked down at the scenery with Jen as she pointed to a cab, taking a puff of her cigarette.

"That's him, that's Liam. He's home." I watched him exit the cab and hand the cabby a card to pay for the ride. "Liam!" She called out. "Oy! Liam!" she beamed down at him. He looked up, saw us both, and smiled. Relief flooded over me. Happiness flooded over me. Mom never intended me to miss. She never intended for me to be alone in the world. And she absolutely never intended me to be such a weak piece of shit that I couldn't chase and hold on to happiness when it was right in front of me.

CHAPTER 11: MY END OF THE EXCHANGE

Connor was next to me, holding me, and I was still slightly shivering. I couldn't help it. I'd never done anything like that before. I'd never even dreamed of kissing someone before I came here; feeling like the climax of my love life would be stifling all inappropriate feelings and just hoping day to day that no one found out I wasn't attracted to girls. And here I was... a week, shaking mess, naked in Con's arms, having just lost my virginity to who, I knew, would be the love of my life. I felt my pulse in my fingertips, still felt him against me, warm; his heart racing at the same speed as mine. Calming down at the same speed as mine. Skin drying at the same speed as mine. I turned into him, catching his expression. Even in this unbelievable bliss, there was still the hesitation inside me, the nagging disbelief that I was allowed to be happy, that perhaps we'd gone too far. This would be the moment that he would realize the whole idea of us being together was disgusting. I looked at him and saw him calculating my expressions, the same way I was calculating his. I didn't think I saw regret. Would he be able to hide it?

I blushed thinking about how different it felt. Different than anything I'd expected...though I hadn't been sure what to expect. There was a flurry of emotion inside me. It felt like I'd rid myself of a giant secret; as though I no longer had anything to hide. Did this change anything? My body felt changed. I didn't feel so ashamed anymore... I didn't feel so disgusted being myself. This was my very first time... I knew that Con had had sex plenty of times before. But this was his first with a guy... I couldn't figure out how he felt. Had I somehow taken advantage of him again?

He closed his eyes and he sighed, not looking at me as he said;

"Don't do it." I hadn't said anything.

"Don't do what?"

"Don't fucking apologize. I mean it." He pulled me into him and I wondered when exactly he'd started being able to read my thoughts. I didn't apologize.

"I love you." I told him. He grinned and kissed me warmly, familiarly.

"Is that code for you want to go again?" I laughed, kissing him back. I'd never experienced this kind of euphoria. I turned away from him, somehow embarrassed again, after everything we'd done, he pulled me toward him, I let him. I lay there, tracing my fingertips over his forearm, needing to do something with my hands. Needing to slow down my thoughts.

My whole life I'd felt like I was born *wrong*. Like I'd never belong anywhere. I always assumed, deep down, that my parents lack of affection toward me was self inflicted somehow, and everyone else would be the same. The isolation wasn't suffocating back then, it was expected, it was all I ever knew. After meeting Con, after knowing him, like I tried to tell him earlier, I finally felt like I belonged somewhere. Someone had seen me for exactly who I was; weak, pathetic, usually kind of stupid... scared. And still loved me. Accepted all parts of me. To the last inch of my bare naked skid, huddled under the blankets together, kissing my ear as I touched on his arm. I could feel his smile in my hair, I could taste his happiness just through the scent of his shampoo on my pillow. He loved me and somehow, the nothingness that I'd always felt I was, made him happy. And I wasn't nothing anymore. I'd love Connor Shay forever.

"I think I'm going to love you forever, Con." He paused his kisses and gave my confession a moment of thought. Genuinely considering.

"Please do." There was a comfortable silence. The 'whirring' of the ceiling fan providing the backdrop of comfort as I slowly started to fall asleep in his arms. I heard rain start to hit the windowpane. A heavy rain. It was calming.

I heard his parents door open. It had to have been significantly late. Maybe Hank needed to use the restroom and didn't want to wake Maggie?

I heard him knock on Connor's bedroom door. Con bolted up next to me. He silently crawled out of bed, throwing on his boxers, his pants. I remembered how nonchalant he'd been when his mom almost caught me in his room this morning. This was the exact opposite. He mouthed words at me. 'Liam, put on your clothes...'. His urgency had my heart racing. I jumped quietly out of bed and found my boxers, put on my pants, threw on my shirt. Mid-pants I heard a knock on Con's bedroom door again.

"Connor?" It was Hank. I heard his door open. "Connor? We need to talk." *What could he possibly need to talk about this late at night?* We heard him realize Connor wasn't in his room. We heard him check the living-room. I heard him at my door and we didn't know what to do. There was no 'acting natural' at this time of night. And our skin was still glowing, the bed was still in disarray, and a redness would not go away all over my being. I saw Connor take a deep inhalation of breath and close his eyes as my door opened, clearly trying to shake off whatever nervousness or anxiety had taken over.

"What are you two doing up?" Hank flipped on the lights. He saw Connor leaning against my dresser with his arms folded. He saw me standing like a complete fool, in jeans, next to my disheveled bed. Neither of us made eye contact with him. My body was shaking for entirely different reasons now and felt myself paling out. "What the fuck were you two doing?" I smelled alcohol on his breath and became all the more scared. How much could he possibly have had to drink in the time we'd all been home from the restaurant?

"It's none of your fucking business." Con muttered, motioning to push passed him, out of the room. Hank stopped him, looking him directly in the eye... looking back at me. He shook his head.. a disbelief enveloping his normal drunken rage. He was trying to repress it.. and couldn't. He was staring straight at his son but deep in his eyes he wasn't there at all. His growling rasp rang through the air. He didn't have a son.

"You piece of fucking, human garbage." He slammed his fist into Connor's jaw and pushed him away from him, to the floor. Con looked up at his Dad... hallow... and laughed.

"If I'm garbage than the apple doesn't fall far then, does it, Dad?" Hank absolutely lost it, he reached down, grabbed Connor by the throat and threw him on the bed. The frame hit against the headboard, knocking a book off of the bedside table. He hit him again. And again. *What have I done?* I lunged in and grabbed his arm, but I was practically a gnat.

"Stop! Stop it... Please, Hank...stop" I was yelling. I heard Maggie rip open the door to her bedroom, running in in her nightgown and robe, confused. She immediately jumped between Hank and Connor and I pushed myself to the back of the room, not knowing what on bloody earth to do. As soon as Hank saw Maggie it's like he woke up, he started to back off. She was fuming, shoving him, vehement.

"Don't you ever lay a hand on *my* fucking son." She hit him in the face slamming him in the chest, pushing him away from Connor. He'd slunk off the bed. He was on his hands and knees on the floor trying to get his head straight. "Who the fuck are you Hank? Who the Fuck do you think you are?" She was so angry she was crying. She pushed him out of the room against the bathroom door. I ran to Connor.

"Con..." He was silent, looking down; I couldn't see his face. He was shivering. I put my hand on his shoulder. My throat

267

was constricting, listening to Maggie screaming at Hank in the hallway. "Con..." He reached up and took my hand in his, still not looking up, and he put it to his lips, and he kissed it. It felt wet. I felt him shaking. Connor was crying. I didn't.... I didn't think it was from the pain. I heard him gasp in a delicate breath of air, and the shaking immediately stopped. He wiped his face. When he did finally look up, he was furious. I heard his soft, ironic, chuckle, and for once, it didn't put me at ease.

Hank was now screaming at Maggie in retaliation.

"God Damnit Margaret, he's not my Son! He's not my Son anymore!" I heard her slap him across the face. It resounded through the whole house. *What had I done?* Connor walked out of my room, and I followed. He stepped into his room, I followed. I watched him grab his backpack, throw in a random assortment of clothes, he threw on a shirt, and made his way to the living room. In the hallway he stopped, and he looked back at me.

"Liam. I love you. I just have to leave tonight."

"No, I'll come with you."

"Hank's too worried about impressing your Dad. He's not going to hurt you. He's not going to let you leave. I'll be back tomorrow." He was devoid of expression. He couldn't afford to let himself feel anything.

"Ok." I wished I could think of anything else to say... I didn't agree... it didn't feel ok. How could he be so composed when I...I wasn't.

He walked into the living room, with his backpack already on.

"I never asked to be your son." He said it in a normal voice, completely composed. "I *fucking* hate you Hank. You're never laying a finger on me again." Maggie got between them again, her body language always trying to protect Connor. Even from the things he might regret saying.

"Con, honey..." She was a mess. A wild mess. Half crying, half fuming. He pulled her into him, and kissed her on the cheek,

"It's ok Mom, I'm fine." He looked back at Hank, vehemently. "And if you hurt her... more than you already have... I promise you, Hank, I *will* fucking kill you." She pulled away from him, they were almost eye level.

"Connor!" she scolded, about to yell at him. But he cut her off.

"No, Mom. I mean it." He carefully wiped a residual tear from her face and moved some hair from sticking to her cheek. They locked eyes and for the briefest of seconds, they were the only two people in the world. Completely understanding one another. And then he left them both dumbfounded. I watched him shut the door behind him without looking back. He'd left us all dumbfounded. There was a huge pang in my gut as the door slammed shut. I was invisible. I backed back into the hallway and leaned against the wall, sliding to the floor. *What had I done?*

I heard Maggie continue in the living room. I'd never heard her voice so emotionless. So low.

"Have you hit him before?" She asked him outright. He didn't answer. "Have you ever hit my fucking son before?" I didn't hear him say anything and I couldn't see them. "You need to leave." I looked around the corner and saw Hank stand up. He started walking toward his keys hanging by the door. She grabbed them from him. "No." I watched him look at her, tears welling in his eyes, his drunkenness probably slipping away from him, realizing what he'd done. As he should.

"Mags. I love you. I'm so sorry. I'll make it right with Connor, I promise you. I don't know... I don't know what's wrong with me." but she didn't have any sympathy.

"Get out of my house, Hank." He left without his keys, without a jacket, without his wallet. There was a crackle of thunder as he'd left the door open behind him. It had really started storming. The pounding of raindrops on the driveway resounded into the house. Maggie didn't forget me.

"Liam?" I stood up and walked into the living-room. I wasn't a Shay. I couldn't hide anything. "Come here."

"I... I didn't mean..." I started to say.

"Not a single part of this is on you. There's nothing wrong with You and Con. Nothing at all. This is all on Hank. You didn't do this. Do you understand me?" She hadn't even taken a moment to compose herself, she hadn't needed one. She went straight to comforting me. She even smiled. I had no idea what she was thinking.

I nodded but I didn't believe her. *What the fuck have I done?* I kept asking myself over and over. I wondered where Connor went. Not ten minutes ago, we were in bed. We were happy. Not ten minutes ago.

"It's going to be ok Liam, this doesn't change anything. Hank's going to quit drinking, completely, after this. And he won't be welcome in this house until he does. If Con lets him." She walked into the kitchen, opening the refrigerator and pulling out a Dr. Pepper. Maggie spoke with confidence but the slight trembling in her hands gave her away. She took a drink. "It's going to be ok." She stared off, just a bit, and repeated it one more time. "It's going to be ok." Neither of us got up to close the door. The rain outside was almost comforting. I sat at the kitchen table, where I could see it falling outside, focusing in on the lull of cascading droplets. She sat across from me with her back to the door. We needed the sound of the storm to drown out the emptiness of our home for just a moment, at least.

"Mrs. Shay. I should never have come here. I'm sorry." I meant it. I could barely list all the things I was sorry for.

She waved my apology away with her shaky hand. "Those two have been at each other's throats way before you got here, Liam. This *isn't* your fault." She reached out and folded her fingers into mine lovingly. "The only thing you've brought into this house is Happiness. For me and Connor. And I wouldn't have changed a goddamn thing. I swear." She smiled away the tension in my shoulders. I took my first real breath since Hank came into my room. Somehow she looked into my soul. "Liam, if you two fall out of love after growing up a little, that's fine... whether you're with Con or not, you'll always be my kid, ok?" She paused, clearly wondering how much more parental advice she could drop into this moment with me, a moment she knew I'd never forget. She smiled and half laughed toward me; "If you decide to go home after this, I don't blame you. But I'm sending Con with you, because I've never seen him so happy in my entire life." Her eyes really did light up, and it made me smile. Even after the emotional chaos that was tonight as a whole. I didn't ever want to leave her.

"I'm not going anywhere." A confidence escaped my lips that I wasn't sure had ever been there before. I noticed movement behind her head, and leaned slightly. Expecting to see Hank or Con in the doorway.

It wasn't either of them.

A soaking, unfamiliar trench coat stepped out of the shadows, right into the house... Maggie saw the fear in my face immediately and shot up out of her seat. I did too. "Liam, Liam, get behind me." I didn't. I wanted to get in front of her.

"Where's Shay?" He asked. He stared at her, dead in the eyes. His emaciated face was sunken and sullen, dark eyes, expanded pupils, a fearfully unstable disposition. She put her hands out, as if trying to calm a startled horse.

"James... James, Hank isn't here. He's not here... he left. It's just me." I could hear a tremble in her voice. The man had a gun,

271

hanging loosely at his side. Dripping water all over the carpet. What had he been doing, wandering around at this hour in the storm?

"Bullshit." He smiled as he said it; an empty smile, a confident head shake of disapproval.

"Jennings, I swear. He's not here. We had a fight, I made him leave."

"He's *really* not here, Sir." I said. He needed to believe her. Mr. Jennings looked over at me. He motioned at me with the gun, still talking to Maggie.

"That's not Connor. Is that the one messing with David?" He had no tone inflections, he only half cared, as if none of that mattered anymore. He was an empty shell of a man. She answered too quickly.

"No. No it's not. He went home. This is my nephew." She lied for me. He could tell.

"You're lying, Mags. Why are you fucking lying to me?" He lifted his hand with the gun, uncomfortably wiping water from his face, stressed, numb. Maggie hurried around the table and stood directly in front of me. He didn't pull the trigger.

"JAMES. Hank isn't here. You need to leave my house before I call the police." He laughed slightly then.

"Oh, what will they do... arrest me?" He walked closer and pointed his gun directly at her, and she froze, becoming gentle again.

"You've known me since we were kids, Jimmy." She walked toward him, I knew that I should grab her, pull her back, but I didn't. I *knew* I should have... but I *didn't*. I was frozen. "I did everything I could to get you back on your feet when you got out of jail, remember? You're not going to shoot me. I'm telling you, Hank isn't here." His eyes squinted, thinking darkly, coming

272

to a conclusion, locking his jaw in resolution and shaking his head emphatically.

"I'm not going back." He practically whispered to her. And then he yelled it.

"I'M NOT GOING BACK!" I couldn't see his hands, she was blocking my view, and I saw her jump out of her skin. The gun shot rattled the entire house. She'd reached him, and already had her hand on the gun when it went off... Her grip tightened on his, in shock, before she fell to the floor. I made a movement toward her and he pulled the gun on me. He didn't shoot. There were tears flowing out of my eyes that I didn't even understand yet. He looked down at her body. He looked back up at me. His eyes were huge and I could tell he was panicking. I was just frozen... thinking that I needed to get to Maggie, before it was too late. I took another step forward, and he backed up. He turned, gun in hand and ran out the door back into the rain. I fell to the floor with Mrs. Shay, and pulled her into my lap. There was blood all over her nightgown, in her hair. On her cheek.

"Maggie... Mrs. Shay... I brushed hair out of her face, water was pouring from my eyes... "it's okay", I reminded her. "Its okay." I stared at her in disbelief. The first person in the entire world to really love me...Connor's mother... "It's okay." I jumped at the shot I heard outside. I was scared, but I couldn't move. I just held her. "It's okay." I whispered.

Hank suddenly came rushing through the door, soaked, out of breath.

"Jennings, his car, it's in the driveway, I heard a shot..." I looked up at him, holding Maggie.

"Mr. Shay..." I said.... "Mr. Shay, she..." I was crying. I didn't know what she was. She couldn't be.

He came over and fell to his knees next to her. He grabbed her from me, he held her. I couldn't move. "Get... Get away from her." He said to me, his eyes clouded, angrily refusing to accept what was happening. I couldn't move. He held her into him. He sobbed. Grotesquely, loudly. "GET AWAY FROM HER!" He screamed at me. I backed up against the table. She was okay. She was okay. She was okay.

"Mr. Shay... is she..." I wanted to ask if she was okay. I was frozen next to the table.

There was no concept of time.

I heard police cars, I heard ambulances. Someone had heard the shot and called it in. They came in... in their uniforms, they pulled Hank away from her. They checked her pulse. I wanted to ask *them* if she was okay. She'd said everything was okay. They took her body away on a stretcher, covered in a blanket; I slightly reached out. Wait.

One policeman had taken Hank to the side and was just saying words at him. He didn't appear to be listening. I saw them point to me. I hadn't moved. I wasn't sure I'd even breathed. A lady police officer knelt down next to me. I hadn't realized I was covered in Maggie's blood.

"Liam...? It's Liam, right? Are you alright, can you hear me?" I was staring toward Hank and the other policeman. "Liam?" I didn't answer. My mind went blank.

Somehow we were standing in the Police Station. People had asked me my account. I told them in a trance. They'd given me non blood curdled clothing. They'd called my parents. Mom and Dad had sent for me to come home immediately. I heard Hank also tell the police that they would be talking to their lawyers, that my name was not to be mentioned in any papers. That I was not to be mentioned in any reports, and that they'd pay whatever they had to. I thought we'd go back to the house. I thought I'd see Connor. I didn't. Hank pulled me aside, before leaving me at the police station;

"William, Don't you dare tell Connor." I looked at him. I was empty... "don't you dare tell Connor you were there. You tell him, I threw you in a cab and sent you home, before Jennings got there. Do you understand?"

"Why."

"You were never there." It's all he said... before he turned around and left.

The police drove me to the airport, watched me get on my flight. Everyone did everything for me. I just... I walked. That's all I did. I didn't speak, I didn't pack, I didn't... do anything. I thought about Jennings in the doorway with the gun... I *didn't* do anything. I thought about Maggie... in my arms... I didn't *do* anything. Maggie asked Hank to fire him because of *me*. Hank had fired him because of *me*. Hank and Connor weren't home... because of *me*. Maggie was.... she was dead. Because of *me*.

The memory of Connor standing on the park basketball court, telling me he liked me for the first-time...Connor dancing with his Mom in the living room, smiling down at her... the only images that would hold still in the giant raging whirlpool of my mind.

———

I stood in front of the door. I didn't know how to turn the knob. I hadn't slept well at the hotel at all. Talking to Hank and Gideon had resurrected some of my frequent unpleasant dreams. I hadn't had them for quite some time before coming back here. My shoes were still kind of wet. I looked down at them, lightly wiggling my toes, slightly dismayed. I looked up, at the door, it was time. I reached for the knob and couldn't open it again.

Jen yanked the door open with a bright familiar smile. She immediately pulled me into a hug.

"We were worried about you! You should have told us you were leaving. We thought you went back to Europe you big Jerk." She pulled me into the apartment. I looked around for Con and saw him standing on the balcony still, not looking at me, not acknowledging my presence. I wondered what he was thinking, how he was feeling. I set my backpack down and scratched the back of my head where a headache was throbbing; smiling back at her.

"Sorry about that. I get a little impulsive."

"Ugh. You look like shit too. The bruising is so much darker already." she reached up and moved my face back and forth, eyeing my black eye and other ailments. Honestly, I hadn't paid them much attention. It hurt, yeah, but Brent and I had gotten into plenty of scraps the last few months; along with the rest of my bandmates. I hadn't even taken any pills the doctors had offered to me. I was always wary of just how much delight I'd taken from the array of pills and liquor that I'd torn my solace from back home.

"I'm okay, I promise. Hardly feel a thing." And then I sneezed, feeling my white-lie tremble through my aches and pains. I had felt kind of clammy, out in the rain, and hadn't quite shaken it from my bones. I thought perhaps it was more so from the secrets inside me, inhaling all of my fervor. I'd taken a hot shower back at the hotel, but still, the chill clung to me.

The last time I saw Con was in the hospital bed, still out of it. Still asleep. Before that... he'd been in my arms, unconscious on the floor... and there had been blood, just like before. I slowly walked to the balcony, Jen followed. He avoided eye contact, staring down at the street below. And then lower, toward his bare feet on the concrete.

"Welcome home." He said, still not looking at me. I'd never seen him like this. We'd completely reversed rolls. I was the shy awkward one, nursing shame in the pit of stomach at all times. I didn't say anything, I reached out to him and pulled him into me. I hugged him; gratefully. Grateful for the smell in his hair, for the warmth in his body... grateful for the sound of his voice that I'd still get to hear for the rest of my life. I was grateful for Jen, leaning in the doorway... safe and sound. And Connor was still here with me.

I knew he was okay when I'd left, the Doctor had said so. But I hadn't *seen* him be ok. I think... I think maybe... aside from Maggie, aside from the birthday, there was a small part of me that believed he wouldn't actually wake up. That someone would tear him from my arms and throw me on a plane back to Europe. But here he was. I hugged him tighter, a constriction developing in my throat, and he let me. He began to realize I was acting strangely and hugged me back. His hand placed on the small of my back, pulling me into him, his other gently on the back of my head, my hair sliding through his fingers.

"Liam? Are *you* okay?" he asked.

"Yes." I lied. I lied through my teeth. I wasn't ok. None of this was fair. None of it. He was here, he was ok. We were together and everything could just be...fine. It could be okay. But I couldn't let it. Con pulled away from me and finally gave me a concerned once-over. Usually he'd be a blank expression, he'd laugh and light a cigarette and say something shitty to lighten the mood. But he didn't. I saw a flash of guilt strike over his face upon seeing my sadness. And probably seeing my beating.

He didn't need to feel guilt. I was almost certain that I'd hurt them far more than any of them had hurt me. They'd definitely deserved it.

"You two are soooo fucking dramatic." Jen laughed from the doorway and I was immediately thankful for her presence. Connor laughed. He kissed the top of my head and made his way into the apartment, slowly and calculated. I could tell he was avoiding any excess movement. He grabbed his small whiskey glass on the way in and made his way to the kitchen where his half empty bottle was sitting. I made a note in my head of just how handsome he looked... even at his shittiest. He poured a new glass. Usually I'd interject... I'd snatch it away from him and urge him to eat real food. But I was about to completely demolish his world, so I may have owed him this. I took a deep breath. And then we spoke at the same time;

"I have to tell you something." Our eyes locked peculiarly and I watched his wall, his defence mechanism of detachment glaze over. He took a sip of his whiskey. Jen sat on the couch, comfortably crossing her legs beneath her. I wondered if I should ask to speak to him alone. But that didn't feel right; if I was going to come clean she deserved to know as well. He smiled at me; a real smile. And he looked down again, almost bashful.

"Thank god." he said, "You go first." I really, really, really didn't want to go first. I knew I'd really be going last. He leaned against the kitchen counter, giving me all of his attention. I was just going to spit it out. I was going to just spit it out all at once and be done with it. Everything would be over. I'd lose him, but at least.... at least we would both really *know*. There'd be no more secrets.

"When your Mom died nine years ago..." His eyes sort of widened. He hadn't seen this coming. I knew Jen was aptly listening behind me as well; my back was toward her and I could feel her gaze penetrating the back of my skull. "When Maggie died, I wasn't already on my to the airport." I waited for him to say something.

278

"Okay." He took another sip.

"I was there. I was there with her, I stayed with her." The words started piling out a little faster. "You left, after Hank went mad, and then she kicked him out.... she... she took his keys so he wouldn't dive drunk, and he left. It was just she and I, and we were just... we were talking." He never broke eye contact. That stoic version of himself that I, just now, was beginning to resent. "Your Dad, he...he left the door open. It was raining."

"I remember." He stated, factually. He wasn't reacting at all. Connor, for some reason, was holding his whiskey glass with his left hand. I noticed how tightly he was gripping the glass, the tips of his fingers were slightly pale. I worried it might break.

"And Jennings, he … he walked right in..." I didn't know how to say it.

"Liam. Stop." Con looked at me, exhausted, rough. But I didn't.

"He walked in, he was going on about not going back to Jail, for whatever that means."

"Stop." I couldn't though, I'd come too far.

"And I was there, I said something stupid, and she moved... she got in front of me to protect me..." I guess I hadn't quite realized how shaky my voice was becoming.

"Please." He said. "Stop talking. Why are you doing this?" He wasn't looking at me, he was looking down at his whiskey glass, shaking his head slowly, calculatingly, rejecting answers to questions he was clearly, silently asking himself in his head.

"Con." I swallowed, "Before she died, she told me… she told me everything was going to be ok." His gaze shot up at me in disbelief; in anger.

"It wasn't; was it?" he shot accusatory. *No. It wasn't.* I told myself, all the way home from Maggie's grave, that I wasn't going to let anything Con said offend me...he couldn't hurt me any more than I was already hurting. His eyes were narrow looking into me. I couldn't begin to imagine what he was feeling. I faltered; I looked down, at my shoes. His voice came out shaking, an attempted repression of the anger I could hear boiling up inside him. "You were there." It wasn't a question, it was a statement.

"Yes." *Because you left me there.* I hated myself for thinking it, but I did. He left me there that night, he left us both. *Because he had to. He couldn't have known what was going to happen.* This wasn't his fault. It was my fault. I felt disgusted with myself for even thinking it. I confessed: "I could have done something... anything...and everything would be different. She got in front of me. I could have pulled her back, *I* could have protected *her.*" Con just stared at me, seething, realizing with me. It was the truth. I could have been gone and Maggie could be standing in this very same kitchen with both of her children, right then.

I heard an annoyed satirical laugh behind me. I'd almost forgotten Jen was still here.

"Fuck you, Liam." I hadn't expected it from Jen... but I knew I deserved it. Con looked over at her. "Fuck you for thinking that Mom was so weak she'd have let a kid take a fucking bullet for her." That's the same sentiment I'd thrown at Hank... one I *knew*, but didn't *feel* to be true. She stood up from the couch and walked over to Connor in the kitchen, snatching his liquor from him and downing it herself. Con corrected her;

"He wasn't a kid."

"He's two years younger than you, we're the same age. He was a fucking kid..." She paused and added, "you predator." laughing again. "I'm kidding; we were all kids." It felt strange. I felt like I was emploding, Con looked like he might want to murder me, Jen... I didn't know what Jen was thinking. It felt surreal, experiencing the moment I'd been dreading for so long. I walked toward Connor and reached out toward him.

"Con, I…"

"Don't fucking touch me." He legitimately flinched away from me. Everything I was worth shrivelled into a ball and dropped to the pit of my stomach.

"Connor, don't be such a Dick…" Jen stood up for me as I sank lower and lower and I wish she wouldn't. I knew this was coming…although, a small part of me didn't *feel* this was coming. No amount of planning can really prepare you for when your heart comes crashing down in a pit of robust fire.

"Jenny… I love you. But you need to leave right now." He shook his head as he said it, going so far as to close his eyes to avoid eye contact.

"No, Fuck you…"

"FUCKING LEAVE." The sound of him yelling at Jen shocked me. It reminded me of Hank. *No.* I grabbed his arm whether he flinched away from me or not. If he was mad at me, if he hated me, it needed to be directed at me. I pulled him toward his bedroom, apologizing lightly to Jen and shut the door. He let me. He walked and stood at the other end of the room.

"You can be as mad at me… you can hate me however you need to; but you don't get to talk to her like that. You know you don't." He laughed, ignoring me.

"Is that why you really came back? To tell me you let Mom die that night?" I didn't respond. *Partially.* "That's why you've been avoiding me? Running out all the time, not reciprocating my affections? You never intended to stay. You just needed to drop this fucking bomb on me so you didn't have to carry it anymore."

"No. That's not it. That's not it at all." He was completely misunderstanding. "I-"

"Just get the fuck out, Liam. You win!" Con's voice quivered. "You just… you fucking win. You want me to hate you, right? That's what you want? Fine. I fucking hate you." He paced…

281

laughed, shook his head angrily...answering more questions I'd never get to hear.

And then he was apathetic… his usual self… completely devoid. Completely apart from me. "Look, I'm sorry. I take it back. You're forgiven, everything's fine. Jen was right, you were just a kid. That's not on you." He didn't even have hate left for me. He was indifferent.

"I'm trying to tell you-" He wouldn't let me finish, let me get a word in edgewise, I started to panic and I watched his soul dying beyond the anger in his eyes.

"I'm sorry, for once, Liam. I'm sorry I ever kissed you...I'm sorry you ever came to our fucking house, I'm sorry we ever met. I'm sorry for the alleyway with Claire's boyfriend, for David fuckin' Jennings back in highschool... I'm sorry I ever loved you." He spoke slow and concise, the way he always had. Confident, unadulterated.

"You're sorry you ever loved me?" I repeated back to him. "Loved?" Past tense. I wasn't supposed to let his words hurt me. My insides weren't supposed to wrenching, my pulse wasn't supposed to be stopping. He didn't mean it… he couldn't have meant it.

"The only thing I'm *more* sorry about, Liam… is leaving her there with *you* that night. And maybe for not slamming my fucking door in your face when you showed up again." I wasn't supposed to let his words hurt me. I couldn't… breathe. But this is what I'd expected. It was what I'd expected. His expression was unflinching, not an ounce of vulnerability. I'd never seen this version of him before... *Wait*... Yes I had...that first night in the kitchen. The night with the lasagna. When he was scared of Hank. Every time he was scared of Hank.

"Connor…" He was going to let me speak, which was a kindness I didn't deserve. But I wasn't going to let him fucking do this. I wasn't going to let him push me away before he got what he needed. "You're afraid. But you need to let me finish." He wasn't expecting that. He just looked at me. I sat on the bed, turning my back to him, facing the door so it would be easier to talk... avoiding eye contact. Behind me, he continued to let me speak. "I... couldn't come back because I thought I'd *killed* Maggie." I knew about fear. It boiled up into my throat, and I shoved it deep inside as tears spilled silently out of me. If this was the last conversation I ever had with him... I wanted to tell him the truth. My whole truth.

"What?"

"Hank fired Jennings because of me. He hit you that night, and you left, because of me. Maggie made Hank leave, a domino effect of everything *I'd* caused. Connor... you lost your mum because the universe gave you *me*." I swallowed hard as he listened. "And this whole time... I thought you'd already realized that. That you...you *hated* me...And I walked through that door and you immediately *loved* me without an ounce of it missing from that last night I saw you. And I remembered what it felt like to be... To not be empty...until I'd noticed that you never realized what I'd *done*." I looked over at him, and he didn't budge. *This is really it.* "I told myself that I was coming to win you back. That I could convince you to stop hating me, and somehow we'd work out. But you *didn't* hate me because you didn't *know*. And I was relieved and terrified... and then I couldn't tell you because I was afraid." I breathed somehow; a survival instinct in my DNA I hardly noticed. "I wanted to do the right thing... you bloody well have to believe that I wanted to.. but I just couldn't...I couldn't lose you ... I couldn't wait another nine years for you to forgive me. I don't have another 9 years in me to learn how to forgive myself again. I barely made it the first time." Nothing. He gave me nothing in return. I paused, hearing Jen leave out the front door. I didn't have the

283

courage to look at him again. I never would. "You're always...
you're always telling me not to apologize, Connor... but I... I've
never been more sorry for anything in my life than..." I somehow
breathed again, "stripping us of everything we had. Leaving us
both alone in the world. You and Maggie were all I've ever really
had." I was absolutely shaking. I'd never spoken this aloud before.
I felt almost wobbly as I stood up, not looking behind me, too
afraid to look at him. I didn't want the last thing I ever saw to be
hate. Or worse, to see that detached fear inside him that I'd
caused... that I'd caused the same way Hank had. It was through
that familiarity that I knew his hatred was pure. That it was abiding
and resolute.

I put my hand on the doorknob... and heard his voice, soft,
behind me; constricted, heavy.

"*She's* all I'd ever had, Liam. You were nowhere near that
category." Connor always had a way with words.

I turned the knob. Something inside me shut off again and I
knew I wasn't going to make it long once I walked out this door. I
wasn't lying; I didn't have the strength in me to forgive myself for
leaving him a second time. I pulled it open, shut it behind me. He
didn't follow. I grabbed the backpack I'd set down, found the
phone I'd left the first time on the counter and stuffed it in my
pocket, still shaking. I tried to convince myself, somewhere in my
subconscious that there was an odd peace in having said it all. A
finality.

I knew that I was walking into an eternal nothingness. I
knew exactly what was waiting for me back home... the endless
wandering nights, the band, the drugs that I wish I'd had even in
this moment to stop the shaking. To finally stop the shaking like
they had before. And this time, when I ran out of inertia, like
before, I had nothing holding me back; knowing that the damage
I'd done was permanent, that there wasn't anyone or anything I

needed to live for. My end of the exchange was never important though; he had to know the truth. So he could stop punishing himself. So he could really live.

I walked out the front door. I walked down the hall. I turned a corner; a corner of reprieve where no one could see me before leaving the apartment complex...before leaving. Before leaving him alone again. I didn't...I didn't mean for any of this to happen. I slammed my back against the wall, I couldn't breathe and my instincts weren't helping me this time. I slid to the floor, I gasped in a breath and I cried... pulling my knees up to my chest, I cried explicitly like the small 15 year old I had been, holding Maggie's body. My guilt and my self loathing poured down my face and through my fingers the same way her blood trickled through her nightgown onto my clothes. I couldn't believe there was a version of myself that ever thought Connor could love me again... that could even dream of it after what I'd done. How had I ever convinced myself that I'd ever deserved to be happy?

And then I felt a hand... on the top of my head, fingers in my hair. And I looked up.

He was there. He must have bolted from the apartment moments after me. He fell down toward me, pulling me into him, letting me cry into his clothes, with all of the gentleness I didn't deserve, all of the forgiveness I would never be able to give myself. His voice was gruff.

"Liam, It's not your fault. None of it was ever your fault. I'm sorry." But I couldn't respond, I couldn't think, I couldn't...have pride or self respect... all a worthless piece of trash like me could do was cry.

And somehow, for reasons I couldn't and will never understand...he let me.

"You're so dumb." He finally said, "So fucking dumb for carrying that around all this time. And for thinking I'd let you leave again. But I'm a fucking idiot.. I've always been a cowardly fucking idiot… I'm probably always going to be a fucking idiot." He paused, collecting courage and sound in his voice box. "You've always been my everything, Liam. I don't know why I can't just *say* it… all the time. All of the Fucks… remember? I'm sorry." Somehow he slightly laughed and it got me breathing again.

I could tell he was trying his best not to sound pathetic. "I um." He cleared his throat, "I love you." And I laughed, unexpectedly. Perhaps the unrealized relief was overflowing. I laughed and almost couldn't stop. I don't know why it sounded so funny coming out of his mouth; so honest, it was almost startling. Maybe this was why he was so guarded.

"Oh, I really hate you, William Alexander Clarke...the third. I really do." He laughed indignantly back at me. "Just an unadulterated, scolding hate…" He kissed me on the mouth, ignoring how pathetic I was. Maybe reveling in it. Come to think of it; he'd never minded me being pathetic...or weak.

"You know, Jen's right." I said, wiping my face like a child. "We really are very dramatic." He laughed too, painfully standing up using one hand to balance him against the wall and the other reaching down, offering to pull me up me up.

"You fucking started it." He didn't let go of my hand once I was standing.

CHAPTER 12: CONNOR

Of course I couldn't let him walk out of my life. Of course I knew that everything terrible in the world that had ever fucking happened wasn't his fault. Only his own Liam-Specific stupidity could ever convince anyone of that. Somehow I'd even let him convince me for a second... I wasn't thinking clearly... I never thought clearly when it came to Mom. But her death was really my fault... and Hank's fault...and of course, James Jennings fucking fault, and everyone, and everything in between. Least of all, Liam's fault. It was the entire universes fault because every intricate, tiny decision, from the blinker-driven instances in the hold of traffic, to the amount of humidity in the air, to the slight breeze that influences even a microorganism of sway in the mind of a human being is to blame for every action. For every reaction. Nothing is ever one person's fault. And... Jen was ultimately right. Margaret Shay never would have cared. The only thing she'd ever cared about was if we'd all felt strong...and brave...and capable.

He was texting my phone again. It vibrated violently on the table and I watched the light blink with contentedness. Weeks later, it was 3 o'clock in the morning and I sat at my local Denny's, utilizing the smoking section to its full potential. I stretched, with my laptop in front of me, blowing smoke into it's screen, grateful for the lack of ache in my bones that was slowly subsiding from being jumped in the alleyway. I didn't check it. I knew it was him. It was always him. I closed my eyes listening to the sound of distant chatter from other tables; the roadtrippers sleepily ordering food in the corner, the waitresses and cooks in the back, wide awake, used to their own strange lively hours, catching up on a shifts-worth of gossip back and forth that transpired between their off time. I heard pancakes sizzling in the back, noticed the lack of music on their speakers tonight. I was grateful; the silence had helped me think...helped me type. Helped me tie up the loose ins and outs of my manuscript. I'd sent it to Folly in an email; told her to print it out herself if she wanted to edit it. The joy of me being perfectly healthy after my near death experience had lasted a plethora of seconds until she'd been hounding me again.

Waitress Emilia came and quietly poured my coffee. Before, I'd have loved the lack of interaction; tonight I noticed the slight frown on her face.

"What's wrong?" I asked her. She glanced into my eye contact slightly surprised.

"That uh… that guy the other night, you saw me with at Liam's show…"

"Yeah?" I did remember. It was about three nights ago. Liam was amazing.

"He just stopped texting out of the blue. I don't know, I think I messed something up." I considered for a moment.

"I know that guy. It's uh…" I tried to recall his name from the Poli. Sci class we'd had together a few years ago. "Fred?" She laughed.

"Dave." She corrected me. It made me smile.

"Right. Dave's actually a complete Dick, hun. He has two kids from two different women a few cities over. you're better off." I tipped my cup to her. She laughed. Out loud.

"Is that true?" It really was. I did know who she was talking about. I'd just forgotten his name. I wasn't sure if she'd be hurt if I affirmed.

"Yep. But Emilia, you have more to offer the world in your pinky finger than he does in his whole being. He's worse than a dick… he's a complete moron. And you're not." She laughed again, gratefully.

"What are you doing out so late Connor? I hear you're spoken for-"

"He's torturing me, that's what he's doing." a familiar, groggy, sleepy, wonderful voice interrupted us behind her. Liam came around and plopped himself into my booth, still in his pajamas, half asleep. He had walked all the way down here like a zombie and it lit an exhausted laugh inside me. Emilia laughed too, and head back to the kitchen to get him some water and probably a spinach omelette. His usual order... day or night.

"You just wake up so beautifully." I joked, taking another puff of my cigarette. His arms were folded in front of him on the table, a makeshift pillow for his head. He'd just gotten back from a gig about midnight. He'd gotten about 2 hours of sleep max and clearly he felt it with his eyes closed, mumbling into himself.

"Yeah well, I figured out why Bassanio left Antonio.. I had to tell you." I smiled enigmatically, recalling the thousands of conversations we'd had about that book in highschool. The Merchant of Venice. "He fucking failed him in his stupid Creative Writing course." I laughed. Genuinely. And he didn't get to see it through his eyelids. But the sound made him grin. That sideways smile he would give me when I rumpled his hair, and he'd push my hand away laughing.

"Jenny called me today." I informed him, my cigarette dangling from my lip as I clicked the windows power button to shut down my computer.

"Mmmhmm?" I was losing him. He'd be asleep long before his water got here.

"She's moving back to the states. Possibly to get her masters degree. I was thinking maybe we'd rent a house... somewhere slightly off campus. The three of us. Makes the most financial sense....she should be back sometime before Christmas." He woke up slightly.

"Yeah?" he said, rubbing his eyes with a yawn. "I'm all in." I shut my laptop and scooted out of the booth.

"Apparently Hank's flying all the way out there to help her pack. Father of the fucking year award, right?" Ever since Liam had visited Mom's grave, he'd become awkwardly silent whenever Hank was brought up. Like there was something else he wanted to tell me but couldn't. I didn't care. We'd been through hell and back and were fine; nothing could be worse. Whatever it was I'd be ready.

"Come on, idiot. Let's go back to bed." He scooted out reluctantly, and just fell into my shoulder with his eyes closed, happy and tired.

"We could still be there if you'd stop leaving in the middle of the night and making me come get you." I couldn't sleep lately. I still had a painstaking anxiety that the happiness we'd created would come crashing down over us somehow; that secrets would come bubbling to the surface, feelings would change, or God would simply burn our fucking building to the ground for no good goddamn reason. But it was better. He'd always stumble like a zombie, blocks away to retrieve me, dragging me back. Emelia was used to me walking out. I usually paid for my coffee in advance, and she oddly never charged Liam for anything...ever. I suspected she'd had a bit of a crush on him; she'd gone to every single one of his shows. She knew he was mine... it was nice to enjoy someone who shared my same hobbies. I liked Friend Emelia.

The night was nice and cool on our faces. Almost too cool. Winter was approaching. Liam had stumbled out in a short sleeve shirt and pajama pants. He must have been freezing. I took off my jacket and handed it to him, saving my cigarettes and lighter, moving them to my jeans as I took another one out and lit it. He didn't even fight me on the jacket. He was growing pleasantly entitled to my niceties. He held my hand without any hesitation. The last few weeks had helped us both grow accustomed. Fuck, not that I was worried to begin with, but it sounded like Liam could take care of the both of us. The likelihood of being jumped, together, just for walking down the fucking street was minimal. I knew this because I'd pulled up statistics and presented it to Liam to talk him out of his acute paranoia that had settled in just as my bruising started to clear up. I'd also had to go out of my way to explain to him, like a child, that being gay hadn't gotten me beaten up. The fact that I was an antagonistic prick landed us both in the hospital. Yet another instance of nothing being his fault.

The university had already put up it's holiday lights around campus. The swirling bright trinkets wrapped around every light pole, outlining each building, lit up the night in a way that almost dampened the daytime. The air was more crisp; I could taste it. I'd found Christmas decorations hidden in the linen closet that Liam had already childishly picked up somewhere. And I had to admit… somewhere beneath my satire and chronic obsession to remain aloof, I was pleased.

I was pleased with the hidden Christmas decorations; Pleased with the warm, pulsating happiness flowing from Liam's fingers into mine, pleased that Jenny was moving back within arms reach. I could finally be there for her the way I should have been this whole time. I felt like I'd been asleep for so fucking long. Like I'd wasted so much time. It was a lot easier to forgive Liam for anything that had ever happened than I thought it would be. I was almost on the verge of even forgiving myself.

"Jeff told me Claire got back with that hot guy." Liam volunteered, breaking our silence; keeping ourselves awake.

"Ch. You mean the kicked-me-in-the-fucking-face guy?"

"Right. That one." He really pissed me off. I dropped his hand and walked ahead of him. "Oh, come off it, Con." He laughed at me. He'd done it on purpose. We walked up the three flights of stairs. I looked at the corner that I'd found Liam broken down, and remembered how lucky I was to have realized what a fucking, selfish, piece of shit I'd been for so long. I'd really stumbled upon it, right in that moment. I'd never considered that all this time he'd been alone too. That I, in fact, had been the one to abandon him. When he needed me most. All those years ago. I knew that I'd never do it again, I'd never leave him for a week, a day... a minute. He became an absolute moron when I wasn't around.

I'd found a crumpled up piece of paper in the living room earlier this week. It was a poem that Liam had started writing; clearly before all hell broke loose, before the hospital... maybe it was a song. There was one line in particular that he'd written that kept echoing through my head today;

Oh suprise, suprise,
I'm yours but you're not mine.

I needed it out of my head. It's catchy tone really would make a good song, if he switched up a few lines to get his syllables in the right places; elongated a few thoughts here or there. We reached the door and he fished for his apartment key in his pajama pocket. His face was slightly red from the cold, the tips of his ears tinted. He clumsily dropped the keys. It was late, and it was dark. It made me smile that he'd come all the way to Denny's in his pajamas. That he couldn't sleep without me. I *was* his. I was *unquestionably* his.

"Liam." he looked slightly up at me. I had one hand grasping his, the other gripping my laptop, but I kissed him, pulling him by the hand, never letting go, passionately. He smiled into me, with a sleepy;

" I love you too", feeling my unspoken words. He turned to unlock the deadbolt. We went inside and shut the door of our home behind us.....heading back to bed, to get lost again in the

292

chaos...No. the clarity. To finally *find* ourselves in the clarity of our affections.

I knew exactly what I was getting myself into. And I'd absolutely fucking waited long enough.

Made in the USA
Columbia, SC
12 November 2018